DEAD WEIGHT

'Let me earnestly recommend this Caribbean tale to flying action-novel fans, and others. Good plot, nice easy writing and hard work behind it all'

The Times

'A constant action, no-holds barred, speed-of-light adventure story which grips from beginning to end'

She

'A really thrilling adventure story in the best British tradition'

The Listener

'A cracking murder-and-mayhem yarn set in the steamy West Indies against a background of gold smuggling. A thrill-a-page novel, is definitely not for the squeamish'

Grimsby Evening Telegraph

BRIAN LECOMBER is uniquely qualified to write DEAD WEIGHT. Not only is he a commercial pilot, but he was also Chief Flying Instructor of the Antigua Aero Club for eighteen months. His first novel, TURN KILLER, was acclaimed for its authentic flying background.

'It isn't often that a new writer such as Brian Lecomber jumps straight to the top of his class . . . TURN KILLER is very well done'

Sunday Mirror

Also by the same author,
and available in Coronet Books:

Turn Killer

Dead Weight

Brian Lecomber

CORONET BOOKS
Hodder and Stoughton

Copyright © 1976 by Brian Lecomber

First published in Great Britain 1976
by Hodder and Stoughton Limited

Coronet Edition 1978

Printed and bound in Great Britain for
Hodder and Stoughton Paperbacks,
a division of Hodder and Stoughton Ltd.,
Mill Road, Dunton Green, Sevenoaks, Kent
(Editorial Office : 47 Bedford Square, London, WC1 3DP)
by Richard Clay (The Chaucer Press) Ltd.,
Bungay, Suffolk

ISBN 0 340 21999 8

Acknowledgments

THE CHARACTERS IN this book are all imaginary, of course: but the aircraft and the islands are totally real, and several of the events described are based on fact. It is, therefore, very difficult to know where to start and where to stop when it comes to thanking all those people whose actions, wittingly or unwittingly, provided the material upon which the story is based. There are, however, a number of parties to whom I would like to publicly record my genuine and heartfelt gratitude. Those of them who I think will not sue me are listed below.

Art Farmer, of Seagreen Air Transport, Antigua, for helping me when I'd run out of aeroplanes; M. Claude Deravin, of Air Sport, Guadeloupe, who provided the background to the banana-spraying business in the West Indies; Nigel Brendish, of Harvest Air Ltd, Biggin Hill, who lent me a Pawnee to try the sequences used in the story; the Beech Aircraft Corporation of Wichita, who provided the technicalia I'd forgotten since I last flew a Beech 18; David Whitter, of ICI, who was invaluable on airport fire-fighting techniques; and Duncan Baker — if he's not in jug — for letting me fly his Gemini all those years ago. Also, I would like to thank all those people — particularly Chris Widdows — who were involved in the Antigua Aero Club during my tenure as Chief Flying Instructor, plus Messrs Lycoming, Rolls-Royce, and Pratt & Whitney for never letting me down during those long, long hours over the Caribbean Sea.

BRIAN LECOMBER

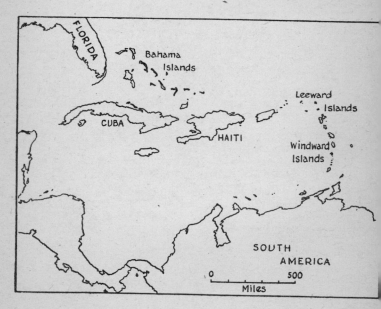

Virgin Islands

Culebra

Vieques

Puerto Rico

St Croix

CARIBBEAN

FLORIDA

Bahama Islands

Leeward Islands

CUBA

HAITI

Windward Islands

SOUTH AMERICA

0   500
Miles

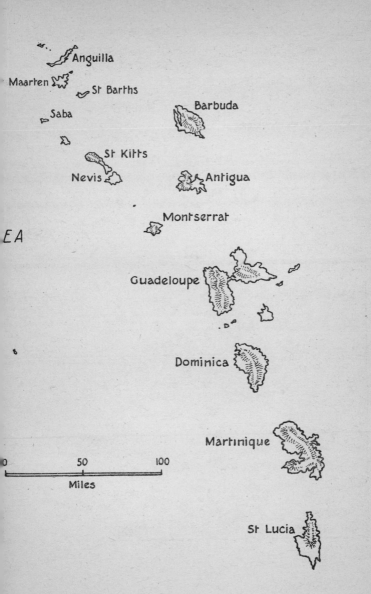

Anguilla

Maarten St Barths

Saba

Barbuda

St Kitts

Nevis Antigua

Montserrat

E A

Guadeloupe

Dominica

Martinique

0   50   100
Miles

St Lucia

Part One

I

WINTER. PITCH-BLACK night reluctantly giving way to sodden, watery daybreak. The old Miles Gemini, registration letters smeared over with heavy grease, growling in low across the Channel with me squinting anxiously into the murk worrying about where the hell we are and how hungover the RAF radar operators in Norfolk and Suffolk might be.

Everything grey in the cold dawn light. Solid grey overcast above, drizzling grey mist all around, icy grey sea below. The greyness crawling into the cockpit like light into an old, old tomb, fading the eerie glow of the instruments and showing up a thousand scuffs and scratches in the shabby wood and leather. My watch says that if we're where I think we are, we have eighteen minutes to run to the coast. *If* we're where I think we are . . .

The daylight reminds me just how cold I am.

After two hours of grinding through the December night the cold has penetrated through gloves, boots and heavy flying suit until now my very bones are deep-frozen. My hands and feet are blocks of ice on the controls, and my brain seems to have congealed inside my skull. 'Warmth' is a word with no meaning: I can't imagine being warm ever again.

And if *I'm* cold . . .

I crank my head round to examine the three passengers. They are even worse off: nobody told them a Gemini isn't heated unless you set fire to it, so they didn't come dressed for the trip. Earlier, as we dodged through the night across France and Belgium, they were shivering and vomiting. Now, stomachs empty and no energy left to shiver with, they look like a trio of adverts for Rent-a-Corpse. Faces that match the sickly dawn light, bodies huddled down into expensive but inadequate overcoats, eyes closed as if to shut out the cold and the flat unending blatter of the two Gypsy Majors. Only the stench of them lives on; the bitter, curdled tang of airsickness transcending the Gemini-smell of petrol, wood and glue.

Refugees, Smith said.

They do not look like refugees to me.

I pull my eyes away from them and glance at my watch again. Fifteen minutes to go.

Well — maybe, anyway.

I ease the throttles back a fraction and trim the nose a touch lower. The altimeter hesitates, then sags backwards from its dizzy 500 feet. Right place or not, it's time to get down *real* low; crawl in on our hands and knees under the east coast radar net. I hope.

The change in the monotonous growl of the engines wakes up the man beside me. Or maybe he wasn't asleep anyway: I neither know nor care. I'm just aware of him grunting and then stirring, probably leaning forwards to peer through the windscreen. I don't bother to look at him because I'm too busy doing some peering of my own. You have to be careful letting down low over water in bad light: it's a bloody sight easier than you'd think to fly slap into it.

"Iss getting near now?"

His voice irritates me. "Shuddup. I'm concentrating."

He shuts up.

We grind on down, the Gemini the only living thing in a world of clammy grey emptiness. The altimeter needle passes 300 feet ... 200 ... 100 ... and suddenly the un-moving wrinkles of the sea are changing, becoming a million individual wavelets tumbling by just underneath the nose. The surface is the colour of tool steel — which is about what it would feel like if we flew into it at this speed — and looks very cold indeed. I shove the throttles back up to 2,050 rpm, niggle at the starboard lever until the noise settles down to the steady snarl of synchronisation, and try not to think about the climb performance a Gemini doesn't have if one engine goes on strike. Then I wind the trim back until we're a little tail-heavy. Sneeze-factor, they call that: if you sneeze or otherwise stop paying attention for a moment, it ensures that the aeroplane goes up rather than down. Some of the time, anyway.

The man in the right-hand seat coughs loudly, hawks, spits on to the cockpit floor, and then subsides. When I snatch a quick glance across at him, he is watching me with a sort of bleary morning-after disapproval. Well, maybe he doesn't like his pilots young and fresh-faced and fair-haired . . .

Or maybe after this kind of trip he just doesn't like his pilots, period.

He is Eurasian — or something. Good suit, costly overcoat, gold cuff-links. Thin sharp face clean-shaven, crinkly black hair well-cut. Age hidden by the same bank account that bought the clothes: anywhere between forty and sixty. Definitely *not* the refugee type — not unless they're breeding a whole new class of refugee, anyway.

Well, maybe they are. Maybe it takes a new class of refugee to afford to be air-lifted into England on the illegal-immigrant run . . .

He still isn't quite what I had in mind.

"Iss near now?" he asks again. "We are soon arriving?"

I dig out my best this-is-your-captain-speaking voice, but keep my eyes looking forward through the windscreen.

"Yep. Quite near. Quarter of an hour to the coast, another twenty minutes to the airfield."

He nods, and leans forward as if he expects to see something in the murk. Maybe he even believes me.

I wish *I* believed me.

"Where we go? Which air'drome?"

I frown at the rumpled sea rushing at us out of the mist. Smith said not to tell anyone the destination — but that was so nothing could leak out beforehand. It can't do any harm now: he wouldn't be daft enough to use the same place twice.

"It's a disused RAF field in Suffolk. Place called Great Ashfield. Used to be a bomber station during the war."

Sharp-face nods again and sits back. The name obviously doesn't mean a thing to him. Well, that's fair enough: apart from being a tiny dot out there in the clag that I've got to find, it doesn't mean anything to me, either.

Not back then, it doesn't.

The Gemini rumbles on with wraiths of moisture flickering around the propeller arcs. I want a cigarette — but the damn thing's a non-smoker, of course.

Ten minutes to the coast.

"You wanna drink, boy?"

I glance right again. Sharp-face has a smooth new Gladstone bag on his knees and a smooth new bottle of something in his hand. He closes the top of the bag as I turn my head.

I get my eyes back on the cold grey sea.

"No thanks. Never touch it." I don't, either.

Not in those days, I don't.

He grunts again and swigs. The scent of aniseed joins the other smells in the freezing cockpit.

Eight minutes to go.

The daylight should be getting stronger now — but it isn't. The mist is the colour of old washing-up water, and the visibility is worse than ever. Fine drizzle peckles on the windscreen and creeps into the cockpit in a dozen icy runnels. Typical winter warm-front weather — except that according to the forecast, *this* bloody front wasn't supposed to get here for another seven hours. I check the gauges for the thousandth time — oil pressures okay, temperatures okay, heading 275 — then go back to biting my lip and wondering how the hell I'm going to find out where we are when we *do* hit the coast.

"Don't you have no vices, boy?"

I go on staring into the murk and try to analyse the accent: at least it makes a change from trying to analyse our position. Maybe it's French North African with the liquid of Arabia plus a dash of American somewhere . . .

Hell — that sounds like it *is* our position.

"Hey — I talkin' to you. Don' you have no vices, hey?"

Season with a dash of Afrikaans . . .

"No," I tell him. "Only running . . . refugees."

I don't know what I expect — but what I get is a laugh. Loud and clear and harsh over the rumbling of the engines. I jump six inches out of my seat — and when I come down, the sneeze-factor has pulled the nose up. I shove forward angrily against the trim-pressure and take her back down to the grey sea.

"What's so bloody funny?"

He ignores that. For a few moments there's just the sounds of Man with Bottle. Then, sneeringly: "How old you, boy?"

"Twenty-one." *And if you want to spend the rest of the flight worrying about my inexperience, that's up to you . . .*

"This the firs' time you done this?"

"Yes." I do not add that it's also going to be the last.

14

"Why you doin' it?"

I think of why I'm doing it. Think of Jenny and our unborn child.

"Money," I tell him.

It seems to satisfy him. It's his language. He nods, swigs again, then leans back and closes his eyes.

Four minutes to run. I check the gauges again, and go on thinking about Jenny.

*   *   *

She was crying when I left.

I tried not to tell her what I was doing — said I was just delivering an aeroplane for somebody — but she knew I was lying because nobody delivers aeroplanes on this night. This night you spend at home with your wife unless you're doing . . . something like this.

And so she cried — and I held her and stroked her hair and mumbled inanities that neither of us believed about how it was a perfectly normal flight and not the slightest bit dodgy or nasty. Our tatty little sitting room, with its tenth-hand furniture and the pile of unpaid bills on the mantelpiece, seemed to close in around us and mock her tears and my lies.

Then it was time to go.

She ran out of the room while I was stuffing the last bits of flying kit into my holdall. When she came back she'd washed away the tears, put on a tiny, trembling smile . . .

And she'd fetched my present.

I sat down on the sofa and opened it. The card said *I love you forever, Bill darling* — and inside the little parcel was a pair of gloves. Really good ones: warm, properly stitched, good-quality supple leather so I could wear them for flying without my hands feeling like cricket bats on the knobs and switches. The sort of gloves that cost real money: money she must have scrimped and saved out of the meagre housekeeping for weeks. Money that must have meant missing her occasional hairdos and cutting down on make-up and new pairs of tights and all the other little luxuries . . .

Thinking about that made it a little easier to go. I kissed her one last time, strapped my kit on the back of the BSA, and pointed it off towards the quiet private airstrip in Hertfordshire.

Okay, so it's wrong. But Jesus — what can you do? You're

twenty-one and twenty, married two years, and the mortgage on the cottage makes a hole in your combined wages that you could drive a Comet through. Then your wife gets pregnant — and you lie awake nights wondering just how the hell you're going to manage with another mouth to feed and only one pay-packet to do it on. You even think of giving up flying — since anything pays better than flying instruction — but flying's the only thing you know and anyway you wouldn't be happy doing anything else ...

And then the letter arrives. Dear Mr Scott, Eagle Airways wish to refer to your application of ten months ago, and are pleased to offer you the position of First Officer flying Viscounts. The offer is subject to your agreeing to the usual contracts, etc. — and also, of course, to your having achieved your Commercial Licence and Instrument Rating in the period that has elapsed since your last interview. And you've got the Commercial, all right — but an Instrument Rating means a further twenty hours training on twins, which costs £400 or more ...

And, that, you certainly haven't got.

So then Smith pops up, with his gold teeth and his shady deals. Just one trip with a load of illegal immigrants — and the problem's solved. £350 in fivers and tenners — and then heigh-ho for three gold rings and the right-hand seat in a Viscount. And Jenny being able to have new dresses and go shopping without having to count the pennies. And it isn't even as if it was a real crime, when you think about it: all you're doing is breaking a few out-dated immigration rules and giving three homeless refugees a new start ...

So you take the job.

And it's not until you get your first good look at the passengers that you start having doubts. It's not just that they're too well-dressed: it's more that they don't ... well, *act* like refugees, somehow. Or not like you imagined refugees, anyway. Cold and sick they might be — but they're not frightened, not even nervous. They almost seem as if they're used to this sort of thing ...

Ah, the hell with them. I glance down at the new gloves on my hands and think about Jenny again instead. *I love you forever, Bill darling.* I think about how I love her, too. And about our child to come. And about the things I'm going to do for them both when I've got the new job.

I have no way of knowing that our forever has already ended.

* * *

0756, Greenwich Mean Time. We should be at the coast . . . *now*.

And ninety seconds later, we are.

For a long moment, my frozen brain refuses to accept it. We *can't* be that close to the estimate after an hour of nothing but dead-reckoning in the shifting winds of an oncoming warm front . . .

But we are.

The faint grey line in the mist hardens, rushes back at us — and then suddenly it's *here*, cold white surf thumping on a desolate beach. We're so low I can see stones and driftwood in the sand as we flash over the water-line. Then I look forward and there's a clump of trees leaping at us out of the mist and . . .

Christ! Man!

I thump the throttles wide open and haul back hard on the stick. The engines blare in surprise as the Gemini rears up into the murk. At 300 feet I shove the nose down to where the horizon would be if there was a horizon, and try to get a grip on the wild thumping of my heart. I knew the visibility was *bad*, but . . .

My hands are trembling with shock as I bring the throttles back to cruise power and ram my head against the side window looking for landmarks. We might have popped up on to somebody's radar screen pulling up like that — but if we have, it's just too bloody bad. With the visibility down to maybe three hundred yards in the mist there's no way I'm doing any more hedge-hopping: next time we could end up decorating a tree or a pylon before I've even seen it.

Behind me in the cabin there's a sudden babble of voices as the passengers come out of shock. Without looking at them I yell: "Shuddup! Just tell me if you see a road or railway or town."

They shut up. I go on staring downwards, tension balling up in my guts. I have to know where we are, and I have to know *now* . . .

Below is nothing but soggy brown-green fields unreeling out of the mist. We could be over Suffolk, Norfolk, or bloody Timbuctoo. My kingdom for a big road or a railway or a disused airfield . . .

A one-pub village looms up on my side and I nearly break my neck looking for some other landmark to pin it down. But there isn't anything, of course: short of flying down the main street and reading the shop signs there's no way of telling it from ten thousand other villages littered around the East Anglian coast.

Damn, damn, *damn*!

I keep heading due west. The flat, dreary-looking countryside slides past close below, and I try to forget that we might be boring straight into RAF Bentwaters' Approach Radar. A minute goes by. Two minutes. Still nothing identifiable. My hands and face are clammy with sweat in spite of the cold. Maybe we should have followed the coast instead of coming inland. Maybe . . .

Sharp-face bawls: "Railway!" — and two seconds later I see it myself. A double track going roughly north-south. I stand the Gemini on its right wing tip and circle over it while I fumble with the quarter-million map. Unless we're in the wrong county altogether that's got to be the track from Ipswich up to Beccles and then Yarmouth. So all I've got to do now is follow it until it passes some other landmark which'll give me a definite fix.

Assuming we *are* in the right county, of course. And also assuming we don't wake up the entire population of England en route . . .

The hell with it. I tighten the turn for a few seconds, then roll out with the railway streaming past under the port engine. If we *don't* follow the damn thing we're just going to stay lost, and that's all there is to it.

For interminable minutes we stay lost anyway. There's nothing but the railway and a few odd roads and the same cold dismal farmland. The cloud-base gets steadily lower, and so do we. The Gemini feels very loud and very conspicuous down here, and I carry on sweating.

Come on, *for God's sake! There must be* something . . .

Then, suddenly, there is. Houses and gardens rush at us out of the murk. I whang the Gemini over on its right ear again, and haul it out on an easterly heading to stay over open country. I'd like to see the shape of the town — but we can't go snarling over the rooftops at 250 feet. The population'd probably be able to read our engine numbers, never mind the smeared-over registration.

I hold 090 degrees for exactly two minutes while we blare over more fields and occasional narrow country lanes, then turn north again. Almost immediately we cross a single-track railway going south-east . . .

And then, so suddenly I don't see it coming at all, we're over an aerodrome.

I crank into another steep turn and stare down at the criss-cross of the dull wet runways. The place is deserted, thank Christ. There are no hangars, no control tower — nothing but a few rambling chicken-shed affairs on one of the taxiways. Must be a disused war-time airfield or something . . .

Well, don't just sit there, man — WHICH bloody disused war-time airfield, for Chrissake?

I keep the turn going and get busy with the map again. At first glance it looks hopeless: the whole of Suffolk seems to be covered with the crossed circles of disused airfields. But I'm looking for one with a town to the south-west and a couple of railway lines nearby . . .

And a few seconds later, I've got it. A place called Halesworth. I hope. Repeat, hope.

Well, we can soon prove it: if this *is* Halesworth, then there's another disused airfield — Metfield — six miles due west. I make a rapid correction for variation and guesstimated wind, and roll out of the turn on a heading of 275. The time is 0816: if I'm right, we should hit Metfield at 0820.

If I'm right . . .

I want a cigarette very badly.

Sharp-face skews round in his seat and looks behind the wing at the place I hope is Halesworth.

"That not there we landing?"

"No. Another twenty minutes yet."

"We are late," he says flatly.

"We're lucky to get there at all in this weather, chum. And Smi . . . er, your driver'll wait."

He just grunts. Someone in the back starts vomiting again.

I divide my attention between my watch and the bedraggled landscape unrolling out of the mist. I also do some worrying about what the hell we're going to do if Metfield *doesn't* show up. If that happens we're going to be really lost — and we could be charging straight into Honington or Wattisham's radar . . .

Amazing how much you can sweat when you're numb with cold.

At 0820 a disused airfield materialises out of the drizzle and slides back under the starboard wing.

Metfield.

I let go of a very old breath, shove the power up a little, and bend the Gemini left to 260 degrees. Fourteen minutes later I pick up the railway line between Ipswich and Bury St Edmunds, follow it west for two miles . . .

And suddenly, we're there. Great Ashfield.

*   *   *

I circle once, losing height slowly with half flap down and the engines throttled well back for maximum hush. In the mist and the drizzle the place looks exactly like any other disused aerodrome — dreary, overgrown, and utterly desolate. Crumbling runways like pointless motorway sections going from nowhere to nowhere in the midst of empty farmland. Apart from the little blue cube of Smith's Dormobile it seems totally deserted: it could be some abandoned alien graveyard on another planet . . .

Yet suddenly, I have a bad feeling about it. For all I know there could be a hundred people down there, hiding in the mist and rain. I want to ram on the power, pull up into the murk, get the hell out and away . . .

Oh, yes — and away where to, Scott? Going to lob into Denham, are you? Or how about Heathrow, while you're at it? Just stop bloody panicking and start bloody thinking, man . . .

I drag my hand over the clamminess on my face, shove a few brain cells into full-fine pitch, and stare downwards over the slowly-revolving left wing tip. The east-west runway's dug up halfway along, just like Smith said, so it'll have to be a cross-wind landing on the north-south. Well, that's all right: I can land south and get off north. That'll give me a cross-wind from the left on take-off — which is the only way a Gemini'll take *any* cross-wind on take-off — and it'll also give me a fast turn-around since the van's already parked at the south end of the runway anyway. With any luck I'll be back in the air and heading for home base in less than five minutes . . .

Okay, then. Let's get on with it.

I'm aware of the passengers stirring as I roll out of the turn and lower the wheels, but don't look at them because I'm too busy flying. I've got to get this *right*: if we have to open up and go round again we'll probably wake up half of Suffolk. The half we haven't woken up already, that is.

At a hundred feet I bank on to a short final approach and pull the throttles back some more. The engines mutter and pop as the runway floats up to meet us out of the drizzle. Full flap *now* —

threshold sliding under the nose — power right off *now* — ease back on the stick — hold it — back more, back, *back* ...

And the Gemini rumbles on to the ground in a neat three-pointer.

For a few seconds the wooden fuselage echoes up hollow-sounding bonks and thuds as the tailwheel bumps on the unkempt surface — and then we're down to taxiing speed and I'm easing on a whiff of power to keep us trundling along towards the Dormobile.

We've made it. I've just completed the first crime of my life.

It is not a nice feeling.

Over on the left the long-abandoned control tower watches us with the sightless eyes of its broken windows. Twenty years ago at this hour of the morning that tower would have been crowded with people waiting for the bombers to return — but now it's deserted and bleak in the rain like an old, uncared-for tombstone. Nobody waiting except the ghosts of aircrews gone by — and nobody coming. No Lancs, no Halifaxes, no Super Forts. No heroes, no cowards, no thundering Merlins.

Just a dirty little people-smuggler, scuttling through the graveyard.

Near the end of the runway I brake gently, swing the Gemini nearly all the way round with a burst of left engine, and stop. For a long moment we all sit there, with the rain crawling on the windscreen and the Gypsies making dry husky blatting noises into the grey morning. Then sharp-face twists in his seat, trying to look backwards at the end of the runway.

"Mistah Smith in that van there?"

I just nod, without moving. I suddenly feel very old and cold and tired. I don't even bother to wonder how he knows Smith's name.

"How we get out, now?"

I come wearily back to life and unfasten the upward-lifting window-cum-door by my left elbow. The cold wet morning pours in along with the engine noise as the stay locks into place to hold it open. Sharp-face fumbles with his seat-belt a moment, then clambers out behind my back on to the left wing, thumping my ear with the Gladstone bag as he goes.

I call: "Get off the *back* of the wing," and he nods. But he doesn't get off at all for a moment — just stands there on the walk-away with the slipstream plucking at his coat while he stretches the kinks out of his back and looks around.

Suddenly, he goes rigid.

"POLICE!"

I whip my head out of the doorway, and look behind. Blue uniforms are pouring out of the Dormobile, fifty yards away.

The Eurasian drops the Gladstone bag, spins like a trapped animal — and starts forwards.

I howl: "NO — BACK!" and smash the left throttle open to blow him off the wing, away from the scything propeller. The engine coughs, blares — and in the same instant he realises and twists frantically, trying to stop himself. For a frozen moment he hangs there in the thundering slipstream, arms flailing in dreadful slow-motion. Then one foot goes over the front of the wing, he tumbles on to the engine cowling . . .

And there's a massive chopping *thump* as his head and arms disappear into the propeller-arc.

For a split-second the prop sprouts a halo of red like the fire round a catherine wheel — and then the engine explodes into tearing, Screeching vibration as the wooden blades break up. Bits wallop into the fuselage and fly out in a great arc as I slam the throttle shut and knock the magneto switches to Off. The engine runs down eccentrically, bangs back fit to jump out of the wing, then finally stops with the splintered, reddened remains of one prop-blade pointing straight up at the dull grey overcast.

Quite slowly, the body slides off the cowling. Blood, bright red and steaming in the cold air, hoses out of the stumps of the arms and the pulp where the neck used to be. For a moment it sprays over the engine nacelle like a sudden coat of paint . . .

And then the corpse flops to the ground with a sickening double thud, and there's nothing but a cloud of steam rising up over the leading edge of the wing.

I sit there staring at it for what seems like a long time before I realise, vaguely, that people are shouting from a million miles away and the right engine is still ticking over unconcernedly.

So I stop that one too, then turn the master switch off and climb slowly out to meet the police.

*   *   *

Half an hour later, when they tell me that sharp-face's

Gladstone bag contains about 20 lb of pure heroin, I am not even surprised. I just sit there in the police car looking at the handcuffs round my wrists and the blood on my new gloves, and don't say a word.

Way off in the distance, I can hear the sound of church bells.

It is Christmas Day, 1963.

Part Two

2

MONDAY OCTOBER 21ST, 1974. A bad day right from the start. But then most days that begin at four in the morning are, quite apart from the date.

I crawled out from under the single sheet, staggered across the room in the hot darkness, and got the alarm clock shut up with the fourth or fifth swipe. After that I groped around for the light switch, found it, then stumbled back and sat on the edge of the bed with my eyes tight shut. Little blobs of light swam around in the redness as I tried to get enough brain cells cranked up to decide whether I was going to be sick or not.

Last night's half-bottle of Scotch and two Mandrax pills lay like a dead cat in my guts. I was sticky all over with the night-sweat of the tropics — but in spite of the ever-present heat, I somehow seemed to be feeling cold from the inside outwards. I was shivering, too. Hands, knees and stomach muscles all flutter-ing uncontrollably. I hunched forward and hugged my arms round my chest, trying to stop the shaking and warm myself up. It didn't work.

My brain churned over sluggishly. There was a long moment of fuzzy confusion before it produced a definite idea.

Weather, Scott: check the weather.

Oh, yeah. Weather . . .

I lurched to the window, leaned on the lever that opened the jalousy-slats, and bleared out at the night. The sky was deep blue-black and starlit, and palm trees rattled gently in the warm trade wind. The bad-eggs stench of rotting copra drifted across from the ramshackle loading wharf on the other side of the road, and a cock crowed in the shanty town off to the right. There's always a cock crowing somewhere in a West Indian Village.

Weather okay. Time to move, then . . .

I made it to the shower, and stood under it for a long time. Cold, of course: guest houses on the island of Dominica don't provide hot water at four in the morning. Or at any other time, come to that. When I'd finished I drank about a pint of water to combat the dehydration of last night's whisky, thought about shaving — and then looked at my trembling hands and un-thought again. The mirror showed an untidy stubble on my face, but it'd be a bloody sight more untidy if I scraped off half an ear to go with it.

The mirror also showed some other things, too: things that went a bit deeper than a sun-and-wind tan and a thirty-six-hour beard. Some of them were superficial and obvious — like the long scar and the slightly closed left eye from the Islander crash in Borneo and the missing tooth from the gun butt in the face in Biafra — while others were a bit more subtle. There was the absence of laugh-lines around the mouth, for instance, contrasting oddly with the deep crows-feet round the eyes from too much staring into too many skies from too many cockpits. And then the eyes themselves, too: gummy with hangover and lack of sleep, but also . . . empty, somehow. The sort of eyes you find in cheap boarding houses in crummy countries all the world over. Eyes that are a thousand years old and only have nightmares to look back on and nothing to look forward to . . .

I shuddered, and quit looking in the mirror.

Eleven years can be a very long time, sometimes.

Moving slowly and deliberately, I got myself back to the bedroom and got dressed. Jack-shirt and jeans and open sandals, all stinking faintly of banana oil and yesterday's sweat. Then I went round the room picking up my belongings and stuffing them into my battered old flight bag.

The Scotch bottle was last of all.

I picked it up, and it shivered in my hands. There was an inch left in the bottom. Not much — but maybe enough to give me the jolt I needed. Maybe enough to get my brain into gear and stop the shakes . . .

I unscrewed the cap and sniffed it. I wasn't going to drink it, not first thing in the morning — not on a flying day, anyway —

28

but maybe the smell would wake me up or stop me wanting it or something. Maybe.

Then I remembered the date. October 21st.

The whisky went down in two long gulps. I left the empty bottle on the rickety dressing table, and went out into the night.

*   *   *

I got to the little jungle airstrip just before five — drenched in sweat, aching in every joint, and with a slow, determined pain behind the eyes. Wrestling Jean-Claude's battered old Chevvy truck up five miles of steep, un-made track through the Dominican rain forest in the dark hour before dawn is not the best of therapies for a four-engined hangover.

I pulled the Chev on to the short gravelled runway and swung it round in a U-turn. The headlights swept across the green-black jungle on the uphill side of the strip and came to rest on the Piper Pawnee in the open-fronted, tumbledown hangar. I trod the park-brake on, switched off the engine, and clambered carefully down out of the high cab. After the noise of the motor, the living quietness of the tropical forest was eerie. Palm fronds clattered softly. Water dripped; a million drips off a billion wet leaves combining into a constant low rustling sound. Insects whirred and chirruped, matching the ringing in my ears, and somewhere in the blackness outside the truck's lights an early parrot cawed once, then shut up. It was very hot, and suffocatingly humid.

I leaned into the cab, fished out my torch, and walked slowly down the light-path to the Pawnee. It reared over me as I got near it, droop-nosed, chunky and aggressive, the way all purpose-built crop-spray planes look. Its mission in life in Dominica was to plaster the banana plantations with oil in order to discourage the *cercosporoise* fungi — and *my* mission in life on this bleary hungover morning was to knock off the last 300 hectares of the current contract in the northern foothills before the heat of the day wound itself up to full power and created too much turbulence for further low flying.

This unhappy state of affairs occurs at around ten thirty or eleven a.m. — and *that's* why a crop-spray pilot in Dominica has to get his hangover out of the sack at four in the morning. If you aren't tanked up and ready to go in the relative calm of first light, then you miss a large chunk of the working day. Pilots *have* been

29

known to sleep late and then try to keep flying until midday, but it tends to be a non-habit-forming vice. The last bloke Jean-Claude had who tried it gave himself a dramatic cremation over about five acres of plantation, and was buried along with the bits of his Thrush Commander that they couldn't separate from the body.

I shuddered at the memory and looked down at my hands, trembling with their own built-in turbulence. Drinking and crop-spraying is something else that's non-habit-forming, too...

Still, at least it was my last day. I wasn't a full-time spray pilot: I only came down to Dominica two or three times a year, when Jean-Claude's running out of spare jockeys at his main base on the nearby island of Guadeloupe happened to coincide with my running out of anything more profitable in the instruction and charter line back at my base in Antigua. This time I'd been here for five days, after stopping off on the way back from a cargo charter down to Caracas — and now, I only had two or three hours spraying left to do.

Hallelujah.

I snicked on the torch, tried to ignore the throbbing in my head and the corpse in my guts, and got started on the daily inspection.

Twenty minutes later, the Pawnee was ready for battle. Fuelled-up, checked-over, and loaded up with 900 lb of banana oil in the spray-hopper in front of the cockpit. Banana oil is a light-grade SAE 5 mineral oil with a few per cent of a chemical called Benlate added, and the stirring of the mixture in the hopper had left me feeling sicker and dizzier than ever. I shoved the Pawnee out of the hangar — and then, of course, it started to rain. I slammed the cockpit hatches shut and made it into the hangar just as the first few heavy drops swelled suddenly into the car-wash deluge of a typical Dominican shower. It thundered on the roof and dripped in through the holes for five minutes — and then stopped as abruptly as it had started. It does that ten or twenty times a day in the rain forest — which is why there *is* a rain forest, of course — and every time it happens, the humidity goes through the roof. I wiped ineffectually at the prickly sheen of sweat on my face and neck, and sat on a spare wheel nursing a Thermos of coffee and waiting for the dawn.

It wasn't long coming. Within ten minutes the darkness had given way to hot, muggy daylight, sunless under the brooding grey clouds round the mountain peak above me. The jungle-covered slopes of Morne Diablotins materialised and became solid, and the chittering of the night insects wound down to make way for the dawn chorus of squawking and grunting from the depths of the forest.

The view was breathtaking. Even in my state and being used to it as well, I walked out on to the strip and looked.

Jean-Claude had his private spray-strip hacked out of the jungle on a muddy shoulder 2,000 feet up the north-west face of the Devil's Mountain. That's about as far away from the world as you can get anywhere in the West Indies — nobody lives that high, and there's no villages for miles around — but it *is* reasonable central to the plantations in the north, and the altitude means that you can drive to work, which saves time. It also means that the scenery is incredible.

On my right, the rain forest reared up from the side of the runway a thousand feet or more into the base of the standing cloud-cap that invariably shrouds the old volcano's 5,000-foot peak — and to the left, through a few low places in the down-slope trees, I could see the foothills dipping and swaying hundreds and thousands of feet below, like a vast rucked-up green carpet.

Then the sun came up.

I didn't get it first hand because I was on the wrong side of Diablotins and anyway the sky was mostly obscured by the heaps of cumulus over the mountains — but I knew when it happened, all right. You couldn't miss that. The hilltops to the north suddenly shone with silver which rapidly became brighter, then spilled over and turned to gold in the valleys. Mist and low stratus streamed and roiled from one green-coated bowl to another, chasing itself away from the heat and light.

Time to move.

I hauled myself up into the high, roomy cockpit, settled in the seat with a fumbling of straps, then pulled on a sweat-stained old crash helmet and sat watching my hands as they flicked the master and port magneto on, gave the primer one stroke, and pressed the starter button. The propeller chunked over once, twice — and the Lycoming thrustled into life, its busy rumble flattening the jungle sounds and raising a squadron of startled parrots out of the forest.

Three minutes later, I was ready to go. I closed the big window-cum-doors, then trod the park-brakes off and taxied to the very end of the strip before pivoting round and pointing

31

the long nose up the runway. The place was tight enough anyway — just over 2,300 feet — without wasting any of it. The jungle, green and dark and hungry, leered at me from the far end as I stood on the toe-brakes and opened the throttle all the way. The engine wound up to its characteristic band-saw howl, and the airframe quivered in sympathy: I glanced quickly at the gauges to make sure the racket *did* represent full power, then let go of the anchors. We started to roll.

By the half-way point the airspeed was clawing into the sixties and the controls were coming properly alive. I gave it a few moments more, *felt* backwards gently on the stick, and the Pawnee lifted smoothly into the air.

Half a second later the throaty blast of the engine suddenly chopped back several hundred decibels. Taking most of the power output with it, of course.

* * *

Jesus God! Partial engine failure!

Everything shaking wildly. The Pawnee sagging back towards the runway. No room to get down again and stop . . .

I had a split-second vision of going into the trees with 39 gallons of fuel and 150 gallons of banana oil on board — and then I was grabbing the big lever marked HOPPER DUMP VALVE and whanging it all the way forwards to the Emergency Dump position. Eight hundredweight of oil sploshed out in seconds as the whole bottom of the hopper yawned open. The Pawnee bounced soggily upwards . . .

But not enough. The trees at the end of the runway were *here*, rushing at me, rearing up. A huge old breadfruit filled the windscreen, blotting out the whole world. The stall-warning light blazed urgently as I tried to haul the shuddering nose up over it — but there was no way I was going to clear it, no way at all. For a split-second I was flying into a tunnel, fast-moving dark green all around. Then a giant lurching *smash* — whirling green explosion in the prop — leaves and branches hammering on the airframe and whipping past the cockpit like missiles. . . .

And then I was out the other side. Sudden miraculous clear sky ahead. The Pawnee staggering and juddering like a drunken vulture, bits of tree streaming off the wings — but still, incredibly, flying.

Jesus, thank you — but don't leave yet . . .

We mushed down towards the tree tops, waffling in a semi-stall and shaking like a road-drill. I dropped the nose a whisker, juggling the sloppy controls, trying to ride the razor-edge between stalling completely and pushing her down into the forest. For long seconds she carried on wallowing and sinking — and then the bright red glare of the stall-warner flickered and became intermittent, and I was holding my height. Just. The jungle roof rushed past five, ten feet below, then gradually dropped away like a frozen green waterfall as I flew straight on and the mountain curved off to the right.

I carried on wrestling, trying to hold my height and fighting for precious speed at the same time. Slammed the stick and rudder round the cockpit to keep her steady in the turbulence and cursed the heavy, unresponsive controls. It was a battle I couldn't win: with the engine delivering 1,900–2,000 rpm instead of its normal 2,550 maximum, I'd already got all the speed I was ever going to get unless I was prepared to trade off height for it. Well, maybe I would — but not yet. I kept her squashing along in a nose-high attitude with the airspeed wandering around sixty mph, and started grabbing round the cockpit with my left hand, trying to find the trouble. Snapped both magnetos off and on in turn. No improvement. Banged the fuel tap off and on. Ditto. Juggled with carburettor heat and mixture, and even tried half a squirt of primer.

Nothing helped. The engine just went on making sick-sounding *braka-braka-braka* noises and trying to shake itself out of the airframe. Must be a cracked inlet manifold or a seized tappet or something . . .

Jesus. I draw in a long shuddering breath.

So okay — now what? Quick! Down into the valleys and look for a straight bit of road to land on? No go — not in Dominica: there *ain't* no straight bits of road. And there ain't no straight bits of anything else, either, not for miles. Just wall-to-wall bloody jungle . . .

So?

So back to the strip — right?

Right. Providing the engine doesn't quit altogether on the way round the circuit, of course. And further providing she doesn't shake herself to bits and that nothing vital gets crunched going through that tree . . .

Ah, shuddup.

33

Still whanging the soggy controls about in big urgent jerks, I cranked on about fifteen degrees of left bank. Real British Airways stuff. The Pawnee curled slowly round, out from the mountain. The engine went on sounding like a very old tractor, and the long matt-black cowling was a blur of vibration. Sweat poured down my face as I tried to convince myself that the shakes *were* all coming from the engine, and not from some tree-clobbered part of the airframe which might be getting ready to part company altogether ...

Then I was downwind, and nothing had fallen off. Yet. I rolled carefully out of the turn, hung my chin on my shoulder, and stared over the left wing tip at the livid green wall of the mountain. From this elevation — or lack of it — the airstrip was invisible, hidden by the trees. I *thought* I knew where it was, but ...

I took another deep breath, swallowed on a throat full of sand, and went through the pre-landing checks. Tried to stop myself thinking what was going to happen if I'd lost a wheel going through the top of the tree ...

Then we were abeam the runway threshold — or at least, where I *hoped* the threshold was — and I was bending the Pawnee into another turn. The shivering nose crawled slowly round the sky until it was pointing at the steep-sloping forest. I rolled out, blinked the sweat out of my eyes, and tried to stare the strip out of the trees as they floated back towards me. For long moments there was nothing but the curtain of green: no gaps, no hangar, no runway...

And then I had it. I saw the dirt-road leading to it first — and two seconds later a tiny clearing with the end of the airstrip poking into it. I was a hundred feet above its level — too far out — take it in — just a few seconds more, Mr Lycoming ...

Yes, *NOW*.

I muttered: "Okay God, I have control," pulled back what was left of the power, and dropped in over the trees still turning left to get lined up with the runway. We touched down in a bonkety three-pointer, and rolled to a stop in the middle of the long shiny splodge of the oil I'd dropped on the way out.

I let go of a very old, shuddery breath. Thank you, Piper Aircraft Corporation, for a real fast emergency hopper-dump facility...

It really *was* being a bad day.

3

THE ISLAND OF Dominica is about thirty miles long by fifteen wide. Not very big — but since most of it goes more or less straight upwards and most of the roads only wander round the coasts, it takes a long time to get anywhere from the interior unless you happen to be a helicopter or a parrot. Jean-Claude's ancient Chev was neither, so it was nearly ten o'clock by the time I chugged into Melville Hall, the island's public airport on the east coast.

Melville Hall has to be about the prettiest strip in the whole Caribbean. The runway points east at the sparkling blue sea, and has banana groves on the north side of it and tall, dignified trees and a babbling river behind the economy-sized terminal building to the south. The whole thing is tucked away in a valley between the hills — which doesn't seem too sensible a place for an airport until you realise that *everything* in Dominica is tucked away in valleys between hills — and has the charm of a small well-painted country railway station.

What it does *not* have, however, is a decent telephone connection with the neighbouring French island of Guadeloupe. It took me twenty-five minutes of wrestling with the system to get through to Jean-Claude, and then another ten minutes of Anglo-French misunderstanding to get the message across that the Pawnee was *mal d'induction manifold*. When it did finally trickle through, Jean-Claude expressed concern over the shock to my system and then rather more concern over the shock to the Pawnee's airframe engendered by passing through the top of the tree. I told him that when I'd checked it over afterwards it had seemed to be okay — apart from looking like a flower stall after a hurricane — and he sounded much relieved, and said he'd send an engineer down to sort out the motor *toute suite*. I replied that that was nice, but that I couldn't hang around here until it was fixed because there might be business waiting for me in Antigua. Jean-Claude said he was sure there wouldn't be — which was probably accurate, but less than tactful — and then the phone gave a last despairing crackle and cut us off.

So that was that. I had a swift beer in the restaurant, went and breathed alcohol fumes over Customs and Immigration clearing outbound, and then stumped out to the sun-blasted apron.

And my Beech 18.

She was sitting on the corner of the tarmac where I'd left her five days ago — since she was much too big to get into the spray-strip — and coming to the boil nicely as the heat of the day hitched into overdrive. She wasn't a pretty aeroplane, but then no Beech 18 is. They're a squat, knobbly, blunt-all-over low wing monoplane with distinctive (and inadequate) twin fins, a pair of Pratt & Whitney Wasp Junior nine-cylinder radial engines, and a distinct air of utility-before-grace. On top of these natural advantages, my particular 18 also had a distinct air of scruffiness-before-grace, too. She was a 1946 D18S model, and her twenty-eight years of life had not treated her kindly. A fairly recent Acrylic re-spray in white had covered up some of the dents and scratches and corrosion — but as soon as you got within twenty yards of her it was obvious that the paint job was nothing more than a desperate layer of make-up on the face of a wrinkled old whore.

I did a careful external inspection and then opened the Air-stair door, climbed in, and pulled it up and shut behind me. The inside of the fuselage, stripped of its eight seats for the Caracas job, was hot and stuffy and stank of oil and aluminium and old, forgotten cargoes. I hauled myself uphill to the cockpit and flopped into the pilot's seat. The hard, faded green leather was at hot water bottle temperature from standing in the sun, and I could feel the back of my shirt sticking damply to both it and me.

I sighed, fastened the bedraggled seat belt, and went through the motions of starting up. The left engine caught immediately, but the right one got itself flooded. (Okay, okay — *I* got it flooded then. It's easily done: Wasp Juniors flood in the tropics if you give them a wet look.) I eventually persuaded it to start by playing pat-a-cake with the throttle and mixture: it half ran in a gale of coughs and bangs, then cleared itself with a final snarling belch and picked up on all nine. The black smoke-screen it had pumped out was whipped away in the slipstream, and I settled the revs back to the clattering rumble of 1,200 rpm and started going round the cockpit checking things.

Five minutes later, I was lined up on the runway and ready to go. The tower said: "Alpha Whisky yo' cleah take-off" in a broad Bee-wee — British West Indian — accent, and I shoved the throttles up to the stops. The engines ran up in a huge rasping thunder, and we left the ground halfway along the runway. With no cargo, she even had an illusion of performance.

After getting the wheels up and organising climb power, I turned left and rumbled up the sky on a northerly heading for Antigua via overhead Guadeloupe. The deep green slopes of Morne Diablotins crawled past the left wing tip, and the base of the huge cumulus ramparts round the summit formed a menacing grey roof at 3,000 feet above my head. I levelled off just below the base and started wondering whether another Lucky Strike would prove instantly fatal.

Ten miles north of the Dominican coastline I said good day to Melville Hall and clicked the frequency to 118.4 MHz to talk to Le Raizet Approach, Guadeloupe. The first thing *they* said was that my transmission was the French equivalent of crappy . . .

And the second thing was that they had an aircraft missing, and would I be prepared to help with the search?

* * *

My immediate reaction was *No I bloody wouldn't*, 'cos I've got a stinking hangover and a stinking overdraft and I need to go home to Antigua and get a beer for the one and some paid-for flying for the other . . .

But you can't say that. Not if you've got an empty aeroplane and no schedule to keep.

Soddit.

I pressed the mike button on the control yoke and said: "Roger, Le Raizet: Alpha Whiskey has fuel for two hours' searching. Who's gone down and where d'you want me? Over."

The radio made bacon-frying noises for a moment, then the French voice came back again.

"Ah . . . Alphair Wheeskey, United States Coas'guard One-twentee is in ze sairsh area. Please contac' 'im on one-two-one-decimal-fife. Ovair."

I said Ta very much and switched to 121.5, the international emergency frequency. Coastguard 120 — presumably one of the tatty Grumman seaplanes they keep at Roosevelt Roads in Puerto Rico — came back instantly out of the ether in a very Georgian drawl.

"Gladta have yew-all with us, Lima Alpha Whiskey. Ah . . . we're lookin' for a Twin Commanche, November 2332 Romeo, who wen' missin' late las' night on a flight from Coolidge, Antigua to Caracas. He was goin' down the islan' chain, an' his las' report was overhead Guadeloupe. There wasn't any Mayday call an' of course there ain't no Goddam radar roun' here, so we don' really know where he is. But at the moment we're workin' on the assumption that he wen' inna th' sea someplace between Guadeloupe an' Dominica, on account of Dominica was the next place he shoulda reported. So we'd be real glad if yew-all'd take a patch from the north coast o' Dominica to ten miles north o' that, if yew don' mind, centred on the 174 radial of the Guadeloupe Papa-Papa-Romeo beacon. Yew'll be lookin' for a coupla life jackets: accordin' to the flight plan, they din' have no dinghy. Yew get all that okay?"

I said Sure. It was all bloody vague — the kite might be hundred of miles away for all anybody actually *knew* — but like the man said, you've got to start somewhere. I eased the throttles back a bit, cranked the Beech into a descending left turn, and then sat back and thought about it.

Twin Com N2332R: I knew that kite. It was — or had been — one of my business competitors in Antigua.

It was — or again, *had* been — owned and operated by a guy called Cas McGrath. Shortish, American, and nasty. Lousy pilot, too, by repute. I'd never flown with him myself — but I'd certainly seen him land that Twin Com like a piano falling off a fifth-floor roof a few times. In fact, come to think of it, he'd arrived at Maiquetia, the civil airport for Caracas, while I was waiting for take-off clearance there six days ago. He'd dropped it on there like a coal delivery, too.

I pressed the mike switch again: "One-twenty, Alpha Whiskey: confirm pilot of 32 Romeo was named McGrath?"

"Standby." I visualised him turning up the report. Then: "Yeah, that's affirmative, sir. Yew-all know him?"

"Yeah."

"Yew-all got any ideas based on that, sir?"

I thought for a moment. You can't just say 'he was a lousy pilot' — and come to think of it, they already knew that anyway. Any airman in the Caribbean who doesn't carry a dinghy *and* hasn't got the sense to yell Mayday when he gets bother over water has to be eight-eights ivory from the neck up.

I thumbed the button and said: "Negative, One-twenty: I didn't know him that well. Does it say who else was on the aircraft?"

"Ah . . . yeah. Guy called Hawkins. L. Hawkins. That's all — jus' the one passenger. Hope he wasn't a friend of yours, too."

"Nope. Neither of them were. Call you back later. Out."

L. Hawkins. That'd be Larry Hawkins, dollar to a dime.

Poor old bastard.

Larry Hawkins was one of Antigua's characters — and believe me, you practically need two heads to be a character in that place. He was a fit little old guy of about sixty, an expatriate New Yorker. He didn't actually have two *heads* — but he certainly had two something else in full measure, because he was the best customer the brothels on the island ever had. Which isn't bad going at sixty. Villa Yolande's and Joey's were going to miss him if he'd ended up as a shark's breakfast. Or at least, they were going to miss his bankroll.

Larry worked for a guy called Harvey Bouvier — a big fat crook who ran a chain of souvenir shops up and down the islands. So maybe McGrath had been doing some work for Bouvier . . . ? Well, if he had, he was welcome: I'd done some myself here and there, and it was a bloody sight more trouble than it was worth. Harvey was the kind of twisting bastard whose cargoes always weighed twice as much as he said they did, and might well vary considerably in content from the manifest to boot. And when you'd got all *that* sorted out and done the flight, it took you a year and a day to screw the charter fee out of him.

All of which, of course, was exactly no help at all in finding Twin Com 32 Romeo or the survivors thereof.

I levelled the Beech off at 500 feet, then played with throttles and pitch levers until the engines were grunting over at 1,800 rpm and the fuel-flow meters had slid back to thirty-four gallons per hour per engine. That's what the Flight Handbook laughingly calls 'best economy cruise' — although you can take it from me that it doesn't feel particularly economical when the fuel bill comes in. Especially when it's a non-profit-making flight.

I sighed, wiped the sweat off my dark glasses with the tail of my shirt, and got my eyes down on the bright, sun-glaring surface of the ocean.

* * *

Two hours later I was still at it. Grinding up and down in ten-mile search legs and slowly melting in the sticky heat. Once every minute I'd blink the sweat out of my eyes, mentally divide the shining sea into strips, then methodically march my gaze along each strip in turn, searching.

And every time, I'd find precisely nothing. No little yellow life-jackets. No sea-dye. No smoke flares. Nothing.

Swanning around at low level in the heat of the blazing noonday sun had turned the cockpit into a steam-bath. Perspiration dripped off my chin, ran down the lenses of my sunglasses, and plastered my clothes to my body. My hands left damp sweaty smears on the control yoke, and the steady blattering of the engines pounded at my headache like a blunt instrument. I lit a Lucky Strike, blew smoke at the fuel gauge, and dreamed about five or six long cold beers while I twiddled the gauge selector switch. Then I sagged back in my seat and got my eyes down and looking again.

Nothing, nothing, nothing, bloody nothing.

The controller at Guadeloupe had been doing a pretty good selling job on the search all morning: practically every aircraft going through the area had come on to the emergency frequency and offered their services to the Coastguard at least *en passant*. A LIAT — Leeward Island Air Transport — Avro 748 and an Air Guadeloupe Twin Otter had hung around for fifteen minutes each, and at one point we'd even had a Caravelle screaming through the search area at 100 feet and 250 knots. He was more of a danger to traffic than any practical help, since his chances of spotting anything at that lick just didn't exist, but I suppose the thought was there. Or maybe he was just a frustrated fighter pilot.

Right now, there were four of us on the go: the Coastguard, me, an Air Sport Cessna 337 from Le Raizet — and, of all things, a Flamingo Air Charter DC6. Quite what *he* was messing about on a search for a Twin Com for, I couldn't imagine: but he'd broken his flight plan from Maiquetia to Antigua half an hour ago, and here he was still at it, combing a patch down south of Dominica. Maybe Flamingo Air, based in Miami and reputedly financed by the CIA, were getting a rush of altruism to the corporate brain. If they *weren't*, someone was certainly going to have to do some fast explaining to a non-flying accountant about why he burned all that fuel.

And it wasn't even achieving anything, either. Flamingo Air had found precisely the same as all the rest of us — which was exactly damn-all. No oil slicks, no wreckage — nothing whatsoever.

I crushed out the Lucky, glanced at the fuel gauge and the clock, and decided that Scott's contribution, at least, was over. Coastguard said, "Thank yew-all very much for yore help, sir," when I told them I was going home to Antigua, and I bent the Beech away to the north and managed not to make any snide cracks about thank-you's not paying fuel bills.

*   *   *

Antigua is roughly triangular, with the base of the triangle in the south and each of the sides about thirteen miles long. The eastern half of the island is flat and parched, while the western seaboard is ringed with a jawbone of humpy young mountains topped by patches of tangled jungle. It's the same pattern on all the West Indian islands: where the land's flat you get dry prickly scrub, and on the high ground, where the orographic clouds form and double or treble the rainfall, you find the jungles.

In Antigua's case, the whole thing is surrounded by a coastline of beautiful white-sand beaches, threaded with the baubles of the luxury tourist hotels. From the air, the contrast between the hotels and the tin-roofed shanty towns of the interior is very marked indeed.

People who wonder why Antigua has a colour problem should look at the place from the air occasionally.

The Beech and me flew in over the south coast at exactly two o'clock in the afternoon, rumbling downhill through the usual puffs of fair-weather cumulus. There weren't any other aircraft about, so the tower said, "Alpha Whisky yo' cleah lan' numma wun." I growled up towards the northern tip of the triangle, turned right over the festering sprawl of St John's, Antigua's 'capital city', and lobbed down on to Coolidge Airport's single active runway, taking the usual pasting in the turbulence between the low hills on either side of the approach.

There wasn't much on the apron — just one 707 and a sprinkling of LIAT Islanders — so they let me park in front of the terminal building. I pulled the mixtures back into lean cut-off, opened the throttles to prevent detonation as the engines clattered to a stop — and then there was blessed silence, apart from the lowering whine of the gyros and the buzzing in my ears. I climbed out with a handful of general declaration papers, cleared Customs and Immigration, and then headed for the airport restaurant for a few of the burnt cow-turds they serve up as hamburgers and a couple of fast, cold beers.

The beers were cold, all right — there'd be a general strike at Coolidge if anything went wrong with the beer-cooler — but the restaurant, as usual, was hot as a first solo's armpit and stinking of a mixture of yesterday's jet exhaust and last month's meatloaf. All the terminal facilities on the airport are housed in one long, low building alongside the apron, and since this building is blessed with neither air-conditioning — except for the control tower at the end — nor blast-fences, the heat and the stench are permanent features. Still, I suppose it could be worse: if they *did* have blast-fences you'd get the meatloaf full strength.

I finished the beers, which came straight out of my pores again as sweat in the early afternoon heat, then went back out into the blazing sun and taxied the Beech down to the aircraft park at the top of the disused 10–28 runway. I left it alongside the other half of Scott's Mighty Fleet — a single-engined Cherokee 180 — and walked back up the taxiway to my clubhouse, set back in the dusty scrub near the eastern corner of the apron.

'Clubhouse', if you want to be pedantic, was rather a grand term for the place. It was actually an old paint-shed I'd bought from West Indies Oil eighteen months before, and had plonked down by a Pam Am fork-lift truck on the end of the row of tatty-looking airline cargo sheds which sit alongside the small service road at the back of the apron. I'd cut some new windows in it, added a veranda about the same size as the original shed,

42

and painted the whole thing a tasteful shade of dog-sick cream. It still bore an unmistakable air of paint-shed if you looked at it from certain angles — but it *was* a clubhouse. It even had a sign on top saying Leeward Islands Aero Club. I'd painted *that* myself, too.

I fumbled with the combination lock for a moment, let myself in, and opened up the shutters to let the trade wind blow through. It still looked the same as it had six days ago: pictures of aeroplanes thumb-tacked to the walls, a pile of old magazines and the tech-log clipboards scattered over the table, and a two-week-old student briefing on the blackboard. It was hot, dingy, and inhospitable — but at least it hadn't been burgled, which was something.

There were three envelopes on the floor, where someone had pushed them in under the door. I picked them up, thought about opening them, and then decided they could wait until drinking time. I stuffed them in my shirt pocket and headed for the phone to drum up some business.

*   *   *

By six forty-five in the evening I'd done two training flights in the Cherokee, taken bookings for another five or six hours on it during the next few days, and worked up a thirst the size of a dry swimming pool. I'd also been told by at least four separate people that 32 Romeo hadn't been found yet. I watched my second student woosh off in his Boeing-sized Lincoln, then taxied the Cherokee to overnight parking, tied it down, and walked back up the service road. The sun was setting redly behind the hills to the west as I went, turning the standing cumulus over Boggy Peak Mountain into heaps of blood-red cotton wool. By the time I got to the clubhouse the daylight was fading with the incredible speed of the tropics, and the evening chorus of whistling and chirruping from a million crickets and tree frogs was cranking itself up in the dusty scrub all around.

I switched on the lights, hauled a new bottle of Johnnie Walker out of my battered flight bag, and settled down on one of the veranda benches to catch up with my mail.

The first of the *billets-doux* turned out to be landing fees for the Beech for the third quarter of 1974 — $770, Eastern Caribbean currency. That was £160, or about $380 US at the current rate of exchange.

Well, they'd wait a while for *that*. Next, please.

The next was the fuel bill for the months of August and September. $2,274 EC. That *would* have to be paid, or they'd stop serving me juice. I gloomed at it a moment, then picked up the last one. The envelope bore the insignia of Seagreen Air Transport, the Antigua-based cargo outfit who did my maintenance.

That was the one I was *really* worried about.

I ripped it open, laid the bill on my knees, and scanned down it, skipping the details, until I came to the total.

$3,724 EC.

Oh, Christ.

For a long minute I just sat there looking at it, stupidly hoping I'd mis-read the figures. Then, when I'd finally convinced myself I hadn't, I took a long gulp from the bottle and stared out unseeingly across the terminal apron. The last of the daylight was draining away, and the airport lights were sticky yellow pools in the hot buzzing dusk. A group of vehicles were clustered around a glistening 707, and the passenger steps were being towed away.

$3,724. For the Courtesy of Your Early Settlement.

I tried to think about it sensibly — but I couldn't. All I could think was *what the bloody hell made you buy that fucking Beech . . . ?*

I knew what had made me buy it, of course: I'd had a dream of expanding from a flying school into a charter business, and making enough money to sell up and go back to England and start a small flying club there . . .

Only it hadn't quite worked out that way.

I'd started the school in Antigua on Christmas Eve, 1972 — a year and ten months ago. It had been a good operation, too: what with no competition, practically no bad weather, and an affluent section of the population who had nothing else to do but drink and water-ski, I'd spent more hours in the air each day than most of the airlines. I'd got the hire-purchase on the Cherokee paid off in the first eight months, and made a cracking good profit in the next eight. Wizard. Scott's a genius — if somewhat twitchy and hitting the bottle a bit after flying nearly 1,900 hours in sixteen months without a break.

So then I'd had my bright idea about expanding. I did some slick talking at the Canadian Imperial Bank of Commerce, mortgaged the Cherokee for the difference between what I had, what I needed, and what they'd let me borrow, hitched a ride to Miami with Seagreen . . .

And bought the Beech. The cheapest, nastiest kite among all the cheap and nasty kites languishing in the sales lots at Miami International, waiting to finish their careers in some steamy Central American republic. I hadn't had any illusions about her age and condition — but I hadn't had any choice, either. If I was going into the charter business I *had* to have a twin — and she was quite simply the only twin on the whole airport that I could afford. So I bought her.

That had been in June — and since then, things had gone downhill like a concrete parachute.

The problem was two-fold: (a) that there simply wasn't enough work around for a kite the size of the Beech — everyone always seemed to want something a bit bigger or a bit smaller — and (b) that I was too under-capitalised to afford another instructor to take over the flying school while I applied myself to finding the answer to (a). In short — buggered. The classic pattern of an aviation operator whose ideas are too big for his bank balance. My own fault, and nobody else's. As my bank manager put it, I was a good pilot but a lousy business man.

The problems weren't eased any by the Beech's propensity for swallowing expensive bits and pieces on what seemed like every second flight, either. Since I'd had her the tailwheel lock had broken, a magneto had packed up, the electric flap motor had burnt out, a tyre had burst on landing — which was exciting, for a few seconds — and the bloody radios had fizzzled out about once a week. And then, to cap it all, the starboard prop had run away — chewing up the constant speed unit beyond repair, of course.

Hence the current bill for $3,724.

I hauled the crumpled pack of Luckies out of my pocket, disentangled one, and washed down the first drag with another go at the bottle. Out on the apron, the 707 started firing up engines with a series of *whine-screech* noises.

Now, I was on the verge of bankruptcy — and there wasn't a damn thing I could do about it. I couldn't even fly the Beech up to Miami and sell it again: nobody wants a kite on the Leeward Island register, and by the time I'd had her overhauled

45

for a new American Certificate of Airworthiness I'd probably clear about a third of what I owed on her.

The Boeing's engines spooled up to a keening howl, and it started to move. Silver, blue and white livery glistened darkly in the lights as it swung ponderously round towards the western taxiway.

British Airways. The Monday evening flight to England.

My lovely, longed-for England.

For a moment I thought about it, my mind reaching back for the sort of rose-tinted pictures an exile remembers after seven long years. The soft green fields, the wood-smokey reds and browns of autumn . . .

Irritated, I swallowed another mouthful of Scotch and tried to snap out of it. I was tied to Antigua now — tied with bonds of steel and aluminium and bad debts, at least until such time as the whole thing folded up round my ears. For me England was a hell of a lot farther away than eight hours in a Boeing . . .

Suddenly, I was sick of both the airport and my own thoughts. I stuffed the bills back into my pockets, and went inside to fill in the day's flying in the aircraft logs.

I was just finishing when the car arrived. It thumped off the service road, crunched on the gravel in front of the clubhouse, and slithered to a stop just short of wiping out the veranda.

It was a blood-red Ford Maverick. Harvey Bouvier got out of it.

4

HE WAS A big fat man, with a big fat manner. Vile tartan
Bermuda shorts, garish sea-island shirt, and the heavy-jowled
rubbery features and crinkly grey hair of the caricature New
Yorker. He looked and sounded like an over-weight middle-aged
slob — but if he *was* a slob, he was a very bright one. Everyone
who'd been on the wrong end of one of his innumerable deals
would vouch for that — and many of them did, regularly, in
every second bar on the island.

The boards of the veranda creaked as he bounced up the single
step. Behind him, the other door of the car opened and a large
black man got out slowly and looked around.

Harvey grabbed my hand in a paw like a young octopus and
boomed: "Hey, Scotty — howaya? Goodta seeya, boy!"

I said Hi, backed away a pace, and retrieved the remains of
my hand. Harvey's Bronx voice was like a Pratt & Whitney at
climb power, and catching it between the eyes at close range
wasn't improving my headache. In fact, his whole presence wasn't
improving it: I wasn't in the mood for Harvey Bouvier tonight.
I made what-can-I-do-for-you noises and hoped there wasn't
anything.

But there was, of course. Harvey wasn't the social-call type.

He moved past me into the clubhouse, and stood there looking
round like a dog who can't remember where he's buried his bone.
It wasn't rudeness — or not conscious rudeness, anyway — it
was just that he was one of those nervous-energy types who can't
stand still for more than five seconds at a time.

"Well, look, I think I gotta job for ya," he said. "A flyin' job.
Good one."

47

"Working for you?" I asked. After the last couple of times, the prospect did not enthral. This time it was going to be cash in advance — *and* I wanted to see what I was carrying before the crates were sealed.

I got ready to break this to him — but he made a small throw-away gesture and said: "No — not for me. This is another guy: ya don't know him." He picked up my board rubber and started examining it for microphones.

"What sort of job?"

"He'll tell ya that himself." He gave the rubber a last suspicious stare, and started in on the chalk.

"Well, where is he? And what's his name?"

"I can't tell ya his name, but he's down at English Harbour. On a yacht. I'll take ya down an' bring ya back here."

I thought about it while Harvey doodled on the blackboard. It all sounded bloody suspicious — a typical Harvey idea, in fact — but on the other hand, people on yachts in English Harbour were the sort of people I needed to know right now. It costs about five dollars a minute to breathe on those charter yachts — so if this guy was dossing down there, at least I shouldn't have any trouble getting paid. And it might be a perfectly legal job, in spite of Harvey.

Might be . . .

Well, it wouldn't do any harm to find out I thought.

"Okay," I said. "Let's go."

Harvey nodded, brushed chalk-dust off his hands, and headed back to the Maverick. The big black guy, who'd been leaning against the driver's door, un-leaned and opened it for him.

Harvey said over his shoulder: "Ya've met Sherman before have ya, Scotty? No? Okay — this is Sherman. He's my assistant. Sherman, meet Bill Scott."

We nodded to each other briefly, then Sherman went back to staring round into the darkness while Harvey got himself folded up behind the wheel. I'd seen *that* kind of assistant before — and he wasn't the kind you hire for the typing and phoning, either. He was the sort of help you get in when your business requires people to be creamed every now and then — or when you need a factor to discourage other people from creaming you. Sherman looked as though he might be pretty good at the job, too: he had a granite-hard jet-black face set in a permanent scowl, suspicious eyes, and a body like a ship's cylinder block.

I switched out the lights, locked up the clubhouse, and got into the car. They put me in the back, and Sherman sat in the front passenger seat. That didn't surprise me: a typing-and-phoning assistant would have done the chauffeur bit, too. . .

But a bodyguard needs both hands free.

* * *

If the ancient bastions of the British Empire are your thing, then English Harbour is a fascinating place. The harbour itself is a deep blue bite out of the scrubby green hills of the south coast, and the Royal Navy built a fortified dockyard there for the West Indies Fleet back in the Spanish Main days of the 1700s. They abandoned the joint in the mid-nineteenth century, and it went to rack and ruin for a hundred years until it got resurrected as a tourist attraction after the Second World War. Now it's known as Nelson's Dockyard and comes complete with old buildings of red brick and ship's beams, an Anglo-tropical pub-hotel called the Admiral's Inn, and a small wooden museum containing Arawak relics and Lord Nelson's Very Own Bed. It is also one of the big centres of the charter yacht industry in the Caribbean: rich Americans go there in the winter tourist season to loaf around on the boats drinking in atmosphere and dry Martinis. One or two of them even remember to go sailing. The charter fleet probably makes a bigger dent in the United States than the Royal Navy ever did: some of those yachts hire out at $8,000 US *a week*.

We pulled up in a dark corner of the Admiral's Inn car park, and walked in through the old stone archway and down to the quay with Sherman sticking close by Harvey's shoulder and me tagging along behind. There were ten or fifteen yachts moored up stern-to, and maybe another twenty or more out in the harbour. That was about usual for this time of year: the big stuff turns up during October-November to catch the start of the season. They made a fine sight, if you were in the mood to appreciate it — all soft lights, furled sails, and gleaming wood and chrome. Schooners, ketches, yawls, sloops, catamarans the size of young aircraft carriers — you name it. Everything from sleek ocean racers like *Gitana IV* to nasty old Rhine barges with three masts banged in 'em and a lot of fancy woodwork to please the tourists. The quayside was peopled with clumps of tanned young Americans in cut-down jeans and tee-shirts, busy telling each other who was

49

sleeping with who and what a dreadful season it was going to be. Nobody took the slightest notice of us, and we made it to a dark corner behind the old Officers' Quarters without bumping into anyone I knew.

When we got there, Harvey fished a small flat torch out of his pocket and flashed it four times out over the water. I couldn't make out which boat he was signalling — there were three or four anchored out in that general direction — but whoever they were, they were on the ball. A rubber Zodiak dinghy buzzed up in less than five minutes, Harvey and me piled in without a word, leaving Sherman behind — and then we were off and planing, with the outboard wailing angrily.

We whizzed across the harbour in the moonpath, bucking over the small wavelets, made a few turns round some of the boats that weren't showing lights — and then shot into the deep black shadows of a mangrove thicket about a hundred yards from the quay. I started to ask What The Hell — and then the moon went behind a cloud and we puttered out again and ambled quietly across to a long, seaworthy-looking yacht moored more or less in the middle of the harbour. So now I knew what the hell: anyone watching casually would have thought we were joyriding and lost interest — and anyone watching seriously would have needed infra-red eyes and a very lucky location to spot which yacht we ended up at.

The yacht we *did* end up at was a bloody great yawl — nigh on a hundred-footer, by the look of her. Her long sleek hull gleamed softly white in the star-light, and her low superstructure seemed to be all polished wood. She carried no outside lights at all, but there was a dim blue glow from the curtained windows of the deck saloon. As we came up on the side of the stern away from the Dockyard I saw her name. *Krakatoa*, registered in San Juan, Puerto Rico.

Rich man's boat.

The guy who'd been piloting the Zodiak shinned up the three-step boarding ladder first. I couldn't see much of him in the dark — only that he was white, about middle-aged, wearing a dark-coloured open shirt . . .

And a gun.

I couldn't see exactly what it was, but it was something pretty hefty in the pistol line. He had it berthed in a holster strapped to the left side of his chest under his shirt. The long dark shape of it was plainly visible when he stood up on the deck and looked around.

I seemed to be getting into bad company.

Harvey went up next, surprisingly agile for his bulk, and I followed him. The deck was light-coloured wood, and the chrome-plated winches glinted as the moon came out again. The whole afterdeck was clean and tidy, the ends of the sheets neatly curled up on the sail locker for'ard of the binnacle. There was a clean smell of warm wood and varnish in the air.

Harvey said, "Come with me, Scotty," and walked forward. Our erstwhile chauffeur stayed on the stern. I took a last look round, noticing the shadowy figure of another guy sitting on the fo'c'sle hatch up in the sharp end, then did what the man said. Harvey picked his way into the cockpit, waited for me for a moment, then clumped down a short flight of steps into the saloon. I went down after him and stopped at the bottom, blinking in the sudden light.

Harvey said: "Bill, meet Mr Hans-Jürgen Ruchter."

So I quit blinking, and met him.

*　　　*　　　*

He was standing rigidly at ease in the middle of the saloon: one of those men who radiate power and authority without moving a muscle. I started forward to shake hands in the True British Manner — and then stopped again. Some men, you don't shake hands with.

He was tall, maybe six-two, and solid with it. But it was his eyes that hit you first: they were very light blue — and totally, utterly cold. Their still, unblinking stare seemed to bore through my skull and thump into the wall behind me.

I'd met eyes like that before. Killer eyes.

The face matched them, too: broad, bleak, and set hard in the 1940 Master Race expression of stony disdain, as if they'd machined it out of Krupp steel in the days of the Hitler Youth and he hadn't moved it since. His hair was close-cropped and fair, he was lightly tanned, and he looked fit and tough. The perfect German officer. I couldn't guess his age within ten years — but I could certainly tell his era. You could almost hear the jackboots tramping.

He wore a dark blue silk shirt and a pair of snow-white trousers, both of which looked as though they'd been delivered by the best tailor in the Reich the day before. His surroundings fitted him, too. The inside of the saloon was all polished wood, dark leather, and silk drapes the same colour as his shirt. It was rich, even tasteful if you like that sort of thing — but somehow, it managed to be as cold as the man himself. You got the feeling that he'd decided to have the best and ordered fifty storm-troopers to make it so — and they'd carried out his orders to the letter, and there it was. Plonk. Efficient as a Panzer charge, and about as much personality.

Of course, it takes money to be that cold and efficient. *That* stuck out all over, too. I began to feel very small and shabby in my faded jeans and sweat-stained bush shirt.

Ruchter watched me taking it all in. When he thought I'd finished he said: "Good evening, Mr Scott." His voice was deep and harsh and slightly guttural — and as expressionless as his face. He just opened his steel-trap mouth and the words came marching out — no inflection, no emphasis, nothing.

I thought of clicking my heels and saying 'Heil Hitler' — but then unthought pretty quick. He looked the sort who might be a bit sensitive about that kind of crack.

"Sit down, gentlemen."

Harvey and I parked ourselves opposite each other on the deep leather-covered bench seat which ran round three sides of the saloon table. Ruchter remained standing: he would, of course.

"What would you like to drink?"

I said Scotch, and Harvey elected to blow his mind on tomato juice. He never touched alcohol — which alone made him a character, on Antigua — but he was a compulsive eater. He'd already homed in on a cut-glass bowl of peanuts, and he shoved a couple in his mouth and started chewing mechanically as his eyes wandered round the saloon. Nervous energy again. I wished I had his problem: I'd rather have an overweight gut than a pickled one any day.

Ruchter pressed a bell-push, and a blue-shirted steward marched in and got busy at a fold-away cocktail cabinet. That figured, too: *Herr Reichmarshals* don't mess about with bottles themselves. Might dent the image.

When the steward had gone Ruchter raised his cognac, fixed me with his cold stare, and said: "*Prost*, Mr Scott. To a success-full association."

He sipped. I gulped. I had a feeling I was going to need it.

I was right.

Ruchter put his glass down and said metallically: "Mr Scott, I have a proposition to make to you. I wish to have three small cargoes of merchandise delivered to Puerto Rico without passing through Customs. I want you to carry them in your aircraft. For this, I am willing to pay your normal charter fees plus thirty thousand dollars US."

*   *   *

I nearly choked on the whisky. It didn't surprise me that it was a smuggling job — not after the way I'd been brought here — but it *did* surprise me that it was $30,000 worth of smuggling job. That was big, big money in these parts: Christ, I knew people who'd smuggle the main runway out of Coolidge Airport for half that. Ruchter's 'small cargoes' must be something very special indeed . . .

Then it hit me — the way Harvey and Ruchter must have known it would.

Thirty thousand US dollars!

That was about 60,000 bucks Bee-wee — and that sort of bread would clear me with the bank and then some. I could get rid of the Beech, buy another trainer, and build up the flying school again. Get another instructor, branch out to Montserrat and St Kitts . . .

Or for God's sake, Scott — you can go HOME, man! Just sell up here and go. You won't have to find an employer in England at all — you'll have enough money to buy a couple of Chipmunks and start your own flying club . . .

Just for a moment, I saw it. A small green-grass airfield on a gentle summer evening . . . a little wooden clubhouse with two red-and-white Chipmunks outside . . . the friendly *blatta-blatta-blatta* of a Gypsy Major . . .

Then the dream dissolved.

I said, "No."

Ruchter's eyes narrowed like gunsights.

"You must think about this . . . very carefully, Mr Scott." His voice was still the same, cold and flat. "These cargoes are not drugs, and the risk to you will be minimal. And if you do not undertake this, you will be bankrupt before the end of the year."

So they'd been checking on me. Well, fuck 'em — I still wasn't getting involved in smuggling. No matter what.

53

Not again.

"No."

It came out as a husky croak. I cleared my throat into the silence that followed, and stood up.

"Sorry, Mr Ruchter — but no. Definitely. Thank you for the offer, but I can't help you. Now, if you'd have me run back to the Dockyard ..."

Harvey said quietly: "Bill, you *are* gonna do this."

I looked at him. He was studying the peanut bowl, carefully making a selection with his thick fingers. He didn't even raise his eyes as he spoke.

"Cos if you don't," he went on, "I'm gonna tell the Immigration people about Great Ashfield."

I sat down again. Very slowly, like an old, old man. There was a roaring in my ears, and I could feel myself going cold all over. I reached for my drink. My hand was shaking so much I slopped half of it over my knees. The glass chattered against my teeth as I gulped down the rest without tasting it.

They *had* been checking on me ...

"How did you ... find out?" I heard myself whisper.

Harvey shrugged. "That don't matter, Bill. I checked on ya 'long time back. I got contacts for that sorta thing."

Yeah, you would have. But he was right — the details didn't matter. The only thing that mattered was that there was always *someone* who checked ...

"What ... good would it do you, to tell?" My voice was a dry rasp.

Harvey raised his eyebrows, shovelled a handful of peanuts into his mouth, and chewed on them rhythmically while he spoke.

"Well, if they find out about that they'll take away ya work permit, right? So then ya'd be finished in Antigua — an' then, maybe, ya'd change ya mind about doin' this job."

I managed to say "Why?" although I already knew the answer.

He swallowed noisily, and waved a big hand at me. "Fuck, Bill — ya wouldn't have no choice. Ya'd be broke an' in debt an' ya wouldn't be able ta work — an ya ain't even a fuckin' limited company. Ya'd *have* ta do the job ta square yaself — if ya didn't, ya'd be in debt for ya whole damn life. *Think* about it, huh?"

But I couldn't think about it. Not right then. All I could think about were the ghosts that were bubbling up out of the past to haunt me again.

The face of the Eurasian, grey in the dawn light ... a wooden prop turning, turning ... the judge, his voice echoing in the quiet courtroom ...

Jenny ...

The nightmare closed in, the way it always did. I mumbled, "Scuse me — want some air," and made the long climb on to my feet. Neither of them moved as I pushed past Ruchter, picked up the half-full Scotch decanter from the cocktail cabinet, and stumbled up the steps to the deck.

Outside in the hot night, I leaned against the side of the saloon and tried to get a grip on myself. It didn't work. All I could see were the ghosts — and all I could hear was a mocking voice in my head saying *someone always checks ...*

I lifted the decanter.

*　　*　　*

I don't remember all of the trial. Just a few fragments like old film stills of the dusty courtroom, the white wigs, and the bland unresponsive faces of the jury. And the charges, of course: I remember the charges. Three counts of 'securing or facilitating the entry into the United Kingdom of an illegal entrant', one of 'being knowingly concerned in the fraudulent evasion of the prohibition on the importation of certain goods, namely twenty-one pounds of heroin', one more of being in possession of a controlled drug, and a final couple concerned with entering and leaving the country without clearing Customs.

There were no charges arising from the death of the Eurasian. All they did was hold an inquest on him. Accidental death.

I admitted the illegal entry counts but pleaded not guilty to the heroin charges on the grounds that I hadn't known the stuff was on board. The jury didn't believe me.

I was sent to prison for four years.

As the judge passed sentence, I was looking at Jenny. Her face was white as parchment — and then she crumpled up, and sobbed and sobbed as if she was never going to stop.

That night, we lost our child. Jenny had a miscarriage at two a.m., and had to be rushed to hospital for blood transfusions.

I did my time in Wandsworth. I remember seeing the place for the first time, getting out of the Black Maria in the courtyard and looking up at the grimy, forbidding walls all round — but after that, memory blurs into a sort of greyness. Most of the events I can recall are disconnected and out of order: I don't know whether they happened at the beginning of the sentence, in the middle, or at the end.

I remember the last time Jenny came to see me, though.

It was in the autumn of '64. You can guess what about. She wore a red plastic mac over an unseasonable print dress, and she looked wonderful. My wife. My whole life. The afternoon sun streamed in through the window and lit up her silky blonde hair while she talked. I didn't hear a lot of it because I was just sitting and looking at her. I remember she told me he was an insurance salesman. Solid, reliable, liked children. I heard my voice mumbling inanities and saying I didn't blame her and I hoped she'd be happy. Then suddenly it was time for her to go and I was watching her getting up and saying an awkward goodbye...

And then the last seconds had ticked away and she was gone. I don't think she saw the big, slow tears trickling down my cheeks: I think they didn't come until after the door had closed behind her.

The divorce procedure was quick and simple. All I had to do was sign.

I never saw her again.

*   *   *

I found I'd slid down to a sitting position on the warm deck of the *Krakatoa*, with my back against the saloon and my knees drawn up to my chest. Sweat was running down my face, and my hands were sticky and trembling. The night was close and quiet. I could hear the tiny lapping of water on the hull and the gentle tonging of halyards knocking against the main-mast in the muggy breeze.

A dozen yards away the sentry on the stern stood immobile in the moonlight, watching me. I ignored him, and took a hefty swig from the decanter. The whisky ran like friendly fire into my stomach. I made a brief attempt to cough up my sandals, then fumbled out a new pack of Luckies and tried to light one. It took three matches to do it, because they kept going out in my shaking fingers. I stared out over the water at the happy lights of the Admiral's Inn and the Dockyard. The sound of steel band music floated thinly across the tropical harbour, 3,700 miles away from a cold little room in Wandsworth prison.

Three thousand seven hundred miles — and ten years. Exactly. To the day.

Happy bloody anniversary, Scott. Have another drink...

If I closed my eyes, I could still see her. The picture had endured, sharp and clear, all down the empty years. The print dress, moulded to her body... the sun in her hair... the hurt in her eyes...

I still loved her.

I had another drink.

* * *

They kept me inside for two years, eight months and ten days, then let me out at two o'clock in the afternoon on October 8th, 1966. Full remission. I was twenty-four years old, silent and unsmiling, and cold and numb deep down inside. There was no-one waiting for me at the gate, no-one waiting for me anywhere. So I walked out into Heathfield Road alone, and began the second part of my sentence.

That's the part that never ends.

Maybe it would've been easier if I hadn't tried to get back to flying. But flying was my life: the skill in my hands and head the only thing I had left out of the wreckage. It was a rusty skill, after nearly three years in prison — but the Board of Trade hadn't taken my licences away, so within a fortnight I'd got them all re-validated.

Then I went job-hunting. Which wasn't fun.

I'd known it was going to be difficult, of course — but nothing could possibly have prepared me for just *how* difficult. I wasn't an ordinary ex-con looking for an ordinary job: I was a pilot who'd *used an aeroplane* to smuggle people and dope, and killed somebody in the process. And *that* made me about as employable in aviation as a ten-year leper. It was no good explaining that I hadn't *meant* to smuggle dope or kill anybody. It was no good saying I'd been young and hard-up and that bringing in three refugees had seemed a very small crime at the time. It was no good telling people I was a hundred years older now and a very different person...

It was no good explaining anything. So I didn't even try. Just went from interview to interview, counting the pennies from the Prisoners' Aid people, until the money ran out altogether.

Then I got a job serving petrol in a garage. That lasted until the till was a pound short one night. Then I got fired.

So I got another job serving petrol — this time on an airfield. I fuelled, oiled and washed aeroplanes during the day, and served in the flying club bar at night. For three months I didn't tell anybody any of my past: didn't even tell them I could fly. At the end of that time I went to the club manager, gave him the full story, and asked him if he'd let me stand in as a part-time instructor occasionally.

He fired me on the spot.

The next morning I spent the last of my money on a tourist-class boat ticket to Canada.

I'd started running.

*   *   *

I went to the Budworm Project in New Brunswick first. They looked at my logbooks and licences and said "Sure, buddy — we gotta job for you." That went fine for a little while — and then some Canadian pilot who'd been flying in England arrived, and he recognised me. He didn't deliberately lower the boom: he assumed my employers knew about my past, and chatted to one of the boss-men in the bar about what a reformed character I seemed to be.

Which, of course, made me an unemployed reformed character.

The next job was instructing. That lasted six months, and then I was fired again. Discreetly, of course — they'd call it 'made redundant' now — but still fired.

The buzz gets around.

An industrial smuggler offered me a job after that, flying contraband down to the States from a field near Montreal. He was the first of several, over the years. I turned them all down.

Maybe I shouldn't have bothered.

The Biafran War blew up. I bummed my way to Portugal and got a job flying an ex-RAF Anson for a charity organisation. Food in and refugees out, alongside a hodge-podge collection of other freelance pilots in ancient Connies and Daks. Most of them were doing what I was doing — but some were carrying guns instead of butter, and word got out. A bunch of reporters caught up with me at Faro Airport — and a story appeared in a British Sunday paper about how Bill Scott, ex-dope runner, could now be found grinding in and out of a place where guns fetched a king's ransom . . .

The charity outfit dropped me like a hot brick.

I turned down the offers of the gun-running boys, and moved on. This time it was Malaysia, rumbling over the jungle in clapped-out DC3s . . . until the Immigration people refused to renew my work permit.

Then it was the Sudan, crop-dusting. Then Borneo, in Islanders. Then New Zealand. Then Texas. Then Zambia. Sometimes it was hard to remember all the places I'd run to — but it was never hard to remember the way they'd all ended up. *That* was always the same: I'd last six weeks or six months or a year — and then someone, some shadowy *someone,* would get curious and start checking back . . .

And then I'd be out in the cold again, looking for another new start in another new country.

It's a vicious circle, too, of course. As your history of 'redundancies' and lost work permits grows, so you get more and more suspect. If you admit your background you don't get a job — and if you don't admit it, you become a man without a past. And employers and immigration officials get curious about that kind of person. . .

So, as the years go by, hope curls up at the edges and eventually dies. The running gets harder and harder and lonelier and lonelier — and the list of places you can't go back to gets steadily longer. Then it takes more and more whisky to help you forget, and more and more pills to make you sleep at night . . .

Until, in the end, there comes a day when you can't run any more at all.

It looked like that day had just arrived.

*   *   *

The choice was a joke. Stay clean and get busted more than ever before — or do another smuggling job, and get a new start. Make enough money to go back to England and set up my own flying club instead of trailing around after jobs I wouldn't get . . .

Full circle. Bloody funny.

And the funniest thing of all was the efforts I'd made to go straight for the last eight years. If I'd given in to the offers and the pressures I'd have made a fortune — but I hadn't given in. That was the real hoot. I hadn't smuggled so much as a bottle of wine since I walked out of Wandsworth — and all it had brought me to, after eight empty years, was here and now. Broke, busted — and blackmailed.

You've paid your debt to society, Scott — except for the last few instalments, of course. We'll just keep asking for them as the years go by . . .

I found I was chuckling, down at the black water. It wasn't a pleasant sound. I stopped it abruptly.

It was no choice at all, really.

I heaved myself upright, the saloon walls doing most of the work. In the cockpit I stopped and took a long pull at the decanter. Then I clumped slowly down the steps into the saloon.

They were waiting for me — Harvey expectant, and Ruchter without any expression at all.

I said wearily: "What am I going to be carrying?"

5

RUCHTER SAID, "Four million dollars' worth of Krugerrands."

I felt my way to the deep leather seat and slid down on to it. Then I splashed whisky into my glass and had a short consultation for medicinal purposes. He still seemed to have said what I thought he'd seemed to have said.

"Four — *how* much worth of *what*?"

"Approximately four million US dollars' worth of Krugerrands. A Krugerrand is a South African gold coin. I have something over 20,000 of them, to be transported into Puerto Rico."

His voice was as flat and metallic as ever. He might have been talking about carrying a load of old bottle tops into a Salvation Army post. I fumbled for a Lucky Strike and tried to think of something more intelligent to say than Jesus Christ Almighty.

Harvey, who'd finished the peanuts and was now busy picking his teeth, shifted his bulk on the seat and hauled something out of a back pocket. It flashed in the light as he tossed it to me. I caught it.

"That's a Krugerrand, Bill," he said. "The current market value's £84 in your British money. It's about eighty-five per cent gold, with some copper an' things ta make it hard."

I looked at it, turning it over in my hand. Somehow, I'd always imagined gold coins as being big and yellow with pie-crust edges — but this thing was neat and conventional-looking and no bigger than the old British half-crown. It wasn't even the proper yellow colour of gold; there was a sort of orangey tint to it. One face said SUID AFRIKA and showed the bust of an old guy with a bushy beard — Paul Kruger himself, probably — and the other had a bas-relief of a springbok or some such animal,

61

the words KRUGERRAND and 1 OZ FYNGOUD, and the date of the coin, 1972. The only things that made it special were its brightness — gold doesn't tarnish like nickel-alloys — and its weight. I tossed it on to the table and it landed with a good solid clunk.

Nice to have your money do that.

After a moment I pulled myself together, got a few sections of brain back on line, and said: "*Why*, for Chrissake? I mean, why d'you want the bloody things taken into Puerto Rico, of all places?"

Ruchter said coldly: "That does not concern you."

"Yeah, but I mean . . ." I ran down, waved an unlit Lucky about while I tried to sort out what I *did* mean, then started again. "Look — the whole thing's bloody crazy. Even *I* know it's against the law to peddle gold in the States or Puerto Rico — but you could take them almost anywhere else in the world perfectly legally. Why on earth don't you run 'em up the Cayman Islands or Switzerland or somewhere, and save yourself thirty thousand bucks and a load of risk?"

The killer-blue eyes narrowed. "I do not require your opinion, Scott. Your job is to transport the cargo — and that is all. Is that perfectly clear?"

I glared at him. It was clear, all right. The bastard had me bang to rights. I was stuck with doing the job whatever, and he didn't have to tell me a damn thing about it.

There was silence for a few moments while he gave it time to sink in, and then he started speaking again. It came out like a field marshal briefing a battalion for an attack.

"You will carry the coins to San Juan Airport in three separate loads within the next ten days. Bouvier is acting as my agent, and you will arrange with him as soon as possible where the coins are to be stored in your aircraft. He will tell you when to carry out the flights, and he will arrange the loading in Antigua and the unloading in San Juan: you will not be present during these operations. He will also provide you with genuine cargoes, and pay you $10,000 in United States currency before the first flight and after each of the other two flights. Is that clear?"

I was probably looking sand-bagged again. I was certainly feeling it. After a bit I managed to say: "Why *three* flights? Why not do it all in one go?"

"I prefer the risk to be spread, rather than concentrated in one operation."

I nodded slowly. I saw what he meant: if I got knocked off on one trip out of three he'd only lose a third of four million instead of the lot. It made sense — from his point of view, anyway. From *my* point of view, it just trebled the risk: if *any* of the trips came unstuck, the actual amount I was carrying was likely to be academic . . .

I took a quick swig of Scotch, and then said: "Suppose I *do* get caught? Will you come and bail me out — or will you send Harvey along to spring me with a stick of dynamite?"

Not tactful, of course. There was a short, aching silence. I could hear ropes slapping faintly on the mast, somewhere out in the night a thousand miles away.

Then Ruchter said slowly: "If you *are* caught, Scott, you will not mention me or Bouvier at all. You will say you did not know the coins were in your aircraft. Do you understand that?"

Just to see what would happen, I leered at him and said: "And if I *do* mention you. . .?"

This time, the hush was electric. Harvey fidgeted as if he was going to say something, then didn't. Ruchter just stared at me with his cold eyes for a long moment — and when he finally spoke, his voice was like a wind off a glacier.

"If you mention me, Scott, you will be killed. Possibly before you go for trial, certainly when you come out of prison."

*   *   *

If anyone else had said that I might have laughed — but coming from Ruchter, it wasn't funny. Not even a little bit. This man lived in a different world — a world where that kind of threat wasn't intimidation, but a simple statement of intention. Here, on his cold sumptuous yacht with its armed sentries, it was all too easy to believe. If he said I'd be killed, then I'd be killed. Just like that.

I shivered in the hot night.

Harvey stirred again, then cleared his throat into the silence and said: "Shit — what're we all worryin' about? If ya get caught — which ya won't — ya couldn't prove anythin' against either of us anyway, Scotty. Ya'd *have* ta say ya din' know the stuff was there — that's the only way ya might get away with it."

Get away with it? With my record? I shifted the remains of

my glare round to Harvey. It bounced off him. He was busy collecting up his pack of Camels and looking like a man who was ready to leave. He was sweating heavily. After a moment he hauled himself to his feet and looked at me.

"I guess that's it, Bill. You an' me better be goin'. We can talk about hidin' places an' times an' things later."

I said: "Why d'you think Cas McGrath went down?"

* * *

They weren't expecting that. Harvey folded back on to the seat with an audible *whoof*, and Ruchter's head snapped round as if the Führer had just walked in the door.

Bullseye.

Ruchter was the first to recover. He said harshly: "What do you know about McGrath?"

I took my time over firing up my cigarette with a table lighter the size of a young nuclear reactor, then gave him another friendly home-town leer.

"Nothing, until now," I told him. "I was just guessing — and you've just confirmed it."

He wasn't amused. For a moment I thought he was going to break his face producing an expression — but in the end he just said metallically: "What made you . . . guess?"

"Nothing very much. I was on the search for the Twin Com today, and the US Coastguard told me that Larry Hawkins was in the kite. Larry worked for Harvey, so that probably meant McGrath was, too — and it just sort of occurred to me that he might have been the ideal candidate for this job in the first place. After all, you'd hardly have planned all this with the idea of blackmailing me into carrying the stuff at the last moment. A pilot — a *willing* pilot — would've been the first thing you'd have fixed up. So — Cas McGrath. Right?"

Ruchter thought about it for maybe ten seconds, then said: "Yes. That is substantially correct."

I leaned back. "Okay then — so now I want to know *why* he disappeared. Was he carrying Krugerrands? Did it have anything to do with this business? Or what?"

That reached them, all right. Ruchter's eyes became suddenly opaque, and Harvey went white as a sheet and very still. He started to say something, but Ruchter cut across him.

"Are you suggesting that McGrath's disappearance may not have been accidental?"

Now it was my turn to get shook. "Yes, of course I am. D'you mean it hadn't occurred to you?"

"That is correct," he said slowly. "It had not occurred to me." The eyes swung round on to Harvey like a pair of naval guns. "Nothing you told me gave any indication that there may have been a connection."

Harvey spread his hands on the table, palms up. There were big beads of sweat on his temples.

"Well, shit — nothin' I know suggests there *is* any connection. We ain't had no other kinda trouble . . ." He sputtered out like a wet fuse.

Ruchter went on looking at him for a moment, then turned back to me. "What is your opinion, Scott? Was there anything . . . suspicious about this accident?"

I thought about it. *Was* there? — or was it just my imagination getting overheated? My sweat-sticky forearm unzipped from the polished table with an audible *zzwip* as I picked up my glass. I swallowed, then said slowly: "What was he doing? And what *had* he done — on this job, I mean?"

Ruchter hesitated. Then: "He carried out two flights to San Juan for me in the last week. They were completely successful, and the coins are now secure in Puerto Rico. He was to have completed the transportation over the next ten days. I do not know what he was doing last night."

Harvey said quickly: "He was on an ord'nary job for me. Carryin' Larry Hawkins an' some woodwork for the shops. I gotta do a lotta shiftin' stock about, this time of year. They were goin' down at night 'cos Cas hadta get back here by mid-afternoon today."

I nodded slowly. Something twitched at the back of my brain — but then it was gone. After the day I'd had, nine-thirty in the evening was a bit late for subtleties. I yawned mightily.

Ruchter was waiting.

"Well, look," I said slowly, "all I can really say is that a complete disappearance like that, with no radio call or anything, is a very rare thing these days. It's *got* to be suspicious."

That didn't advance the cause very much. I thought a bit more, then had another go. "I mean, a Twin Commanche's a sound, modern aeroplane. It can get engine trouble and it can get radio trouble — but it isn't likely to get trouble in *both* engines, *and* the radio, all at once. If he'd had an engine quit it wouldn't have affected his radios and he'd have been able to carry on on one anyway — and if he'd had a radio failure it wouldn't have put him in the drink. But he went down with no word, no nothing — so whatever it was must have been something real sudden and final." I paused, watching them, then added: "Something like a bomb going off, for instance."

If I'd expected a big reaction, I'd have been disappointed. Harvey frowned, and Ruchter just went on being Ruchter.

"Is that what you think happened?" His voice was as flat as ever, like a pool of acid.

"Hell — I just don't know. But like I said, it must've been something very unusual. You're the people who know what's going on — *you* tell *me* if it could've been anything like that."

There was a short pause. Then Harvey said thoughtfully: "Fuck, Bill: I don't see how it coulda been. If — ah — anyone was after the Krugerrands they'da hijacked a load or somethin' — not stuck a bomb on the airplane."

"*Is* anyone after 'em?"

Ruchter said firmly: "No."

I looked at him. "You *mean* no — or none you know of?"

"I would know."

Hmmm. I thought about that in the silence that followed. Maybe Ruchter and Harvey were thinking about it, too — but if they were, they were keeping it to themselves.

After a bit, Harvey said: "Look, shit, Bill: they might turn up yet. They mighta . . ."

"Ah, come *on*, Harvey." I blew smoke. "They're not going to turn up now, chum. You either find people in the drink in the first couple of hours, or you don't find them at all: *you* know that." It was true, too. The ocean currents round the West Indian island chain go every which way: if you don't know *exactly* where someone went in, the area of possibility expands so much after ten hours or so that you couldn't hope to cover it even if the whole of Pan Am and the US Navy pitched up to help. And then there's the sharks, of course . . .

Harvey waved his hands around for a moment, then said: "Well, look. Airplanes *do* go down mysteriously sometimes, don't they? I mean, this ain't the first time, or anythin' like that?"

"Oh no, of course it isn't." I drained my glass, thought about pouring another dose, and then decided against it. The decanter was wearing out anyway. "No — there can always be sudden disastrous fires, pilots not looking at the map and flying into a mountain, going to sleep at the controls, that sort of thing. But it's bloody rare nowadays — so much so that when someone *does* go down without a word, you certainly can't rule out sabotage."

He nodded slowly, chewing a fingernail. "I still don't see why anyone shoulda sabotaged Cas, though. I mean, if anyone'd known he was carryin' the Krugerrands they'da known about us, too. An' then they'd gone for us or maybe hijacked Cas or somethin' like that — not just stuck a bomb on the airplane. There'd be no reason for doin' that: nobody coulda gained anythin'."

"You'd know about that: I wouldn't."

I mashed my cigarette into an ashtray. I felt very tired and old. There were still a hundred things I wanted to know — but I wasn't going to get any more answers tonight, that much was obvious. Suddenly, I was sick of the pair of them — and of this rich, grand yacht with its luxurious precision. All I wanted was *off*.

I said: "Let's go."

We went. Nobody shook hands. Harvey led the way, and Ruchter's cold, hard stare followed me up the steps.

* * *

We got back to the airport at ten thirty, crunching up to the same place in front of the clubhouse. Stupidly, I was slightly surprised to find it looking exactly the same as I'd left it. Maybe I'd sub-consciously expected it to be bristling with cops or something. . .

Come on Scott, quit dozing.

I shook myself fully awake. Harvey was talking to Sherman, who nodded, got out, and went and sat on the darkened veranda out of earshot. Then Harvey turned to me, his heavy face dimly green in the glow of the instrument lights.

"I wanna come along tomorrow night so ya can show me where ta hide the stuff in ya 'planes," he said. "That be okay? Willya have time ta sort it out by then?"

"Er, yeah, I guess so." Then I realised what he'd said. "Hold it. D'you mean both kites? You want me to use the Cherokee, too?"

"Yeah, we might. For one trip. Vary the pattern, see?"

I frowned. "Suppose I get an engine failure? You know the risk of single engine over-water flying. If I have to ditch, you'll lose the lot."

And you might lose a few bits of Bill Scott, too. Still, that particular danger was old acquaintance.

Harvey shrugged and said: "Why should ya ditch? Ya been flyin' round here for two years without ditchin', aincha?"

Well, that was true — but it didn't mean it couldn't happen tomorrow. In fact, statistically it probably increased the chances. I'd done something like four hundred hours single engine over-water flying since I came to Antigua, and there was such a thing as taking the pitcher too often to the well . . .

Still, if that was how they wanted it, who was I to argue? It was their gold-plated dime.

I said: "How much do these things weigh? And how big are they?"

"The whole lot's between 1,570 and 1,590 lb. They're packed in hard polythene tubes of twenny-five each, an' each tube's about three inches long. I got 'em in a stack 13 inches by a foot by 41½ inches: that'll give ya some idea of the volume."

"*You've* got 'em? You mean they aren't on the yacht?"

He frowned — but it was too late by then: the brick was dropped. "Yeah," he said reluctantly. "I got 'em hid ashore. It'd be kinda stupid ta keep 'em on the yacht."

"Why would it?"

He shrugged, spreading his hands. "Well shit, jus' gen'ally, ya know? I mean, suppose Customs decided ta have a swoop, lookin' for drugs or somethin'?"

I nodded. That made sense. The Dockyard Customs *do* get off their butts and turn the odd yacht over for drugs every now and then. I couldn't quite imagine even an Antiguan Customs officer suspecting Herr Ruchter of holding riotous pot-parties — but nevertheless, it *could* just happen.

After a moment I said: "Why *is* Ruchter having these things taken into Puerto Rico? It seems bloody silly to me."

Harvey waved his hands again. "Shit, I don't know, Scotty. I don' ask those sorta things."

I glared at him in the dim glow of the instruments. "Like hell you don't," I snarled. "Come on, chum — *why?*"

"Well, goddamit — I guess he thinks he can make a profit outa sellin' 'em there, or somethin'."

"Yeah, but why *there*? I mean, it's illegal for people to own gold in PR and the States — so why the hell doesn't he take 'em somewhere where it *isn't* illegal?"

Harvey pulled an enormous cigar out of his pocket and started unpeeling its cellophane cover with his big hands. After a bit he said: "Well — did ya know this gold-owning restriction in US territory's gonna be lifted soon?"

"No."

"Well, it is. On January 1st next year — that's in nine weeks' time. That's why the price of gold's been goin' up so much lately. People think there's gonna be a sudden rush of American buyin'."

"So?"

"Well — I'm only guessin', now — maybe Ruchter's gotta customer in PR who wants ta buy now before the price goes up any more, and's prepared ta pay over the market value ta get 'em illegally."

I thought about that, then said: "Sounds like a bloody big risk for a bloody small return, to me."

Harvey bit the end off the cigar and spat it out of the window. "Depends what ya call small, Scotty. If he just makes ten per cent over the market on what you're gonna carry, that'll be an extra $400,000."

That was a point. I tried to visualise a sum like $400,000, but failed. Then I had another thought, and said: "Look, if the price of gold's going up so much, why doesn't Ruchter just hang on to the damn things?"

He waved the cigar. "I toldja, Bill — I dunno. Maybe he figures the price ain't gonna keep goin' up after January, an' wants ta unload 'em now while it's still high. That sorta thing's happened before — everyone buyin' furiously just before a new market opens up, an' then the price comin' down in a rush afterwards. Or maybe he's got some sorta tax-evasion reason, as well. I jus' dunno."

I grunted sourly, and reached for my cigarettes. I had a sort of general feeling of being handed a load of horse-crap — especially when Harvey put on his innocent face and claimed he didn't know anything from anything — but not being a bent accountant, I couldn't actually prove it. I wore out my brain on it for a couple of minutes, then gave up and tried another angle.

"Why doesn't Ruchter take the bloody stuff up to Puerto Rico himself? It'd be a hell of a lot easier to hide it and land it from that floating gin-palace of his, *and* he'd save himself $30,000."

Harvey puffed cigar smoke like a sugar cane railway and grinned. "He don' wanna take the risk. He'd rather pay someone else ta do it."

I winced, thought again — and then said: "So who's hooking the coins out of the aircraft at San Juan? Some of your guys?"

He hesitated. Then: "Yeah, that's right. I got shops up there, as ya know. Ya don' hafta worry: those guys're good at that sorta thing."

Yeah, they would be. With Harvey's sort of business interests, they'd undoubtedly been spiriting stuff out of San Juan Airport without the blessing of Customs for years. In fact, that was probably how Harvey came to be mixed up in this in the first place: his sort of organisation would've been just what Ruchter was looking for.

I still didn't see *why* he wanted them taken into Puerto Rico, though. The risk seemed enormous, even for $400,000 . . .

Out on the airport there was a blasting thunder of jets. I looked across the dim yellow-lit apron in time to see a 707 leaning on its nosewheel as it slowed under reverse-thrust. The evening Pan Am from Miami. It got down to a crawling pace, and the scream of the engines died away to the anxious whine of ground-idle as it nosed off the runway among the blue taxi lights, looking like some big nervous animal unsure of the smell of the airport apron. It obviously hadn't got a whiff of the restaurant yet.

When I eyes-fronted again, Harvey was opening the car door. I followed him out. Sherman stalked quietly off the veranda and got in the other side. Harvey got back in himself, and looked up at me out of the window.

"Seven thirty tomorrow evenin', then?"

"Yeah, okay," I said wearily.

He nodded. "Don't worry so much, Bill. This'll be the easiest money ya ever earned."

I seemed to have heard that somewhere before.

I watched the Maverick crunch off the gravel and zoom away towards the terminal, then fired up my ageing Moke and headed for home.

6

I WAS UP early the next morning, in spite of two Mandrax pills and a hangover like the Day of Reckoning. I stumbled around for half an hour showering and shaving and drinking pints of water, then got myself out to the sun-warmed veranda with coffee and cigarettes.

I'd been lucky with home, that year. I had a millionaire's house on a hill — literally. It was a white-painted L-shaped bungalow with a lush tropical garden on a terrace hacked out of a hillside on the north-west coast. The owner was an American beer-making magnate who brought his wife and his drinking problem to Antigua for a month or so around Christmas every year, then rented the place out to me and my drinking problem the rest of the time.

I sank down on one of the plastic-and-aluminium veranda chairs, stared out through the gently rattling coconut palms at the wide blue horizon of the Caribbean Sea, and tried to convince myself that last night really *had* happened, that I really *was* being blackmailed into smuggling four million bucks' worth of gold coins into Puerto Rico for an ex-Nazi thug called Ruchter. By the time I'd battled my way through my second cup of coffee I'd convinced myself, all right — but I still couldn't see *why*. The $400,000-profit theory had sounded faintly reasonable last night: but now, in the hot light of morning, it didn't seem to stand up so well. It was still a hell of a lot of money, of course — but it *was* only ten per cent of the value of the gold, and a return like that hardly seemed worth risking thirty-three per cent at a time for.

So — what?

After half an hour of pondering and watching the humming birds as they flickered around the oleander and hibiscus, I was no nearer the answer. The whole thing seemed crazy — and the more I thought about it, the crazier it got. There *had* to be some other reason I didn't know about . . .

I gave it up, and drove to the airport for breakfast.

*　　　*　　　*

The heat and the stench of the restaurant nearly made me retch as I walked in — but I kept walking. You have to eat something sometime, even when your stomach *is* a big furry ball trying to climb out through your throat. I picked a table near the open doors leading to the apron patio, where the jet-exhaust had the upper hand over the cremation smells from the kitchen, and ordered up two toasted ham sandwiches and a can of chocolate milk. The waitress said "He come soon, nah", and finally wandered back with it fifteen minutes later.

I spent the time glancing over an abandoned copy of the *Antigua Times*. The headline blared POLICE SEARCHING FOR BLACK POWER ARMS DUMP, and the lead story said that the brave Antiguan police were combing the Shekerly Mountain area for guns they believed were being smuggled on to the island from Cuba for the use of the Black Power militants. I wished them luck: *I* wouldn't have liked to be a black copper wandering around Shekerly Mountain looking for those thugs. The Black Power had gone all political that year: instead of knocking off the occasional whitey they'd aligned themselves, more or less, with the Afro-Caribbean Liberation Movement, and the extremists were coming to the aid of the cause by fading the odd black cop and heaving bombs into government buildings, which presumably achieved something. I was still trying to work out just what when my morning banquet arrived, and the sandwiches heaved a bomb into my guts. I tried to ignore the churning, bought six cans of take-away Heineken, staggered back out into the sun, and drove the Moke down to the clubhouse. From there, I walked to the aircraft park at the top of the runway.

A Flamingo Air DC6 had moved in alongside the Scott fleet sometime during the night: probably the same one that had been on the search yesterday. I spent a few minutes wondering whether *that* could have anything to do with the gold smuggling, and eventually came to the conclusion that it couldn't. So then I stood in the shade of its vast port wing, and applied myself to the problem of where to stow four million dollars' worth of Krugerrands in a tatty old Beech 18.

It *was* a problem, too — largely because of the weight of the goddamn things. Harvey had said the whole lot weighed 1,590 lb, which meant that each of the three loads would be 530 lb or thereabouts. That was the same as three-and-a-third ICAO-standard people — and if I went shoving that sort of dead weight into a wing tip fairing or similar I'd only have one side of the aeroplane leaving the ground.

I looked at the Beech, shimmering in the heat-waves coming off the white concrete, and thought about it. The hot trade wind ruffled my hair and made a low moaning noise as it squeezed itself under the DC6. So okay — the weight consideration ruled out the tail assembly, the fuselage aft of the cabin, the nose compartment, and the wings outboard of the engine nacelles. So that only left the inboard wing sections, which were already filled up with fuel tanks and batteries and things — or the fuselage underneath the cabin floor. Right?

Right.

I walked over to the bitch, opened the Airstair door, climbed up into the cabin — and then just stood there for a moment, crouching under the low roof and breathing softly in the heat. The atmosphere was like a sauna on piecework. After a little while I lurched up the sloping floor, wriggled into the cockpit, and opened the pilots' side-windows in the pious hope of creating a through-draught of fresh air. It didn't work, of course: there ain't no fresh air at Coolidge Airport at ten o'clock in the morning. Only hot air.

I sighed, staggered back to the aft luggage space, and dug out a bag of tools.

Ten minutes later I had the main inspection hatch in the floor up. I fished a rubber-covered torch out of the cockpit, sat down carefully on the edge of the hole in the floor, and peered into the gloomy depths below.

At first glance, the whole area seemed to be filled with control cables, heater-trunking junctions, wires, pipes, rods, and about eighty-four miles of inch-diameter steel tubing running in every-which direction. There didn't seem to be enough spare space to stash away a dollars' worth of dimes, never mind 7,000 Krugerrands . . .

Or was there? Just how much space *did* I need?

I leaned back against the cockpit bulkhead, lit a Lucky Strike, and tried to remember the figures. The whole lot made up a volume of — what was it, for Chrissake? — oh yes, twelve inches by thirteen by forty-one. That was it. So a third of that would be . . . just over a cubic foot.

Christ, there ought to be room for *that*.

I bent forward and had another look. After a couple of minutes' staring, the hodge-podge of bits and pieces started to make sense. The young Forth Bridge of steel tubing under my feet and for'ard was, in fact, the cross-bracing of the truss-construction centre-section of the aircraft. The Beech 18 doesn't have a solid mainspar between the engines: instead, it relies on a multi-tube affair rather like a racing car space-frame. From where I sat there seemed to be a damn sight more frame than space — but you *could* reach down to the outer skin of the underside in places. So you could put a layer of Krugerrands *there*, another layer *there*, and . . .

And then I remembered the weight again 530 lb. If I parked 530 lb on a couple of square feet of thin-gauge alloy outer skin, I was going to end up rolling down some runway in a glittering arc of gold coins when the whole lot dropped out the bottom.

So that was out. I pulled on the cigarette, tried to ignore the sweat streaming down my face, and thought about it some more.

Five minutes later, I had the answer.

Several of the centre-section members at the front and rear of the framework were welded up into vee-shapes or cross-shapes — and there was one pair of vees, just to the left of the aircraft centre-line, which were both in line with each other fore-and-aft and didn't have any odd pipes or cables in the space between them. I could drop a couple of two-foot long planks of wood in there and the vees would cradle them like the ends of a saw-horse — and then, with the addition of a couple of flat, overlapping end-pieces to stop the coins sliding out of the planks or the planks sliding out of the centre section, I'd have a vee-shaped trough big enough to carry all the Krugerrands in the world.

There's a clever boy, Scott. In your state, too.

Someone bawled "Eh, Missah Scott!" and I nearly swallowed the Lucky Strike.

*　　*　　*

My instant reaction was Oh-my-Christ-it's-the-Law — but it

wasn't. It was Simon Appadoo. His jet-black face was poked round the doorway, grinning at me.

Just one of my students. Probably looking for a flying lesson.

I hauled myself up and clumped quickly down to meet him, before he could take it into his head to come in. Silly, of course — since there was absolutely no reason why I shouldn't be poking around in the guts of my own aeroplane — but because *I* knew what I was doing I had the illogical, naked feeling that anybody seeing me would, too. Pure guilty conscience — *and you'll have to snap out of that, Scott. You've got to start thinking like a criminal again* . . .

The realisation didn't cheer me up any.

Simon, it turned out, did want a flying lesson — and *that* didn't cheer me up, either. He was one of my perpetual head-aches: he had all the aptitude of a retarded oran-utang, and furthermore he stank to high heaven of sweat. I sighed, thought about telling him I wasn't flying today — and then decided it might be better if I did fly, so as not to show any break in the normal routine. I told him to pre-flight the Cherokee, and that I'd join him when I'd had a last look at the — er — trim cable run in the Beech.

That's better, Scott. Just don't overdo it, now . . .

We spent a sweaty hour grinding round the circuit with my temper getting shorter and his body odour getting longer. By the end of the session I was hoarse from talking and the inside of the Cherokee smelt like a week-old cargo of fried eggs. I gave him a brief lecture on his faults, sent him away to re-read the Gospel according to *Flight Briefing For Pilots*, and watched him drive away with profound relief.

Then I dug out a saw and a couple of odd planks of wood, and started work on the Scott Patent Gold Trough.

*   *   *

It wasn't fun, sawing and nailing in the midday heat in my condition — but by two o'clock I'd finished it. The end product was a vee-shaped trough about two feet long with wooden squares blocking off each end. It looked like a crude miniature cattle trough — but it took my weight when I stood on it, fitted properly into the centre-section, and might even be passed off as a tool tray when it didn't happen to be carting 7,000 Krugerrands around.

What a clever boy, Scott . . .

After that, I started on the Cherokee. I taxied it down to a quiet corner of the aircraft park, drank a couple of Heinekens while I poked around it looking for hiding places that wouldn't put the centre of gravity way out of limits, and finally came to the conclusion that the coins would have to go under the rear seat or nowhere. Removing the seat-squab and the panel beneath it was an awkward business — there seemed to be far more half-hidden screws than the structure could possibly warrant — but after twenty minutes of sweaty irritation I'd got them out. That left me looking at the centre-section mainspar — on which the front of the seat rested — and a small compartment just aft of it which was cluttered up with things like flap rods, control cables, and fuel lines.

I sat on the spar, lit up a Lucky which immediately went soggy in my sweaty fingers, and frowned down at the lack of space. There was room and floor-strength for maybe a double layer of Krugerrands about nine inches square in a couple of places, providing I made a couple of wooden trays to spread the load and stop the things rolling about . . .

But that didn't add up to anywhere near a cubic foot's worth.

I thought about it some more, and finally decided that the only way was to stash 'em there and also inside the centre-section mainspar itself. The centre-section in a Cherokee is a simple box-section girder about two-and-a-half inches wide by ten deep, and the walls of it have four lightening holes back and front plus slots at the bottom for the control cables to run through. If I stuck a wooden bridge over the cables to stop them getting jammed, you could bung a load of coins in through the lightening holes. The wing attachments at each end formed a barrier which would prevent the tubes of coins sliding up a wing if I forgot myself and did a side-slip somewhere.

It wasn't a *good* idea — but it did have the merit of being the only idea I had.

The main snag — apart from the fact that the combined spaces probably still didn't add up to a cubic foot — was the time factor: the loading and unloading was going to take a hell of a long time if you had to take out the seat and the deck panel and then fish around inside the spar in the dark.

It was still the only idea I had.

I gloomed at it for a while longer, then took the necessary

measurements, hauled myself out of the sweltering cockpit, and trudged back to the clubhouse in the sun to start sawing again.

I finally got finished at six-fifteen — an hour and a quarter before Harvey was due to arrive. The day's sweat had curdled to gluey stickiness, I had a headache like a road-drill behind my eyes, and my port index finger was throbbing painfully where I'd thumped it with a hammer in the course of nailing up one of the wooden trays for the Cherokee. I walked up to the terminal, washed in the controllers' air-conditioned Gents, then braved the restaurant for the second time that day and ordered a beer and an egg sandwich and chips. The food took half an hour to arrive — being a fairly complicated order by Coolidge Airport standards — and when it did materialise it was about as appetising as a dead rat. I ate it anyway, stopped the resulting cat-fight in my guts with a couple of fast Scotches, and was back in the aircraft park at exactly half past seven.

*   *   *

It was dark then, of course — and Harvey frightened me out of ten years' growth by shining a torch at me from inside the Beech. Security-minded bastard. I pulled down the Airstair door and joined him. The coming of night hadn't improved the atmosphere in there any, and I could feel a new instalment of sweat breaking out all over.

I heaved up the hatch in the floor and showed him the Scott Gold Trough. He said, Yeah, that was fine, and I told him to tell his guys to leave it out in the cabin when they'd finished unloading.

Then we moved on to the Cherokee. I'd screwed everything down properly so as to show him exactly what was involved — and it took me twenty minutes and a barked knuckle to get it all unscrewed again by feel and occasional flashes of torchlight. He grumbled about the time factor — especially when he saw how long it would take to unload the awkward cavity in the mainspar — but I shut him up by pointing out that it was the only possible place in the whole aeroplane and suggesting that it'd be safer to do all the trips by Beech anyway.

That left us standing outside in the warm night, listening to the trilling of cicadas in the dusty grass behind the aircraft. Harvey chewed a finger-nail for a bit — and then said abruptly:

"Okay, Scotty: the first run'll be tomorrow, in the big airplane."

I got a sudden hollow feeling in the guts.

"Ya'll go ta San Juan in the afternoon an' stop overnight," he went on. "Ya'll get a legitimate cargo the nex' mornin' — woodwork an' stuff ta bring back here. The Krugerrands'll go on board tonight, so you jus' forget 'em. Go ta San Juan normally an' leave the 'plane in the Transit Aircraft Park. Ya know where that is?"

My mouth was dry. I fired up a Lucky, which didn't help, and said: "Yeah. That's the one between the terminal and Runway Ten, right?"

"Right. Opposite where the North Cay DC3s park, an' Shamrock an' Air Haiti an' all those. Where the Pan Am cargo buildin' is. When ya get there, park on the very end of the line, okay? Try'n get behind somethin' else if you can, too: ya wanna be out in the dark an' tucked away as inconspicuous as possible."

I blew smoke and said: "Yeah — but you don't usually ask where to park, you know. You just go where Ground Control tells you."

"Uh-huh. But if ya say ya stoppin' overnight they'll almost certainly park ya there anyway. If they don't, ya might hafta get engine trouble an' stay another night: then they will putcha there. We'll letcha know if that's necessary. Where ya gonna be stoppin'?"

I started to name the cheap hotel in the Calle San Jose where I usually stayed — and then changed my mind. If I was earning $10,000 for the trip at least I could afford to worry about it in comfort.

"The El Convento, in Old San Juan. Calle Cristo, I think."

Harvey nodded, hauled one of his enormous cigars out of his shirt pocket, and lit it. The fallout billowed away on the warm night wind. When it was going properly he said: "Okay, Scotty: the next trip'll probably be the day afta ya get back. That'll be Friday. I might wancha ta use the Cherokee for that. I'll let ya know."

I just grunted. Then I said: "How're your guys going to get the stuff away — down that little road alongside Pan Am?"

He stiffened for a second. Then he said slowly: "Howdja know 'bout that road, Scotty?"

I shrugged. "It's no secret. That and the little side-door into the terminal near Pan Am Cargo have been used before. That bloke Ben what's-his-name got picked up with a load of hash from

Guadeloupe around there, didn't he? I mean, if you're relying on that road, then all I can say is I hope your guys don't talk when they get knocked off."

Harvey looked at me for a few moments — and then grinned, in the moonlight. A slow, confident grin.

"My guys might use that road or they might not," he said. "But they *won't* get knocked off. I can guarantee that."

I leaned against the Cherokee's port wing. "*How* can you guarantee it? You got some of the airport staff working for you?"

The grin slipped a few notches. He puffed on the cigar, frowned, and finally said: "That's my business, Scotty. It's safe — that's all ya need ta know."

I shrugged again. It looked as if he *was* using the airport staff — but I didn't really give a damn. He could use the Holy Ghost for all I cared; just so long as he wasn't putting his trust in the Lord and that little road . . .

We started walking towards the clubhouse, our sandals making small flip-flap noises in the buzzing night. When we were nearly there, I said: "What about the money, Harvey? Ruchter said the first $10,000 before the first flight."

He produced a big generous-uncle smirk and waved his cigar at my Moke, parked alongside the hut.

"Ya already got it, Scotty. Ten thousan', under ya car seat. Now, aincha glad I got the job for ya?"

I just looked at him. The smirk faded. He stopped walking, and spread his hands.

"Well, aincha? I mean, doncha like money, or somethin'?"

He really meant it. I snarled: "Ah, fuck off," and turned away and trudged away through the prickly scrub to the clubhouse. When I got there and looked back, he'd gone.

*   *   *

The money was under the driving seat, just as he'd said. A stiff brown envelope, with a slab of $100 dollar bills in it about half an inch thick. $10,000.

The price of selling your soul. Or a third of the price, anyway.

I dropped the envelope into my flight bag, and drove home. I wanted a drink.

7

I SLEPT LATE the next morning, finally coming to about nine thirty with the usual nuclear-sized hangover. I spent until early afternoon puttering about the house, clearing up and dusting and trying to stop my nerves sticking a foot out of my body, then drove to the airport via the Canadian Imperial Bank to deposit my $10,000. I wasn't very happy about shoving in a wodge of hundreds just like that — but I could hardly carry it around with me in my spare socks, and when it came down to it, it *was* the bank's money, anyway. They had the grace not to ask when the rest might be coming in.

When I reached Coolidge I offered myself a snack in the restaurant as I drove in past the terminal. My stomach, which was reacting to tension by trying to hide in a quiet corner under my ribs, crawled out and did a slow roll and then crawled back in again.

No food, then.

But I *did* want a drink.

I chugged straight down to the clubhouse, unlocked it, carried my flight bag inside, and dropped it on the table. It landed with a solid clunk. I fished around in it . . .

And came up with my gun, in its leather under-belt-holster.

I weighed it thoughtfully in my hand. It was a good carry-about gun — a little Smith & Wesson .38 Special revolver with a two-inch barrel — and before I'd left home this had seemed to be one of those times when it might be a good idea to carry it about. But now, I wasn't so sure: it would provide a degree of protection against elements unknown, certainly — but on the other hand, it could also get me into a lot of trouble. It wasn't licensed — you hadn't needed a licence in Biafra when I'd got it — and it rather obviously wasn't a target pistol or a gat for rubbing out mongeese. If anybody's Customs happened to find a shooter like *that* on board they'd probably take me and the aircraft apart on the spot looking for bazookas and dismantled jet fighters.

After a few minutes' pondering, discretion won. If elements unknown *did* have a go at me I'd have to throw rocks and run like hell. I opened up the store cupboard and stashed the Smith & Wesson away underneath the inhibitor-plug in a spare Wasp Junior cylinder.

After I'd locked up the cupboard again, I looked at my hands. They were shaking.

I hauled the Scotch bottle out of my flight bag and lowered the level a bit. The spirit flowed down into my guts like purifying fire, loosening the knot of tension as it went. I capped up the bottle, put it back in the bag, and examined my hands again. They were still.

Stupid bastard. Stupid, weak *bastard : . .*

I promised myself for the thousandth time that I'd stop drinking tomorrow, then walked up to the terminal to deliver my outbound general declarations and file a flight plan.

*   *   *

I got down to the Beech twenty minutes later — and the first thing I did after a careful external inspection of the crate was to shut myself up in the hot stuffy fuselage and peer suspiciously out of the windows. I don't know what I expected to see — but there was nothing and nobody around.

So then I opened up the inspection hatch in the floor. And there they were.

They filled the wooden trough from end to end. Row upon row of white-ish, translucent polythene tubes with the gold sheen of the coins gleaming faintly through them.

Seven thousand Krugerrands. One-and-a-third million dollars' worth.

Suddenly, I was a rich man. I had an aeroplane all fuelled up and ready to go. I could fly to the Caymans or South America or anywhere in the world. I could live in luxury for the rest of my life . . .

I could also get very dead. I dropped the hatch down and

fastened it. Then I heaved myself into the roasting cockpit, fired up the engines, and taxied the most expensive Beech 18 in the world up to the terminal apron en route to the runway.

I was going to Puerto Rico.

*   *   *

Apart from my imagination, the flight was completely un-eventful. I lifted my wheels off Coolidge's runway at 1625 local time, turned out over the ocean on a heading 300 degrees magnetic, and spent the next fifteen minutes drumming slowly up to the relative coolness of flight level eight-zero. Outside, the cotton wool puffs of fair-weather cu drifted serenely past the wing tips, then sank away into the blue depths below.

Inside, however, serenity was notably absent. Scott, William, thirty-two, white, was getting himself wound up like a clock spring.

First of all I worried about the coins shifting during the take-off and dropping out of the bottom of the bitch somewhere over the ocean: then I worried about getting a return-to-Coolidge signal, and jumped six inches out of my seat every time the ear-phones crackled. And after I got over *that*, I started in worrying about the engines. That gave me unlimited scope — since all aero-engines immediately go into auto-rough whenever you think about them on the over-water flight anyway — and I spent the rest of the climb finnicking with throttles and pitch and listening to all sorts of pops and bangs and clanks which were taking place only between my ears.

Eight thousand feet.

I carried on up another 200 feet, lowered the nose to the cruising position, and waited until the airspeed crawled round to 150 knots indicated. Then I brought the props back to 1,900 rpm, nit-picked at the starboard pitch lever until the engines were synchronised, and lowered the nose a whisker so that she slid down to 8,000 exactly. It's known as 'putting her on the step': you get a touch more airspeed for the same power setting. Every pilot has his own theories as to *why* it works — mine's that the props get settled into a fractionally coarser pitch as you slide down to the height you want — but the only thing we all *know* about it is that it does work.

The airspeed stabilised at 157. Have a banana, Scott.

Or better still . . .

I reached into my flight bag, fished out the Scotch bottle, and took a couple of medium-small snifters. Well — maybe medium-medium snifters, then. They did the trick: the jangling nerve-ends subsided, and I stopped jumping at crackles and bangs out of the other.

Stupid, stupid *weak bastard . . .*

I called up Coolidge, told them I was crossing their zone boundary level at eight-zero, and clicked the frequency to San Juan Centre on 125.8.

*   *   *

Eighty minutes later I started descending towards the north-east tip of Puerto Rico. San Juan had their usual heavy traffic — *this* part of the Caribbean didn't seem to be suffering from any recession — and as I slid down out of 8,000 I could see two Prinair Herons below, a 707 steaming north, and an ancient C46 lumbering up through the scattered cumulus in the direction of St Croix.

Off to my left, the vast standing cloud cap over the Luquillo Mountains was etched out in brilliant orange as the evening sun sank behind it. I rumbled down alongside its bellying mass, passed through the fragments of cu over the sea, and popped out under-neath with the coastline running under the nose and the mountains of El Yungue rain forest bubbling up out of the coastal plain to the left of that. Down here the traffic was even thicker: there was another Heron about a mile off my port wing going the same way at the same speed, a Grumman Goose of Antilles Air Boats crawling along the coast at low level, and a DC3 threshing its way upwards ahead. I picked my way between them, terminated the Instrument Flight Plan, and switched to Approach Control.

And suddenly, there was San Juan.

It's a big city, San Juan — or big by Caribbean standards, anyway. It covers maybe twenty square miles — and when you've been stuck on the tin-pot islands down south for a while, a twenty-square-mile metropolis looks about ten times the size of New York. I positioned to join on the downwind leg for Runway Seven at the *Aeropuerto Internacional*, and Approach handed me over to Tower as I was getting started on the pre-landing checks. The Tower Controller said: "Victah-Papa-Lima-Alpha-Whisky yore clear' finals numba t'ree behina Prinair Heron" without drawing a breath, and I did a wide circuit over the city to let the

83

Heron get well ahead. The skyscraper hotels in the exclusive Condado and Miramar areas slid beneath the wings as the undercarriage rumbled down and eventually lit up the single green light on the instrument panel.

As I turned finals, I was worrying again. Suppose some of the Krugerrands *had* shifted? Suppose they were lying on the thin bottom skin of the fuselage, and . . .

Ah, shaddup.

The headphones said: "Lima-Alpha-Whisky yore clear ta lan' numba one."

I acknowledged, trundled the flaps down all the way, and concentrated on holding ninety-five knots dead-on. Sweat dribbled down my temples as the runway floated up and back. The threshold slid by underneath, I eased back on the throttles — back a touch on the yoke — back more . . .

The Beech wheeled on tail-up without a quiver.

I stayed ready on throttles and brakes — a Beech 18 landing isn't over until you've got out and closed the door — but for once she rolled out straight as an arrow, without any of the usual darts off to the sides.

Tower said: "Nice landin', Lima Alpha Whisky" — they get a lot of Beech 18s bouncing halfway into orbit at San Juan — "take the nex' exit onya right an' contac' Ground one-two-one-poin'-niner."

I said Thank you and Good-day, and did as I was told. Ground Control threaded me through the expanse of taxiways on to the main apron, shuttled me past the sprawling wings of the terminal building . . .

And then told me to park alongside a Dorado Wings Aztec in front of Pan Am Cargo.

I swallowed dryly and said: "Ground, Alpha Whisky'll be night-stopping tonight and maybe tomorrow. Will I be okay there all that time?"

There was a moment's silence. Then "Ah . . . rahger, Alpha Whisky: ah guess we'll put yo' in the Transit Park if yore gonna be here that long. Turn lef' from yuh presen' position an' park where th' two other Beech 18s an' th' Super Constellation are. Yuh see them okay?"

I breathed out. "Affirmative. Good-day, sir."

"G'day, Alpha Whisky. Ah . . . Prinair 984, hold where y'are a moment . . ."

I reached out and turned the radio volume down, gave the starboard engine a whiff of throttle to swing us round, and trundled over to the Transit Park with the motors making satisfied husking noises. After a couple of minutes snorting and jockeying I'd got her nicely tucked away in an inconspicuous slot in the rear of the double row of parked aeroplanes. The Super Connie, battered and scarred from years of slumming around Central America, blotted out my view of the Pan Am building altogether. I was pleased about that: by the look of the poor old Connie, nobody was going to be moving her for a good many nights to come. I pulled the mixtures into lean cut-off and opened the throttles, then went round the cockpit turning off switches and fuel taps while the props grumbled to a stop. After that I closed the throttles again — and then just sat there for a moment, listening to the dying whine of the gyros and steeling myself for the next bit.

The clearing-Customs bit.

*   *   *

To get to Customs and Immigration from the Transit Park you walk a couple of hundred yards across the apron, go under an archway to the right of Pan Am Cargo, and in through a small doorway near one of the arrival/embarkation wings of the terminal building. Having got that far, you then get lost in a maze of corridors unless you've been there before and happen to remember which way to go. I had, and did. Immigration found an odd corner for his rubber stamp in my dog-eared passport . . .

And then I passed through the barrier into the Customs area.

There was a scattering of touristy-looking people milling about, so there wasn't much choice of unoccupied Customs men. I drew a middle-aged, sour-faced Spanish-American with a pot-belly and bad breath. He took my general declaration, then had a quick rake through the contents of my flight bag.

Then he said: "You goin' out tonight, o' stayeeng?"

"Staying. Leaving tomorrow morning."

"Uh. You breeng anytheeng in?"

"Eh?"

"Cargoes — you not breeng cargoes with you?"

"Oh — no. I'm picking some up to take back in the morning."

"Uh. I like to look in you airplane, okay?"

My stomach did a vertical hesitation roll into the back of my throat. "Sure," I said easily — or at least, I meant to say it easily: it probably came out like a busted doll saying 'Mama'. "I'll take you out to it."

He nodded, and picked up his cap. We filed out, and I led the way across to the Transit Park with every nerve sticking a foot out of my body and twanging furiously. It wasn't exactly *unusual* for the US Customs to look in a cargo-less incoming aeroplane — but on the other hand, it certainly didn't happen every time . . .

We reached the Beech, and I opened it up. Pot-belly hauled himself inside and clumped uphill to the cockpit. I followed him. I don't know what he was looking for — but he started in as if he was getting warmed up to take the crate apart rivet by rivet. He unfolded a couple of maps, slid the wind-scale out of my navigational computer and squinted down the slot, then knelt on the floor with much grunting and panting and peered under the pilots' seats. I felt fresh sweat prickling on my face — and it wasn't just the heat in the cabin, either.

After a moment he pulled himself up again, backed out of the cockpit, and turned round. Crouching under the low roof he took a slow, all-encompassing look around the inside of the fuselage.

He was standing on the centre-section inspection hatch.

Then he grunted: "Iss okay. Le's go."

We clambered out. I wanted a drink. Or six.

*　　　*　　　*

The next morning was the way most of my next mornings were, but with acute nervous tension sprinkled on top. In spite of the pills and the bottle, I'd spent most of the night lying awake listening for the howl of police sirens and the tramping of feet. Now I had a mouthful of sand, a head full of sharp rocks, and my guts doing press-ups on the El Convento's breakfast coffee and Disprins.

I was out looking for a taxi in the Plaza de Armas by seven thirty.

I got one in the end, and then spent the next half-hour chewing my finger-nails up to the elbows as we bludgeoned our way through the honking, heat-shimmering thrombosis of bright-coloured traffic out of Old San Juan and along the length of Baldroity de Castro Avenue. When we finally fetched up at the airport I gave the driver a ten-dollar bill without waiting for the change and started to head for Pan Am Cargo, who acted as my handling agents in San Juan. Halfway there I changed my mind, and weaved my way towards a side door out on to the tarmac. The Customs guard who was propping up the wall nodded casually and waved me through when I told him I wanted some paperwork out of the aeroplane.

Two minutes later I was in the Transit Aircraft Park.

The Beech was exactly as I'd left it, which somehow surprised me. There was no reason why it shouldn't be, of course — but I was mentally prepared for anything from an armed guard to a charred wreck, so it was something of a surprise to find it sitting placidly in the sun surrounded by nothing more sinister than the usual oil stains under the engines. I hauled the door down and climbed in. The fuselage was empty: no corpses lying around, no squads of cops hiding under the pilots' seats.

Just the empty gold-trough, sitting on the floor.

For a while, I just stood there making deep-breathing noises. Then I kicked a few brain cells into gear, hauled the bag of tools out of the rear baggage compartment, and up-ended it on the floor. Spanners and screwdrivers cascaded out with a crash that went through my morning head like a squadron of Phantoms. I chucked half of them in the gold-trough and slung the rest back in the bag. Then I stood back and surveyed the effect.

It was all right. Now, I didn't have a Krugerrand-carrier at all: I merely had a sort of Modern Art-ish tool tray.

Who's *still* a clever boy, then?

I closed up the kite, wandered round a Flamingo Air DC6 which had turned up overnight, and made my way to Pan Am's Export Cargo palace to see if my legitimate freight had arrived. It had: four crate-sized crates of it. Trust Harvey to get his money's worth — especially when it wasn't his money anyway. The Pan Am people spent ten minutes filling in the forms and raising an Airwaybill, then another five assuring me that the cargo would be loaded up pronto, if not sooner. I picked up the cargo manifests and wandered along to Customs and Immigration.

I was met by my pot-bellied friend of the evening before. He took the paperwork and studied it intently. I lit a Lucky Strike and watched a pretty coffee-coloured girl going through the barrier inbound. I wasn't even paying attention to this part of it: no country's Customs are very much interested in what goes *out* of the place . . .

Pot-belly said: "We wanna search yore airplane f'you don' mind, Captain Scott."

8

I WENT VERY cold, very suddenly. For an instant that felt like a week, I couldn't think of a thing to say.

Eventually, I managed to croak: "Why?" Not exactly a brilliant contribution, but at least it showed I hadn't died on the spot.

Pot-belly produced an elaborate Spanish-American shrug. "Jus' routine, senor. We search outboun' airplanes sometimes, jus' at random. Come this way, plis, to wait."

I hesitated for a second, then went. There was no point in making a fuss beyond the bounds of natural indignation: any real tantrums on my part would only make them search longer and harder than they were going to already. Pot-belly led the way to an unmarked door at the side of the Customs hall, and ushered me into a cream-painted cubular room with a table, two plastic chairs, and no windows. I shivered as I went in — apart from the air-conditioning grill it could have been a room in Wandsworth Prison — and tried to dredge up something to say that might come under the heading of natural indignation.

For a moment, my mind stayed blank. Then I coughed, frowned, and said: "I'd be obliged if you'll be as quick as you can. It's costing me money sitting on the ground while you guys have your fun."

It was nearly right — but not quite. Pot-belly's face went stiff and official at the word 'fun'. He said woodenly: "We will be as queeck as eez possible, senor. Plis to sit down."

Then he went out and locked the door behind him.

I sat down, and fought with panic.

It was the locked door that did it, of course — just as it was designed to. Leaving the suspect to stew an hour or two in a small locked room is the oldest softening-up trick in the book — and with me, it worked better than they could ever have imagined. It took me straight back ten years, back to other keys turning in other doors and locking me up for weeks and months and years and taking away life and youth and hope . . .

And now it was happening aagin. They'd caught me on the second bent flight of my life — and they were going to put me back in a prison cell for another three or four grinding, unending years. I'd be thirty-six or seven when I came out and I'd never fly an aeroplane ever again . . .

I screwed my eyes tight shut, clenched my fists until they ached, and resisted the desperate urge to pound the door and yell and scream to be set free.

It was several minutes before I remembered the whisky.

When I did I grabbed up my flight bag, fished around in it with quivering hands until I came up with the bottle, and prescribed myself a couple of deep, steadying slugs. The spirit flowed into my guts like warm quicksilver — and slowly, the panic wound down a few notches. I took another gulp, which emptied the bottle — and lo, I could think again. Not well and not much — but maybe enough to keep my eyes off the locked door and my mind off the memories of prison . . .

I screwed the cap on, dropped the bottle back in the bag, and tried to tell myself that I was worrying about nothing. The Beech was clean, unloaded last night: I was in the clear.

That made me feel better until I remembered two small snags.

The first was the question of Customs' reasons for searching me. Pot-belly's line about a routine random check *might* just be true — but if it was, it was a routine I'd certainly never heard of. A check on incoming aircraft and cargoes, yes, sometimes — but not on outgoing stuff. No-one's usually bothered about what goes *out* of a place . . .

Unless, of course, they've had some sort of tip-off.

I frowned at the wall and thought about it. If they *had* had a tip-off they ought to fire their tipper-offer — since he'd at least got the direction wrong, being as how I'd been bringing the coins into Puerto Rico, not taking them out — but what worried me more was the thought of there being an informer at all: that implied the existence of a third interested party whom I'd never even heard of . . .

Ten minutes' concentrated effort on that produced no ideas whatsoever beyond the fact that I wished to speak to Harvey Bouvier on the matter, so I gave it up and turned to snag number two: namely, *was* the Beech as clean as it ought to be? I cursed myself for not checking under the inspection hatch when I went out to the bloody thing — because now, for all I knew, there might be a tube or two of Krugerrands rolling around among the cables and stringers in the bottom of the fuselage. I tried to convince myself that Harvey's boys wouldn't be the types to overlook odd tubes at $5,000-worth a time — but they *had* been unloading in the dark, and one or two *might* have fallen out of the trough and slipped down out of sight . . .

I took several deep breaths, and thought about prison again. I was still thinking about it when they came to me two hours later.

* * *

The door was opened by Pot-belly, who looked hot and grubby and peevish. He didn't come in, though: he just looked at me expressionlessly for a second, then stood aside to let another man in and went away again, slamming the door behind him. That left me with a visitor who looked like a typical American rancher: crinkly tanned face, hard grey eyes permanently narrowed from staring across too many prairies in too many noon-day suns, and a greying flat-top crew cut. I got up as he walked over to me and stuck out his hand.

He said: "Bill Scott? Ah'm Bob Morgan, Cen'ral Intelligence Agency."

I felt myself getting cold again. Remembered the Flamingo Air DC6 out in the aircraft park. The CIA airline.

His hand was dry and firm, and he even smiled — a sort of tight little rule-94-in-the-regulations smile. I bounced it back, slightly sickly: rule 95 in the Gold Smuggler's Handbook says you always smile back at the local representative of God. Then I jumped in with the natural indignation.

"Were you responsible for having my aircraft searched?"

He didn't bat an eyelid. "Yeah," he said calmly. "Ah'm afraid ah was. An' now ah'd like to talk to you a moment, f'you don't mind."

The voice matched the looks and the smile — a deep Western drawl, neither friendly nor unfriendly but at the same time making it abundantly clear that we *were* going to talk, whether I minded or not. They probably have something in the regulations about *that*, too.

I said: "Why?"

"Let's take a seat, Mr Scott, an' ah'll tell you."

We sat down. He parked himself squarely behind the table and leaned his forearms on it as if it was a desk. *His* desk: a man behind his own desk has a psychological advantage. I had just enough Scotch in me to think about pulling my chair up to the other side of the table and doing the same thing — but I also had enough in me so I didn't want him catching the full blast of it. I left the chair where it was, a couple of feet out and angled to one side. Sat down, crossed my legs, and worked at keeping Natural Indignation pasted firmly on my face.

"Okay," I said. "Why?"

The grey watchful eyes settled on mine.

"We-ell," he drawled slowly, "we kinda thought we might find some contraband on board."

"I'd worked that out for myself. What kind of contraband?"

He fished something out of his shirt pocket and put it down gently on the table.

It was a Krugerrand.

"About 40,000 of these," he said.

*　　　*　　　*

My first reaction was *Jesus, they* did *find an odd tube or two in the Beech*. Sweat started out on my temples, and I could feel the natural indignation curling at the edges.

Morgan seemed to be waiting for me to say something.

"What is it?" I asked. I tried to keep my voice normal, but it seemed to have developed a mag-drop. Morgan didn't notice — or didn't give any sign of noticing, anyway.

"It's a Krugerrand," he replied. "Ain't you seen one before?"

"No." I picked it up and looked at it, more so I didn't have to keep looking at him than anything else.

"What is it — gold?"

"Yep. Worth nigh on $200."

I gave a little whistle that came out like a tyre going down. "And you've lost 40,000 of them?"

"Not exactly *lost* 'em, Mr Scott," he drawled slowly "It's rather more that we're tryin' to *find* 'em. We kinda think they may be bein' smuggled down south from aroun' these parts.

There's severe restrictions on gold dealin' in an' out of US territory, as you may know."

Yeah, didn't I just . . .

I waggled my head meaninglessly and looked down at the coin again. It was a 1972 model. To keep the ball rolling, I said: "Well, you seem to have found one of them, anyway."

His eyes were still on my face. "Yeah. We picked up a . . . ah . . . small consignment just recently."

I actually felt the short hairs move on the back of my neck.

"Oh? Where?"

The rule-94 smile came out again for a second. He said: "Around" — and then just sat there waiting for me to say something else. The interrogation-by-silence technique: or, more likely, giving me time to wonder whether 'around' meant inside my Beech. I so wondered, and tried not to show it.

After a moment I put the Krugerrand back on the table, coughed into the silence, and said: "Where do they come from, these coins?"

"South Africa."

"Yes, I can see that" — careful, Scott — "but where did the 40,000 you're looking for come from?"

He said calmly: "Cuba. We think they're the payment in the Isla Bealta deal. You know about that?"

I felt myself nodding like a clockwork Mandarin. There was a massive fuzzy roaring in my ears, and my guts were performing a slow motion inverted snap-roll. I knew about that, all right.

I just hadn't known I was involved in it.

My face seemed to be frozen. I heard myself say: "Who's doing it, then? I mean, who's moving them?"

Morgan looked down at the coin, and poked it an inch or two along the table with his finger. Then he looked up at me again. When he spoke, his voice was almost casual. Almost.

"We-ell . . . we kinda thought you might be."

Christ, what was the bastard playing at? Had they found the bloody coin in my aeroplane, or hadn't they . . .?

I cleared my throat again and said: "Well, I'm not." It sounded a bit flat, even to me. I raked up a few shreds of indignation, sprinkled them on top, and had another go. "Definitely not. Why the hell pick on me?"

There was a short silence, while the grey eyes watched me carefully. Then he said softly: "Ah know you're not — *this*

93

time, but ah'm sorta wonderin' if you have in the past — or might do in the future."

I tried to stop myself reacting. *He knew I wasn't this time* — so they hadn't found anything in the Beech! I wanted to shout, jump, run in the free open air with relief . . .

I frowned and said again: "Why? Why should you think I might be involved?"

His hands moved in a small gesture. Then he said slowly: "We-ell, firstly, you been in the right places at the right times. An' secondly, our records show that you been . . . ah, involved in smugglin' before. So, we have to kinda ask ourselves if you might be doin' it again: ah guess you can unnerstand that, from our point of view."

So there it was.

My record.

My rotten, stinking, lousy bloody record again. I might be able to hide it from the Immigration authorities on a tin-pot island like Antigua — but the CIA'd have it on file, all right. They wouldn't shout it around or share it — but all the time it would be there, quietly gathering dust in some archive, waiting to be hauled out if the need ever arose . . .

Suddenly, I felt very tired and old. I ought to get angry: ought to point out that fifty other pilots must also have been in the right places at the right times for this, wherever those places and times were: ought to tell Morgan that I'd been going straight for ten years, and that it was inhuman to hound a guy and hound him and hound him to the ends of the earth . . .

I just nodded wearily.

The interview was over. Morgan showed me out.

*　　　*　　　*

Customs had left half the inspection panels off the Beech, of course. They always do, after a proper search: they're not obliged to put them back. I spent five minutes walking round the kite cursing in every language I know any swear-words in, then dragged out the tools and got to work in the screaming midday sun.

It was a pig of a job. The white-painted parts were just hot — but the black anti-glare bits, like the inboard sides of the engine nacelles, were fit to grill a four-course meal on. They certainly grilled my fingers without the slightest hesitation. It took two hours to get everything back on — two hours and a whole lot of temper. By the time I'd finished I was slippery with sweat from head to foot and had a splintering headache — and then I had to tramp back to Export Cargo and supervise the re-packing of Harvey's crates of Haitian woodwork, since Customs had been mauling them around as well. It was a pity they hadn't found something illegal in there — because if they had, it would've been Harvey's baby fair and square: a pilot isn't responsible for the contents of his manifested cargo.

And right now, Harvey wasn't exactly my favourite people.

I finally lifted my wheels off San Juan at five past five in the afternoon, and headed uphill for flight level nine-zero. When I got there I set the power at 28 Hg and 2,100 rpm, put her on the step, and then settled back to catch up on any thinking. The first thing I thought about was Isla Bealta — and the second thing was how I'd like to lynch Harvey Bouvier for not telling me what I was getting into.

You may have forgotten about the Bealta thing: it never made a lot in the American and European papers, not like Anguilla. But it certainly made a blazing row in the New World while it lasted — *and* in the United Nations, too.

Isla Bealta was a privately owned island. That in itself isn't unusual in the Caribbean — several of the tiniest islands are privately owned, particularly down in the Grenadines — but Bealta was special in one very important way. All the rest of the private dots lie inside some other island's territorial jurisdiction: but Bealta, sitting fifteen miles off the south coast of Haiti all on its own, was *outside* territorial waters — and that, of course, made it a tiny principality. About two miles by three, totally barren and non-productive apart from one luxury hotel which never had any guests — but nonetheless a principality. The owner could call himself King or Grand Duke or whatever the hell he liked . . .

And he could also, of course, make his own tax laws. Which made the place worth its weight in platinum.

According to rumour the island changed hands fairly regularly, the demand for it shifting according to which civilised nations were stopping up which particular tax-avoidance routes at any given time. The Mafia — inevitably — were reputed to have owned it for a period, then a group of Dutch businessmen from Curacao, and then a series of shadowy figures who were rumoured to be everybody from the Kennedys to Idi Amin but who never quite came forward to be counted. I had a vague recollection of hearing it had been sold to another unidentified purchaser shortly after I came to the islands twenty months back — and now, or three weeks ago to be exact, it had been sold again.

And the day after the sale, Haiti had moved a detachment of troops on to it and set up a canvas garrison in the grounds of the Bealta Hotel.

Baby Doc Duvalier — son and successor to Papa Doc — explained the invasion to the world by announcing that he'd discovered "a Cuban communist plot to take over Isla Bealta". Most of the world yawned mightily and took no notice — since it was customary for Haiti to accuse Cuba of responsibility for everything from the Second World War to the smells in the Port-au-Prince drains — but after a week or so, reports started to trickle out which suggested that for once, the Haitian government was actually telling the truth. Several foreign newspapers carried stories about a number of Cubans, among them a government official from Havana, holed up in the Bealta Hotel waving the deeds to the island and screaming at the Haitians to get the hell off their property.

And *that*, of course, was something else again.

*　　　*　　　*

It is commonly supposed by the general public of the Western world that Fidel Castro more or less shot his bolt with the missile crisis in '62 — but this ain't so. He may have stopped trying to muscle into the big league games — but he hasn't stopped inhaling Russian aid, and he certainly hasn't stopped pushing the Gospel According to St Fidel around the rest of Latin America. Haiti, being right next door to Cuba and admittedly rotten to the core to boot, has been one of his prime targets for years. He's supplied arms and finance to the rebels in the hills, sparked off border incidents between Haiti and the Republic next door, and even mounted guerrilla operations of his own. The Organisation of American States slapped trade and diplomatic sanctions on to Cuba because of these activities ten years back — and every time a motion comes before the house to end these sanctions, Edner Brutus from Haiti is conspicuously

96

among those abstaining or actively putting the boot in against it.*

So what with one thing and another, trying to get his hands on a place like Isla Bealta was a stunt right up Fidel's back alley. Maybe he didn't quite know what he was going to do with it when he'd got it — but if the chance came up he'd certainly grab it first and worry about little details like that later.

It looked like the chance had come up.

The stage things were at now, nobody had actually *proved* he was grabbing it — not stone cold bang-to-rights proof, any-way — but on the other hand, nobody had much doubt about it, either. The Cubans in the Bealta Hotel claimed they were mem-bers of a private investment group and nothing to do with that wicked Fidel at all — but since they refused to name the princ-ipals of the group, their story was beginning to smoulder a bit round the edges. Castro himself had denied complicity — naturally — but then rather spoilt the effect by protesting to the United Nations in the next breath about "Haiti's unprovoked invasion of the freedom-seeking state of Isla Bealta". That master-piece of diplomacy got the Haitian delegation up on their hind legs in the UN, with the net result that now the whole affair was being investigated by that ponderous body.

Early reports indicated, predictably, that the investigation was not exactly proceeding apace. The UN were not only hampered by the natural secrecy and bloody-mindedness of the Haitians and the Cubans, but they were also up against a stone wall in the matter of tracking down the seller of the island and Castro's alleged front-man who'd been the ostensible purchaser. Both these parties had tucked themselves away behind a maze of paper companies and concrete lawyers all over the world — and the UN, thrashing about in the jungle of company law in places like Liechtenstein, Switzerland and the Caymans, had no more hope of finding the principals in the transaction than they had of organising an Arab-Israeli winter sports day in Cyprus. The

* Two weeks later, in November 1974, the OAS Conference in Quito again voted to continue the sanctions against Cuba. A campaign to end the sanctions — headed by Columbia, Costa Rica and Venezuela — lost its steam after the United States, Guatemala and Haiti announced their intention to abstain, and several other nations came out openly against it. The Brazilian Foreign Minister commented that "only guarantees from Castro that he will cease his actions of intervention" would cause the sanctions to be lifted. No such guarantees have ever been offered by Havana.

general consensus of opinion was that they'd fumble around for a year or so until everybody had forgotten about the issue, then quietly arrange for Haiti to keep the island on condition that *they* didn't flog it to Moscow or the Catholic Church or anybody.

So that was the position at the moment — except that now, thanks to Agent Morgan, CIA, I knew who the seller was.

None other than Harvey's friend and mine, Mr Hans-Jürgen Ruchter.

*   *   *

I shoved the revs up to 2,200, which started the fuselage drumming like a tractor race in an echo chamber, and trimmed slightly nose-down for max continuous cruise. I wanted to have a talk with Harvey.

9

I LANDED IN Antigua at 1830, whizzed through Immigration and left Customs and some porters fiddling around with the cargo, and headed straight for the clubhouse and the phone.

I couldn't find the bastard.

There was no reply from his home, and his shop in St John's said they hadn't seen him all day, didn't know where he was, didn't know when he'd be back, and who's this calling? I put the receiver down, lit a cigarette, and took a gulp out of the fresh bottle of Scotch I'd just bought from one of the airport souvenir shops. It didn't help.

I looked out over the hot airport and said "Damn and blast", aloud. That didn't help, either.

The only thing I could think of now was to start searching the whole bloody island by car. That wasn't such an impossible project as it sounds, since Antigua's a pretty small island and Harvey's was the only red Maverick on it, but I could certainly think of jollier ways of spending an evening.

Damn and blast again. I stood up to go — and the phone rang.

For an illogical moment I was convinced it was Harvey. I snatched up the receiver and snapped: "Leeward Islands Aero Club?"

It wasn't him, of course: it was a local construction company who wanted a tractor tyre and a few other things picked up from St Croix in the Virgin Islands as soon as I could, or sooner if possible. I said Sure, I'll do it tomorrow and Sure, business was fine, and rang off.

Then I slung the Scotch bottle into my flight bag, the flight bag into the front seat of the Moke, and headed into town. It started to rain as I drove out of the airport.

* * *

I found him two hours and one rubberised Chinese meal later, in the place I should have tried right at the start.

Joey's brothel.

It was raining properly by then, thundering down with tropical intensity in the hot, black night. I parked the Moke behind the red Maverick, sat there for a moment listening to the water roaring on the canvas roof like an automatic car-wash, then took a deep breath and sprinted through the puddles to the doorway. The distance was only about thirty yards, but I arrived looking like a wet cat and feeling as if I'd just swum home from Puerto Rico.

It wasn't a high class place, Joey's: not one of those establishments that get into the tourist brochures described as 'country clubs' or anything like that. Inside, it was bare and uninviting. No decoration, no sexy nooks and crannies, no soft lights, and no decent furniture to get busted up by drunken trouble-makers. Just a big, empty-looking room of old bleached boards and flaking pink paint, lit by three or four garish psychedelic strip-lights and equipped with a few battered, un-matched tables and chairs scattered around a plain, badly stocked bar. A sagging door in the far wall said NO ADMITTANCE. That was the door to the bedrooms. Guess how I knew.

The only people in the place were four girls — two dancing with each other, one studying the tone-deaf American juke box, and the fourth sitting on a high stool beside the bar — and Harvey's man Sherman, sitting with his back to the wall near the NO ADMITTANCE sign, where he could watch the door on to the street. There was no trace of Harvey himself.

Well, I could guess where he was.

I nodded to Sherman, and walked over to the bar. He didn't nod back: just watched me impassively with his hard brown eyes. There was a half-finished bottle of Fanta orange on the table in front of him, so maybe he was getting carried away with the evening's general debauchery.

I reached the bar and peered over it. Joey himself was slouched in a low chair behind it. He was an enormous fat man, black as coal, with a narrow-brimmed felt hat perched ridiculously on the very front of his huge head, right down over his eyebrows. He always wore that hat. On another man it might have looked funny — but with the rest of Joey to go with it, you didn't feel like grinning. He had one of the most brutal faces I've ever seen anywhere in the world: small, cold black eyes, wide flat nose several times broken and starting to show the grizzly effects of syphilis, and a thick-lipped sneering mouth that never ever smiled, just opened and closed like a trap as he breathed.

I asked for a Scotch. He grunted, and reached under the bar without stirring in his chair. There were pouring noises, and a faint tang of whisky struggled to get through the stench of disinfectant and Negro sweat.

The girl on the bar stool said: "Yo' wanna buy a drink fo' a girl, mista?"

I looked at her. She was a pretty coffee-coloured mulatto with big, slightly slanting eyes. She was wearing short red hot pants, a black string vest, and a big false smile. Nothing else.

I said: "Sure, but that's all I'm doing tonight." Joey gave another primeval grunt, reached up and plonked my Scotch on the bar, and gave the girl a glass of something that might have been rum and Coke but was more likely just Coke and Coke.

"Two dolla' fifty."

I paid him, hitched myself on to a stool, and took a small fast swallow of Scotch à la Joey. It tasted like cut-price jet fuel. Out of the corner of my eye I could see Sherman, still leaning back in his chair, still watching me.

The record on the juke box finished, leaving the sound of the rain drumming on the tin roof like a Voodoo dirge. The two dancing girls sat down at a table and pouted at me hopefully. Their jet-black faces were shiny with sweat in the muggy heat.

The girl at the bar slid off her stool and pressed herself against my right side. Her body was warm and soft and gently moving. One hand still held her glass.

"Yo' shore yo' jus' wanna drink, honey?" she whispered. "Yo' shore yo' woun' like a fuck as well?"

The delicate approach.

I leered at her tiredly. "Not at the moment, baby. Maybe later."

A slender brown hand stroked the inside of my thigh and then slid up between my legs. I could taste the smell of her in my nostrils; a mixture of mustiness and cheap brassy perfume.

"Yo' shore, honey? I fuck real good."

I picked up her hand and moved it away. Not that I didn't like it — but any second now she was going to be stroking the Smith & Wesson, hanging inside my trousers in its little under-belt holster, and telling me how well-endowed I was. And Joey might not like the idea of people carrying gats around the place.

It didn't stop her. She took my hand and pressed it between her own legs. The drink in her other hand didn't even quiver, but her eyes got big and round.

"Ooh, dat *good*, honey," she breathed. She held my wrist and pulled my hand slowly up and down. The warmth of her thighs ran up my arm like fire. "Dat *real* good. Le's go fuck now, huh . . .?"

At that moment, Harvey walked in.

He appeared through the door marked NO ADMITTANCE, checked to make sure Sherman was still on sentry-go, then looked round the room and saw me. His eyes went blank with surprise for a moment, then he flip-flapped over to the bar on loose sandals. I pushed Hot Pants gently aside and slid off the stool. She seemed about to say something, then got the message and melted away.

Harvey boomed: "Hiya, Scotty — come fr'a bit o' pussy?"

"Nope. I came to see you. Come and sit down."

I led the way to a table as far away from everyone else as possible, feeling Sherman's eyes on my back as I moved. Harvey hesitated a moment, then dropped a five-dollar bill on the bar in front of Hot Pants, said "Bring me a Coke an' a Scotch, willya," and flip-flopped over and thumped down on a chair opposite me. There was sweat on his face and he stank of sex and disinfectant: Joey's girls performed a crude sort of after-service with the disinfectant.

"Wassa trouble then, Scotty?" His voice was throttled back to a deep underground rumble. He glanced quickly round the room, then added: "Kinda stoopid ya comin' ta see me here, huh? Why'ncha have a good fuck then come up ta my house or call me?"

I ignored that, and let him have it right between the eyes. "I want to know why Ruchter got paid for Isla Bealta in Kruger-rands," I said quietly. "And also, why he brought the bloody things here to Antigua."

That shook him, all right. His face and hands went suddenly very still. The rain rumbled loudly on the roof, shutting us in a cocoon of tension a million miles away from the other people in the place. Two beads of sweat rolled down his jowls as he stared at me.

After a moment he said hoarsely: "Whatdja mean, Isla Bealta — " and then had to stop while Hot Pants swayed over to the table with our drinks. She gave me a leer like an open cash-register, then swayed back to the bar. I got in before Harvey could get his mouth open again.

"Don't waste my time with any bullshit," I snarled. "I've had enough bullshit from you to last me all year. Just answer the question — starting with how he came to get paid in Krugerrands."

"How d'ya know . . .?"

"Just bloody answer, chum!"

He stared at me for a few more seconds — and then spread his hands on the table in a slow what-the-hell gesture.

"Shit, Scotty . . ." He swallowed a couple of times. "Well, shit — why not? He hadta get paid in something. The — ah — buyers wouldn't deal through a bank, an' he wouldn't take a traceable cash currency. So — Krugerrands were as good as any-thin'. They're handier an' easier ta sell than pure gold, an' they ain't numbered."

I studied his face for a moment, then nodded. "Okay — so now tell me why he came to Antigua — and why he wants the damn things moved into Puerto Rico, of all places?"

Harvey took a fast swig of Coke. "He had — sorta — security reasons."

I leaned back. "Security reasons. Bloody great. What you mean is he was about half a jump ahead of a mob of Cubans howling for their money back because the deal went phut. And since the word had got out about the Bealta payment, he was stuck with a load of coins he daren't shove into a bank anywhere in the world because everyone from the CIA to the Upper Tooting Boy Scouts would be watching for him to do just that. Okay — I see all that. I even see why he brought them here to Antigua, since you and Cas McGrath were based here and you were going to run them from here to Puerto Rico for him. But what I *don't* see is why the hell Puerto Rico at all? Why for the love of Christ take 'em somewhere where it ain't even legal to own 'em?"

Harvey frowned, chewed a fingernail for a moment, and then said slowly: "Well — ah — ya answered that yaself, Scotty. Every cop an' intelligence agency in the world's lookin' out for that money. There's no way he could sell it legally without someone gettin' tipped off. Even the Cayman an' Swiss banks ain't that secure — not against people like the CIA when they're really tryin'. An' even if they were, he'd lose his coin premium sellin' ta banks an' dealers."

I said impatiently: "Okay, so it's hot money; I know that, for Chrissake — but that still isn't the reason for taking it into PR. Why doesn't he flog it to the Mafia or someone somewhere else . . ."

"Lemme finish, willya? I'm fuckin' tellin' ya why." He breathed heavily for a moment, wiped at the sweat streaming down his face, and then went on. "Sure he could sell it ta someone like that — an' whatdja think he'd get for it, huh? Half its value? A quarter? It's *hot* money, Scotty, like ya said — an' that's expensive ta get rid of." He stopped, wiped his face again, and then added: "Unless, of course, ya find some place where there's an illegal demand for it."

I frowned, then said: "Puerto Rico?" right on cue.

"Right. There, it's a seller's market. He can *charge* a premium there instead of paying one."

"They really want gold that bad up there?"

Harvey shrugged. "A few wise guys do. They wanna quick turnover before the price goes down again. They're not payin' a hell of a lot over the normal price — but it *is* better than Ruchter'd get anywhere else, an' it *is* secure. I think the guys buyin' the stuff are takin' most of it up to the US mainland to sell again quick."

I nodded slowly. I was beginning to see daylight, now. "So that's why Ruchter's taking such a big risk with the stuff," I said. I was talking half to myself. "He's stuck with selling it illegally, and he wants to get rid of it now, quickly, while the demand lasts. And breaking the gold-trading law doesn't matter a damn to him, because he's got nothing to lose anyway. If the Yanks catch up with him at all they're going to hit him with everything from busting the sanctions against Cuba to high treason, or whatever your guys call it. That'd put him away for about ten lifetimes and most of the hereafter — so on top of *that* lot, a little thing like running gold into Puerto Rico nine weeks before it got legal anyway wouldn't make tuppence worth of difference one way or the other. I see his point . . ." I took a quick gulp of jet fuel, then looked up at Harvey again and said: "Okay — but why isn't he having the stuff run up to the mainland United States himself? Presumably he'd get even more for it there."

Harvey had another go at his fingernail. Then he said: "Well — ah, my organisation's used ta workin' in San Juan, for one thing. An' then Ruchter lives in Puerto Rico, see? Runs a chain of hotels there an' in the Virgin Islands. So he wants the money there anyway."

"So what? He could take it there anytime."

Harvey spread his hands again. "Yeah, sure — but if he did, he'd hafta smuggle it in."

"What the hell for? You can take dollars into PR, surely to Christ?"

"Sure ya can — but if ya push four million in through any sorta bank transfer, ya get the Internal Revenue on ya doorstep. So — ya gotta smuggle it in. So I guess Ruchter wants ta get all the smugglin' done in one go."

That was a point, of course. I thought about it for a bit, while the rain rumbled on the roof. Then something else occurred to me. I said: "Look — surely the Cubans are going to get on to friend Ruchter any moment? I mean, they must be mad as hell about spending all that money on Bealta now the Haitians have moved in. I'd've thought they'd have been looking for *Herr General* to get their money back."

Harvey grinned. "Fuck — ya don' wanna worry about that. Ruchter's good at precautions against that sorta thing."

I glared at him. "Precautions! He sits there fat, dumb and happy on the biggest yacht in English Harbour and you call that *precautions*? My Christ, mate — I'm surprised he hasn't had a bunch of Cuban thugs blow his head off already. If that's his precautions, then all I can say is God help you if he ever does anything in the open!"

Harvey frowned again, scowled, then dug a cigar out of his shirt pocket and concentrated on pulling the cellophane off it while he decided how much to tell me. I poured the remains of my first Scotch into the one that'd just arrived, and waited. I had nothing but time.

After a long moment, he said slowly: "It ain't quite like that, Scotty. Nobody knows Ruchter or me's involved at all. The deal was in another name, like the ownership of the island, an' he had somebody else make the pick-up. The stuff was transferred ta his yacht at sea. So he ain't got no need ta hide: he's just a rich businessman takin' a vacation."

"Oh, yeah?" I leaned forward, and leered at him. "Then how come I was stopped and searched by the CIA in San Juan this morning? And how come they had a sample Krugerrand which they said was part of the Bealta money?"

The cigar ground to a halt halfway up to his mouth, and his face went suddenly dead white under the suntan. I hadn't known that was actually possible, before. I watched him, and enjoyed it: you don't often get treats like that.

After a moment he said slowly: "You were stopped by *who*?"

"The CIA. One Agent Bob Morgan, to be precise. He's been here in Antigua, too, I think."

I told him what happened. It took a little while, because he wanted to know exactly what Morgan had said — particularly on the subject of where the CIA had picked up the 'small consignment' of Krugerrands that Morgan claimed his sample had come from. At the end of it he sat and chewed the cigar for maybe five minutes, while the colour crawled slowly back into his face. I lit a Lucky Strike, wiped at the sweat under my chin, and stared around the flaking pink room. Hot Pants, over by the bar, caught my eye and stroked her hands over her hips suggestively. One of the other girls put another record on the juke box, and the steel band warble of *Limbo Like We* bounced around the stagnant bar like a clown at a funeral. The rain drummed a mournful bass background, and nobody danced.

Typical Thursday night in your Friendly Home Town Brothel. Then Harvey said abruptly: "I guess it's okay, Scotty. The CIA've had a look at ya now. They won't do it again. We'll go ahead like we planned."

*   *   *

Jesus! I nearly choked on my whisky. When the world stopped swinging on its hinges I croaked: "You can't be serious!"

But he was, of course.

"Fuck, why not? Like I said, the CIA's had a look at ya now. They won't get Customs ta take ya apart again after they din' find anythin' today. An' they were only bluffin' anyway: if they were serious about it they'da searched ya goin' *in* ta San Juan, *and* they'da tipped off the Antiguan cops about ya record. An' as well as that, they certainly ain't picked up any of *our* Krugerrands, that's for sure. I reckon what it is, they just gotta sample of their own an' they picked on you 'cos of ya record."

I pulled out a damp pack of Luckies and got one fired up. The juke box ran down, and the sound of the rain closed in again. My hands were gummy with sweat.

And suddenly, I was angry. Real, deep-down angry.

Always, somebody telling me what to do. Go here. Go there. Do this. Do that. Go away. And for eleven long years, I'd taken it. I'd jumped when they said jump, gone when they said go. And now . . .

Now, I'd taken all I was going to.

I could feel my face going tight and cold as the anger welled up out of my guts. I leaned forward and blew smoke. My voice seemed to come from a thousand miles away.

"Listen, bastard: I don't seem to have made myself clear. I'm *quitting*. I agreed to smuggle some coins for you: I *didn't* agree to being the fall guy for the CIA. So I'm through. Finished. You *got* that?"

For a moment, there was a brittle silence. Then Harvey cleared his throat, spread his palms, and said slowly: "Ya remember what I told ya . . ."

"Yeah, I remember." I said it softly — but it stopped him as if he'd run into a wall. "You told me you'd tip off Immigration about me, didn't you?"

He didn't say anything. Just sat there watching me.

"Okay," I went on, very quietly. "You do that. But just remember that when you've done it, I shall kill you."

Have an Oscar for subtlety, Scott. And another one for stupidity, too — because if you really mean to kill someone, the last thing you do is tell them about it . . .

But right now, I didn't care. Whether or not I'd be capable of doing it in the future I didn't know — but *now*, at this moment, I could have shot him as easily as swatting a fly.

He seemed to realise it. He sat very still and white, staring at me. Drops of sweat rolled down his face in the heat.

The silence lasted a long time, filled only with the rumbling and gurgling of the downpour. Then, very slowly, the fury began to drain away. I found I had my right hand on the butt of the Smith & Wesson, poking out from my waistband under my shirt. I took it away, leaned back, and picked up my drink.

Harvey stirred. When it didn't get him shot he turned his hands over on the table, palms upwards, in a slow gesture that might have been defeat.

"Okay," he said. His voice was hoarse. He cleared his throat and had another go. "Okay, Scotty. Maybe ya right: we shoulda told ya what was happenin'. But I thought ya'd prob'ly turn the job down if ya knew it was anythin' ta do with Bealta . . ."

"You were damn right, too."

"Yeah." He frowned. "Yeah. But look, Scotty, ya *can't* quit now." I started fizzing again, but he pushed his hands and head forward and hurried on. "Look — I mean — if ya'd said no at the start, before ya knew what we were doin', that'd've been one thing. But now ya know all what's going on: if ya quit now, Ruchter's gonna think ya're a security risk. Ya unnerstan' what I'm sayin'?"

I understood, all right. I gave him a glare that should have knocked his teeth down his throat and snarled: "Tell Ruchter to go stuff himself."

Harvey waved his hands about helplessly, exercised his face through anger to fatherly concern and back to anger again as he tried to think of something else to say — and then seemed to give up. He made a massive slow shrug, and started to heave himself on to his feet. It seemed to be a long journey.

When he got there, he looked down at me and said heavily: "Okay, Scotty. I'll tell him what ya said. But I'm gonna do ya favour, pal — I ain't gonna tell him 'til I've talked t'ya in the mornin'. So you sleep on it, huh? Think about earnin' another twenny grand on one hand, or havin' Ruchter mad at ya on the other. Jus' think about it."

Then he left.

Sherman got up and glided after him like a pet panther, raking me with an expressionless black stare as he went. I watched them go and then sat on, nuzzling my drink and wondering just how big a mistake I might be making. The peeling bar-room seemed hot and empty and echoing, and I felt very tired and lonely. I swallowed the last of the jet fuel and told myself it was time to go. I didn't move.

A shadow fell across the table. It was the girl in red hot pants.

"Yo' wan' some Wes' Indian pussy now, honey?"

The rain thundered on the roof. I dropped the stub of the Lucky on the floor and trod on it, then looked up at her.

"How much for the whole night?" I asked.

*   *   *

At three in the morning it was still raining. It rumbled on the corrugated iron over my head like a pair of Pratt & Whitneys at cruise power, and rushed and glugged and chuckled down unseen drains and crevices. It also dripped through the roof somewhere with a steady *plink-plink-plink* like a Chinese water torture.

I lay awake in the darkness, chain-smoking and listening to it and sweating.

Especially sweating.

The normal night winds of the Leewards seemed to have abandoned the island to make way for the hammering rain. The result, in the tiny airless bedroom, was heat and humidity that bore down like a solid, tangible weight. My body was slippery with sweat from head to foot, and the single sheet was limp and rumpled underneath me. Even the air itself seemed exhausted: there wasn't the slightest breath to shift the musty smell of the girl sleeping beside me or the joss-stick tang of the slowly smouldering mosquito coil.

I stared into the blackness and tried to forget the heat by thinking about England. In the good days. Eleven — no twelve — years ago, now. In our little cottage in a Buckinghamshire village, newly married. Hard up, struggling with the mortgage, struggling to graduate from instructing to big-time flying . . .

But happy. At the time, I never realised how happy.

I reached over the side of the bed and picked up the bottle. The whisky tasted dull and acrid, and made my head ring in the stifling darkness. I put the bottle down again, and went back to my memories.

We'd been long on hopes in those days. I was a good pilot, and I was headed for the airlines. We both thought I could do it. So we scrimped and saved and I got my Commercial, and then we scrimped and saved again for the Instrument Rating.

We were still saving when Jenny got pregnant and Smith came along and our lives ended at a place called Great Ashfield.

I stirred, pulled on my cigarette until it glowed red, and blew smoke into the darkness. I didn't want to think about Great Ashfield — but I couldn't help it. It's always the same when I try to remember the good times: my stupid brain runs on past the little haven of happiness that was our marriage, and scans down the long empty years that came afterwards. No airlines, no home . . . and no Jenny. Just the bum jobs and the running and long, downhill slide . . .

And now the downhill slide had brought me to this time and place. Lying on a stinking bed in a cheap West Indian whorehouse trying to choose between the risk of going to jail again and the threat of getting my head blown off.

Because that was what it came down to, all right: a straight choice between carrying on in the teeth of the CIA's investigations, or quitting and getting the Antigua branch of the Waffen SS down on my neck. It had been one thing to shout my mouth off at Harvey a few hours back — but it would be something very much else if Herr Ruchter got seriously peeved, and I knew it. And he *would* get seriously peeved if I quit, too: Harvey was right about that. *Mein General* would undoubtedly regard anyone who knew as much as I did as a very considerable security risk indeed ...

The bed creaked as I hauled the bottle up again and took two or three swigs. The girl stirred and murmured, but didn't wake up.

So all right, Scott: just how much *do* the CIA know? Do they seriously suspect you — or did they just pick on you because of your record? And that Krugerrand Morgan had: did that really come from a consignment of the Bealta money — or was it just a sample he was carrying about for general inspiration and the prompting of suspects?

I blew more smoke and listened to the rain. The steady thunder of it didn't hold any answers.

There was something else that bothered me about the CIA, too: something that nagged from just under the surface of conscious thought. I rubbed a sweat-sticky hand over my sweat-sticky face and tried to pin it down. Was it to do with Morgan having me searched outbound instead of going in? Or maybe something he'd said, or not said ... ?

But it was no good, it was gone. My brain was trudging round in weary circles and refusing to pick up the right thread. I stubbed my cigarette out on the floor, and reached for the bottle again.

Beside me, the girl rolled over and came drowsily awake.

"Wha' time it, honey?"

I squinted at my watch. " 'Bout three thirty. Drink?"

"Huh?"

"Would you like a drink?" I jiggled the bottle, but the sloshing of the whisky was lost under the rumble of the rain.

"Oh ... No." She moved, and a warm hand slid up my leg to

my crutch and started doing things. "Yo' like t'fuck some more?"

I took a last swig of Scotch, dumped the bottle on the floor, and lay back on the damp, reeking bed. My head seemed to be going round and round in the darkness and the heat. I rolled over on my side and smelt the musky sweat of her as I reached out.

"Sure," I said.

IO

I MADE COOLIDGE AIRPORT by eight thirty in the morning. The weather had dried out, even if I hadn't, and the sun blazed down out of a fresh blue sky studded with cheerful white blobs of fair-weather cu. I couldn't be bothered to drive home for a shower, so I stopped off at the terminal instead and had a long cold wash in the controllers' cloakroom. It was a waste of time; soap and water could never wash away the mugginess in my head, and the blistering after-storm humidity outside raised a new sheen of sweat in the time it took to drive from the tower to the clubhouse.

After unlocking the place I spent a couple of minutes studying the Note to Self about today's charter to St Croix, then stumbled around opening up the store cupboard and re-stashing the Smith & Wesson and its holster. In the hot light of morning I didn't know why I'd bothered to take the bloody thing last night anyway. I hadn't really been intending to shoot anybody, and all I'd got from carrying it about was a sweaty raw patch under my belt where the butt had chafed. I shoved it back in the P & W cylinder, locked the cupboard again, and was just about ready to start on the day proper when the phone rang.

It was Harvey.

"Hiya. Scotty." He sounded brisk and cheerful — or as brisk and cheerful as a Bronx voice ever sounds. "Glad I caughtcha so early."

I just grunted.

"Well — watcha decided?"

I looked out over the bright sunny apron. A LIAT Avro 748 fired up its starboard engine in a steady rising whine, then got started on the port. I thought about Ruchter and his sentries on the lush, immaculate yacht down in English Harbour.

"I'm going to carry on," I said.

"Hey, that's great, Scotty." There was relief in his voice: maybe he hadn't been looking foward to carrying the bad news to the Fatherland. "I knew ya'd change ya mind. Ya worryin' about nuthin', pal."

I grunted again. Some nothing.

"Okay," he went on hurriedly. "I wancha ta do the next flight this afternoon, in the Cherokee. Park at the same place in San Juan, an' stay overnight again. I ain't got no cargo for ya, but if anyone asks ya can say ya got business with John Bennett. He's my shop manager in San Juan, an' he'll confirm it. His phone number's 343-2020. Okay?"

I said: "No, not okay. I've got a charter to St Croix today — and anyway, how the hell are you going to load up the Cherokee in broad daylight?"

There was a momentary hesitation. Then: "Well — ah — fact is, Scotty, it's loaded already."

"What?" I whipped round and stared out of the window towards the aircraft park. I could just make out the Cherokee through the wriggling heat-haze over the white concrete, sitting placidly opposite somebody's Apache and almost in the shadow of a Seagreen DC3. It didn't seem to have grown horns yet — but all the same, I felt new sweat starting out on the palms of my hands as I looked at it.

A million and a third in gold. Jesus.

"When the bloody hell did you do that?"

"Two nights ago. While ya were in San Juan. It was pissin' with rain here, like it was last night, so I took advantage of it. Got about 4,000 inta it, which was all it would take." There was a moment's heavy breathing, then: "How'dja come ta be takin' a charter today anyway? I toldja ya'd prob'ly be doin' the next trip today."

"I took it on last night. Before I saw you."

"Oh." He didn't seem inclined to pursue that. "Well, can't ya cancel it?"

I thought quickly. I could, of course — but on the spur of the moment, I decided I wasn't going to. No real reason, except maybe that cargo flying was my business and this was the first business decision I'd made for myself for a while. The hell with the bastard: let him stew for a bit. If the coins had been sitting in the Cherokee for the last thirty-six hours then another day wasn't going to hurt them.

I said: "No."

"Well, can ya go ta San Juan when ya get back?"

I thought again. "Yeah, I could do. But I don't know when that'll be — you know how it is when you've got to wait for cargo. I might get off for San Juan at a reasonable hour, or it might be pretty late at night. Would that matter?"

"Ah — I don't think so, but it might." He brooded on it. Out on the apron, the Avro raised its nagging whine and nosed off towards the western taxiway. It was the morning island-hopper to St Kitts, St Maarten, Beef Island and San Juan. I wished I was on it.

Then I had my idea.

"Look," I said. "Why don't I do this St Croix job and then drop into San Juan and see what happens? It's only another 150 miles round trip — and then we'll *know* if the CIA are on to me, if they search me again. Then if it's okay I can take the — er — your cargo, tomorrow."

That appealed to him, all right.

"Yeah," he said slowly. "Yeah, that's a real good idea. You do that."

*   *   *

So I did.

And apart from the weather — I ran through last night's storm-belt over the ocean both going out and coming back — I didn't have the slightest trouble. I got to St Croix just before noon, found my cargo with less than the usual number of threatening phone calls, then got straight off again and jiggled my way through the crowded sky into San Juan. I told Customs I was over-nighting, watched them slap a bond certificate over the door of the aircraft to cover the cargo-in-transit, then wandered off and had a few beers in one of the airport bars. Then at four o'clock I went back to Customs and said my San Juan cargo had fallen through and I was leaving now — and they came out and removed the bond-sticker without twitching an eyebrow. There was no sign of Pot-belly or Morgan, and they didn't even want to look in my flight bag. It looked as if yesterday's search *had* been a one-off thing . . .

I got off the ground at four thirty, and rumbled back in over the north-west coast of Antigua just before sunset.

*   *   *

The tower said: "Alpha Whisky yo' clear t'land: wind one-one-zero at one-two, gustin' two zero."

I clicked the transmit button in acknowledgment, shoved down the rest of the flap just before the threshold, and settled the Beech on in a three-pointer. She gave one stiff-legged little bounce — and then tried to skew herself off the right-hand side of the runway. I caught her with brake and a quick burst of starboard engine, slowed down, unlocked the tailwheel, and turned off at the first taxiway, consoling myself with the thought that you can't win 'em all and that most people don't even *try* three-pointing Beech 18s . . .

The apron was seven-eighths Boeings and DC8s: either the tourists *were* coming back this year or — more likely — the traffic-planners had screwed it up and got a whole week's aeroplanes arriving in two hours on a Friday afternoon. I found a slot between BWIA and Air Canada, stopped the engines, and clambered out with hands full of general declarations and cargo manifests. The sun was well into its evening dive towards the hills to the west, but that hadn't stopped the heat. It came up off the dusty white concrete in waves, aided and abetted by the dragons' breath of taxiing jets. I could feel my face and armpits going sticky with sweat as I walked over to Customs and Immigration.

A gang of Bee-wees from the construction company were waiting to pick up the cargo. I dug out a Customs officer, distributed the paperwork, then left them to get on with the unloading and clearing of the goods while I ambled along to the restaurant for something to eat.

I should have known better, with all those jets on the apron.

The place was wall-to-wall tourists, mostly American, all reeking of sun-tan lotion, and all inclined to peevishness about the statutory West Indian trade gap between ordering and getting served. The waitresses were reacting in the usual way — pouting sulkily and going even slower than ever — and I hovered in the doorway for a moment toying with the idea of driving up to the Sugar Mill hotel instead. But they'd probably be just as crowded *and* twice the price, so I ended up grabbing a table to myself as a party of Yanks left in disgust, and putting in a bid for sausage-egg-and-chips with a passing waitress who mistook me for someone who might leave a tip. The fast twilight came and went, leaving the restaurant lit by the sort of watery yellow arc lights you find in aircraft hangars and railway stations, and the banquet turned up after twenty minutes. Cool greasy chips, a vulcanised egg, and a pair of sausages that looked like Arawak relics. I sighed, poured ketchup over everything in the hope of making it taste of something other than dead mongoose, and got started.

I was halfway through when the law arrived.

* * *

It clumped in through the door in the shape of one of Antigua's senior Customs officers and a size-twelve plain clothes copper I knew slightly by sight. The pair of them marched straight over to my table. I wished I *had* gone to the Sugar Mill.

When they reached me, Customs gave me a stony official stare from under the peak of his uniform cap and said: "Good evenin', Missah Scott." He had a sneering, high-pitched voice, and he made sure it carried several tables around. He was the sort of black man who'd enjoy paying an Official Visit to a white man in a crowded restaurant.

I replied "Evenin' " round a mouthful of lukewarm chips, then added, "Why doncha siddown?" as they both pulled out chairs. They ignored that. Customs kept his cap on to perpetuate the Official Visit image, and glared at me with hot suspicious eyes behind his horn-rimmed glasses. He didn't like me — I'd won an argument with him once — and it was showing.

I waved my fork at the police contingent and said to Customs: "Who's your friend?"

Customs' broad black face went stiff and angry — but before he could think of anything suitably nasty to say, the friend chipped in for himself.

"I'm Inspector de Lima, Antigua Police Force," he said calmly. "I'd like to ask yo' a few questions, suh."

I looked at him. He was big and coal black, neatly dressed in blue trousers and a crisp white shirt — and he didn't seem the slightest put out about me being rude. His liquid brown eyes were watching me steadily, without haste. Noting how much I was sweating, the set of my mouth and eyebrows — the little things that unconsciously give you away when you start telling lies.

De Lima might just turn out to be a pretty good cop. I began to get a small hollow feeling in my stomach.

I said: "Go ahead. Ask away."

De Lima just nodded, and then pointed his face at the bar for a moment. A waitress whizzed over immediately with two Carib beers, and whizzed off again without leaving a bill.

I swallowed. A consignment of chips went down like wood-shavings. "What d'you have to do to get service like that here?"

De Lima frowned at the bottles, then looked up with a small sad smile.

"Be black perhaps, suh," he said.

"And a policeman, too."

He nodded. "Yeh. That too, maybe."

"Haven't got much chance what with one thing and another then, have I?"

De Lima produced his small smile again, plus the beginnings of a shrug to match. If he was niggled, it certainly didn't show. He drank a mouthful of beer, put the bottle back gently on the table, and then said: "I hear yo' had yo' plane searched in San Juan yes'day, suh."

I'd been expecting that, so I didn't react. Just shovelled another portion of lingering death into my mouth and said through it: "S'right. They didn't find anythin', though."

He nodded, his face impassive. I expected the next question to be What were they looking for? — but it wasn't. Instead, he said almost casually: "What were yo' doin' in Joey's las' night, Missah Scott?"

For a moment I just gaped at him. Then I waved a forkful of Arawak relic and said: "Well, at the beginning of the evening Miss Bardot and I had a little caviar on toast washed down with the Bollinger '42. Then we danced a few numbers to Mr Sinatra's excellent little band, and after that we watched the cabaret while . . ."

"Quite so, suh." This time he didn't smile, and his eyes had gone hard. "Now, what were yo' *doin'*?"

"Bloody screwing, of course: what the hell else d'you do in Joey's?"

The eyes stayed hard. "That unusual place fo' white man to go screwin', suh. Mos' white men go to Villa Yolande."

I shrugged and leered. "So I felt like a bit of local colour."

Customs fidgeted at the 'local colour' bit, but de Lima ignored him.

"Did yo' meet anyone there?"

I thought fast. If *I'd* been seen . . .

"Yeah. Harvey Bouvier. The guy who runs the souvenir shops. *He* was screwing, too."

"Yo' got business wi' Missah Bouvier?"

The first half of the egg curled up in my stomach.

"Some. I carry freight for his shops now and then. Woodwork and stuff." I took a mouthful of sausage, mainly to give my face something else to do besides sit around looking guilty.

"Yo' shore yo' din' meet no-one else?"

"Sure I'm sure. Unless you're interested in a little Santo Domingan whore called Nina. Who else d'you think I'd meet?"

He leaned his elbows on the table and twiddled the beer bottle in his big hands for a moment. Then he looked up and said deliberately: "I bin wonderin' if yo' might've met some Black Power people, suh."

I felt my jaw sagging open stupidly.

"Met some . . . *Black Power* people?" I echoed. "*Me?* You're off your ever-lovin' rocker, mate!"

De Lima just shrugged. "Maybe, suh," he said evenly. "But I have to ask, jus' de same."

"Well, the answer's no. Definitely no. Why the bloody hell did you think I might've been?"

He took another small swig of beer, keeping his eyes on my face. Then he said slowly: "Well, suh, I bin wonderin' if yo' bin bringin' them guns in yo' plane."

*   *   *

After a while I found I had my mouth open again, with the kitchen-stench walking in. I jacked it shut, decided he *had* said what I thought he'd said, and croaked: "What the *hell* makes you think that?"

For a moment, he just went on watching me thoughtfully. Then he said: "Well suh, *someone* bringin' them in. We find a big dump of Russian guns an' explosives 'round Injun Creek recen'ly, an' we think they more on Shekerly Mountain. An' they din' jus' walk on to the islan'."

I waggled my head meaninglessly. They didn't walk on to the island, indeed — they're been smuggled in from Cuba, and everyone knew it. Even the *Antigua Times*. But why the hell *I* should be a suspect for the smuggling . . .

"Why *me*, for Chrissake?"

De Lima didn't answer. Just studied me for a few moments more, then turned his head and looked at Customs, who'd been following the proceedings with interest. Customs made sure the regulation scowl was in place, and leaned forward.

"Yo' bin to St Croix today, Missah Scott?"

"Yep."

"An yo' got nuthin' to declare to Cus'oms?"

"Nope. Your men are dealing with the cargo now."

His eyes gleamed triumphantly behind the glasses. "My men are *searchin'* yo' cargo now, Missah Scott. An' afta that, we wanna search yo' plane." He sat back to observe the effect.

I turned back to de Lima. "Why?" I asked again.

He picked up his beer bottle, swallowed, and trotted out another of his slow shrugs. "Yo' got searched in San Juan, suh: they musta had a reason fo' that. An' then yo' in Joey's las' night an' St Croix today."

"What the hell's that got to do with anything? D'you always tell Customs to search a guy just 'cos San Juan's had a go at him and he spends a night in a whorehouse?"

Customs steamed. De Lima didn't react at all.

"No suh," he said calmly. "But when there's enough evidence fo' suspicion, we gotta look into it. Joey's is known to be used by militants here, an' St Croix is a strong Black Pow' place. We think the arms may be comin' through there from Cuba. So . . . we gotta check."

I nodded slowly. I hadn't known that about Joey's before — and now I did, I was beginning to see the light. If the cops thought they might scoop up some Black Power in the place they were probably keeping a regular watch on it — and last night's watch would have reported the presence of one Bill Scott. Hence de Lima checking on my activities of yesterday and today — and hence him putting two and two together and making five. It wasn't unreasonable, in a left-handed sort of way: St Croix *did* have a bad rash of Black Power and *was* dead in line to be used as a staging-post between Cuba and Antigua — and if no-one had seen fit to enlighten the Antiguan authorities about my San Juan search, then for all they knew I *could* have been taken apart on an arms hunt. I could have added to their store of knowledge on the last point myself, of course — but I damn well wasn't going to. I'd rather have de Lima suspecting me of running guns than gold any day . . .

I frowned, shoved the last of the chips into my mouth and a bit of indignation into my voice, and said: "It's a bit bloody thin, mate, isn't it? I mean, you can't get much more circumstantial than that lot."

De Lima leaned massive black forearms on the table and made a small gesture with his hands round the beer bottle. His face was totally expressionless.

"Sho' it is, suh. But like I say, we only checkin'. Yo' not bein' accused of anythin'. Not yet."

There wasn't anything to say to that, so I didn't say it. I turned to Customs again. "Go ahead and search, then. It's not locked."

The man was looking sullen. Maybe he was disappointed because I hadn't Broken Down And Confessed All — or, more likely, he was just disgruntled at de Lima stealing his thunder. I grinned — which was unwise of me: if there's one sure way of making a Bee-wee official lose his cool, it's to laugh at him.

His face snapped shut. "We no' do it now," he said truculently "We do it later. Yo' plane groun'ed 'til we finish. Yo' move it to de parkin' area now. Dey already a man wid it."

I wiped the grin off my face. He was delaying now because he couldn't spare the men for a thorough search — not with five jets on the apron — but if I *really* upset him he'd be perfectly capable of stringing this thing out for days on end just to prove how powerful he was.

Or he might even decide he wanted the Cherokee searched, too . . .

That thought went home, all right. I stopped even thinking about grinning. New sweat prickled on my temples, and I could feel de Lima's eyes on me. I kept my face turned towards Customs. "D'you want to search me personally?"

"No. Jus' yo' plane."

"Right. You won't need me, then." I pushed my plate away and stood up. "I'll be at home if you want me. I'm sure the Inspector knows where that is."

For the moment he seemed about to object to that — something on the lines of I ought to be there while they did it, maybe — but then he changed his mind and nodded. Probably he didn't have much idea about where to start searching a Beech 18, and didn't want me watching when he made a fool of himself. I nodded to both of them, picked up my flight bag and the bill, and turned to go.

De Lima said casually: "Yo' got yo' passport dere, Missah Scott?"

I stared at him for a moment, then dug it out and handed it over. He thumbed through the pages while I stood and sweated. You can learn a lot about a man by reading his passport . . .

After a while, still thumbing, he said casually: "Yo' bin to a lot of places, Missah Scott."

I felt my face going still. I said: "I like to get around," and held out my hand for the passport.

De Lima took no notice. Just went on with his reading, turning the pages over slowly and squinting at some of the more illegible place-stamps. The PA system started to announce the departure of a Pan Am flight, got the number wrong, and subsided with a metallic whistle to think things over before having another try. The big fans on the ceiling flapped round slowly and achieved exactly nothing: I could feel the sweat running down the front of my face and collecting stickily under my chin. Several people at the crowded tables were watching me curiously.

After what seemed like an age, de Lima got to the end. He slapped the passport shut, handed it back — and then said softly: "Yo' don' seem to bin to Englan' fo' a long time, Missah Scott."

Something inside me went still and cold in the evening heat. I said: "I don't particularly like the place," and heard my own voice sounding harsh and forced.

De Lima's steady brown eyes watched me to the door as I walked out.

* * *

The coming of darkness hadn't made any difference to the heat on the airport apron — but now, I didn't feel it. It didn't even start to reach the block of ice in my guts. Even the sweat on my face felt cold as I trudged over to the Beech.

It was happening all over again. People asking questions about the past . . .

I'd been down this road before.

I glanced in the open door of the Cargo In Bond shed as I passed it. Three Customs men were pulling the crates of my freight apart, while the gang from the construction company looked on glumly. I wouldn't be getting any more work from *that* source . . .

There was another Customs guy standing by the Beech, staring vacantly out into the black night. I told him to get in, followed him, and hauled the door shut with a wallop. Then I cranked up the engines, growled at the tower, and taxied down to the disused runway with vicious blasts of throttle. I parked the kite alongside somebody's tatty old red-and-white American-registered Piper Apache — which was as far away from the Cherokee as I could get it — and left the ape sitting woodenly in the co-pilot's seat with his brain switched firmly to Off.

By the time I'd walked back to the clubhouse it was starting to rain. I ran the last few yards through the warming-up drops, and made it to the veranda just as it got down to it in earnest. I let myself in, switched on the light — and then sank down on a chair and tried to do some fast thinking.

The thing that worried me most was whether my pet Customs man might take it into his bloody-minded skull to search the Cherokee as well as the Beech. There was no reason why he should, of course — the Cherokee hadn't been off the island for weeks — but that was absolutely no guarantee that he wouldn't. It all depended on his reaction when he found the Beech was clean: he might get discouraged and pack up and go home — or he might get all uptight and turn over everything I owned out of pure spite. He was that kind of guy, and my face was the wrong colour.

I sat and sweated in the hot, humid night, and wished to hell that I'd taken the Cherokee to San Juan today as Harvey had wanted. Stupid, pig-headed bastard, Scott . . .

For a minute or two I considered whizzing off in it right now — but then sanity prevailed. I couldn't go without clearing Customs and Immigration outbound — not unless I wanted to be clapped in jug as soon as I landed, anyway — and such a move at this particular moment would almost certainly be construed as Scott taking it on the lam. And I could guess what would happen then . . .

So — what? I lit a Lucky Strike, thought about it a bit longer, and finally came back to my original conclusion that it was so nothing: there was damn-all I *could* do apart from crossing my fingers and toes and sweating it out.

It was going to be a bloody long evening.

I stood up, pitched the cigarette out of the doorway, and got busy filling in the day's flying in the Beech's tech-log and calling Shell about re-fuelling and oiling. When that was done I opened up the store-cupboard, fished out my Smith & Wesson and its holster — since I didn't want Customs finding *that* if they decided to extend their snooping to the clubhouse — and then shut up shop again and drove the Moke home through the pounding rain.

11

THEY WERE WAITING for me in the house.

In happier times I might have seen them first — but tonight I was busy worrying about other things, and walked straight into it. Just opened the door, flicked on the light — and *whammo*.

For the first few seconds I didn't know what had hit me. Then the world slowly stopped doing torque rolls and inverted spins, and I found I was pinned up against the doorpost with a rock-hard black forearm jammed across my throat.

I was also looking down the loser's end of a silenced gun.

From a very long way away, an American voice said incongruously: "Good evenin', Mr Scott. If you promise not to do anythin' silly, René'll let go of you."

I stared at the barrel of the gun. That and the black fist which was holding it were the only things I could see from my position anyway. The muzzle yawned at me like a young railway tunnel.

Do something silly? Who, *me*? I gurgled " 'Kay."

It came out a bit squashed, but it seemed to be what American Voice wanted to hear. He said something I didn't catch — and suddenly the forearm and the gun weren't there any more.

I sagged against the wall, coughing and choking and blinking the tears out of my eyes. It was a minute or more before I got my brain unscrambled and my eyes uncrossed enough to take an active interest in things. Well — an *interest*, anyway: most of the active was coming from the wall. I leaned on it weakly and bleared at them.

There were three of them. One white, one black, and one in between.

The white one, a tall man in a cream shirt and khaki trousers, was leaning casually against the cane-fronted plates cupboard and watching me with an interesting mixture of amusement and concern. He had the right kind of face for that — long, narrow, and expressive. He was bald, except for a few streaks of gingerish down on each side of his head, but it didn't make him look old. I put him in his early forties.

Number two was a typical coffee-coloured Spanish-American. Tight negroid hair, heavy features, toothcomb moustache — and obviously nasty with it. He rocked on the balls of his feet as if he was ready to jump on someone any second, and glared at me with hot, hungry black eyes.

But he wasn't the one who really worried me. That was the third one. The black one.

The one with the gun.

He was wearing dark glasses and a green felt hat — and he was nursing that gun as if it was a baby. It was a big bastard, a Browning Hi-Power or something similar, and he was holding it in his right hand and resting it on his left as though touching it with both paws doubled his enjoyment. The sight of him took me straight back to old Haiti in the last days of Papa Doc, and a seedy street in Port-au-Prince where three Tontons Macoute — the Haitian secret police — had beaten me up and robbed me. This guy was wearing white shorts and a red-and-black shirt instead of the Tontons' invariable raincoats — but apart from that, he was exactly the same. The cheap sunglasses stared at me blankly, inscrutable and lethal. The gun did likewise.

I shuddered. Him, I *was* frightened of. The other two might get nasty if I gave them reason — but that one would kill instantly, without the slightest warning, like a striking snake. You could almost smell it.

The white man un-leaned from the cupboard and waved a hand at the chairs round the dining table.

"Come an' sit down, Mr Scott. I got somethin' I'd like to talk to you about." He had a sort of neutral American-broadcaster's voice, with an unmistakable ring of authority.

I stayed where I was and croaked: "Who the hell are you?"

"I'm Chris Lashlee." He waved at the coffee-coloured party. "That's Alvaro Mariano, an' the guy with the pistol an' the bad manners is René Heurtaux."

I finally got myself stood up without Marshall Aid from the doorpost. "Thanks for telling me. The cops'll be glad to know.

Now you can fuck off and give yourself a running start while I call them."

Dead tactful, of course.

Lashlee wasn't worried. He gave me a friendly, lazy smile and walked over to the dining table himself. His long body moved with the easy loose-limbed grace you expect in a West Indian rather than a white man.

"Now, you don't wanna do that, Mr Scott. Not 'til we've had a little talk. You couldn't prove anythin' anyway."

Well, that was true enough. On my right, the black man shifted his weight as if he was about to do something.

I sat down.

Lashlee joined me, twisting a chair at right angles to the table and lounging on it with long-legged ease. The other two stayed where they were.

"Now then, Mr Scott." His quizzical blue eyes rested on my face. "I'd like to talk to you about 40,000 Krugerrands."

*   *   *

Well, I couldn't say I hadn't been expecting it. Lashlee and Heurtaux were a surprise — I'd subconsciously been thinking in terms of an all-Cuban delegation out of the same toybox as Che Guevara and the rest — but *some* sort of visitors on these lines were exactly what I'd been worrying about for the last twenty-four hours.

I assembled an expression of resignation and said: "The Isla Bealta money."

Lashlee turned on a big happy smile and flapped a long slender hand in approval. "Yeah, that's it, feller. I wanna know where it is, an' I'll be happy to pay you for tellin' me."

"That's nice. I'll bear it in mind if I happen to find it in my next Corn Flakes packet. *Now, fuck off!*"

I could've put that better. There was a small noise behind me — and something cold and hard ground into my neck just under my starboard ear.

I froze.

Lashlee's smile had disappeared like a patch of sunshine snuffed out by a fast-moving cloud. His voice had an edge to it to match.

"Listen, feller, don't fuck about with me. We been waitin' for you to turn up for a long time, an' we're not in the mood for

126

funny stories. You're transportin' them Krugerrands an' I wanna know about it right *now*. Okay?"

I started to say "I'm not transporting anythi . . ." but then I ran down. The gun was pressing into my neck harder and harder. I had to move my head away from it — and the pressure went on and on, so that I leaned sideways and further sideways until I ended up with my head on my outstretched left arm on the table. And still the pressure kept on increasing: he had the muzzle right on the nerve at the back of my jaw, and the pain flared and shrieked in my head.

The only thing I could see properly was Lashlee's right hand, resting on the table about a foot away from my nose. It was narrow and hairless, with long, sensitive fingers. It moved languidly, turning over on its back in a gesture of sweet reason. His voice floated down from somewhere above me.

"I told you not to fuck about with me, Mr Scott. Now I want some *answers*, see?"

I made a noise like the last of the bathwater running away — and the pressure of the gun disappeared. I sat up slowly, rubbing my neck, and turned to look at Heurtaux. He was standing back a few feet with the gun pointing right between my eyes. The flat black face and the sunglasses watched me impassively.

"Okay then, feller. Let's hear it."

I twisted my head back again. "You *were* hearing it," I said hoarsely. "I ain't carryin' the damn things."

Lashlee leaned forward a little and pulled a long thin cigar out of his shirt pocket. His mobile face shifted to the sort of expression you use on a kid with jam all over his face who insists that he doesn't know where the larder is.

"Feller," he said carefully, "if you're silly over this I'm gonna have René an' Alvaro persuade yah — an' that'll be a painful process. Now you already said you know it's the Bealta money I'm lookin' for — an' you wouldn't know that unless you got somethin' to do with movin' it. So I ain't gonna ask you nicely again. Understand?"

I nodded, swallowed a few times to get my throat into some sort of working order, then said: "I know about it 'cos the CIA told me."

That stopped him. He froze in the act of lighting the cigar, and stared at me over his cupped hands. Behind him, Mariano's eyes snapped to attention as well. He'd know about the CIA, all right: most Cubans are authorities on the subject.

"Go on."

"The CIA had Customs turn me over when I was going out of San Juan a couple of days ago. They didn't find anything, but a CIA man called Morgan interviewed me. He told me what they were looking for and where they'd come from — so unless you happen to have mislaid a different eight million bucks' worth of Krugerrands, you've got to be after the same thing. Right?"

There it was. I'd got it said. I sat back and went on rubbing my neck. Now they knew that (a) I'd had some dealings with the CIA — even if they *were* a little less than cordial to date — and (b) I'd been pronounced clean.

Who's a clever boy again, then . . .?

Lashlee finished lighting his cigar, blew smoke at the ceiling, then studied his feet while he thought it all through. It didn't seem to please him very much: annoyance, irritation and calculation walked across his mobile face in quick succession.

Then he looked up at me again and said slowly: "Why should the CIA pick on you partic'ly, feller?"

That was a point. I hadn't thought of that. Maybe I wasn't such a clever boy . . .

I shrugged and said: "I dunno. Why did *you* pick on me? And who are you, anyway? You representing the Cuban interest, or what?"

He didn't answer: just sat there regarding me through a thin blue haze of tobacco smoke. I was doing a bit of fast thinking myself, too, about such things as what to say next now that I'd used up my first line of defence . . .

I never finished the thought. Lashlee nodded over my shoulder at Heurtaux — and a split-second later something crashed into the back of my head with a huge distant wallop. For a moment I was aware of the table coming up and clouting me in the face, almost in slow motion — and then nothing.

I never even felt myself hit the floor.

*   *   *

Consciousness came back in odd, unrelated fragments. Something cold and rough grinding into my cheekbone . . . voices and shufflings from a long way away . . . red light on one eyelid and none on the other . . . hot sick throbbing feeling all over and a big dull pain in my head . . .

I slowly realised I was lying in a heap on the pink stone floor. The random thought came that I'd fallen out of bed and the nurses hadn't seen me yet, so I had to tell them. I groaned and rolled over. My head thundered and rocked. I was going to be sick.

Then a voice from somewhere said: "Where's the Krugerrands, feller?"

A bit of reality started to trickle back. I tried to get my brain cranked up to say something, but the effort only made things worse. The whole red and black universe was pitching, rolling and yawning.

"Where are they?"

The words lapped and receded like waves, merging into the huge humming in my ears. I heard another voice I dimly realised was my own mumbling: "Wha's fuckin' . . . Krug'rands . . . ev'body wanna . . ."

Then I *was* sick.

I managed to pull myself over on to one elbow as my guts heaved up into my throat — and then the world was full of the sour taste and smell of vomit. I heard it splattering on the floor, heard myself coughing and spitting and trying to blow it out of the back of my nose . . .

And then it was over. I let myself roll over on to my back and just lay there, weak as a kitten. The voices went on, but I ignored them.

After a time, I got round to opening my eyes. The first thing I saw was the light on the ceiling. It was a big white glass bowl, and it hurt to look at it. I hitched up my right arm and slid it behind my neck. The movement produced a fresh bellow of pain at the back of my skull — and it also brought three vague blobs into my range of vision. I blinked several times, and got them more or less into focus.

Lashlee, Mariano and Heurtaux.

They were standing in a tall triangle against the white corrugated asbestos of the ceiling, looking down at me. I could see the twin dark reflections of myself in the lenses of Heurtaux's sunglasses. I could also see his bloody gun. Even now, he was still pointing it at me.

I swallowed dryly on the taste of puke in my throat and croaked "Water . . ."

Lashlee said: "René, go get some water from the kitchen." Then the white face swooped down from the ceiling as he squatted behind me. "Now — you gonna tell me where the Krugerrands are?"

I swallowed again. "I ain't *got* the fuckin' things. Did tell you."

Heurtaux came back with a glass of water. I started to prop myself up for it — but Lashlee put a hand on my chest to hold me down and the black man just stood there with it, waiting.

"Listen, feller — where are they?"

It seemed to be very important not to tell him — but right now, I couldn't for the life of me remember why. Much easier, surely, to tell him and get a drink of water and then they'd go away . . .

Only they wouldn't go away, of course. Or at least, they *would* — but they wouldn't be leaving me in any condition to talk about it . . .

I mumbled: "Don't know where they are. Bloody fuck off . . ."

"Okay, feller, have it your way." Lashlee stood up and looked at Heurtaux. "Throw the water over him, René."

Heurtaux giggled, then threw.

It hit me in the face with a swamping splosh that left me gasping and coughing. I rolled over on to my side and tried to squeeze my lungs out through my ears. Fresh pain banged through my head as the spasm went on and on . . .

Then, suddenly, I was being hauled on to my feet. Un-gentle hands yanked under each armpit while the world rocked and swayed dizzily and a vast roaring noise filled my head. Lashlee's voice floated across from a long way away.

". . . pardon me if I don't take your word for it," he was saying. "We're all goin' out to the airport right now an' take a look in both your planes."

Then they dragged me out.

*   *   *

We went in my Moke. Lashlee drove, Mariano sat beside him, and Heurtaux parked himself and his gun in the back with me. It started raining again after the first hundred yards — big, heavy drops that clawed on the canvas roof and leaked in through the sidescreens. The jolting and swaying as we thumped over the un-made road out of Dickinson Bay started my stomach doing barrel-rolls again. For a while I tried to ignore it by concentrating on the supersonic headache in the back of my skull — but in the end the barrel-rolls won, and I unclipped my sidescreen and spewed the rest of my guts out into the warm wet night. Heurtaux chuckled as I did it: the low, sadistic chuckle of the fully paid-up psychopath.

After that, I slumped back in my seat and switched to worrying about what Lashlee was going to think when he found at least one of my aircraft knee-deep in Customs men.

And, of course, what Customs were going to think when Lashlee and Co turned up to do some searching of their own . . .

It was the second point that really worried me. There wasn't a great deal Lashlee *could* do except stand around gaping — but my pet Customs man was going to be more than slightly suspicious when I pitched up with three strangers who obviously didn't know what was going on. He might not exactly be the brain of Antigua — but even *he* wasn't going to believe that I'd just sort of forgotten he was tearing my aeroplane apart . . .

I was still thinking about it, with my brain staggering around drunkenly between my ears, when we turned into the airport entrance.

Oh, Christ . . .

I mumbled thickly: "Stop in th' car park . . . wanna talk to'you."

Lashlee gave no sign that he'd heard — but when he reached the terminal car park he pulled into a space under a line of tamarind trees and switched off lights and engine. The rain thumped on the roof, and the yellow lights of the terminal starred and wavered in the water running down the windscreen. Lashlee twisted in his seat to peer at me in the near-darkness.

"What d'you wanna talk t'me about then, feller?"

"I . . . er . . . y'oughta know . . . Cus'oms're searchin' my aircraf' at the moment."

There. I'd got it out. My tongue felt like a roll of old carpet in my mouth.

Lashlee's profile was still and silent for a moment. Then he said: "Why're they doin' that?"

I coughed, making the pain flare up in my head and spots float in front of my eyes. "They thin . . . think I'm bringin' in guns. For th' Black Power people."

Mariano gave a quick snort that might have been laughter. Very bloody funny.

Lashlee said: "What makes 'em think that, feller?"

I shrugged. The inside of the car was hot and muggy, and I was starting to feel sick again. I wiped at the sweat trickling down my face and tried to put one thought in front of the other.

"They . . . heard 'bout me getting searched in San Juan. An' then I wen . . . went to a brothel the Black Power use last night, an' St Croix today. They think the guns're comin' in from St Croix."

Lashlee's voice raised its eyebrows. "That sounds sorta thin, feller."

I shrugged again. "This is Antigua, chum. An' they ain't actually accusing me of anything. They're just checking." I blinked at the terminal lights and thought sluggishly that I seemed to have been through this conversation before . . .

Lashlee nodded slowly for a moment, and then made up his mind. The silhouette of his head turned to Mariano, and he said: "Go take a look in the parkin' area. See what they're doin'. You can make like you're fetchin' somethin' outa the airplane."

"Is rainin' out there," Mariano objected. It was the first time I'd heard him speak: he had a standard Spanish-American accent along with the standard Spanish-American fear of rainwear. "Carn' yo' drive down?"

"No. Just git goin'."

He got. The wet night spattered in as he climbed out — and then the sidescreen flopped back into place and he was gone. I watched him splosh away into the darkness to the east of the terminal, and hoped he was getting very wet indeed.

The silence closed in again. Lashlee lit one of his thin cigars, I rested my head against the hood-frame and wondered if the back of my skull was going to fall off, and Heurtaux just sat stock-still with the gun across his knees. A twee canned voice from the terminal PA system floated across announcing the departure of Air Canada's Sunjet Flight 743, bound for somewhere-or-other up north. I looked at the lights of the scruffy check-in desks fifty yards and a whole world away, and wished I was getting on it. Anywhere-or-other would do nicely: I wasn't fussy.

Heurtaux read my thoughts and stirred in the muggy dimness beside me. "Yaw no' goin' nowhere," he growled. His voice was deep for a black man, and the accent was French-but-not-French.

I guessed his native language was Creole, the patois used in different forms in Haiti and Dominica.

I turned my head to look at him, trying not to wince at the fresh flare of pain. I said: "D'you miss the Tontons Macoute?"

His head moved, the sunglasses catching the yellow electric light from the terminal. The gun lifted off his lap and ranged on my stomach with a waving motion. He didn't say a word.

I shut up and stayed shut up.

Mariano came back after ten minutes, yanking the sidescreen out of the way and plopping wetly into the front seat. His shirt was soaked and plastered to his shoulders, and he was panting. The inside of the Moke immediately started misting up.

"They there. Inside the Beeshcraf', movin' round' weeth flashlights."

"Uh-huh." Lashlee pondered on that a moment, then said: "What about the other plane, the Cherokee?"

"I no see an'one there, but I doan' go over close 'cos they washin' me from the Beesh. The Beesh park 'longside us."

Lashlee nodded and drew slowly on his cigar. The atmosphere was damp and stifling hot and my body was gritty with sweat. I tried to get my brain fired up and ready for what was coming next, but it was obviously out in sympathy with the headache. The only thought it came up with was that Lashlee and Co must be the proprietors of the tatty Apache I'd parked beside. As a deduction, that wasn't bad for a man in my state — but in terms of practical assistance, it was rather less than helpful.

Lashlee turned to me and said: "They searchin' just the Beech, feller, or both of them?"

"Just the . . ." Then I saw it coming. "The both, er —"

Too late, of course.

Lashlee's outline didn't move. "Bend his hand, Alvaro," he said.

Mariano twisted in his seat, reached over the back of it and grabbed my forearms. I gripped both hands together and pulled back against him . . .

And something walloped into my mouth with a sickening *thump*.

When my head stopped pitching and rolling I was aware of two things. One was a blasting toothache in every chopper I possessed — and the other was a searing, twisting pain in my left wrist. I got my eyes un-toppled and looked down. Mariano was gripping my hand in both of his, and bending it in towards the elbow. I scrunched over sideways in a futile, instinctive attempt to bend the arm with it, but he just chuckled and increased the pressure. I ended up wound into an awkward S-bend with my left ear ground hard into the hood frame and electric bolts of agony shooting up my arm.

Lashlee drew on his cigar, blew smoke, and said calmly: "They're just searching the Beech, right?"

I heard my breath coming out in a long tortured whistle. I tried to move my other hand to lash out, but it seemed to be clamped to my side. I mumbled "Righ'" through rapidly swelling lips — and the pressure eased a fraction. My head pounded and roared. Lashlee was speaking again.

"So we'll go an' look in the Cherokee," he said. "They won't be interested in that." He twisted in his seat and started the engine.

I struggled wildly for a second, collected a fresh blast of pain for my trouble as Mariano leaned on my wrist still further — and then blurted desperately: "Wait! F'you go now Customs'll see you an' come an' look too. Why'ncha leave it 'til later?"

He blipped the throttle and glanced back over his shoulder. "So what if they do?" he drawled. "You said there's nothing in it anyway."

Yeah, I did, didn't I . . .

Lashlee stirred the gearlever, found reverse with a quick *snunk*, and we started to move. I tried to think fast — but my brain was struggling in a swamp of agony. The only thing it would produce was a picture of Customs coming over to the Cherokee to see what was going on . . .

Oh, the hell with it.

I croaked wearily: "There's a load of Krugerrands under the rear seat of the bloody thing."

*   *   *

Lashlee graunched the gears into first, pulled forward into the parking slot again, and switched off the engine. Mariano let go of my hand, and the three of them sat there in a satisfied silence for a moment. I hauled myself slowly into a normal sitting position and wondered just exactly how bloody stupid I'd been.

Then Lashlee said: "Where'd you get 'em from, feller?"

This time, I *did* think fast. I thought about the destiny of Scott when Lashlee knew all he wanted to know, then about the further destiny of Scott — if there was any left — when Ruchter found out who'd told him . . .

"I dunno," I said. Mariano seemed about to move, so I hurried on. "Look, if I *did* know, I'd sell you the information and get the hell out — but I don't. I get all my instructions by phone, and I don't know who's calling."

"What sort of instructions?"

I had a sudden inspiration. "I don't know, yet. I've only heard from the guy twice, so far. Once was Monday, when he made the proposition, and the other time was Tuesday when I told him where to hide the stuff in the aircraft. He said he'd have it loaded up ready for a trip tomorrow. He hasn't even told me where I've got to take it, yet. He's going to ring again in the morning."

It was the best I could do on the spur of the moment — but it sounded bloody thin, even to me. It evidently sounded thin to Mariano, too. One enormous hand whipped over the seat-back, grabbed the front of my shirt, and jerked me forward so that my face was within inches of his.

"Yo' lyin' bastard," he snarled. Flecks of spittle landed in my face. "Now yo' jus' . . ."

"*Shut up, Alvaro!*" Lashlee's voice sounded like the snap of a small pistol. "We'll get the story later. Just siddown an' shut up."

Mariano hesitated, then slowly let go of me and subsided. I sank back into the seat and tried to look cowed and terrified.

Lashlee turned to me and said: "What makes you so sure Customs ain't gonna search the Cherokee as well as the Beech, feller?"

I shrugged — gently, so as not to excite anybody. "I'm not *sure* at all. But there'd be no reason for it. How much artillery can you hide in a Cherokee?"

"They really *are* lookin' for guns, then?"

"Yeah."

"Hmmm." He thought for a moment. The rain pounded on the roof, punctuated by loud *thocks* as one of the tamarind trees dripped on us. Then: "So you're just trustin' to luck they don't look in the Cherokee?"

I shrugged again. "Yeah. There's nothing else I could do."

"No chance of taxiin' someplace else on the airport an' unloadin' it quick?"

"No. Unloading'd take half an hour or more. They're stowed under the rear seat panel and inside the centre-section mainspar."

"Shit." He thought again. I wiped uselessly at the sweat running down my neck and listened to the crashing-surf noises in my ears. After a bit he said slowly: "I guess we'll have to fly the bastard off the island."

I swallowed on a throatful of sand. "I already thought of that. I reckoned it was one sure-fire way of making them search it."

"Where were you thinkin' of goin'?"

I nearly said 'San Juan', but stopped myself just in time. "I dunno. Anywhere."

"Just by yourself?"

"Yeah."

"That *would* look suspicious, maybe." The cigar glowed while he pondered on it. Then: "Look, we'll make it a student night cross-country exercise. Give 'em a line 'bout it bein' good weather for instrument flyin', an' take Alvaro an' René along with you. Alvaro's a pilot, so don't go gettin' no funny ideas. You'll go to St Kitts: they close at around ten, an' their security's pretty slack. I'll follow you in the Apache, an' we'll switch the stuff over later on. That all clear?"

I shook my head, and then wished I hadn't. It made my brain roll round my skull like a pin-ball. "No. We'd never get off with three people on board. Those coins weigh 600 lb or more: if we pile in three people on top of that we'll be totally WAT-limited."

"What?"

"WAT — Weight And Temperature. Come on — I thought you were supposed to be a pilot."

He was — but not that kind of pilot. The nearest he'd come to WAT-limitations was the simple weight-and-balance calculations as understood — some of the time — by private pilots.

He said: "You mean you'd be overweight?"

"That's it. By a hell of a long way."

"So what? It only means a longer take-off roll, and you've got nine thousand feet of runway here. You'll get off eventually."

Privately, I agreed. A Cherokee would probably stagger off with a bathful of concrete on board — eventually. But I said: "No, we won't. The max all-up weight's 2,400 lb and it's got full fuel. If we bung in three people as well as the coins the total'll be something over 3,000 — and we won't get off with that, in this heat, never mind how long the runway is.' I was juggling the figures a bit, but it sounded reasonably convincing . . .

I hoped.

Lashlee absorbed it for a few seconds, then nodded. "Okay. Just you'n Alvaro. You do the flyin' an' Alvaro'll watch. Now let's *go*."

I leaned down, hauled my flight bag out from under the front passenger seat, and started filling in General Declarations. Even with Heurtaux out of the way I was still far from happy about the idea — the chances of anyone believing I was giving an instrument flying lesson on a night like this seemed pretty remote to me — but I obviously wasn't going to get anywhere by arguing any more. And the Antiguan Customs *might* just swallow it: after all they were the world's greatest non-experts on flying matters, and they'd certainly swallowed taller stories than that in the past . . .

They did swallow it. Or maybe it was just that they'd lost interest in me anyway after failing to find the Crown Jewels in the Beech. Either way, they cleared us outbound in ten seconds flat without even bothering to turn down their transistor radio. We walked out of Customs and Immigration with me looking glazed and wobbly and Mariano following behind me looking watchful.

Five minutes later I drove the Moke through the rain towards the aircraft park. Mariano sat beside me with his left hand under his shirt, holding the silenced Browning pointing straight at my stomach.

12

IT WAS NO good trying to hide our approach, so I did the next best thing: drove briskly and confidently across the disused runway, parked on the grass behind the Cherokee, and climbed out immediately with my flight bag under my arm. Through the driving black rain I could just make out the humpy shape of the Beech on the other side of the tarmac, about a hundred yards away.

They were still searching it. The interior lights in the cabin were on, and one or two torches were moving around the outside, underneath the wings.

I fished in my flight bag, came up with a small flat torch, and started the pre-flight inspection. The warm rain thumped on my head and shoulders, and my brain clanged around between my ears every time I bent down. Mariano followed me round with his left hand still underneath his shirt. Maybe he thought I was going to hit him over the head with a wing or something.

I finished up at the starboard wing root, near the cabin door, and looked across at the Beech again. Two of the torches had got together under one wing. As I watched, one of them flashed brighter, pointing at us. At a hundred yards through heavy rain it showed about what you'd expect it to show — nothing — but it did prove they were at least slightly interested . . .

I climbed on to the wing walk-way and opened the door, trying to ignore the hollow ball of tension in my belly. Mariano hauled himself up after me, and I waved him into the left-hand seat out of sheer force of instructor's habit. He edged past me, sat down, and slid across. I followed him in and left the door ajar.

The inside of the cockpit was hot and steamy. It smelt of old sweat, warm leathercloth and aluminium. I dumped my flight bag on the floor by my right knee, did up the lap-and-diagonal harness without looking at it, and felt a tiny fraction better. Here, I was home. My hands moved around the cockpit in the darkness, switching on the master and boost pump, shoving the mixture into rich and setting the throttle for starting . . .

And then we were ready to go. The next bit was the noisy bit. I turned the key.

The engine churned over a couple of times, then caught with a steady flat rumble. The hot wet night poured in round the door, and the drops of water on the windscreen scuttled into a million glistening streaks as the slipstream started to blow them off. I peered out at the Beech while my left hand ran round switching on radios and lights. The two torches were both pointing at us now . . .

I wanted to slam open the throttle, point the nose down the disused runway, and GO. Away into the wet darkness, away from someone stepping out in front of us with a torch, away from a recall signal before we got off . . .

The radio warmed up with a sudden hot-sausage noise, and I snatched up the mike. I swallowed a couple of times, and tried to keep my voice normal as I went through the rigmarole of departure.

"Coolidge, Victor Papa Lima Echo Mike pre-flight check and taxi, Special VFR Golden Rock, St Kitts."

Crackling silence. Then: "Echo Mike, Coolidge read yo' strength fife. Yo' cleah to de holdin' point o' de western taxiway. Runway in use zero-seven, QFE one-zero-zero-niner, QNH one-zero-one-zero."

I acknowledged, released the park-brake, and pushed on a little growl of power. The yellow cone of the landing light swung across the line of parked aircraft opposite as we turned towards the taxiway to the main apron. For an instant it lit up the snub-nosed twin-engined profile of Lashlee's Apache — and then it was brushing across the Beech, showing two white-shirted Customs men crouching under the port wing watching us. I tried to make out if one of them was my favourite enemy, but we were too far away. We sploshed through a few puddles — and then we were alongside them and the two torch beams were shining squarely in the left-hand windows. I tried to tell myself for the fiftieth time that they *were* only interested in the Beech: that they had no conceivable reason for stopping the Cherokee . . .

Mariano snarled: "Look at 'em — act nach'ral," and I fought down the temptation to pour on the power and scuttle past as quickly as possible. We ambled on at snail's pace with the engine mumbling gently . . .

And suddenly, we were turning on to the taxiway and the torch beams were gone.

I let go of a vintage lungful of air and wiped ineffectively at the sweat on my face. Mariano just sat watching impassively in the red glow of the instrument lights, the pistol resting across his legs. He didn't seem to have felt the tension at all: maybe he was used to hijacking 707s, and sneaking out a pipsqueak Cherokee wasn't worth raising a worry over.

Two minutes later, we were ready to go.

The cockpit went suddenly quiet as I slammed the door and twisted the top catch, and the temperature immediately soared into the Turkish bath league. My headache went with it. I picked up the mike in a sweat-slippy hand and got us cleared for take-off, then pulled out on to the runway, aimed down the tunnel of blackness between the lights, and opened the throttle. She rolled slower than usual with the weight in her — but when I eased back on the yoke at sixty-five mph she growled into the air without a quiver.

At 300 feet I raised the flaps and glanced across at Mariano. He was still watching me unblinkingly.

*   *   *

We ran into the weather as we passed through 2,000 feet.

It came suddenly, the way it does at night under heavy cloud cover. One second we were rumbling uphill with the lights of Antigua falling away below and behind — and the next we'd plunged into the utter, impenetrable blackness of the biggest cloud I could find. The world shrank to the size of the dim-lit cockpit, and I got my eyes down and scanning the instruments.

Then seconds later we hit the turbulence.

It started with a couple of mild warning judders — and then a giant hand swiped us from underneath and rattled us like dice in some vast cosmic cup. The Vertical Speed needle jumped to its maximum 2,000 feet-a-minute Up and stuck there, and the altimeter wound round like a demented clock.

I snatched the power back to half throttle before we went into orbit, and slammed the controls around trying to keep us right-side up. We were alternately walloped into our seats and yanked up into the straps. Maps and pencils jumped around the cabin — and I waited for the crunch that would be several thousand Krugerrands leaving through the thin bottom skin of the fuselage.

Three thousand feet . . . 4,000 . . .

Sudden fire-hose rain smashed against the windscreen. The noise was fantastic — an enormous mind-numbing roar. Water trickled into the cockpit in a dozen places, and the engine ran rough as the paper air filter element got saturated. I whanged the carb-heat to Hot: there isn't much danger of ice in a tropical storm-cloud, but the hot air intake in a 180 doesn't have a filter to get clogged. The engine smoothed out again.

Five thousand . . . five-and-a-half and slowing a little . . .

Still fighting, I whipped my eyes off the dancing instruments for a second and snatched a look at Mariano. The Browning was still pointing straight at my guts — but his face was turned towards the dials, as any airman's would be.

You won't get another chance, Scott. GO . . .

I yelled: "You have control — gonna be sick!"

And let go of everything.

Instantly, we slammed to the right like a snap-roll. Mariano swore and grabbed with both hands, keeping the gun in his left. I doubled up, making retching noises that were lost in the roaring of the rain, and reached down as if I was groping for a sick-sack in my flight bag. For a few seconds he was totally occupied with suddenly being handed a strange aeroplane on instruments in vicious turbulence . . .

And then I rammed the muzzle of the Smith & Wesson into his face and bawled: "Just keep flying with two hands, matey!"

Half a minute later the Titans spat us out into bright clean moonlight at 6,400 feet. The air smoothed out as if we'd driven on to a vast tarmac road.

*   *   *

Up here, it was a beautiful night. The sky was deep blue-black and vast, sprinkled with the diamonds of a million stars. Below, the rolling snow-fields of the five-eighths cloud cover were touched with the cold silver luminosity of the moon. The same light painted our wings an eerie pale white and crept faintly into the cabin, dissolving the claustrophobic effect of a small cockpit in cloud and fading red glow of the instruments into sudden insignificance.

I took no notice of it at all.

Mariano was still flying with both hands on the yoke, his gun gripped awkwardly in his left and pointing uselessly up at the cabin roof. Keeping the .38 grinding into his cheekbone, I said clearly: "In a moment, I am going to reach across and take your gun out of your hand. Be advised that if you make the slightest movement, or if your hand leaves the yoke before I've got hold of the gun, I shall shoot immediately."

He believed me totally: there's nothing like meaning it for making people think you mean it. I stretched my left hand awkwardly across his body, got a firm grip on the silencer of the automatic — and his hand opened slowly and carefully as I lifted it away.

I sat back, rested my gun-hand on my lap, and un-cocked the Browning and dropped it into my flight bag. Mariano sagged in his seat as the Smith & Wesson left his head. He seemed to have been tensed up about something.

"Okay," I said. "Now put the carb into cold, set the power to 2,400 rpm, and turn on to a heading of 030. And don't get any clever ideas about turning the aeroplane on its back or anything, because if you do I shall shoot first and correct it later. Understand?"

For a long moment, he just stared forward into the night. I cocked the Smith & Wesson with an audible *cl-click*. The muscles in his jaw worked and then, slowly, he reached out and adjusted the power and cranked us into a gentle right turn.

Keeping my eyes on him, I reached out with my left hand and switched off nav lights and beacon. Now we were anonymous, a tiny dot sliding through the black night. Someone close above us might have spotted our moonlit wings, but I wasn't worried about that. With no radar in the area, no-one was going to *get* close above us.

I glanced at the clock on the panel, then picked up the mike and told Coolidge I was switching to Golden Rock and a very good night to them. They good night-ed back, and I clicked the frequency 118·3.

Golden Rock, at the foot of their mountain in St Kitts, were weak but audible. I gave my call-sign, asked about their weather — which was lousy — and then said: "Echo Mike is on a navigation exercise of uncertain duration. I'll call you with an estimate in half an hour or so." There was a pause while the controller contemplated the stupidity of any instructor doing a single engine over-water nav exercise at night — and then they said, "Roger, Echo Mike," rather doubtfully, and I put the microphone back on the hook.

It was 2132, local time. About five minutes to run to where I was going.

Time for a little talk with Señor Mariano.

* * *

I started at the wrong end of the thing, of course. Maybe I was more concussed that I thought — although the way I felt, *that* didn't seem possible.

I said: "Are the three of you from Cuba?"

He didn't answer.

"Listen, pal," I said conversationally, "it doesn't matter to me whether we arrive where we're going with you dead or alive. And if you don't answer my questions, it's gonna be dead."

He didn't quite believe me — but he didn't quite *dis*believe me, either. In the eerie light of the moon and the instruments I could see his jaw muscles working again, and fat blobs of sweat rolling down his face. I hefted the revolver, and wondered if *I* believed me . . .

Then he said: "*Si.* From Cuba."

I lowered the gun. "Who's Lashlee, then? How's he come into it?"

"He . . . 'andle the deal fo' Habana. Buy the islan' een his name."

I nodded. That was what I'd thought. The middle man behind the other middle men behind the smokescreen of lawyers and phoney companies. The man who handled the money. The man who was going to have to explain to Havana how come the deal got cocked up . . .

I glanced at the clock on the panel again. 2134. Three minutes to go. I wished the little men with hammers in my head would take a tea-break so I could think straight.

"Did you sabotage 32 Romeo? Put a bomb on it, or something?"

" 'Oo t'ree-two Romeo?"

"November 2332 Romeo: Cas McGrath's Twin Commanche.

143

Went missing on —" Christ, when was it? It seemed like years ago " — Monday morning."

He hesitated. Then: "No."

I lifted the gun again. "You *sure* about that? I wouldn't like to think of you getting dead because you lied to me."

The jaw muscles worked for a moment. Then he said quickly: "We din' do eet. We ask fo' heem to be . . . stopped . . . by someone else. We no' in Antig' then."

"What someone else? The Black Power?"

"*Si.* Yes."

The time was 2135, coming up '36. I snatched a quick look out of the windows: still heavy cloud cover below. Sod it. I dialled up the St Maarten radio beacon on the ADF and then said: "Why did you have him killed?"

"We din' mean to. They get eet wrong. We jus' wan' you stopped. Grounded. No' keeled."

You . . . ?

I squeezed my eyes shut for a second to promote Thought, then said: "You mean both of us? McGrath and me?"

He hesitated again, then: "*Si.* But we don' wan' yo' keel — jus' groun'ed."

"Nobody tried to ground me."

"Yo' off de islan'. Then when we hear o' thee crash, we come to Antig' ourselves. We been lookin' fo' yo' las' two days."

I nodded, thinking briefly of Wednesday night in San Juan and Thursday night in Joey's. If I'd gone home at all in that time . . .

I shook my head to clear it — which was less than clever, in my state — and tried to concentrate on the double tasks of sorting out my position and figuring what to ask him next. The St Maarten beacon was off the air or on the blink — as usual — so I clicked the VOR frequency to 108.2 in the faint hope of getting a cross-bearing from St Croix. Then I said: "*Why* did you go for me and McGrath? I mean, why pick on us?"

"We know one o'you carryin' the Krugerran's."

"How d'you know?"

He paused. I waved the gun again. He glanced at it, sweating, then said: "We know thee coin' comin' out o' Antig', an' we know when. Yo' an' heem were de on'y ones there from Antig'. So we know it mus' be one o' yo', but we don' know wheech."

I tried to make sense of that, but lost it somewhere. Delivered in his broad Spanish-American accent it would've been complicated enough at the best of times — and right now, under the influence of mild concussion and a splitting headache, the times were anything but best. I gave it up after a few seconds and bleared at the VOR, which was refusing to pick up St Croix. Too bloody far away, of course. The Antigua beacon told me I was on the right line north-south, but my kingdom for a cross-bearing.

I said: "How did you know the coins were coming from Antigua?"

"We . . . find some at de other en'."

I frowned at the instruments. If they'd got on to the Puerto Rico end that might explain why they didn't know about Ruchter — but if Harvey's organisation had sprung a leak surely to Christ they must know about *him* . . .

"D'you know who gave me the job?"

"No."

I frowned some more. He might be lying or he might not — but short of mentioning Harvey's name point-blank there was nothing I could do about it. And if I did that, I *would* have to kill him . . .

The clock said 2137. There was no more time.

I said: "Let go of the controls and put both your hands on top of the instrument panel."

He hesitated, then did as he was told. The Cherokee droned on steadily through the calm clear night.

"Now look out of your side window."

His head turned slowly, reluctantly. I suppose he'd guessed what was coming. I transferred the Smith & Wesson to my left hand, hooked his automatic out of my flight bag, and gripped it firmly by the barrel. Then I braced myself against the straps, swung back as far as I could in the confines of the cockpit, and hit him over the right ear. Hard. He slumped forward against his shoulder-strap without a sound, and his hands flopped limply into his lap. Out for several counts but not actually dead — I hoped.

So now all I had to do was get rid of him.

13

I UN-COCKED THE .38 and shoved it under my right thigh, dropped the automatic back in my bag, then spent a few seconds rolling Mariano's seat back to the limit of its travel and re-tightening the straps. Then I grabbed the controls, corrected the pitch-up caused by his weight shifting, and rammed my nose against the side window and stared out and down.

Still five-eighths clouds. A deck of moonlight, broken strato-cu a couple of thousand feet below with occasional bottomless black holes in it. Scattered thunderstorms rearing up past me on all points of the compass, eerie pillars of silver-white candyfloss violence pushing their anvil heads ten or fifteen thousand feet into the velvet night.

Bugger, bugger, bugger, *bugger* . . .

I knew what I *wanted* to do, all right: I'd thought of it ten seconds after Lashlee announced we were going flying and I'd remembered the Smith & Wesson in my flight bag. What I *wanted* to do was lob into Barbuda . . .

But now it looked as if it wasn't going to be possible.

Barbuda is a flat, scrub-covered coral island ten miles long, about twenty-five miles north of Antigua. It's part of Antiguan territory, actually — although no-one seems to have told the Antiguan Customs that yet. About the only things on the place are flocks of flamingoes in the steaming swamps to the north, a tiny native village with matching tiny native airfield in the west, and a high-priced secluded hotel on a scrubby peninsula in the south.

Which, among its amenities, has its own private airstrip. And *that* was what I was interested in.

From the point of view of a clandestine landing to dump off an unwanted passenger, it was ideal. It was five miles from the village, and the Paradise Point Hotel hadn't opened for the winter season yet — so the whole southern half of the island ought to be completely deserted. There wouldn't be any runway lights — but on a clear night with a bright tropical moon, that shouldn't be an insurmountable problem. You could spiral down from about 5,000 feet with all your lights off and the engine throttled right back, pick out the light grey line of the runway against the dark grey mass of the scrub — and Robert would be your proverbial uncle. You might have to use the landing light for the last few seconds of the approach but by that time, with any luck, you'd be too low for it to be visible from the village anyway.

If you had a clear night with a bright tropical moon . . .

Which I, of course, hadn't.

In fact, the way things were at the moment I couldn't even find the island, never mind the runway. I could cure the island problem by dropping down underneath the clouds and rumbling along the correct radio bearing from Antigua until I stumbled over it, of course — but I still wouldn't be able to find the runway until a patch of moonlight came along, *and* I'd be advertising my presence with the engine noise. The growl of a cruising Lycoming carries a long way in the quiet of a West Indian night.

In short — screwed.

I throttled back to the rumbling murmur of 1,900 rpm, started a gentle turn over the place where I thought Barbuda *ought* to be, and stared down at the silver-white clouds below. If I got real lucky I *might* just see something through a hole . . .

Nothing, of course.

Bugger, again.

I glanced at the clock. 2140. I could drop off the edge of the world on the strength of the nav exercise story for maybe half an hour before people started screaming for Echo Mike over the radio. And it was already ten minutes since I'd made the call . . .

I passed a sweaty hand over my aching head, continued staring down at the rolling clouds and the black holes, and tried to think of an alternative method of getting rid of Mariano. I'd already decided that I was going to Puerto Rico tonight to get rid of my load of coins double-pronto — and one thing was for dead sure: I wasn't taking him with me. That would produce enormous complications. If he came round before we landed I'd have to let him go — since I could hardly march him through Customs and Immigration at gun-point — and I had enough problems in San Juan already, without having him on the loose. And if he didn't come round, then I'd really have some explaining to do: the Puerto Rican *Policia* were likely to become very officious indeed about a guy with my reputation tooling in with an unconscious — or dead — Cuban gunman decorating the left-hand seat.

Still, if I couldn't see Barbuda . . .

Then I did see it.

Or at least, I hoped I did. What I actually saw was a tiny pin-prick of light in one of the black holes almost directly underneath me. It was there for a second like a spark in the bottom of a deep, dark well — and then it was gone, hidden by the movement of the clouds on the trade wind. I slammed the Cherokee over on its right wing tip and stared downwards.

Nothing.

Had it been the lights of Codrington, Barbuda's village? Or had it been a boat? Or my imagination? Or . . .?

The clock said 2143.

Only one way to find out, chum . . .

I closed the throttle and rolled the Cherokee over and down into a steep spiral dive. The wind noise wound up to an urgent rushing roar as the airspeed clawed round the dial: 130 . . . 140 . . . 150. . . . The giant hand of G pressed me into the seat and sagged my cheeks. The elevators were rock-heavy, and I dropped a leaden hand on to the trim wheel and wound it full back. The black hole and the pale woolly clouds rotated round the starboard wing tip and floated up to meet me. Down through 5,000 feet . . . 4,000 . . . three-and-a-half . . .

And suddenly, we were *there*. The cloud-tops rushed past the nose for a few seconds in a tumble of silver luminosity — and then they were gone, too, and there was only blackness and the G-force and the invisible sense of twisting. With the moonlight gone I couldn't tell whether I was in the hole or in cloud. I held the spiral and whipped my eyes down on to the dials: 2,800 feet . . . . 2,200 . . . remember the altimeter-lag, Scott . . .

I don't know exactly when we came out the bottom. I was flicking my eyes from instruments — windscreen — instruments — and suddenly, on one of the flicks to the windscreen, there was the sea. Shining faintly with moonlight in places, blotched black with cloud-shadow in others . . .

And the dark mass of Barbuda, complete with the speckle of lights that was Codrington village, lying like a stain on the sea about a mile away to the east.

Bathed, for the moment, in a patch of moonlight.

I slammed the Cherokee out of the spiral with the nose just to the left of the southern peninsula, where the Paradise Point Hotel was. The airspeed dribbled back as I used the speed of the dive to hold on to precious altitude as long as possible: 120 ... 110 ... 100 ... the wind noise dropped back down the scale to the steady hiss of a normal glide approach. At 80 I let the nose sag down a little and re-trimmed.

Eighty? You're into-wind and heavy, Scott ...

All right: 85. I lowered the nose a whisker more and listened to the engine chuntering over slowly and unhappily. You're supposed to give an aero-engine periodic bursts of throttle during a prolonged glide to warm it up and clear the plugs — especially this one, which ran over-rich at low throttle openings and tended to oil itself up more than most — but bursts of engine make a noise ...

I kept my hand away from the loud lever and let it run rough. The hell with it.

Eighteen hundred feet ... 1,700 ... and the peninsula sliding up to the leading edge of the port wing, the weaving crescent line of the white-sand beach clearly visible in the moonlight. Can't see the runway yet — but it's there, all right. Somewhere in the dark shadow at the top of the spit of land ...

Okay then, Scott: you're the bloody-minded instructor who insists on students doing forced-landing practice on moonlit nights — so now let's see you do it. For real. Remember what you tell 'em — don't try and look slantwise at a field, get overhead and look straight down at it ...

I eased the Cherokee round to the left in a gentle turn that ought to end up directly over the strip, and tried to push my forehead through the side-window looking down. The altimeter sagged back through 1,300 ... 1,200 ...

And then I noticed the cloud shadow.

* * *

It was sliding up from the east, loafing on the fifteen-knot trade wind — and gobbling up the faint silver sheen of moonlight on the water into dense, impenetrable blackness as it came.

Now it was crossing the bay on the far side of the little peninsula. I could actually see it moving. In a minute, maybe less, it would be crawling across the strip.

Jesus!

I stood the Cherokee on its left ear and kicked on full top rudder. In the surprised pause you get before an aeroplane starts a sudden side-slip, I snatched a glance down over the left wing.

The runway was bang underneath, a fuzzy line of grey across the base of the peninsula.

And then we were slipping.

People'll tell you that a Cherokee 180 won't side-slip very well — but people are wrong. It won't slip in a straight line worth a damn because it hasn't got enough rudder control — but in common with most piston-engined aeroplanes, it'll do one hell of a slipping *turn.* You wham on about eighty degrees of bank, give it full opposite rudder — and then, when it falls out of the sky like a concrete parachute and every instinct tells you to push *forward* to slow down the rotation and maintain control, you pull *back* instead. *Then* it'll slip all right . . .

I pulled back now. Hard.

The Cherokee dropped like a stone, the fuzzy grey line pivoting round underneath the wing tip. The airflow shuddered and moaned at the unusual angle of attack and the stall-warning light flickered nervously. I kept my eyes on the strip and reached down for the flap lever. As we passed through a right angle to the runway I banged down two notches. That's something else the book tells you not to do — use flaps in the slip.

The hell with the book.

I slammed us out of the turn as we came in line with the dim slash of the runway. The cloud-shadow was already painting the far end in creosote. We slid over the sandy beach — full flap *now* — strip floating up fast — scrub on each side suddenly showing in black-and-grey detail . . .

And then the moonlight going out as if someone had turned a switch. Everything black. Total darkness at twenty feet.

We were stalling, falling. Dropping into a black hole with the engine lumping quietly and the wind whispering through the last few seconds of flight. I was going to hit a tree, fly into the ground, die in the dark . . .

Then I was stabbing at the line of switches — and the landing light flicked out like a yellow flame. It picked up grass, white

coral dust — and the world snapped into place. *Too low, man!*
I hauled back on the yoke . . .

And the Cherokee thumped heavily on to the ground and
rolled along with the undercarriage making hollow bonking noises
on the uneven surface.

*   *   *

I braked as hard as I dared, whipped the mixture into lean
cut-off to stop the engine, then snapped the landing light and
master switches off as soon as we were down to walking pace.
We came to rest with a final small crunch on the coral gravel. I
unclipped the door and opened it — and then just sat there
for a long moment, breathing heavily and letting the hot sticky
night walk into the cockpit. The whistling and trilling of crickets
and tree frogs in the low scrub mingled with the dying whine of
the gyros and the singing in my ears. Everything seemed quiet
and soft and fuzzy after the harsh rumble of flight.

There were no other sounds. No shouts, no engine noises —
and no lights anywhere. The hotel, two hundred yards away
through a belt of scrub and a grove of coconut palms, was lost
in the darkness and quiet as a mass grave.

I'd done it.

Suddenly, I felt weak and shaky. Sweat poured down my face,
and I wanted to be sick again . . .

It was Mariano who snapped me out of it. He stirred and gave
out a low groan like a creaky door — and if I hadn't still been
strapped in I'd have done a vertical take-off without the aeroplane. Just for the moment I'd completely . . . well, not *forgotten*
him, exactly, but certainly sort of mislaid him in my mind under
the press of events. Which was not a very safe thing to do with
a character like him. I came back fast to the here and now.

He was still slumped in his seat, but his drooping head was
making small weak movements like a man thinking of coming
round after a long drunken stupour. I unclipped my straps, then
picked up the .38 and pointed it vaguely at him while I reached
across and undid his harness. He pitched gently forward. His
right hand pawed feebly at the air as he went, but the muscles
weren't answering the helm yet and he ended up bonking his
face on the control yoke and then staying slumped up against it
as if he was praying to the instrument panel. I reversed the

revolver, raised it up to the roof — and hammered him medium-hard on the base of the skull, where the thick ropes of the neck muscles disappear into the cranium. That shouldn't kill him ...

It didn't. He just sort of sagged down a bit lower and made deep-breathing noises like a very old pair of bellows.

I slipped the Smith & Wesson into my belt, tried to ignore the raging pain in my head, and clambered out and knelt on the wing walk-way. Then I leaned into the cockpit, slid the right-hand seat back out of the way, and got to work hauling out the remains. He was a lot more difficult to shift than I'd expected — a sleeping body is a completely dead weight with all sorts of bits sticking out of it to get tangled up with things in a confined space like an aircraft cabin — but after a couple of minutes' heaving I had him assembled in an untidy heap on the walk-way. By that time my headache was threatening to punch its way out through my ears, and I was long past caring whether Señor Mariano collected a few extra dents or not. I stood up shakily, leaned against the door-opening, and pushed him off the back of the wing with my foot. He arrived on the ground like a sack of bananas falling off a lorry.

I stepped down after him, grabbed his wrists, and dragged him into the scrub at the side of the strip. There, I laid him more or less on his front and turned his head to one side so he wouldn't choke on his tongue or the ground. For a moment I thought about searching him — and then I glanced round and saw the Cherokee. It was sitting there in the primeval scrub like a great white spaceship, approximately twice the size of a Boeing 747 and shouting its presence to the whole of Barbuda and several islands beyond ...

Come ON, Scott: just get bloody moving, man ...

I got bloody moving.

*   *   *

The departure wasn't as difficult as it sounds. I did a hurried pre-take-off check before starting the engine, then fired up and taxied smartly back to the threshold. After the sweaty quiet of the night the Lycoming sounded like a prolonged atomic explosion to me, of course — but down here on the ground, with five miles of trees and scrub between me and the village, the chances of anyone else hearing it just didn't exist. You can hear a light aeroplane *in the air* at five miles because there's nothing between it and you except sky — but you certainly won't hear it on take-off at that range. I swung round at the end of the runway, snapped on the landing light, and opened the throttle. The Cherokee lifted off the coral about two-thirds of the way down the strip. I immediately throttled back about halfway, left the light on just long enough to vault the trees at the end, then clicked it off again and held her down as low as I dared over the black water of the bay. The engine snored over at 1,800 rpm, and with two stages of flap down we floated along at about sixty-five mph.

Noise Abatement Procedure for leaving the island of Barbuda undetected — I hoped.

I *should* be all right — rumbling off at ten or twenty feet *should* make me no more audible than a noisy car, and you wouldn't hear that five or six miles away — but I had to admit that the theory had hope sprinkled on top pretty freely. I'd certainly never tested it before — and I felt about as incon-spicuous as a brass band hiding in a phone box. I kept her down low and headed straight out to the east for five minutes, eyes glued to the vague oily blackness of the water and fighting the instinctive urge to pour on the coal and rear up into the safety of the wide open sky. Low flying over water at night is a non-habit-forming occupation: at any given second you can get hypnotised by the rushing dark surface below and fly straight into the sea — and *that* won't be like ditching: you'd probably bounce end-over-end once and then go straight to the bottom like a jet-propelled brick.

When I finally eased on a little more power and ran away into the sky, jacking the flaps up as I went, I was pouring with sweat and tensed up like a clock-spring from head to foot. I opened the little storm window, tossed Mariano's automatic out wide so it wouldn't hit the tail as it went, and then slumped back in my seat and lit up a crumpled Lucky with hands that wouldn't stop shaking.

At 1,000 feet I pushed the throttle up to normal climb power, turned due north to begin a wide circle round Barbuda, and started trying to raise St Kitts on the radio.

*   *   *

I finally got through as we passed 2,500 feet. Golden Rock were snarky about me not calling them for forty-five minutes — and snarkier still when I told them I was at 6,500 feet over the north coast of their island and changing my flight plan to go to San Juan. The controller grumbled and grumped and gave me a mini-lecture on filing *full* flight plans even for training flights, and I apologised humbly because he was dead right. It was perfectly legal for me to change my destination — once you've booked out through Customs and Immigration for a foreign trip you can go where the hell you like — but filing incomplete flight plans and going radio-silent for long periods *is* bloody silly, there was no arguing with that. I got him more or less soothed in the end, levelled off at 6,500 feet — feeling that since I'd lied about my position it was only fair to get at least *one* part of the flight plan right — and spent the next two-and-a-half hours grinding through the wide black night over the Anegada Passage and on into the infamous Bermuda Triangle. I kept a listening watch round several frequencies for Lashlee's Apache coming up after me from the south, but didn't hear anything. I wished that meant he wasn't following — but I wasn't fooling myself: he could be using any of three or four wavelengths and he'd only be talking for a few seconds very occasionally anyway.

I brushed my wheels on to Runway Seven at San Juan at twelve minutes to one in the morning.

14

*I'd been waiting in the Cherokee when Lashlee and Heurtaux
had turned up. They'd arrived at the same time as the US Customs
and there'd been a gunfight right there on the airport apron. I'd
been blinded by flying Perspex as the windscreen got shot out, and
now they were charging me with first degree murder and the
hospital wouldn't give me a gun to shoot myself with ...*

I woke up on the thin edge of screaming out loud. Lay there in
a muck sweat for a long time, blinking at the shafts of morning
sunshine pouring into the white-painted Spanish-style bedroom
and trying to separate fact from nightmare through the fog of
drink and Mandrax in my head.

Gradually, memory filtered back.

There hadn't been any gunfight: incredibly, there hadn't been
any trouble at all. After clearing inbound at San Juan International I'd stood in a phone booth in the empty, echoing airport
concourse and sweated for fifteen minutes while a bored overseas
operator got me a collect call to Harvey Bouvier in Antigua.
Harvey had been sleepy and irritable at first — but he'd got un-
sleepy bloody quick when I gave him the one a.m. news, especially
when I came to the bits about Lashlee and Mariano and Heurtaux.
He'd sounded as if the idea of a Cuban delegation horning in
hadn't occurred to him before — which, if true, wasn't very bright
of him, considering he'd known the source of the Krugerrands all
along. I gave him a minute to let it sink in, and then followed it
up with the most interesting part of all: namely, that I was expecting Lashlee and Heurtaux to land at San Juan any moment, hot
on my trail from St Kitts.

That really shook him; I felt the impact from three hundred

miles away. He said a sort of telephonic equivalent of 'oof', and then there was a period of heavy breathing and distant crackles while he put in some fast thinking. I just stared out at the near-deserted concourse and left him to it: I was in no condition to do any more thinking of my own.

At the end of it, he'd come up with the bright idea that I should guard the Cherokee for half an hour while he arranged for it to be unloaded. I'd argued for a couple of minutes, then given in. Much as I disliked the idea of sentry-go with Lashlee and Heurtaux on the prowl, it *was* the obvious thing to do: I didn't want the *Aeropuerto Policia* dropping in on Lashlee trying to pinch my aeroplane any more than Harvey did. So I cursed Harvey up, down, and sideways, hung up the phone, and headed out to the yellow-lit apron where I'd parked the kite as conspicuously as possible alongside Pan Am Cargo.

Then I'd sat in it for forty-five minutes, pretending to fiddle with the radio while I waited for Lashlee to come taxiing round the nearest wing of the terminal. It was a bloody long forty-five minutes, but the Apache never came. I was too exhausted to wonder why.

At the end of it, a yellow official airport car zoomed up, slowed down to a walk just in front of the Cherokee's nose, and then accelerated away into the darkness beyond the yellow lights. Just like Harvey had said. I slammed the radio back into place, started up, and taxied after it to the Transit Aircraft Park. There'd been no sign of it when I'd got there — again, just like Harvey had said — and I'd simply got out, walked to the terminal, and found myself a taxi to the El Convento.

Which was where I was now. Room 210.

Hallelujah.

I lay under the single sheet for a while, wondering fuzzily and futilely why Lashlee *hadn't* turned up, then gave it up, got slowly out of bed, and sat on the edge of it with my head in my hands. What with the usual hangover plus the fading echoes of concussion, I felt like something that'd been dead a year. I picked up the phone and ordered coffee and Disprins from room service, bleared at my watch and found it was nearly eleven a.m. — and then had to lurch over to the bathroom to vomit rakingly into the toilet bowl. By the time I'd got back the coffee arrived, so I sucked it down slowly and tried to get the day organised in my pounding brain. Common sense told me to go back to bed and be ill in a civilised manner — but I couldn't do that. I had things to meet, and people to do. Or something.

I had, for example, told Harvey to get the last batch of Kruger-rands loaded into the Beech last night double pronto as soon as Customs had finished mauling it around, and have Seagreen put back any panels that Customs had left off first thing this morning. So by now, barring snags such as my friendly Customs Officer getting really awkward and grounding the aircraft for life, she ought to be all ready and waiting.

Which meant that I ought to get moving.

I sighed, got dressed in the clean shirt and trousers I carried in my flight bag for emergencies, and got moving.

* * *

I made it to San Juan Airport just before noon. No-one arrested me as I walked in, and Customs and Immigration cleared me outbound without a murmur: the CIA was nowhere in sight. I walked out to the Transit Aircraft Park in the midday heat . . .

And Lashlee's Apache was parked on the end of the line three aeroplanes away.

When I first saw it my guts did a flick-roll and landed upside-down in my throat — but after a moment's panic I got myself under control again. It wasn't as if I hadn't expected to find it here, after all.

The only question now was, where were the contents . . .?

I spent several seconds staring all around — and then shook my head and carried on walking. I'd already thought all this out — and it didn't matter a damn *where* they were, providing they didn't try to stop me leaving.

Providing . . .

I opened up the Cherokee and climbed in. The rear seat panel had just been plonked into place, and the screws were in the ash-tray. The cavity underneath it was empty: both the gold and the wooden trays were gone. I did deep-breathing exercises of relief for a bit — and then set about giving the Cherokee an internal and external inspection the like of which it hadn't seen since its last C of A check. It took me twenty minutes and re-doubled my headache in spades — but at the end of it, I was as certain as anyone ever could be that I wasn't going to be taking off with any little surprise packages of cargo on board. Such as bombs.

That done, I strapped myself into the steam-bath heat of the cockpit, pulled my life-jacket on, and cranked up the Lycoming. Ground Control threaded me out between the jets and the Prinair Herons, and I lifted off Runway Ten at 1255 local time.

* * *

The weather, now that it didn't matter a damn one way or the other, was good — almost *too* good, in fact. The forecast winds were a pale shadow of their normal fifteen-knot selves — which was nice for me just at the moment since it meant I wouldn't be bucking the usual head-winds on the easterly flight home, but not so nice for the islands in general since the slackening of the trades invariably means the temperature and humidity going through the roof. It's unusual to get a calm in October, but it often happens for weeks on end in high summer in July and August. Then the islands dry up and burn under the merciless hammering of the sun and everybody, white and black alike, goes around gasping in the torpid heat, short-tempered and wringing with sweat. That's when the rich people leave the West Indies for extended holidays in London, Maine, or Montreal.

Me? You're joking, of course.

I levelled off at flight level seven-five, leaned out the mixture, and spent a few minutes finicking with the trims. Then I stared out into the limitless blue beyond the nose, and thought about what was going to happen now. I reckoned I might get away with the last Krugerrand-run if I was lucky, but after that . . .?

After that, of course, Messrs Lashlee, Mariano and Heurtaux were going to take me apart piece by piece until I told them what I'd done with the stuff.

Maybe it was about time I did take a holiday.

I pondered on that for a while, without coming to any conclusions beyond the theory that if I *did* remove myself for a bit the whole thing might blow over. Lashlee was bound to find out where the coins had got to in the end — you couldn't expect to shift 40,000 of the damn things through P.R. to the States without *something* leaking out to the underworld — and once he had found out, he'd have no more reason for coming after me. A crook on his scale is a businessman: he'd be perfectly willing to pulp Bill Scott in order to get information out of him — but he wasn't likely to have me creamed out of pure revenge after the event.

I hoped.

I lit up a Lucky Strike and blew smoke at the airspeed indicator. Eventually, of course, I wanted to get out of the Caribbean and go back to England anyway — but that wasn't much help *now*. Selling up was going to take time — and if I stuck around for that sort of time, I was undoubtedly going to wake up one morning on the wrong end of Heurtaux's gun. So maybe I ought to go to England for a holiday first, then come back and sell up afterwards . . .

That idea got me dragging out my dream again, and polishing it under the tropical midday sun. Right now, Buckinghamshire would be a blaze of autumn browns and golds: cold brittle mists in the mornings, fallen leaves in the woods, the tang of woodsmoke in the air . . .

Home.

The dream kept me going until the little green humps of Saba and 'Statia materialised out of the blue distance and started crawling back towards me. There was something different about them, I thought vaguely — and then sat there staring at them for another five minutes before I realised what it was: their cloudcaps were missing. It looked as though the forecast had been right: when the trades pack up there are no warm moist winds to be pushed upwards by the bulks of the islands — and therefore no cloud caps. Perhaps the weather men *did* use more than a wet finger, after all.

A few minutes more, and St Kitts showed up. I flicked the radio frequency to Golden Rock, gave the routine position reports and estimates — and then, on impulse, asked did they have an Apache 58 Papa on the ground there? I knew perfectly well that they didn't, of course — but if the controller was feeling chatty the question might prompt him to tell me what the aircraft did last night that had kept it from lobbing into San Juan two minutes after me.

He was feeling chatty.

"Negative, Echo Mike," he said. "Five-eight Papa come in las' night late, an' then go straight out again fo' Sain' Lucia."

"*St Lucia?*" You're more hungover than you thought, Scott: You're hearing things. St Lucia's two hundred miles to the *south* . . .

"A-ffirmative, Echo Mike. Sain' Lucia. Now say 'gain yo' estimate abeam Golden Rock?"

I said: "Abeam Golden Rock four-five" automatically — and

then sagged back in my seat and stared at the instruments without seeing them. *St Lucia*, for God's sake! I just couldn't believe it. Why the *hell* should Lashlee, presumably intent on catching up with me and Mariano sometime before we all qualified for our old age pensions, suddenly turn round and skedaddle two hundred miles in the opposite direction . . . ?

I was still cudgelling my brain about it forty minutes later, when I slotted myself in between the Saturday Boeings and landed at Coolidge.

*　　　*　　　*

Customs weren't interested in me. A sulky-looking officer waved me through the barrier and grudgingly admittedly, when I asked, that the Beech had been pronounced clean last night and was no longer grounded. I hid my relief, put on the best sarcastic leer I could muster, and said Thank You Kindly. He just scowled. There was no sign of the island's Most Popular Customs Chief at all: I sincerely hoped he'd contracted double pneumonia sploshing around in the aircraft park last night.

When I stepped out of the Customs and Immigration hall, the first thing I saw was Sherman. He was standing like a big black rock in the bustling tide of tourists and taxi-drivers, waiting for me. He shouldered three medium-sized hippies out of the way as I came through the door and said simply: "Harvey wan' see you."

Full of the social graces, this guy. I blew smoke past his ear. "Where is he?"

He said, "Come wid me," and strode off without waiting to see if I did. I shrugged, and straggled along behind. Stepping out from the shade into the sun was like walking into an oven: the temperature was in the nineties and the humidity pushing its Velocity Never Exceed. I screwed up my eyes against the shimmering white glare of the apron and followed Sherman down the little road alongside the cargo sheds. Sweat collected instantly under my chin, and the heat-rash round my crutch rubbed itself into gritty soreness as I walked.

You only appreciate the trade wind when it ain't there any more.

Harvey was in the clubhouse — and apart from the front door, the clubhouse was all closed up. I suppose it was his idea of security: it was *my* idea of a quick way to dissolve in the heat.

Sherman stayed on the veranda and I walked inside, blinking in the sudden dimness. Harvey bounced up out of a cane chair, which creaked with relief. He was sweating heavily, his nervous tension sticking six inches out of his body. Maybe he'd had a bad night.

"Hey, Scotty — howaya?"

I rubbed the aching lump on the back of my head. "Okay, I guess. Is the Beech loaded up?"

"Yeah, sure. Seagreen've put the panels back, too. An' I gotcha a cargo ta go ta San Juan, as well: French dolls an' stuff from Martinique."

I frowned at him. "I'm not waiting for it if it isn't here. I want to get off right now."

"Don' worry so fuckin' much, Scotty. It's here an' loaded up already an' I got the manifest raised." He hauled it out of his pocket. "Okay?"

I shrugged and subsided. So long as it wasn't going to hold things up or get Customs on the hop again he could fill the kite with dinosaur bones for all I cared. And it *would* look better if I had a cargo, anyway. I took the manifest and Harvey produced a cigar, started unwrapping it with jerky movements of his big fingers, and said: "When ya goin' exactly then, Scotty? Now?"

"Pretty soon. I'm going up to the tower first to see if Lashlee's on his way in. I'm expecting him to follow me as soon as he finds I've left San Juan — and I want to wait until he's on the ground here, and then get off."

Harvey's head jerked up as if I'd clipped him. "What! Whatda fuck d'ya wanna do *that* for, for Chrissake?"

I swiped at the flies which were starting to make a soup-course out of my sweat. "If he's coming in while I'm going out he'll hear me over the radio," I said. "Then he'll just turn round and follow me again, and land five minutes behind me in San Juan."

"Yeah — but if ya leave while he's here he's gonna take off an' follow ya anyway, ain't he?"

I leered at him. The Scott Plan had already thought of that one. "Oh, no he isn't," I said. "Because I — or better still, your man Sherman — am going to ring up Inspector de Lima of the Antigua police and tell him that Lashlee's kite's got a load of illegal arms on board. *That* should hold 'em up for a bit."

Harvey stared at me for a moment — and then burst out laughing like a Spitfire making a low pass.

"Hey fuck, Scotty! For a guy din' wanna do this job ya sure makin' sure of it. Jeez . . . !"

I just looked at him.

After a while he ran down, put his head back, and bawled: "Sherman!" Sherman appeared in the doorway. "Hey Sherman, go 'long ta the control tower an' find out when an airplane's comin' in for me, willya? The 'plane's . . . ?" he looked at me.

"Something-or-other 58 Papa," I supplied. "A Piper Apache inbound from Puerto Rico. We want to know its estimate for here."

Sherman nodded and marched out into the sun. Not the chatty type.

Harvey finally got round to lighting his cigar. He puffed out jets of smoke like an anxious freight train, and started looking round the clubhouse for something to fidget with. His hypertension was having a field day.

I leaned against the wall, put my flight bag on the floor between my feet, and started searching through my pockets for a Lucky Strike. Then I said: "Okay, Harvey: just who is Lashlee?"

The cigar jerked. "Shit, Scotty.— I dunno. *I* never even seen the guy."

"But you've heard of him?"

"Well, fuck . . ." He chewed his left thumbnail, looking more twitchy than ever. "I — ah — heard the name a coupla times, here an' there. He's one'a them guys who sorta . . . deal between Florida an' the islan's. Ya know what I mean?"

I knew, all right. There's several big-time operators like that around Latin America: shadowy multi-million dollar 'dealers' who rarely come out into the open, but who are nevertheless behind a large slice of commerce between America, Mexico and the Caribbean. There's maybe half a dozen guys at the top of the pyramid: powerful, ruthless men who'll move anything anywhere. Guns into Cuba and the Dominican Republic . . . *ganja* out of Jamaica to the United States and everywhere else . . . obsolete jet fighters to the highest bidder — you name it, they'll supply it. At a price, of course.

I sighed, and rubbed the back of my neck with a sweaty palm. It wasn't really news, when it came down to it: I'd never suspected Lashlee of being a small-time torpedo . . .

I said: "Don't you know *anything* more about him? Like

whether he knows anything about you and Ruchter, that sort of thing?"

Harvey waved his hands about and looked more worried than ever. "I tell ya I don't know a fuckin' thing, Scotty. Last night was the first I knew he had anythin' ta do with anythin'."

I regarded him sourly. I wasn't sure he was telling the truth — you can never be sure, with a man like Harvey — but if he wasn't, there was exactly nothing I could do about it. He'd got himself over to the blackboard and was toying with my board-pointer, nervousness showing through his fiddling fingers.

Suddenly, he looked round at me and said: "How come ya so keen on makin' this last run, Scotty?"

I stared at him. He was watching me narrowly, through a cloud of cigar smoke.

He'd actually meant it.

"I ain't got any bloody choice, chum," I snarled. "It's all right for you and Ruchter: nobody knows anything about you two, as far as I know. But Lashlee knows about me, all right: he knows I've been carrying the bloody stuff. So that means I've got to get out of here for a bit — go on a long holiday or something. So — I need the money. It's as simple as that."

Harvey nodded slowly, as if the point hadn't occurred to him. "Yeah. I see what ya mean."

"I'm so glad," I sneered. Then: "While we're on the subject of money, perhaps you wouldn't mind coughing up for the last trip."

"Well — ah — look, Scotty . . ." He was sweating more than ever. I could see the drops of it rolling down his face and neck. "Hell, look — I was expectin' ya ta go today an' come back tomorrow, wasn't I? Then I was gonna pay ya Monday, before the last trip. But today's Saturday, an' the banks're closed, an' . . . an' . . ."

"And you haven't brought the money," I finished flatly.

"Well — ah — no. I mean, I just don' keep that sorta cash lyin' aroun' . . ."

I glared at him. It was reasonable — the banks *do* close on Saturdays, and it certainly *isn't* sensible to leave $10,000 wrapped up in your dirty socks in Antigua — but the reasonableness also had a distinct smell of Harvey-ness sprinkled on top. I was very aware that after this last trip he wouldn't need me any more —

and what with one thing and another I wasn't exactly going to be in a position to sue . . .

I said slowly: "Suppose I refuse to take this load until I've had the money for the last lot?"

That *really* made him sweat. He went for a circular walk, waving the cigar around agitatedly. I watched him, feeling my own sweat trickling down my back. The air in the hut was old and used-up and stifling.

"Look Scotty — shit, I . . ." he stopped, then started again. "Look pal, ya can't just leave them fuckin' Krugerran's in the airplane 'til Monday. Not with that guy Lashlee comin' here . . ."

He was dead right, of course — I wanted those coins sitting around in the Beech the way I wanted a dose of clap. When the chips were down I was taking them to San Juan this afternoon whether I was paid or not, and I knew it.

Still . . .

I gave him a low, nasty grin and said: "Who can't?"

"Shit, look . . ." He pawed a big square wallet out of the back pocket of his shorts. He was really worried, now. "Look, I'll give ya cheque for the whole twenny thousan' . . ."

"A cheque from *you?*" I kept the grin going. Very low, very nasty. I'd had Harvey cheques before: on the second bounce they went into orbit.

"Well, fuck . . ." He waggled the cigar in one hand and the wallet in the other. "Look — shit — I'll give ya all the cash I got on me . . ."

I frowned, shrugged — and held out my hand for the wallet. He hesitated a second, then handed it over. I mauled through it and came up with a fistful of notes, mostly American $100 bills. A quick count showed there were twenty-four of them — $2,400. That plus a couple of hundred in Bee-wee money and a few of the beautiful 100-franc notes of the French Antilles. Harvey's small change was more than the profit I'd made in the last six months. It still wasn't much of a substitute for ten grand in hard American dollars, of course . . .

But it *was* the best I was going to do right now.

I folded the whole lot double, shoved them in my back pocket, and tossed the wallet on to the table. His eyes followed it — and I bent quickly, hauled the Smith & Wesson out of my flight bag, and pushed it firmly into his stomach. He looked down, saw what it was — and took three fast paces rearwards until he was trying to back out through the wall. I followed him and kept up the pressure.

"Wha'...what..."

"I just want to make sure you *get* this," I snarled softly. "Tomorrow I'm going to be coming back here — and first thing on Monday morning I want my money. *All* of it. By ten thirty. And if I *don't* get it..." I gave an extra-hard jab, nearly losing the gun and several inches of arm in the rolls of fat.

His head wobbled from side to side. He was staring down at his stomach with a sort of horrified fascination. Beads of sweat dripped off his nose in the heat.

"Yeah..." he said weakly. "Yeah..."

I stepped back out of range of his breath and dropped the revolver back in my bag. Harvey came off the wall as if someone had un-pinned him, and dragged in air in a long shuddering wheeze.

"Fuck, Bill... ya din' needta do that..."

"Just lest you forget," I said gently — and then, in the same breath: "Why d'you think Lashlee flew down to St Lucia last night?"

He went very still, and just sort of goggled at me. He looked real shook — but then he'd been looking real shook anyway.

"*St Lucia?*", he stammered stupidly. "St Lucia, las' night...?"

Sherman walked in.

"De 'plane estimatin' Coolidge fiften' minute," he said. "A' five to four."

*   *   *

That was the end of Question Time. I spun round on Harvey.

"Get Sherman to phone de Lima right now," I snapped. "I'm going to do my flight plan and clear outbound."

Then I snatched up my flight bag and started for the terminal at a dead run. Fifteen minutes wasn't long to get cleared and check the aircraft and...

"*Hey, Scotty!*"

I skidded to a halt on the gravel. Harvey was leaning over the veranda rail as if he'd arrived there in a hurry.

"How long'll the trip take ya? I gotta tell my people."

There was no wind, and it'd taken two hours twenty to get back...

I bawled: "About two hours twenty," and started moving

again. I was about halfway to the terminal before a nagging itch from my flying sense made me realise I'd given him the Cherokee's flight time and not the Beech's. Oh well, what the hell — forty minutes here or there couldn't make that much difference . . .

I clattered up the steps to the control tower two at a time, and arrived making race-horse noises and scattering sweat like a fountain. The two black controllers looked round from their Saturday afternoon apron-full of aircraft.

"Hey, yo' in a hurry, Cap'n Scott."

"Yeah. Got a lot to do." I grabbed up a pad of flight plan forms and started scribbling. Coolidge — code MKPA — to San Juan International — MJSJ . . .

"Yo' wearin' a groove 'tween here an' San Juan these days, Cap'n."

"Yeah. Gotta lot of charters there suddenly . . ." Then I was off down the steps to Customs and Immigration, hauling out general declarations and Harvey's manifest as I went. I shot through the two halls jumping colourful queues of incoming tourists, popped back out into the sun . . .

And came face to face with Señor Alvaro Mariano.

For a split-second I did the twist trying to reach the Smith & Wesson in my flight bag — and then sanity returned. We were on the crowded pavement of the terminal with a copper standing three feet away shovelling people into taxis. Mariano seemed as startled as I was, and began backing away. I hesitated for a second — and then just nodded to him and loped off towards the aircraft park. There was nothing else I *could* do: the cops were likely to get officious about it if I stuck a gat in his ribs in broad daylight — and anyway, there was no point. I didn't want him as a pet, and we'd already had a little talk last night . . .

I arrived at the aircraft park with ten of my fifteen minutes gone and sweat pouring off me in torrents. Harvey popped up out of nowhere as I reached the Beech. He seemed to be having a bad time with the heat, as well: his white shirt was blotched darkly down his chest and under his armpits, and he was panting like a puffer fish.

"Ev'rythin' okay?"

I said "Yeah, no sweat" — which was the inaccuracy of the century — and started doing a sketchy high-speed external inspection. Harvey kept up with me, breathing like a walrus and getting in the way at every turn.

"Ya ready ta go, Scott," he panted. "I already had Seagreen check the plane over when they put the panels on."

I nodded, trotted all the way round it quickly anyway — mainly to make sure they *had* put all the panels on — and then opened the door and heaved myself in. The last thing I saw as I yanked the door up and shut was Harvey standing stock-still watching me, white as a sheet in the burning sun. Maybe all the excitement didn't agree with him.

Well, it didn't agree with me, either.

The cabin was filled with four tea-chest-sized crates, all pushed as far forward as they'd go and lashed down under a cargo net. I'd meant to have a quick squint under the centre-section hatch to make sure the gold-trough was securely in place, but the crates were sitting squarely on top of it. I shrugged, squeezed past them to the cockpit, and plonked down in the left-hand seat.

Outside, the heat was bouncing off the concrete in shimmering waves — and in here, under the burning-glass of the windscreen, it was like sitting in a kettle. My sunglasses fogged with a fresh outbreak of sweat as I flicked on the master and generator switches and ran my hands around setting the controls for starting. The left propeller groaned over reluctantly, jerking on the compressions. I counted four revolutions, then snapped the magneto switch to Both and pressed the ignition booster and primer with a couple of spare fingers. One cylinder banged, then another — and then the engine caught in the usual ragged blast, vomiting a gout of white smoke which was instantly whipped away in the slipstream. I set the revs at 1,200, got the other one going, then sat there listening to the harsh blaring clatter while my eyes walked round the panel checking things. After a minute or so I clipped up the lap-strap, pulled the headset over my ears . . .

And almost immediately the radio crackled and said: "Five-eight Papa yo' cleah to lan'. Wind is calm."

I cranked my head round and hung my chin on my left shoulder. I was just in time to see Lashlee's Apache slide down the last hundred feet of its approach, disappear into the quivering heat-haze over the distant threshold, and reappear a few seconds later on its landing roll-out.

There's timing for you, boyo . . .

I pressed the mike-button to speak — and then changed my mind and unpressed it. No point in *telling* Lashlee what I was doing. I screwed a knot in my neck again and watched the Apache scuttle across the apron in front of a re-fuelling Boeing, then swing round and park itself directly in front of Customs. I waited until the props stopped, gave it a little bit longer for luck — and *then* called up for taxi clearance.

Four minutes later, all the checks completed, I rolled down Runway Two-five in the blattering thunder of full power and lifted her off into the burning afternoon sky.

It was 1605, local time.

I climbed up to 8,500 feet on a heading of exactly 300 degrees, put her on the step and fussed around with the trims until she flew hands-off, and then just sat there staring into the vast dome of the sky and listening to the steady drumming of the engines.

I felt old and sick and empty. I promised myself a huge celebration dinner in San Juan tonight, and tried to ignore the hollow feeling in my guts.

I'd been airborne an hour when the troubles began.

15

THEY STARTED FAIRLY insignificantly: nothing more than the oil temperature on the starboard engine creeping up a little from its normal 155°F. I noticed it when it had reached 160, and watched it over the next five minutes as it niggled round to 165. That was the beginning edge of the narrow yellow arc marked on the dial — the Maximum Operating Range. It didn't mean there was a serious problem — not yet, anyway — but it *did* mean I ought to give the matter some attention.

I started by frowning at the gauge and tapping the glass with my finger, which is the way you always start when a dial says something you don't like. As always, it didn't make the slightest difference. I glared at it, then pushed the starboard mixture lever up a little on the grounds that the richer the mixture the cooler the combustion. The right engine fuel-flow needle moved up, the cylinder temperatures backed down to 460°F . . .

But the oil temperature went right on increasing. It was 175 now, and still climbing.

Shit.

I shoved the mixture into full rich and opened the cowl flaps a crack. 180. 185 . . .

Shit, again.

The oil pressure was being affected now, too, sagging down fractionally from its normal 75 psi. That figured: oil viscosity decreases as temperature increases — and so you lose pressure. *Ipso facto.* Or something.

I opened the cowl flaps all the way, and corrected the slight asymmetric drag by winding on a touch of rudder trim. Then I undid my belt, clambered over into the right-hand seat, rammed my nose up against the side window, and stared out at the dull black engine cowling. Looking at the source of the aggro is another standard reflex action and normally achieves about as much as tapping gauges does — but this time, I *did* see something.

A long, wind-smeared streak of black oil, starting at the rear edge of the cowling and running back along the nacelle and on to the wing.

Fuck it!

Now I knew what my problem was, all right. An oil leak — a big bugger, too. Enough of a big bugger, in fact, to drain out so much of the seven gallons of oil in the tank that the remainder was overheating. More oozed out from under the cowling as I watched. It was seized instantly by the slipstream and dragged back along the trail of what had gone before. The top of the wing inboard of the nacelle was dirtily covered in it, and judging by the direction of the flow there must be even more on the underside.

I dragged my eyes away and looked at the gauges again. The temperature was up to 195 and the pressure was down to 60 psi — near the red line in both cases.

Fuck it, fuck it, FUCK IT!

There was nothing I could do about it: the engine had to be shut down before it seized solid and tore itself out of the wing. I hauled myself back across to the left-hand seat, spent ten seconds cursing Messrs. Pratt & Whitney up, down and sideways — and then closed the right throttle, brought the pitch back to fully coarse and the mixture to lean cut-off, and hit the starboard feathering button.

The steady roar of two engines immediately cut back to a surprised asymmetric blare on the left-hand side. The nose tried to yaw to the right, but I was ready for that with rudder. The starboard prop slowed down until it was visible, then finally stopped altogether as the blades finished twisting themselves edge-on to the airflow. I shoved the power on the left engine up to 2,200 rpm and full throttle, reached up to the roof and gave the rudder trim a quick couple of turns, then went round the cockpit whanging levers and switches to get the aeroplane properly cleaned up for single-engine flight.

After that I trimmed her out at 125 knots and sat there watching the altimeter unwind.

Nasty feeling, that.

She'd hold her height on one eventually, of course — but not up here in the rarified atmosphere of 8,500 feet: she needed the denser air of the depths below to give her more power to the engine and more lift to the wings. I didn't know how *much* below — that depends on the density-altitude and the all-up weight and a few other things such as how good a life you've led — but I was fairly confident it'd be at some point before the ocean impinged on our further downward progress. *That* wasn't worrying me . . .

I rubbed the back of my aching head and thought about the factor that *was*. To wit; what does Scott do now?

What I *ought* to do was simple and easily-defined: I ought to turn towards the nearest land and put her on the ground with the utmost convenient dispatch. You don't fall out of the sky when you lose one elastic band on a twin-engined aeroplane — that's what you *have* twin engines for — but on the other hand you don't push your luck by swanning around over the ocean in that state for any longer than you have to, either. *That's* what you have common sense for. So what I should do was put out a PAN call — a sort of watered down Mayday meaning I've-got-a-problem-but-I-don't-need-the-cavalry-called-out-yet — and divert to the island of St Croix, about thirty miles to the south-west. From where I was, crabbing down through 7,000 with the port engine blattering away at max continuous cruise, I could even see St Croix, lying in the blue oily distance like a monster green rat.

That was what I *ought* to do, all right.

But . . .

If I landed at St Croix I had no way of getting the gold off the aeroplane — and no way of leaving again until the engine was fixed. You can fly and you can land on one engine — but you most certainly can't take off. The fault might be something simple like a duff pipe-connection — or it might be a size-twelve problem like a split crankcase, which would mean an engine change. And *that* would ground me on St Croix for anything up to a month . . .

While Lashlee and Co, of course, would be rolling up in a matter of hours.

It wasn't a choice at all, really.

*   *   *

We finally stopped going down at 5,600 feet, which was higher than I'd expected in this heat with nearly full fuel and a cargo-sized cargo *and* a load of Krugerrands. Maybe there was life in the old bi—— sorry, the dear, *nice* old girl yet. I spread some of the sweat around my face with a shirt-sleeve, and spun the time/distance scale of my little plastic computer. San Juan was a hundred nautical miles away, near enough: fifty minutes' flying, at this miserable speed.

I looked over my left shoulder at the good engine and said aloud: "If you will please keep going for another hour I will buy you a premature oil change *and* a new set of plugs." It roared on serenely, unimpressed — and I sagged back in my seat and tried not to think about the consequences if it *didn't* keep going.

At first glance there may seem to be little to choose between a twin-engined aeroplane with one engine out and a single-engine machine which only has one mill to go wrong in the first place — but in fact, the difference is very considerable indeed. If the engine of a lightweight pipsqueak like a Cherokee hands in its dinner pail the aircraft will glide down reasonably flat and slow and civilised to a forced landing or a ditching —but if the *second* engine of a flying brick like a Beech 18 should elect to cash in, the crate will glide with all the grace of a piano falling off a top-storey roof. When you arrive at the water the ditching speed will be about twice that of a Cherokee and the inertia will be ten or fifteen times as great. And as if *that* wasn't enough, the only door into an 18 is way back down the fuselage ...

So, in short, you ain't gonna get out. Whatever happens.

I squirmed in my seat, ran my eyes over the engine gauges every few seconds, and finicked with the port cowl flaps until the cylinder temperatures were a touch lower than usual. That and shoving the mixture into full rich — which I'd already done — were the only things I could do to coddle the motor. I just hoped it appreciated them.

Ten minutes went past. St Croix crept away behind and left, and St Thomas inched up over the horizon ahead of the dead finger of the starboard prop. It looked close enough to reach out and touch — but that particular deception was an old acquaintance, and I wasn't fooled. In the clear air of the Caribbean, untainted by the industrial crud which hazes the atmosphere over most land masses, distances can be very deceptive. St Thomas might look as if it was within gliding distance — but in reality it was a good twenty miles away, and about as much use to me if the port engine quit as a runway on the moon.

I fidgeted for the fiftieth time, and stared at the instruments for the hundredth. All okay. The blazing yellow disc of the sun, ambling over to the west ready for its fast evening dive into the sea, hammered mercilessly into the cockpit and made the sweat run in slippery streams down my face and neck. My palms left damp marks on the control yoke, and no amount of wiping them on my trousers would dry them. The sun also showed up the flakes and bare patches in the faded green paint of the cockpit, and the million tiny scratches round the instruments. The dials were dancing slightly in the booming vibration of asymmetric power, as if the poor old Beech was shaking with some kind of fever.

I knew how she felt.

Another five minutes. Forty still to go.

The untidy disarray of throttles, mixtures and pitch levers on the control pedestal jarred on my flying nerves. I tried telling myself that modern aero-engines very rarely fail and the chances of two going sour within an hour of each other just didn't exist — but myself remained unconvinced. For a start, these engines were anything but modern — and secondly, I was hammering the port one harder than I'd ever hammered it before. It *should* be all right — it wasn't exceeding max continuous cruise — but just the same . . .

The voice of my first flying instructor reached down across the years and echoed in my brain. "*Never commit yourself totally: always have some other plan up your sleeve in case the first one doesn't work out.*" It was one of the most basic principles of safe flying — and since those far-off days in the windy cockpit of a Tiger Moth, I'd drummed it into countless students of my own. And now, because of a bent cargo the size of a small suitcase, I was ignoring it. This time, I had nothing up my sleeve. No alternatives. Either the good engine kept running and I made it — or it didn't, and I didn't.

As simple as that.

St Thomas slid past the right wing tip. I scrabbled around beside my seat, came up with a floppy yellow life-jacket, pulled it over my head, and tied up the ribbons round my waist. It was a useless gesture, of course — but maybe God and Pratt & Whitney help those who help themselves.

*　　　*　　　*

A few minutes later, at 1730, the two little islands of Vieques and Culebra swam into view. Vieques to the left of the nose,

Culebra to the right. Both of them are Restricted Zones, used by the US Navy for pasting missiles in the general direction of the Atlantic Fleet Weapons Range Bravo, down south. On walking-the-missiles days one or both of these zones are active — or 'hot' — which means that the civilian peasantry isn't allowed to overfly. I didn't know whether today was one of those days or not . . .

Which made it time I got on the radio and found out.

I pressed the button and said: "San Juan, Alpha Whisky request status of Vieques and Culebra" very fast, in the hope that they'd just reply and forget about it.

No chance, of course.

"Aircraf' callin' San Juan Radio, say again yo' call sign?"

Blast it. "San Juan, Victor Papa Lima Alpha Whisky, requesting status of Vieques and Culebra."

Pause. Then: "Lima Alpha Whisky, say yo' presen' position an' altitude?"

"Alpha Whisky's ten miles east of Vieques at flight level five-five."

Another pause, longer this time. Then the voice said: "Lima Alpha Whisky, San Juan — we have yo' flight-planned at flight level eight-five, sir, an' estimatin' San Juan at four-zero . . . ?"

In other words, please explain what you're doing lower and slower than you should be.

Blast again.

"Roger, San Juan. Alpha Whisky has a small problem which has meant the precautionary shutting down of one engine. Revised estimate for San Juan fife-fife if Vieques and Culebra are cold."

"Roger, Lima Alpha Whisky. Please advise immediately in future in this sort of instance. D'you wanna declare an emergency an' divert to St Thomas?"

Did I, hell. That was precisely why I *hadn't* called earlier — if he'd known I'd lost an engine half an hour ago, he'd have fed me into St Croix or St Thomas before you could say knife. Now, I was that much nearer to San Juan and in a better position to argue . . .

"Negative, San Juan: it's only a precautionary shut-down and I can restart it if necessary."

Lying bastard. If you re-start that one you'll get a seizure and a possible fire and . . .

Ah, shaddup.

174

San Juan absorbed that for a moment, then said: "Roger, Lima Alpha Whisky. Vieques and Culebra both hot, but maintain yo' headin' an' stan'by: I'll try'n get clearance fo' yo'."

I said thanks, then moved the boom-mike away from my mouth and wiped my face with my sleeve again. Vieques and Culebra *would* be bloody hot today of all days, of course: if I had to go round them it'd add another twenty minutes to the flight . . .

The headphones buzzed and said: "Lima Alpha Whisky, San Juan?"

I slapped the mike back. "Alpha Whisky go."

"Alpha Whisky yo' cleared from yo' presen' position direct to San Juan at flight level five-five. Call abeam Culebra an' crossin' the Puerto Rico coastline."

I pushed out a sigh of relief. He was nice people, that controller . . .

"Roger, San Juan — five-five, call you abeam Culebra and the coast. And thank you very much for your trouble, sir."

"S'okay, Alpha Whisky. But call us a bit earlier nex' time, okay?"

I said: "I hope there won't be a next time, sir — but if there is, I'll do that. Thanks again."

I didn't mind calling him 'sir'. He'd just saved me twenty precious minutes . . .

And my life, as it happened.

Because twenty-one minutes later, just as I was switching to Approach Control five miles east of San Juan, the port engine blew up.

16

When I say blew up, I mean *really* blew up. There was a shattering *BANG* like a vast flat shotgun, and a walloping concussion through the airframe. I shot six inches out of my seat and smacked my head against the side window. The engine was erupting a wind-flattened sheet of yellow-white flame. The prop jerked to a stop with a vast metallic *kerr-runch*.

Then silence, total and appalling. No engines. Nothing but the eerie moaning hiss of the airflow.

The Beech started downhill.

For a few seconds she just sort of staggered as the airspeed washed off — and then she rolled tiredly left and down, sinking like an express lift and curling round like some ridiculous over-fed fighter trying to peel off into an attack-dive. I slammed everything right — a moment's utter panic as nothing happened — and then she responded drunkenly, stopping the turn and plunging straight ahead in a howling, shuddering side-slip, left wing low. The livid green coastal plain filled the windscreen, 5,000 feet below but swelling rapidly.

With the cold detachment of total shock I found myself thinking *the engine's blown itself to bits and probably taken half the wing-skin and the undercarriage with it, so there's asymmetric drag on the left. Better find somewhere to put her down*...

Christ! And how! I stared desperately over the nose at the ground. The altimeter was unwinding crazily, somewhere through the four-thousands. Two minutes, maybe less, and we'd be on the deck whatever...

A giant vicious roaring noise started up over the thunder of the wind. It was several seconds before I realised it was the fire.

My right hand reached out instinctively and whanged the port fuel tap to Off, twisted the extinguisher valve to Left, and yanked the panic-handle. The detached part of my brain sneered *that's for small carburettor fires and it'll be about as much use as pissing on this one* — and it seemed to be right. The roaring went on undiminished. I snatched a glance to the left — and then just stared for precious, irreplaceable split seconds.

The engine was literally a ball of fire — a booming white inferno with great long streamers of tattered yellow flame torn out of it, peppered with streaking sparks of melting duralumin. Under the flames the cowling was a mass of gaping holes, the edges widening like dissolving plastic. A lump of it lifted as I watched, fluttered furiously in the airflow for a second, then ripped off and disappeared instantly.

God in Heaven! Get her DOWN, Scott . . .

Right — but *where*, for Chissake?

There was nowhere.

I searched frantically, dimly aware of my arms and legs quivering with the strain of holding on right rudder and aileron to keep us straight in the plummeting side-slip. To the left were the Liquillo foothills, to the right the sea — and ahead, rushing up to meet me, nothing but jungle and rivers and sugar fields. Nowhere to put a dying Beech 18 at twice its normal landing speed with the remotest chance in hell of walking away . . .

God, come ON! Find SOMEWHERE! You're passing 3,800, you've got maybe ninety seconds left! That road? The seashore? Ditch it . . . ?

The headphones spoke calmly into my ears. A real voice from the real world. A man who would still be alive in two minutes' time.

"Lima Alpha Whisky report lef' downwind fo' Runway Seven."

The airport! Reach the fucking airport!

I looked up the shivering windscreen and right, and saw it. The vee of the two runways pointed at me invitingly, about four miles away. Hard surfaces to slide on, crash-wagons on the spot . . .

The only thing was, I wasn't going to get that far. The Beech's brick-like engine-less glide was going to end in a ball of fire in a sugar field before we'd got even half way.

Unless you re-start the starboard engine, Scott — then *you might just do it. IF it doesn't run out of oil and seize up on the way, of course ..*

*   *   *

I decided on it in the split-second, right or wrong. There was no other alternative. I heaved on the right rudder pedal with all my strength to get the nose pointing at the nearest runway, and sent a hand scrabbling furiously through the unfeathering drill. Starboard fuel tap — on; mixture — full rich; pitch — coarse; throttle — inch open; mags and boost pump — on . . .

Then I hit the feathering button.

For a moment, nothing happened. We just went on plummeting downhill, juddering in the Beech's death throes. The passage in the Flight Handbook which says *The feathering pump takes three seconds to feather or unfeather* flicked up in my mind. It seemed a bloody endless three seconds . . .

Then the blades twisted against the howling airflow. The prop chunked soundlessly over a couple of compressions, spun a few turns, hesitated again — and then disappeared in a blur as the engine caught and ran, the familiar husking clatter almost lost under the boom of the wind and the roaring of the fire. I pulled the feathering button out of engagement, took a fast deep breath — and shoved throttle and pitch about halfway forward together.

The engine coughed and banged furiously, sending a new crop of shakes through the airframe in protest at being opened up from cold. My muscles cringed with it. *Come on, you bastard, come ON . . .*

It picked up on all cylinders in a peal of crackling thunder.

Which, of course, created a whole new problem.

I now had power on the right and drag on the left — so as the engine ran up, the nose instantly swung to port. I shoved all my weight on the right rudder pedal again. For a long moment the swing continued — and then she weaved soggily and steadied as the airspeed crept up a few knots and gave more bite to the twin rudders. I kept feeding on power and began edging the nose up to flatten the descent. After a moment the swing started again and I had to wait for her to accelerate some more. It was a giant deadly balancing act: I had to get the nose high and the speed low to reduce the downhill plunge — but if I got the speed *too* low there wasn't enough rudder control to keep straight. In normal times a Beech 18 will climb on one engine at ninety-five knots with rudder-power to spare — but now, with whatever-it-was hanging down on the left and causing enormous lop-side drag, I needed 110 or more just to keep straight. And at *that* speed I wasn't even going to achieve level flight, never mind climbing . . .

The radio bleated in my ears. "Lima Alpha Whisky, yo' readin' San Juan Approach . . .?" I thought *fuck off* and ignored it, concentrating desperately on the balancing act. More power . . . nose up 'til she's about to yaw . . . more power again . . .

The cockpit was a chaos of noise and vibration. Great tearing cycles of shuddering came through the controls every few seconds, and the blaring of the engine was overlaid by the express-train thunder of the fire. Something went *KERR-RANG* behind me and then started tramping with loud dustbin-lid noises. I nearly jumped out of my skin — and then immediately shut it out. Either it was something important, such as the port wing, or it wasn't — and either way there was bugger-all I could do about it.

Suddenly, the throttle and pitch were up against the stops.

I glanced at the revs. 2,600 — Jesus! Snatched the pitch back to 2,300, and didn't even look at the oil temperature and pressure: if she was going to seize, she'd seize. I did flash an eye at the shivering flight panel, though. The speed was waving around 120, the altitude was coming down through 2,000 . . .

But the descent *had* slowed. The nose was higher, no longer pointing suicidally down at the jungle, and the airport was expanding in the windscreen. Two, two-and-a-half miles to run, and the vertical-speed dancing somewhere around 1,500 feet-a-minute Down . . .

The headphones said peevishly: "Victah Papa Lima Alpha Whisky d'yo' *read* San Juan — over."

Jesus, man — knock off the fucking calculations and TELL somebody something . . .

I thumbed the mike button. I wanted to shout and scream — but the words came out in a dry, terrified croak. The feedback through my head-set was lost under the din of the fire, so I couldn't hear my own voice.

"Mayday, Mayday, Mayday — Alpha Whisky has an engine fire, crash-landing on Runway Two-five. Two miles to run."

Mayday calls are supposed to include rather more than the fact that the perpetrator is about to come in the wrong way down the main runway and spread himself in a flaming mass all over the airport — but the controller didn't argue. No controller getting a call like that would. There was a two-second pause as he shifted into overdrive and hit a few panic-buttons — and then he started scattering aircraft like confetti as he made room for me. I heard him, somewhere in the vague distance, as I fought with the drunken sogginess of the controls and slapped the trims around to ease some of the pressures before my arms and legs dropped off.

"Roger, Lima Alpha Whisky, keep on coming — break, break, Prinair Niner-one-zero break off your approach to the left immediately and hold to the south — break, break, Dorado Wings Two-five turn right from yo' presen' position an' hold over the sea — break, break, Eight-Papa Bravo Echo Romeo, yo' have a Beech 18 with an engine fire half mile ahead o' yo' — d'yo' have contact?"

"Negat — ah, roger, affirmative. Got him now. Big trail of smoke."

" 'Kay — we'd be glad if yo'd try'n get alongside an' give us a fast status report, sir."

"Roger."

I thumbed the button again and croaked: "Echo Romeo from Alpha Whisky: don't come up on my left, or I may roll into you if the wing falls off or anything."

"Roger. Coming up on your right."

The runway over the nose floated nearer — I suppose. To me, spaced-out in the slow motion of disaster, it seemed to hang in the juddering windscreen motionless and unreal; a distant unattainable Promised Landing. I wasn't even terrified — or at least, I suppose I *was*, but I wasn't feeling it. I'd done all I could, now: until the actual landing — if there *was* a landing — there was nothing left except to keep up the muscle-wrenching pressure on the controls and hold the nose up on the tight-rope verge of snapping away to the left. I was braced against the seat-back with my right leg locked and quivering on the rudder, and using both hands on the yoke to hold the left wing up. I tried to look at the starboard engines gauges, but they were shaking too much to be readable. It didn't matter, anyway: I couldn't ease the strain on the motor even if they all jumped out of the panel and waved flags at me. Either it kept running or it didn't, and that was that.

For a few seconds, I thought about Jenny. Then I turned my

head and looked at the fire again. Even the flames seemed to be moving in slow motion as they licked and poured in the gale. The cowling was completely gone now, nothing left but a few splashes of melted alloy on the naked remains of the engine, ahead of the heart of the fire. The top two cylinders were missing, and the rest stuck out like a skeleton in the wind. I looked farther back. The wing itself was alight, along with the top of the nacelle. Black smoke, bar-solid in the airflow, gushed out of yellow-red welding torch flames. That meant petrol or oil, probably both. Well, so it would be: all the tanks were round there. I wondered, distantly, whether a tank would blow up or the mainspur burn through first . . .

The headphones snapped: "Alpha Whisky, Echo Romeo's on your right."

I said: Roger," and turned to look. A shiny blue and silver Beech King Air was sliding up alongside about a hundred feet away. I could see his wheels coming down as he used them to kill his overtaking speed. I could even see a row of white faces in the neat square windows down the fuselage. I had the instant slow-time thought that those people were going to be dining out on the story tonight after I'd ceased to exist . . .

The King Air dropped down a few feet and the voice crackled in my ears again, speaking fast.

"Your left wheel's hanging half down. It seems to be moving in the airflow, so it'll probably go up when you hit. One undercarriage door's banging around, and the flap's buckled and drooping. Good luck . . ."

I swallowed stickily and croaked "Thanks" as the King Air peeled away upwards into the burning blue sky, sucking its wheels back in as it went. I was suddenly terribly alone in the shaking, racketing cockpit. I had to fight back the impulse to jam down on the mike-button and yell for him to come back and sit beside me during the rest of the approach so there'd be someone near me when I died . . .

Then I looked forward again — and there wasn't any rest of the approach. The ground was *here*, two hundred feet below. Swampy scrub rushed under the nose and the glaring white ribbon of the runway reached out to meet me, dancing in the windscreen as the Beech bounced tiredly in the low-level turbulence. I could see the details of the approach lights and the black skidmarks on the threshold . . .

The only thing was, I wasn't going to get there. We were going to be about a hundred yards short, the Beech and me.

About where the low stone-and-concrete rampart of the reclaimed airport land reared up out of the swamp, in fact.

*   *   *

In the instant of realisation a voice screamed in my head *you can always turn speed into height*. Well, I had speed all right . . .

I slammed the starboard throttle shut so I wouldn't yaw myself into the ground — and then heaved back on the yoke as hard as I could, tramping on the rudders to keep straight. The nose hauled itself up for the last time, slow and old and shaking. The howling wind-noise sagged as the airspeed washed away . . .

But it was enough. The Beech mushed tiredly upwards for a few seconds.

The rampart slid by underneath.

Then we were over the end of the runway, and she stalled.

There wasn't a thing I could do about it. She just fell out of my hands from about fifteen feet, exhausted and finished with flight for good. There was a moment's falling sensation, the left wing dropping . . .

And then we hit.

The wing tip struck first, with a jarring *krang*. For a split-second we started skewing round — and then everything else hit at once. There was a vast shattering *CRASH* — the yoke whipping out of my grip and walloping me in the face as I thumped forward into the lap-strap — a hideous drawn-out screeching while giant hands slammed and pummelled the cockpit from all directions . . .

The sliding seemed to go on for ever. The cockpit full of exploding dust, and the screeching and banging like a thousand car accidents strung together. Through the windscreen I caught glimpses of the runway and the airport, shaking and rocking and twisting impossibly. Split-second images registered — a yellow Rapid Intervention vehicle bouncing across the grass, a runway light lens curling through the air in front of the cockpit — then the scene turning like a tracking camera as the Beech skidded round and carried on sideways. The metallic screaming and tearing was fantastic, never-ending . . .

Then it stopped.

Suddenly, incredibly, everything still and settling and utterly,

utterly quiet. The silence thudded on my ears like funeral drums. Dust drifted in the hot cockpit, and the airport was white and shimmering and shocked into stillness outside.

Then the sullen crackling of flames, like a distant bonfire.

God! Man! Get OUT!

I came partially back to life, and un-clicked my seat belt. Hauled myself up into the usual cockpit-crouch on watery legs, and reached for my flight bag. My brain howled *Jesus — just bloody GET OUT!* — but I picked it up anyway. My mind seemed to be wrapped in cotton wool, and didn't have the power to move my body at anything more than snail's pace. I reeled through the doorway between cockpit and cabin, nearly fell over backwards trying to correct for a sloping floor that didn't slope any more, and finally arrived somehow at the door. I twisted the handle and pushed . . .

And it wouldn't open, of course. Bloody stuck.

The distant-bonfire noises deepened suddenly into a menacing hiss, like a God-sized blowtorch.

Fucking hell, Scott — MOVE!

Keeping the handle pressed down I turned my back on the door and stab-kicked rearwards. Hot pain blasted up from my heel.

Nothing else happened.

The hissing wound up louder, punctuated with urgent poppings and creakings. I kicked again, desperately.

The door sagged open.

I shot through it into the sunlight and ran. The solid concrete and grass thumped my feet like being born again. There were people, vehicles, in a moving blur to the right. I swerved towards them and kept going. I could feel my legs and elbows thudding like pistons — but they seemed distant, not connected to my brain. They were mechanical parts of me that were going to carry me back to people and safety and life. The vehicles were getting nearer, figures were moving . . .

There was a huge powerful *wol-oomph* behind me.

I skidded to a stop and turned round. The left side of the Beech was a roaring explosion of orange flame feeding up into a great mushroom of black smoke. The smoke bellied and roiled against the burnished blue sky — except that the sky wasn't blue any more: it was going black all over and yawing and rolling and falling . . .

I felt the stubbly grass come up and hit me in the face. But after that, nothing.

*   *   *

When I came round, there was white everywhere. Like snow. *What the hell . . .?*

Then the white moved, and the waking confusion drained away like the last bit of bathwater. The slopes of the Eiger turned out to be the north face of a clean white coat — and the coat turned out to contain a big black man who was kneeling beside me. Medicine man. Probably counting my arms and legs to make sure I hadn't been seriously hurt. I blinked up at him, grunted something when he said something, then pushed myself up on to my elbows. The effort made the world swing on its hinges and started Atlantic-roller noises in my head — but I had to *see*.

The Beech was a burnt-out, carbonised wreck covered in heavy, oozing white foam.

The tail, some of the fuselage, and the outer section of the left wing still looked more or less reminiscent of an aeroplane — but the left engine nacelle, the inboard wing section, and the place where the left wall of the cabin used to be were nothing but a twisted mass of naked, blackened stringers and spars sticking up out of a sea of foam like an enormous detergent advert.

Jesus . . .

I started pushing myself upwards. It was a long, hard climb. By the time I'd got to my knees I seemed to have reached my current service ceiling. I paused, breathing deeply and watching the world rocking and wavering, while voices lapped and receded in my ears.

"Wen' up so beeg afta yo' pass out . . ."

"De foam exting'sher . . ."

"Yo' jus' lie still an' leave t'all to us . . ."

"That was a fine piece of flyin', man . . ."

"We gotta pull the remains off'n the runway so we c'n open it up agin . . ."

I cranked my head round and bleared in the general direction of the last voice. There seemed to be a shooting gallery of mixed black and white faces, all staring at me. I found a tongue lying around in the sticky cavern of my mouth and mumbled: "Move't inna minute. Wanna lookatit first."

184

There was a new babble of voices. The medical man was saying something about lying still and the ambulance.

"Fuck off," I told him politely, and went on working my way upwards. I got both feet under my backside ... big heave ...

And I was there. Standing. Two or three extraneous hands seemed to be doing most of the work while my head performed an interesting sequence of barrel rolls and flat spins — but I *was* standing. I shoved my tongue into fully-fine pitch again and slurred: "Water — anyone got any water?" Someone actually had. I grabbed the bottle with shaking hands, and drank deeply and spat.

"Lis-lissen ..." I stopped and assembled the words. They wouldn't stand in line properly, but I went on anyway. "S'my aeroplane. My cargo. Right?" Nobody said anything. I waved my head about and carried on. "Ri-right. Mine. So I wanna look't it — inspect it — b'fore it's moved. See?"

They saw — I think. At any rate, nobody tried to stop me. I put one foot in front of the other, moved away from the supporting hands, did it again — and lo, I was walking. The Atlantic-roller noises came and went in hi-fi quadrophonic, the evening sun was hot on my back — but the Beech was jerking slowly towards me.

Then it was here.

Up close it looked like a long-dead wreck under a mantle of film-unit imitation snow. The fire couldn't have been out for more than minutes — but there was no clicking of cooling metal, no shimmering heat waves, no sinister wisps of smoke. The airport fire appliances, designed to chuck out dry powder and fluoroprotein foam fast enough to knock down a 747-sized blaze in under a minute, had swotted my little inferno without even breathing heavily. The only thing they'd left behind them was an incredible gut-churning stench, hanging rank and foetid in the stagnant heat. An acrid mixture of aluminium-foundry plus burnt-out wetness plus a kind of heavy detergent smell.

My empty stomach bubbled menacingly as I sploshed through the foam towards the left engine.

The wing-root and the nacelle had been the real centre of the fire — and now, there was practically nothing left but a mass of blackened, heat-buckled framework dripping dirty rags of foam into the snow-carpet on the concrete below. The outer wing skin had disappeared to well outboard of the nacelle, the fuel and oil tanks had gone, the batteries had gone — everything. And I mean completely gone: nothing left but soggy white-ish ash mixed up in dirty patches of foam, like melted polystyrene tiles.

I found I was shaking my head. This — *mass* — couldn't have been holding together, *flying* . . .

But it had.

I patted the side of the heat-blistered nose and muttered: "Thanks, pal. If I ever called you an old bitch, I take it all back. You were the best aeroplane in the world."

Then I stepped up to look at the engine itself.

It had been torn halfway out of its mountings in the crash, so that now it leaned tiredly forward with the prop-hub ground into the concrete and one propeller blade mashed back under the bottom cylinders like a man standing on his own tie. I shuffled in between it and the fuselage, feeling the wetness crawling over my sandals, and peered down behind it.

Even under the ever-present layer of foam, it looked as if it had been hit by a bazooka.

I scooped off a few handfuls of the stuff — and then just stood there looking like a soap-commercial and stared. I reckon to know my way round the nether regions of a Wasp Junior — but not this one. Not any more. For a long moment I couldn't get my bearings at all — and then I located the remains of a magneto that American Bosch would have had to look at hard to recognise, and worked out the rest of it from there. That lump of half-melted alloy must have been the carb . . . the thing like a used hand-grenade casing was once the supercharger . . .

Jesus, again.

I backed out of the engine and weaved unsteadily round the wing. There were people standing around pointing their voices at me as I went, but I took no notice. The fuselage was streaked with soot and foam, and the Airstair door was still gaping open where I'd kicked it. I hauled myself inside.

It was a shambles. For a start, the tunnel of the cabin was flat instead of sloping — and secondly, half of it wasn't there at all. Up forward near the wing-root the left side of the floor and the outer skin of the fuselage had melted away completely. It was like being inside some monstrous animal which was halfway through being skinned: the sun shone in through the carbonised ribs and stringers and dappled smoky patterns on the charred black lumps which had once been the front two crates of cargo.

The whole interior was covered in black ash and soot, and spattered with dirty brown blobs of foam. The stench was indescribable.

The floor creaked under me as I edged my way forwards.

When I came to the hole I stepped gingerly down into it, putting my feet on the bare stringers. Everything I touched to steady myself seemed to disintegrate into a handful of dirt. I took two or three deep breaths, then doubled over and peered around the charred depths of the under-floor compartment.

There was nothing there. No melted gold. No burnt-out gold-trough.

Nothing.

I staggered out of the aeroplane, made twenty or thirty yards, then sank down on to my knees and retched into the wiry salt-grass at the side of the runway.

The uniformed vultures closed in.

17

It was a period of considerable confusion. Port Authority, Immigration, Airport Maintenance, the Medical Unit and Uncle Tom Cobbleigh and All stood around me in a chattering semi-circle. I sat on the grass and shivered in the hot tropical sunset, incongruous in the soot-smeared yellow life-jacket I somehow hadn't got round to taking off yet, and caught about one question in six as they zapped past my ears. A crew of black maintenance men with an aircraft tractor were busy hitching up enough ropes to the Beech so they could haul it off the runway without it actually falling apart on them. I was paying more attention to them than I was to the questions: after months of hating the sight of the Beech, it now suddenly seemed terribly important that it shouldn't be damaged any more. Ridiculous, of course — its scrap value would be the same fifty bucks or whatever whether it still vaguely resembled a Beech 18 or was rolled up in a ball and delivered in pink ribbons. But one has these silly notions: perhaps it was something to do with the fact that she'd brought me down in one piece before she died herself . . .

Medical Unit said: "Yo' *shore* yo' don' wanna check-up, Cap'n?"

Sure I was sure. Just stick a plaster on the cut over my left eye and forget it. Unless you happen to have a drink about your person, of course . . .?

Medical Unit hadn't. Neither had anyone else. And anyway, Capitan, alcohol is bad for shock . . .

Immigration said he was sorry to trouble me, but did I happen to have got my passport out with me? I started to say no — and then remembered that I *had* brought out my flight bag. Someone found it on the grass where I'd come to rest the first time, and Immigration found a clean corner of a page somewhere for a pocket-kit rubber stamp.

Air France thundered off Runway Ten in a sun-faded old Caravelle. Someone said was I ready to go to the terminal yet? I looked over at the tractor, taking up tension on the ropes in a chorus of shouted Spanish from the maintenance crew, and said sure, in just a few minutes. They seemed to understand.

The last rim of the sun hung on a mountain to the south-west for a moment, then disappeared. The light began to fade.

Then the FAA arrived. The Federal Aviation Administration.

He was a short tubby American, bespectacled and balding, and he'd been fetched away from his dinner. He squatted beside me as the cicadas and tree frogs began their night song with a few tentative pipings and chirrupings, sympathised with the way he reckoned I must be feeling, and asked me what happened.

"I had an engine fire."

A couple of crash wagons flicked their arc lights on, and the Beech was lit up in a harsh white glare in the gathering gloom. The aircraft tractor took up the strain in earnest, engine snarling steadily.

"Was that the same motor you'd shut down earlier on?"

I looked at him. His face was friendly and apologetic — but he knew his job all right. He must already have spoken to Air Traffic Control — which was very quick work indeed.

I knew what was coming, now.

The Beech stirred in the arc lights, then started to move with a slow, rending screech.

I said: "No. I shut down the starboard engine near Vieques and Culebra because it had a bad oil leak. Then the port engine went up when I was about five miles out. I re-started the starboard to get in."

The Beech groaned slowly across the concrete, a large dead animal being hauled away by a tribe of chattering cave-men.

"How d'you mean 'went up', sir?"

The nose lumped gently across the division between concrete and grass. The tractor eased the strain for a moment, then took up again.

"It sort of . . . exploded . . . and then caught fire."

"Ah . . . exploded?"

The tearing noises diminished as the Beech crawled tiredly on to the grass. A DC3 rumbled off Runway Ten and hauled itself away into the dusk.

"Yeah. Bang. Then the fire."

FAA took off his thick, round-lensed glasses and rubbed his eyes with a finger and thumb. Then he said carefully: "Well ... ah ... what d'you think might have caused the explosion, sir?"

Aviation in the Commonwealth of Puerto Rico is controlled by the United States FAA. One of their duties is to investigate accidents which happen within their airspace, regardless of where the aircraft concerned happen to be registered. This man could look at the backside of a Wasp Junior and draw his conclusions as well as I could — and he would, too. And when he did, he'd be wanting to know why I hadn't mentioned a few things before ...

Somebody in the towing crew yelled *"Pare! Pare!* Stop dere. She cleah o' de runway now." The Beech stopped moving, and the roar of the tractor engine died. The show was over.

I said wearily: "I think someone stuck a bomb on board."

*　　　*　　　*

It was full night by the time we got back to the terminal. I borrowed a Staff Only shower to scrape off the soot and sweat of disaster, Immigration went off on a clean clothes hunt with thirty of my dollars, and Port Authority and the FAA disappeared to start yelling into telephones. By seven thirty I was more or less respectable in new shirt, sandals and trousers, and more or less ready to face the world again. Immigration apologised for the fact that the shirt was a gimmick denim number with *'Property of St Croix Jail'* printed on the back in large letters, I said that didn't matter at all, and we chugged along to somebody-or-other's air-conditioned office for the official interrogation by the Port Authority, the FAA, and a fat sweaty Spanish-American *Policia* inspector.

I asked for a large Scotch and got it, and went through the story of the flight from beginning to end. A slightly expurgated version concerning my position when the first engine failed, of course — but apart from that, exactly what happened minus the background. When I'd finished, the inspector started in on the questions.

What made me think it was a bomb?

The fact that it went bang. And that the back of the engine was shattered.

Could not a mechanical malfunction have produced the same result?

No. An engine ingesting a major component might mangle itself pretty badly — but it wouldn't shatter the carburettor, the supercharger, *and* the magnetos all at once. FAA chipped in and said that he'd be making an examination and sending the *Policia* a copy. He didn't sound as if he thought the *Policia* would do much with it when they'd got it — and he was probably right. Unless there was some reason for thinking the bomb might have been shoved on board in their bailiwick, the *Policia* were just going to stick the reports in the files and forget about them. The crime had taken place in Antigua, and they weren't about to go trailing down *there* . . .

Did I have any idea who might have planted such a bomb?

I took a swig of Scotch and thought about Lashlee and Mariano and Heurtaux — all of whom would involve me if they got picked up.

No. No ideas.

Do you have any idea *why*, then, Señor?

I thought of eight million dollars worth of Krugerrands.

No, again.

After that, *Policia* started to lose interest. He asked if I had any enemies just to prove that *he* watched detective films, too, didn't believe me when I said none that I knew of, but didn't follow it up because he didn't really want to know about my enemies in Antigua anyway.

Then the interview was over. Nothing discovered, no evidence of any crime in Puerto Rico, no action recommended. Case opened and closed. *Hasta luego*, and don't slam the door behind you on the way out.

I stood up to go.

FAA took off his glasses and peered at me myopically. He asked: "Where will you be staying tonight, Mister Scott? Just in case we need to get in touch with you?"

Policia gave him a sharp look. The case was *closed*: he didn't want anybody poking the corpse around.

I said: "The El Convento." I couldn't afford it — not any more — but by now I was so broke that it wouldn't make any difference.

"You'll be there all evening will you, sir?"

I shook my head. "Nope. Just to sleep. If you want me this evening, try the bars in Old San Juan."

FAA smiled sympathetically and nodded. I walked out.

*   *   *

By eleven p.m. it was turning out to be a hot muggy night outside and a cold wet night inside. I'd soaked up Scotch and rum in every second bar in the old city, eaten a greasy chicken-and-French-fries in a stand-up café in the Plaza de Colón, and then started a second tour of the place to take in the bars I'd missed the first time round. I was getting smashed — or at least, my brain and legs were staggering round and I was sticky with running sweat, so I *supposed* I was getting smashed — but it wasn't doing any good. The cold ball of failure in my guts remained untouched and untouchable.

I was ruined. Ruined, ruined, ruined. Back to square one, just like eight years ago. Worse, in fact. Eight years ago I'd just been broke: now I was broke *and* thirty thousand Bee-wee dollars in debt.

I was also very, very lonely.

I ended up in The Bear Pit, in Calle Fortaleza. You can buy your way out of loneliness there, once you're drunk enough not to care about the money-look in the eyes of the girls. I hitched myself unsteadily on to a bar stool, ordered a double Scotch without the rocks to make sure I was drunk enough . . .

And that was where he found me. Agent Bob Morgan, CIA.

*   *   *

The first I knew of it was a hand landing on my right shoulder and a voice drawling: "Property of St Croix Jail, huh? Ah hope that ain't too prophetic, Mr Scott."

I cranked my eyeballs round, blinked in the dim reddish light, and recognised him. It was no thrill. I grunted: "Oh, it's you," and turned back to the bar. I wasn't quite *that* lonely.

But you don't brush off Your Friendly CIA Man that easily. The manual deals with that — page 742, para 3, sub-section (a): Approaching Unwilling Suspects In Bars. He pulled up a stool and perched beside me.

"You look like yo're havin' a bad time, Mr Scott."

I grunted again. It bounced straight off him.

"Here yuh had a bit of bad luck comin' in here today." He paused. "Or good luck, dependin' on how you look at it."

I was drunk enough to get hooked. I bleared at him. "*Good* luck?"

He gave me a small crinkly grin. "Sure. Yuh still alive, ain't yuh?"

"Big deal." I eyes-fronted again and nuzzled my Scotch. It seemed to have got used up.

"Let me get yuh the next one."

I shrugged. If I was stuck with him, he might as well buy the drinks. He skewered a passing barman with his eye, and we got served.

He said: "Health," and sipped. I gulped, then tugged a pack of Luckies out of my shirt pocket and even remembered to offer him one. He took it, and lit both from a thin book of matches.

After a bit, he said: "Ah been lookin' at yore airplane. You were right, yuh know. It was a bomb."

I wondered who'd told him about it — and then remembered FAA asking where I'd be tonight. I waved my glass and said: "I knew I was right, chum: I was there at the time." That produced no reaction at all, so after a moment I added: "What type, d'you know?"

He shook his head. "Nope. The full investigation might find out, but I didn't see anythin'. Ah'd say it was an amateur job, though."

"Oh?"

"Well — yuh still had the wing after it'd gone off, didn't yuh?"

True. I nodded sagely and blew smoke out of my nostrils.

He took a drink of whatever-it-was he was drinking, then said: "Your other engine was sabotaged, too: did yuh know that?"

I shook my head, which was a mistake. The bar carried on shaking after I'd stopped.

"No, I didn't. What did you find?"

"Loose connection on the feed pipe to the oil radiator. The locking wire was snipped through, and there were self-grip wrench marks on the gland nut."

I was tired of trying to sound surprised. I just waggled my head again — gently this time — and said "Oh."

"Yeah. Almost looks like somebody wanted yuh to go down, but also wanted yuh to report some kinda trouble first. So it

wouldn't look quite so suspicious as disapearin' just like that" —
he snapped his fingers — "with no word or anythin'."

Deductions in that class were a bit too much for a man in my
state of health at this time of night. I tried for it — but it opened
up to max continuous cruise and walked away from me. In lieu
of having any sensible contribution, I said: "I suppose *you* think
it was tied up with that smuggling you reckoned I was doing?"

His head moved slowly in the dimness. "Well . . . yeah. Ah
guess ah *do* kinda think it's gotta be somethin' like that."

"Well, it ain't." I tried to think of something a bit more convincing to add to that, but couldn't. "It ain't," I said again. Then
I sucked down more Scotch and frowned at my reflection in the
wall-to-wall mirror behind the bar. I seemed to be a little fuzzy
round the edges — but maybe it was just the mirror.

I realised that Morgan was talking again.

". . . to admit it kinda looks thataway." He held up a blunt,
square hand and started counting off on the fingers. "One —
you're there same place, same time when we pick up part of a
consignment that's said to've come from Antigua; two — you're
suddenly comin' in an' outa San Juan an' St Croix like a pinball;
three — someone bombs yore airplane an' tries to make it look like
an accident. Now put yourself in my position, Mr Scott: what
would *you* think?"

What *I* thought was that he'd been doing a bloody sight too
much thinking — but I didn't say it. He *did* sort of have
something, anyway.

*And he had something else, too — something that snagged in
my brain like a splinter you can feel but can't find. I tried to
reach through the whisky-fog and grab it . . .*

But it was gone.

I found I was blearing into the remains of my Scotch and
ignoring the expectant silence which was leaning on my ears.
Perhaps I ought to say something . . .

I said: "It's all circumstantial."

That intelligent observation rolled across the bar and thumped
on to the floor without advancing the cause at all. I emptied my
glass and had another go.

"Has it — " I took a hiccup-break — "has it occurred to you
that I might've been bombed 'cos someone *else* thought the same
way as you? That in the normal line of business I might've jus'

crossed someone's tracks by coincidence an' that's why I got bombed . . ."

I realised I was rambling — and also, that that was probably what Morgan wanted me to do. I shut up, and signalled the barman. He was fuzzy round the edges, too — but then you never did get a very good class of barman in The Bear Pit. Morgan let me buy him a second Bourbon on the rocks — which came up seven-eighths rocks with a thin layer of strato-bourbon at the bottom — and then sipped at it in silence while I tried to get enough brain cells on parade to continue The Case For The Defence. It wasn't a conspicuously successful exercise — but as it happened it didn't matter, because Morgan suddenly changed the subject. Maybe he thought I'd clam up if he kept prodding sensitive areas. Maybe he was right, too: clam up was certainly what I ought to have done.

"What're you gonna do now?" he asked.

"Get bloody drunk. What's it look like?"

"No — ah mean now you've lost yore plane. What you gonna do?"

I gave a slow shrug. "I dunno. I might try'n find whoever bombed it." *Careful, Scott.* "I dunno."

"You could get hurt doin' that. An' they ain't likely to buy you another one."

He was right there, all right. I just shrugged.

"You'll get the insurance on it though, huh?"

There was the rub. Or one of them, anyway. I blew a long, slow streamer of smoke and said quietly: "No, I won't. You don't get covered against sabotage if you're operating in the Caribbean. Not if you're insured with any company I can afford, anyway. The only thing they'll pay for's the runway lights I busted at the airport, and they'll probably argue for five years about that."

AND it was a dead cert that Harvey wouldn't be paying up either. Not after the gold-load had been pinched before I'd even taken off . . .

I managed not to say it.

Morgan was nodding slowly, as if I'd just explained something important. Well, maybe I had, come to think of it: maybe he'd thought I might be daft enough to put a bomb on my own aeroplane so I could collect the insurance . . .

Maybe. I didn't really think so, though.

"So what'll you do?" he asked again.

That was the $64,000 question — and I hadn't got 64 cents' worth of answer. I dropped the last inch of Lucky into an ashtray, swished the latest instalment of oblivion round my glass, and heard myself say quietly: "Just start running again, I guess."

The bitterness in my voice came across like a small thin bell.

"What d'you mean?" Morgan had his head turned towards me, watching my face in the dimness.

"Just that." The words were low and slow and seemed to be coming from a long way away, over all the distant horizons of the last eight years. "Just that. Start running away again. Find a new sleazy job in a new sleazy country. Try'n pay off my debts."

Maybe. Or maybe I've run out of new sleazy countries by now. Or perhaps out of the energy to move on and start again and face the same old defeat again . . .

I wiped at the hot sticky sweat on my face and tipped my drink down my throat. All the maybes of all the years . . .

I nodded, and waved at the barman again. Morgan paid. Then he said: "Is it as bad as all that? You're a very good pilot: that's well known around here, at least. Ah'da thought you'd get jobs easy."

I spread my hands on the bar, palms upwards. For a moment there seemed to be several pairs of them, then they wobbled and fused back into the standard-issue port and starboard.

"People might want these," I said slowly. "But they don't want the rest that goes with them. Big airlines don't want ex-cons, period — and small airlines don't want ex-cons who're going to attract attention from the authorities."

"That happens a lot?"

I cranked my head round and looked at him. "What made *you* pick on me?"

He nodded thoughtfully.

For a long moment, there was silence. I stuck my nose in my glass again and wondered how the hell I came to be confiding in the CIA. Morgan was probably running through a fast mental re-play of everything I'd said to see if he'd missed anything incriminating.

Then he said slowly: "Do they know about yore background in Antigua, Mr Scott?"

I went suddenly still and cold.

"Why? You gonna tell 'em?"

"No-o." He took one of my Luckies and lit it, watching me

through the smoke. "But it kind of occurs to me if they don't, it might make you a good target for blackmail."

I didn't say anything at all to that: just sat there looking back at him in the heat and the dimness, and wondering which part of the CIA manual had taught him to read minds. I knew the silence would make him think he'd struck oil — but I also knew that if I opened my mouth any more I'd probably only prove it. The Scott brain was in no condition for violent evasive action, not at this time of the bottle. Now it *was* time to clam up . . .

Morgan seemed to get the message. He drained his glass, slid off the stool, and reached into his trouser pocket. For a moment I thought I was going to get dragged out at gun-point — but all he did was produce a couple of quarters and drop them on the bar to show that CIA expense accounts *do* extend to tipping. I watched his hands, remembering the last time I'd seen him handle a coin . . .

And suddenly realised what it was that had been nagging at me. I said. "One l'il thing . . ." He stopped and looked back at me. I blinked back at him and waved what I hoped was a suitably drunken hand. It required no big act. "Jus' tell me somethin' . . . where d'you pick up your load o' Krugerran's? The ones you think I smuggled?"

He frowned in the dim light, trying to work out what I was getting at and whether the information came under the heading of State Secrets. Evidently it didn't, because after a moment he grunted "Caracas. Same time you were there."

I just nodded, and turned back to the bar. When I looked round again, he'd gone.

I sat on for another fifteen minutes, nuzzling my Scotch and listening to the answers clicking into place between my ears. At the end of it, I had the whole thing.

For the first time in my life, I was ready to kill someone in cold blood.

I walked back to the El Convento without weaving hardly at all.

*   *   *

It was a bad night. *Real* bad.

Jenny came to me.

It happened quite suddenly. One moment I was lying naked on the bed, drifting into a hot, shallow doze — and the next, I was walking along a footpath through a summer cornfield with

Jenny beside me. For a little while I told myself not to believe it, I was dreaming . . .

And then the longing won, and I did believe it.

The cold, harsh years melted away. I held her hand, and we walked slowly on together through the whispering corn. I felt warm, deep down and swelling inside where I'd long forgotten that you can feel warm. The scars of time, both inside and out, were no longer there. There was only the mellow sun and the warmth and scent and touch of Jenny by my side . . .

After a long time, we came to a little row of farm cottages. The second one of the four seemed somehow familiar. I looked at it for a moment, the rough red brick and the tiny garden facing the cornfield — and then, with a jolt, I remembered.

It was our home.

I said to Jenny: "Let's go home, darling" — but she just stopped and looked at me with gentle, awful compassion.

"We can't go home," she said quietly. "We haven't got a home any more. We haven't got anything."

Then she walked away.

I tried to follow her — but my feet were stuck in the ground. I struggled and struggled and shouted "Come back — I love you . . ."

But she was gone. The emptiness was like a big, cold room.

With terrible slowness, I turned back to look at our cottage. It wasn't there any more. Where it used to be was a ghastly, coffin-like block of flats. The cornfield was a housing estate.

Just the way it had all been when I came out of prison.

I shuddered back to consciousness and a terrible, aching sense of loss. For a period that may have been five minutes or an hour I ran desperately through the corridors of my mind, searching for the room that held the memories that made the dreams . . .

But I couldn't find it. I never can.

18

THE NEXT DAY was Sunday, which gave most of the world's airlines an excuse for not going to Antigua. I got my hangover out to the airport just before noon after struggling my way through the accident report for the FAA — and then found that those lines who *did* have anything going down south were all booked solid. I tried all the relevant desks twice over, went and had a king-sized hamburger that gave me a king-sized bellyache to match, then mooched back to the desks again in the hope of picking up a cancellation.

There was no joy at Pan Am or Eastern — but then I bumped into a LIAT pilot I knew, and talked my way into the jump-seat of the afternoon island-hopper under the irritated glare of a desk clerk who'd just told me for the third time that the kite was full. We taxied out past the forlorn remains of the Beech, and I spent the rest of the flight answering questions about the crash as the Avro 748 whined through the burning windless sky from San Juan to St Maarten, and from there to Coolidge. The co-pilot greased the Avro on to the runway at four thirty in the afternoon, and I nearly dislocated my neck squinting out of the windscreen at the aircraft park as we taxied in.

Lashlee's Apache was sitting alongside my Cherokee, shimmering in the heat.

Five minutes later I pasted the Mark One Innocent Look on the front of my head, and walked into Customs and Immigration along with the rest of the passengers.

The innocent look was a waste of time. Inspector de Lima, who was waiting for me in the Customs hall, didn't even notice it.

* * *

This time, we ended up in the VIP lounge at the end of the terminal concourse. I was glad about that: I figured it meant that de Lima was only rattling my cage on general suspicion rather than anything definite. If he'd really thought he had something on me he'd have marched me off to the airport cop-shop so quickly my feet wouldn't have touched the ground.

I was right, too. Almost, anyway.

We sat down in a couple of imitation-leather armchairs — which was fair enough: we were only imitation-VIPs — and de Lima fished out a notebook and pen and parked them symmetrically on a small coffee table between us. Then he settled his watchful brown eyes on my face, and got under way.

"I hear yo' take off wid a bomb on yo' aircraf' yes'day, Missah Scott?"

"Yeah. I was going to come and see you about it." I had been, too: it would've looked bloody odd if I hadn't started screaming for the cops at *some* point.

De Lima said woodenly: "Yessuh. I sho' yo' were. Now — d'yo' have any idea who might have done it?"

"No. None. I'm hoping you might be able to find out. *If* you can spare the time from doing Customs' job for them, of course."

That got the reaction I'd expected, which was nothing at all. He just said calmly: "Quite so, suh. D'yo' have any idea *why* it was done?"

"No."

He nodded, as if he hadn't expected anything else. Well, he probably hadn't. Then he said: "What were yo' carryin', suh? As cargo?"

"A load of Martinique dolls for the Coral Reef shops."

"Did yo' see them yo'self?"

"No. I only saw the crates. But the bomb wasn't in there, if that's what you're thinking. It was behind the left engine."

"Yessuh, I know that." He made a few notes, then looked up at me again and said: "I wan' know yo' movements fo' the las' three days, suh. Ev'rythin' yo' done."

I shrugged, and gave him my movements for the last three days. Slightly edited, of course. It took about twenty minutes. At the end of it he finished writing in his notebook, thought for a minute — and then said: "What was the purpose of yo' trip to San Juan on Friday night, suh?"

That was the Cherokee flight. I began to get a hollow feeling in my stomach.

"That was a private trip. I got a girl friend there, and I had to see someone on business on Saturday morning."

De Lima flipped back a few pages in his book. "Yo' clear outbound to Sain' Kitts, suh. Why yo' do that?"

Christ. Trying to keep my voice casual, I said: "I didn't think of going to Puerto Rico that night until I was airborne. I only started off with the idea of doing some instrument flying practice between here and St Kitts. You get rusty on that in this part of the world, and there was some genuine bad weather that night."

It sounded bloody thin to me — and it seemed to sound bloody thin to de Lima, too. The sad brown eyes stared at me suspiciously.

"Yo' had a student, then?"

I felt perspiration leaking out on my temples. "No. There was a guy going to come, but some of his friends turned up at the last moment and he backed out."

"What was his name?"

He'd have got that from the general declarations . . .

"Mariano. Alvaro Mariano. Tourist. With a group of guys who flew down here in an Apache."

De Lima nodded. Then: "Why din' yo take his name off the gen'al declarations when he decide not to come?"

"It was taken off — wasn't it? Alvaro said he'd drop in there on his way out of the airport, to save me the trip to the terminal. Didn't the bugger do it?"

The brown eyes bored into mine. "No," he said slowly. "He didn't."

I mumbled something apologetic. There was a pause, during which de Lima wrote a few more things in his notebook.

Then, almost conversationally, he asked: "What *are* yo' smugglin' this time, Missah Scott?"

*   *   *

He's trying to rattle you, chum. That's all — he's just trying to rattle you . . .

He was bloody well succeeding, too.

I stared at him, feeling the Mark One Innocent Look beginning to curl at the edges. It was that '*this time*' bit I didn't like.

"I've told you before — I'm not smuggling any-bloody-thing.

You've already had my aeroplanes torn apart once without getting anywhere: what the hell more d'you want?"

That earned me a small sad man-of-the-world smile with matching shrug. "I know yo' weren't carryin' anythin' *then*," he said. "But I still sho' yo' bin carryin' somethin', somewhere, all right."

"Like what?"

He shrugged again. "I don' know. Yet." The smile faded out and the eyes got watchful again. "It . . . ah . . . wouldn't be the firs' time, suh, would it?"

I got that still, hollow feeling again. From somewhere a long way off I heard myself say: "Meaning . . . ?"

"I think yo' know what I mean, suh." His voice was cold and official, now. "We bin . . . checkin' on yo'. Yo' record come in from Englan' yes'day. Four year in prison fo' flyin' illegal entrants an' heroin . . . " He let the sentence hang in the air.

I took a slow, deep breath. I didn't want to hear the rest — but you have to *know* . . .

"I suppose you . . . the police . . . 'll be objecting to my work permit?"

He nodded. Just once. The broad black face was totally expressionless.

And that was it.

Out.

It hurt. Even though I'd been planning to leave anyway, it hurt. You don't get used to it.

*　　　*　　　*

Forty minutes later I ground the Moke up the steeply sloping zig-zag drive-way to Harvey Bouvier's place on Martin Hill, pulled up alongside the scarlet Maverick, and switched off the engine. The old grey stone plantation house, sitting in lofty arrogance on its hillside miles from anywhere, was very quiet and still in the glaring late afternoon heat. With the tradewinds dead, even the Royal palms and Australian pines in the garden hung still and motionless, waiting for something to happen.

I pulled out the Smith & Wesson, checked the load and cocked it, and walked up the path towards the front door.

It was wide open.

For a moment, I hesitated. A wide open door can mean a lot of things — among them, a party such as Sherman waiting behind it ready to bounce a double-decker bus off your skull as you walk in. I slowed up my approach and thought quickly about going round the back of the house or . . .

Then I decided the hell with it: if they'd already seen me coming there was nothing to stop them saying it with buses wherever I went in — and with the front door, at least *I* knew where *they'd* be.

Maybe, anyway.

I kept walking until I was three or four feet away — and then dived in over the step like a rugby player going for his fourth broken nose. I hit the floor with a meaty thump and had myself jackknifed round and waving the revolver at the space behind the open door while I was still sliding . . .

There was nobody there. I rolled over fast and whipped the gun round the rest of the room . . .

And there was nobody anywhere. The place was as empty as a politician's head.

After a moment, I stood up. Wondered whether to feel silly or frightened, and settled for frightened. My nerves were strung out like a tight wire: empty houses that might not be empty houses do that to me.

I seemed to be in the main living room. There were chairs and sofas scattered about, a glass-topped table on a white driftwood base in the middle of the floor, and a crescent-shaped bar up against one wall. A hi-fi stereo like an Apollo control panel occupied most of another wall.

And then you met the paintings.

I'd known Harvey was a self-styled connoisseur of Haitian art — but what I hadn't known, although I might have guessed, was that he collected pictures the way some people collect stamps: by the carpet-bombing method. *And* he'd hung them all, too: he would, of course. There must have been thirty or forty of them in that room: the walls were covered in them from floor to ceiling. They were mainly tribal scenes in brilliant prime colours, primitive and powerful. On their own some of them might have been good — but all crowded up together like that, they hit you like an explosion in a paint factory. You could even smell them — a sort of musty mixture of heat and paint and canvas, overlaid by the usual white-man's-house tang of mosquito coils.

I dragged my eyes away and got back to the job in hand. There were two doorways off the left-hand side of the room, and an archway alongside the bar on the right.

The doorways first, then . . .

Keeping close to the nearest wall and doing my best to look in all directions at once, I walked over to them. The first one was unlatched, and open a few inches. I took a deep breath — and suddenly whanged it all the way open and jumped into the room.

It was the kitchen. And unless someone was hiding in the deep-freeze, it was empty.

So was the room next to it, which was a bathroom.

I stood with my back to the shower and looked out over the living room again, hearing my breath coming in quick ragged gasps in the heavy silence. My knees were shaking, and my hands and face were damp with sweat. The quietness was solid and tangible, creeping up behind me and running ghostly fingers down my spine . . .

Cool it, Scott. Just cool it . . .

I dragged a forearm over my face, shifted the gun to my left hand while I wiped the right on my trousers — and then walked quietly across the room to the archway. When I got there I crouched down beside the bar — no point in presenting a head at head-height when you don't have to — and poked a cautious eye round the wall.

Empty again.

I stood up and looked around. It was sort of large, dim, window-less anteroom. Roughly D-shaped, with four doors in the curving wall opposite me which probably led to bedrooms or some such. As a piece of house design it would have mopped up the Ideal Home booby prize for wasted space any day — but then those old-time plantation owners hadn't been paying any ten-bucks-a-foot for building land when this place was put together. *And* they hadn't been humping those big stone blocks around themselves, either : if you wanted a bigger room back then you just mixed yourself another rum punch and whistled up a few more slaves out of the sugar fields . . .

Come on, man — don't just stand here giving yourself bloody history lessons . . .

I knew why I was hesitating, though : I was hesitating because I didn't want to start opening those four doors. You can get yourself killed doing things like that. I could feel the sweat going clammy on my face . . .

I strode forward suddenly and flung open the first door on the left.

It was an office. An untidy mass of papers overflowed off a large old desk on to the floor . . .

But that was all. No people.

The silence breathed down my neck again.

The next room was a bedroom — a guest bedroom, by the look of it. It contained a double bed, a white-wood suite, and the deserted, impersonal atmosphere that guest bedrooms assume when there aren't any guests. I walked round the bed to make sure there was no-one playing Red Indians on the other side of it, and arrived at a communicating door which presumably led to the next room along. It wasn't the way I'd intended to go, but there was no point in taking a long walk when a short one would do. I yanked it open and jumped into the room in the approved manner . . .

And something small and hard rammed into my back while a voice bawled "Stand perfectly still!"

*   *   *

I skidded to a halt — or at least, I did a short vertical take-off out of pure shock and *then* skidded to a halt. For a few timeless seconds I just listened to the blood pounding in my ears and waiting for the bang . . .

And then the voice said: "Drop the gun." A guttural accent.

"It's cocked," I told him quickly. "If I drop it, it might go off."

It was true, too — I wasn't trying to be clever. If it went off as it hit the floor the bullet might get either of us — but much more importantly, it might also startle the party behind me into doing something hasty. Such as blowing my spine out through the front of my stomach.

There was a brief pause while he thought about it. I went on keeping still. Then: "Very well: take it by the thumb ant forefinger off the left hant, and hold it out in front of you."

I did what he said. *Exactly* what he said. Ended up holding the Smith & Wesson out at arm's length like a guy carrying a bad smell. The small hard pressure on my spine disappeared, and there was a slight creak of floorboards as the man stepped back.

"Now move forvard one pace, ant put it down on the bed."

I hadn't even noticed the bed before — which was pretty un-observant of me, considering that it was a water-bed the size of a young swimming pool and it was all of two paces in front of me. Perhaps I'd been a little preoccupied. I stepped forward slowly, placed the gun on the yellow coverlet, and then stepped back again. The surface of the bed dented and bounced gently under the weight of it, and little ripples chased themselves away across the cover.

A new voice, harsh and metallic and coming from somewhere off to my left, said: "Now walk two paces this way."

I recognised that voice. I turned my head for the first time since coming into the room — and I was right.

Hans-Jürgen Ruchter. In person.

He was standing in the corner of the room looking very German-military in well-tailored khaki shirt and slacks — and even more military in the way he was pointing a big black revolver at me. None of your waving-vaguely-from-the-hip for him — he was parked sideways-on and sighting at me at arm's length, like a man in a shooting gallery. The gun was pointing rock-steady at my chest — head shots are strictly Hollywood when your target might be about to do something sudden — and the cold blue eyes stared at me unwinkingly over the sights. He looked weirdly out of place against the background of Haitian paintings and voodoo masks scattered over the walls — but it didn't stop him looking thoroughly lethal with it.

I walked towards him — just two paces, like he'd said — and then stopped again.

The gun-in-the-back merchant stepped into my field of vision for the first time — and I recognised him, too. He was the character who'd been piloting the rubber dingy the night Harvey and I went to the *Krakatoa*. Middle-aged, well built, good Aryan stock, and the general air of being the man who whistled up the firing squad when the *Oberführer* gave the word. He was carrying a massive, cannon-like Luger: maybe it brought him happy memories of the good old Wehrmacht days. He dropped it into a holster strapped to the right side of his chest under an open shirt, then picked up the Smith & Wesson off the bed. After peering at it for a moment he held the hammer with his left hand, pulled the trigger, and let the firing pin down gently. Then he dropped it into his hip pocket, fished under the shirt again, and went back to giving me the wooden look over the top of the good old Fatherland Equaliser.

The atmosphere in the room seemed to become a little easier — for everyone except me, anyway. Ruchter lowered his revolver to waist level and said coldly: "What are you doing here, Scott?"

I cleared my throat. "The same as you, I expect. Looking for Harvey Bouvier."

"Why?"

I leaned back against a natural-bamboo dressing table and said: "He tried to kill me by sticking a bomb on one of my aeroplanes. So I'm sort of planning on blowing his head off."

19

IF I'D BEEN looking for big reactions, I'd have been disappointed. Ruchter's killer-blue eyes narrowed a few millimetres, but apart from that he didn't move a muscle. The faithful *feldwebel* did likewise — but he probably only had one expression anyway.

"Explain this." It was an order, hard and flat.

I shrugged, reached up to my shirt pockets — gently, so as not to excite them — and said: "I'm going to smoke." Ruchter's mouth tightened into a thin, hard line — but I took my time about hauling a Lucky out of the crumpled pack and lighting it. Guns or no guns, I'd been ordered around quite enough just lately . . .

"Now explain!"

I blew smoke. "I will in a moment — but first, I've got a question. Did you have Harvey take any of your Krugerrands down south, to Caracas, when he was operating with Cas McGrath?"

Ruchter hesitated a moment, fury smouldering in his ice-blue glare. Then: "No. Everything is to be taken to Puerto Rico."

I nodded slowly. That was all I needed. The final proof.

"In that case," I told him, "I've got some bad news for you. Harvey pinched one or more of your loads of coins and sold them in Caracas — and now he's skipped."

"What do you mean?"

I perched my backside on the dressing table and said: "He and McGrath were taking you for a ride, chum. They flogged a load or two of your coins in Caracas, and they probably had some plan for covering up the discrepancy by staging a fake accident or something near the end of the job. Then McGrath got wiped out halfway through — and that put Harvey in a spot. He figured — quite rightly, if it interests you — that I wouldn't wear the sort of double-cross he'd been working with McGrath, so then he was faced with the problem of being several thousand coins short in the final reckoning. His answer to that was to stick a bomb on board my Beech when I was supposed to be carrying the last load. I imagine the idea was that I'd disappear into the sea, and he'd come to you with a sad tale about how I'd been sabotaged by the Cubans and eight or nine thousand Krugerrands had gone down with me. It nearly . . ."

"Stop!" Ruchter's voice was a harsh parade-ground bark. I stopped. He took a breath to say something, changed his mind for a moment, and finally came up with: "Why should Bouvier tell me you had been sabotaged by . . . ah . . . *Cuban* interests?"

For a few seconds I just stared at him with my mouth open — and then the penny dropped. The last time Ruchter had seen me I hadn't known anything about anything — and if all his news since then had been coming through Harvey he was probably under the impression that this happy state of affairs still existed. In which case my casually mentioning the Cubans must have come as a nasty shock — so that now he was fishing, trying to find out how much I *did* know. He probably even thought he was being subtle about it . . .

In spite of the guns, I grinned at him. If he was that far behind the times this was going to be his big evening for nasty shocks . . .

"What you really mean," I said deliberately, "is how do *I* know about the Cubans?"

That produced the usual reaction — nothing — so I let him have it with drums and percussion, ticking off the points on my fingers.

"Well — for one thing, I know about the deal you did with the Cubans over Isla Bealta. *And* how much you got paid for it. *And* I know who's chasing the money right now — probably a lot better than you do. How's that for a start?"

It wasn't bad. The Krupp-steel face didn't move — but the gun jerked and his eyes slitted down into twin chips of light blue ice. I could hear him breathing heavily in the quiet heat.

Maybe he didn't like people knowing that much about him.

After a short, crackling pause he said: "How did you . . . acquire . . . this information?"

I sucked on the Lucky and blew more smoke. "Oh — it just sort of filtered in over the last few days. The . . . er . . . people representing the Cuban interest gave me some of it, and the CIA supplied the rest."

That hit him amidships, all right. The heavy breathing misfired badly a couple of times — and then he blared: "You have had contact with the CIA?"

I grinned again: it made a change to see someone else getting rattled. Especially *this* someone else . . .

"Yep. I've had a busy few days. I've been searched by the CIA in San Juan and the Customs and cops here, chased all over the show by a guy called Lashlee and two other thugs, and finally bombed by our mutual friend Harvey Bouvier. I suppose you haven't heard anything about any of it?"

I needn't have asked. He was staring at me as if I'd grown two heads on parade.

"No." His voice was slow and harsh. "This was . . . not my information."

I nodded. "I just bet it wasn't. Harvey told you everything was hunky-dory, I suppose? No problems, Scott having a lovely time, wish you were here. Right?"

He made more deep-breathing noises for a moment. Then, slowly: "I was not informed there were . . . difficulties."

I resisted the impulse to let go an hysterical laugh, and just nodded again. It made sense: Harvey wouldn't have wanted Ruchter getting cold feet, stopping the smuggling-runs, and asking for his gold back . . .

I said: "I'll also bet you were surprised as hell when you switched on the news this morning and heard I'd crashed in San Juan. So you come rushing up here hot foot to ask Harvey what-the-hell — only to find Harvey isn't around to be asked anything. Right again?"

There was a tense little hush. I was right, all right — but he wasn't ready to say so. Not yet. The killer eyes bored into my skull for a long moment, while the revolver went on looking at my middle.

Then he said metallically: "Tell me exactly what has happened since I last saw you."

So I told him. Just the straight facts. It took ten minutes. His eyes never left my face the whole time, and the two guns never wavered from my chest. When I'd finished there was a long thoughtful silence while he digested it all.

Then he said: "How do you know that Bouvier has been selling my gold in Venezuela?"

*　　　*　　　*

I stared out of the window for a moment, trying to get it all straight in my mind. The daylight was fading fast, and the sky to the west was orange and yellow with sunset. Somewhere in the garden the first tree-frog of the evening cranked itself up with the familiar *thwee-thwee, thwee-thwee* of the tropics. The bedroom was very hot and still.

"In the end," I said slowly, "it was the CIA agent, Morgan, who gave it to me. He said I'd been in the same place at the same time that they'd picked up a consignment of Krugerrands which was said to've come from Antigua — and when I asked him point-blank, he told me the place was Caracas."

Ruchter frowned. "That may not have been true."

I waggled my head from side to side. "It was true, all right. Remember that Morgan had my aeroplane searched when I was coming *out* of San Juan — not when I was going in. He thought I was picking up the coins in Puerto Rico and taking them down south: he told me that himself. It never occurred to him that I might be bringing them the other way, *into* Puerto Rico — and it never occurred to me to wonder why he hadn't thought of that. The reason, of course, was that he'd picked up a load, or part of a load, in Caracas: he *knew* the stuff was travelling south. Or thought he did, anyway. Maybe I should have worked it out then — after all, *I* knew he'd come up from Maiquetia two days before, because he'd been on the search for 32 Romeo — but I didn't. I was too busy worrying about whether Harvey's outfit in San Juan had sprung a leak."

Ruchter was looking like a bronze statue of someone thinking hard. I stopped to let him catch up. When he did, he said: "Where is Maiquetia?"

"It's the civil airport of Caracas."

He gave a small jerk of a nod. Then: "How do you think the CIA traced my coins in Caracas?"

I shrugged. I was beginning to want a drink. "I don't know. Probably through whoever-it-was that Harvey — or, more likely, Larry Hawkins — sold them to. Harvey was careless there:

maybe he thought Caracas was far enough away so nobody'd be looking hard. It was a bad mistake, 'cos he not only sold 'em too soon, before the heat had died down, but he also let it out that they'd come from Antigua. That's how the CIA got on to me — or that and my record, anyway — and it's also where Lashlee picked up his lead "

"How are you sure of that?"

I shrugged, pulled out the pack of Luckies again, and got one lit. Then I said: "Well, I'm not actually *sure* of it: I mean, I can't prove it or anything like that. But it all adds up. When I was questioning Mariano in the Cherokee he told me they'd got hold of a load of coins 'at the other end' and found out that they'd come from Antigua. At the time I assumed that 'the other end' meant San Juan, and didn't think to question it. But it wasn't San Juan at all — it was bloody Caracas. *That* way, it makes sense. They caught up with Harvey's load in Caracas just like the CIA did, checked to see who'd been in from Antigua at the relevant time — and found that McGrath and me had *both* been in. That was a bit of bad luck for me: I happened to go in there with a cargo at roughly the same time that McGrath pitched up with the Krugerrands. I remember seeing him land as I went out. So Lashlee knew it had to be me or McGrath — and with McGrath rubbed out, that just left me."

I stopped for thinking-space, took a drag on the Lucky, and then went on. "If you want more confirmation, there was Lashlee turning round and flying south after I didn't turn up at St Kitts that night. If he'd asked the controller he'd'd've been told I'd gone north to San Juan — but he was so sure I'd head *south* down the islands for Caracas that he didn't even bother to check it: either that or he left St Kitts before I called 'em up to change my flight plan. Anyway, he went boring off down south after me, probably expecting to hear me on the radio and catch up with me when I stopped for fuel. It must have surprised the hell out of him when he got all the way down to St Lucia without coming across me — and by that time, he'd be running into a fuel problem himself. So he had to lob into St Lucia and wait 'til morning to get topped up, then go back to St Kitts and start picking up the trail again there."

Ruchter went silent for another thought-break, and I blew smoke at the window. Beyond the jalousy-slats the Technicolor sky was fading into an oyster-blue sunset. The crickets and tree frogs were settling down to the night's work in earnest as the daylight faded: their steady whistling and chirruping drifted in through the mosquito screen.

Ruchter said something fast in German, and the Luger-specialist came to life. For a second or two I thought I was going to get shot — but all he did was reach across the water-bed and pull the light-switch cord. A medium-dim light came over the bed along with dark red bulbs in some of the voodoo masks. I relaxed, nerves tingling. Getting jumpy in your old age, Scott . . .

Ruchter said suddenly: "You are suggesting that this man Lashlee was responsible for the sabotage of McGrath's aircraft?"

I nodded.

"Why should he do this? I do not see a reason. McGrath would have been more useful to him alive."

I nodded again. "Right. I got the impression from Mariano that there was a mistake there. The Black Power boys here did the job, and they got their orders wrong or got carried away with the excitement of the thing or something. Lashlee didn't want McGrath killed at all — he just wanted him stopped, until he could get here himself. He wanted me stopped as well, come to that, but I wasn't on the island at the time."

"Why the Black Power?" Ruchter demanded. "Why should the Black Power do anything for this man?"

I blew smoke and said: "The Black Power's getting guns and other aid from Cuba. I suppose they had instructions to come to the aid of the party if they were needed."

Ruchter nodded one of his jerky nods and went quiet, probably trying to digest the idea of people doing things for something other than money. I dropped the end of the Lucky and trod on it, and tried to forget how much I wanted a drink. The daylight had almost fizzled out now, leaving the dim-lit room to close in around us. The voodoo masks glowed eerily on the walls, touching everything near them with a dull, blood-coloured tinge. In another time and place they might have looked overdone or just plain ridiculous — but here and now, in an old plantation house in the trilling heat of the West Indian twilight, they were sinister as a Black Mass. The clean-cut, solidly Teutonic figures of Ruchter and his one-man artillery division looked more incongruous than ever. The only thing that really fitted in was the tangible menace of the two guns: the men who'd used those masks, the voodoo priests of old Haiti, would have understood those ...

Ruchter said: "How are you sure that Bouvier sabotaged your aircraft? Why could it not have been Lashlee who was responsible?"

I stirred my backside into a more comfortable position against the dressing table. "For a while, I thought they were," I said. "But after Morgan told me about the Krugerrands in Caracas I started thinking in terms of Harvey having done it — and then it all clicked. He always did have the best chance: he was lurking around the Beech all yesterday morning and most of the previous night, whereas Lashlee was tied up chasing me all over the Caribbean."

Ruchter made a small gesture with his revolver. "This man Mariano was on Antigua. Or Lashlee could have instructed his ... ah ... associates here to place the bomb."

"True enough — but what they wouldn't have known was when to set the explosion for. Harvey was the only person who knew my take-off time — and I even told him my flight time and left him alone with the aeroplane just before departure. I couldn't have been more bloody helpful if I'd tried."

Ruchter frowned. "You are assuming that this device was operated by a time mechanism. If it had been activated in some other way it may not have needed priming before the flight."

I shrugged, dug out another cigarette, and said: "I think it must have been timed. It couldn't have been detonated by a thermo-couple or an altitude-sensitive capsule, or it would've gone off long before it did. And it wasn't actuated by any of the control systems, 'cos I wasn't using anything when it blew. So — that just leaves a time-bomb device. *And* it'd be the easiest to arrange, too: Harvey probably knocked up something with an alarm clock and a couple of sticks of dynamite — it's easier than you'd think, if you know what you're doing. Then he stuck it in the top of the wheel-well, and set it so it'd go up about two-thirds of the way through the journey. That way there'd be time for the oil trouble to come up on the other engine, and for me to report it, so that when I disappeared it wouldn't look quite so suspicious. It damn near worked, too: I only got away with it because I made a mistake and gave him the Cherokee's flight time instead of the Beech's. The Beech was faster, so I was practically on top of San Juan airport when the bomb went off.

If it hadn't've been for that I'd've been a goner: I'd never have pulled off a ditching with the kite in that state."

I shuddered, remembering how near I'd come to not pulling off the landing at the airport, either. Then I said: "So when Harvey got the news that I'd survived, he got the hell out. He's probably in Timbuctoo by now."

Ruchter was back to frowning again. "You mean Bouvier has left because of you?"

I stuck the Lucky in my mouth, lit it, and blew smoke at the window. It was full dark outside, now.

I said: "Maybe a bit because of me — but mostly, he'd be worried about you. He was going to tell you that last load of Krugerrands went down in the sea along with poor old Bill Scott, remember? So when poor old Bill Scott didn't go into the sea, he was buggered. It was going to come out that there weren't any Krugerrands on board on that flight — and then *you* were going to want to know where they'd got to."

Ruchter's eyes ranged on me like a pair of gunsights. He said harshly: "You are certain there was nothing on board the aircraft?"

"Bloody right, I'm certain. I looked myself — and later on that CIA man looked, too. If there'd been a sniff of a Krugerrand I wouldn't be talking to you now: I'd be in jug."

That seemed to convince him. He absorbed it for a while, then said slowly: "Bouvier told me that you were carrying the final consignment yesterday. There were still approximately 9,000 coins outstanding at that time. They are not . . . where they were hidden here."

I nodded, blew more smoke, and said: "There you are, then, McGrath took two loads north for you — and 9,000 of them south for Harvey."

We had a bit more communal gloom while Ruchter adjusted to that and I did a bit of thinking. Then I added: "You'll probably find half of those 9,000 in Caracas — unless Lashlee or the CIA've collared them — and the other half at the bottom of the sea somewhere."

The killer eyes snapped back to attention. "Explain this."

I waved the cigarette and said: "I'm only guessing, but I reckon McGrath would've shifted 9,000 coins in two loads rather than one. I'm thinking of the weight and volume: 9,000 coins would weigh somewhere around 700 lb — the same as four-and-a-half people — and make a load about a foot by a foot by twenty-one inches. I don't know much about Twin Commanches — but remembering the problems I had with weight and stowage space, I shouldn't think he'd have got all that lot in in one go. It's a hell of a job finding a space to shove that sort of load which is well hidden, strong enough to take the weight, and near enough the centre of gravity. So I think he'd have shifted that lot in two trips: the first load got there — and I'd guess the second was on board when he went down. He was on his way to Maiquetia again on that trip, remember — the US Coastguard told me that — *and* he had Larry Hawkins with him. That night on your yacht Harvey told us they were carrying woodwork and things for the shops — but Harvey hasn't *got* a bloody shop in Venezuela. I should have realised that at the time, but I didn't, of course." I took a deep swig of cigarette smoke and tried not to remind myself that if I *had* realised it I might still have two aeroplanes and a business. "Anyway, that's what I reckon happened."

Ruchter nodded, very slowly, but didn't say anything. The piercing blue eyes were still on my face — but they weren't seeing me. They were looking straight through me and on into some infinite distance beyond. Maybe he was saying goodbye to 9,000 Krugerrands in his own private way: I wouldn't know how a man goes about that.

I let the silence build up for a while — and then coughed and said: "Er — I don't like to mention it at a time like this, but you still owe me some money."

That fetched him away from the Last Rites, all right. His eyes narrowed into the familiar icy stare, and his voice narrowed with them.

"What do you mean?"

"Harvey didn't pay me for the last two trips," I said. "Or at least, he only paid about $2,500, which I sort of prized out of him. So — you still owe me $17,500. I made three trips as per contract: it wasn't my fault there was nothing on board the last one."

There was a short, incredulous hush. Then Ruchter said coldly: "This is not my concern. Your agreement was with Bouvier, not with me."

"Bollocks!" It wasn't the moment to get angry — not standing on the wrong end of two pistols — but I got angry anyway.

"Both of you bastards blackmailed me, both of you hired me — so now you fuckin' well pay me!"

The wrong thing to say, of course.

For an instant, Ruchter just froze. The glittering eyes drilled into my skull, and there was a silence you could reach out and touch. It seemed to go on for a very long time — and when he finally spoke, his voice was hard and metallic and utterly menacing.

"Are you . . . attempting to blackmail me, Scott?"

I got a sudden hollow feeling in my stomach. I hadn't been, actually — but I could see how he'd got the idea. I had enough on him to get him extradited by the Yanks from practically any country in the world, and here I was asking for money . . .

Without waiting for me to reply, he seemed to come to some sort of conclusion about it. He snapped out something in German — and the *Wehrmacht* on my right raised his Luger. For a paralysing split-second I realised what the conclusion was . . .

Then there was a colossal ear-numbing *CRASH* — and the Luger expert dropped his gun, took one dancing step sideways, and thumped down heavily on the bed.

20

FOR A FEW micro-seconds the *bang* and the sudden reek of cordite held the whole world frozen in shock.

Then everything happened at once.

As soon as I realised it wasn't me who'd been shot I dived for the floor, landing on something hard that ground into my ribs. Ruchter leapt for the communicating door where the shot had come from — and tripped over me as I dropped. He flailed, fetched up against the wall with a soundless wallop — and then he was twisting convulsively and shooting into the doorway. He fired four or five rounds in as many seconds, the heavy revolver bucking and flashing in his outstretched hand and the crashing explosions fusing into one gigantic thunder in the confined space. Then he stopped — and over the woolly ringing in my ears I heard a thin screaming noise and a collection of distant thumpings as if someone was leaving at emergency over-boost.

Ruchter started to move. I did likewise — although I didn't know where the hell I was moving *to* — and reached my knees before I suddenly realise what it was that had been digging into my chest. I scrabbled desperately, got my left hand on it . . .

And then heard a tiny, almost insignificant *cli-click*, very close to my head. I looked up — and froze.

Ruchter was towering over me with the revolver pointing straight down into my face. His thumb was just leaving the hammer after cocking it.

I heard myself say quickly, ridiculously, without thinking: "That's your last round: if you fire it, you'll have to re-load."

Incredibly, it stopped him. Only for a split-second, while I stared into the yawning barrel and the black holes of the empty chambers — but it was enough.

Someone giggled.

The shock couldn't have been greater if the Luton Girls' Choir had walked in on a rousing chorus of 'God Save The Queen'. Ruchter's head snapped round as if he'd been slapped — and so did mine, in spite of the fact that there were many more profitable things I might've been doing.

René Heurtaux was standing on the other side of the water-bed, just inside the main bedroom door.

He was still wearing the dark glasses and the green felt hat, and he was cradling a sub-machine gun in his arms. In the eerie red light of the voodoo masks he was pure Tonton Macoute — black, bestial, and deadly. His thick lips were drawn back in a sneering grin.

I thought stupidly *they followed me here*.

Ruchter swung the revolver.

Heurtaux shot him.

He fired in a scything blast, sweeping our end of the room at chest-height. The roar of the gun was fantastic, the concussion walloping on my eardrums. Chips of stone and plaster puffed out of the wall behind me, lit up in the flickering yellow glare of the muzzle-flash. For a moment Ruchter seemed to stand in the gale — and then he was picked up and slammed backwards into the dressing table. For an instant the machine gun bullets pinned him there, shaking him — and then his chest disappeared in an explosion of scarlet, and the back of his head blew out as he took a few rounds in the face.

The firing stopped. The body flopped down with a tumbling thump. The pistol went off as it hit the floor, but after the blare of the machine gun the shot was an innocent-sounding *thock*.

Heurtaux giggled again in the thundering silence.

I knelt where I was, looking over the bed in full view and wondering in stupid slow-motion why I was still alive.

Then I found out.

Heurtaux was smiling through the drifting gunsmoke — the stretched, tooth-filled leer of a psychopath caught up in an orgasm of killing. The sunglasses watched me with an empty blank stare, anonymous and terrifying. The man was a natural killer — he was *enjoying* keeping me alive for another few seconds or minutes.

He wanted to see me grovel and beg and then finally disintegrate under a tiny pressure from his finger . . .

My knees turned to chewed string underneath me — but I went on looking straight at the flat, vicious face. That way, I might live a few seconds longer while he thought of ways to make me cower and cringe . . .

Mariano came into the room behind him. He was holding his right arm in his left, and there was blood dripping from his fingers. He leaned against the wall and breathed heavily: he looked unhappy about something.

Heurtaux glanced at him quickly, then went back to watching me. The smoking muzzle of the machine gun waved around gently, hypnotically, like a snake about to strike.

After a few seconds, Mariano realised what was going on. "Jesus!" he panted. "Fuck'n' shoot 'im, René. We gotta go . . ."

"Va t'en! Shut yo' mouf."

Mariano shut his mouth.

Heurtaux started to advance slowly round the bed. I tried to kick my paralysed brain into gear and think of something . . .

Ruchter's partner, slumped untidily across the bed, stirred and produced a low, gut-wrenching moan.

Heurtaux sctopped and pointed the machine gun straight at my head for a long moment. I felt sweat streaming down my face and heard my breath coming in short, ragged gasps — but still I kept looking at him, staring into his dark glasses. I think I had some silly idea that he wouldn't shoot until I looked away . . .

He giggled again.

Then he shifted the gun a fraction and fired into the feebly twitching body of the German.

This time, I was about four feet from the gun. The muzzle-flash seemed to blaze out straight at my face and the noise was a solid, slamming force. I went over backwards, turning my head away instinctively — and looked straight at the German.

For a split-second he was surrounded by little spurts of water as bullets tore into the bed — and incredibly, impossibly, he was trying to sit up. His mouth was open and screaming soundlessly with the effort and his body was shaking as the water trembled beneath him — but he actually pulled himself up on to his right elbow and got his left hand pawing at the pocket where he'd put the Smith & Wesson . . .

And then it was all over. His legs flailed as bullets smashed his knees — and then Heurtaux sprayed the gun up his body. There was sudden red everywhere and the man was flung on his back . . .

And that was that.

The gun stopped, leaving a tremendous muffled hissing in my ears. I dragged my eyes off the corpse and turned my head again to look at my own death.

Heurtaux was still smiling. His wide nostrils were flaring, and the sinister black pools of his glasses were catching and reflecting the red lights of the voodoo masks as he made little sideways movements with his head. He looked like a man smelling a precious scent — and then I realised sickly that that was exactly what he *was* doing: breathing deeply of the blood and gunsmoke of his own carnage.

Christ! Scott! DO something . . .

But there was nothing I *could* do. The machine gun was still pointing at me negligently, smoke drifting from the muzzzle like a cigarette left in an ashtray.

Heurtaux chuckled, although I only heard a faint echo of it.

Then, still keeping the blank stare of his glasses on my face, he snicked the magazine out of the bottom of the gun, dropped it on the bed, and started reaching into his pocket. My brain registered 'he's out of ammunition and changing the magazine . . .'

NOW! GO! You won't get another chance . . .

I dived forward and grabbed up the Luger from where the German had dropped it. Shifted it from left hand to right, gripped it in fingers that seemed to be large and clumsy and moving at snail's pace . . .

And shot him just as he was slamming the new magazine home.

After the hellish blaring of the machine gun, the Luger seemed to pop like an air-pistol. Only the jolt and the flash convinced me it had gone off at all. I fired again, to make sure. Another pop, flash, and jolt.

The first one shattered his left shoulder and spun him round. The second one missed.

He reeled back a few steps as if he'd been hit by a car, then collided with the wall, bringing down one of the voodoo masks with a silent clatter. His left arm hung uselessly, and blood glistened in the dim light. He'd lost the fresh magazine — but he seemed to have forgotten about it. He rolled over against the wall until he was facing me, the green felt hat getting pushed drunkenly on to one side of his head.

He was still smiling. He raised the empty gun one-handed and pointed it at me.

I shot him again.

I don't know where I hit him — but his mouth made a soundless "*Oooof*", and he dropped the gun and started to crumple.

Then I remembered Mariano, and whipped round to cover the door where I'd last seen him.

He wasn't there.

A small cold voice in my head snapped *Find him! Otherwise he'll get you when you leave* . . .

I hauled myself on to my feet. My legs felt like wet noodles, and I swayed against the bed for support. I took two long, shuddering breaths — and then lurched round the bed and out into the dark, cool anteroom.

Nobody shot at me.

I went on into the living room.

Nobody shot at me there, either.

I ended up at the front door, which was still open. Sagged against the wall in a dark patch of shadow just outside it, the Luger heavy in my hand, and stared out into the moonlit garden. The palm trees were unmoving against the navy blue sky, the whirring of the night insects added to the roaring in my ears — but that was all. No other sounds, and no movement anywhere.

So now what?

I could go out and look for Mariano in the darkness — but what good would that do me? The chances were he'd just taken off for the tall timber anyway — but if he *hadn't*, and he had a gun, all he'd have to do would be sit in a dark patch somewhere and wait for me to go blundering into him.

And in the meantime, of course, the cops'll be heading this way hot foot . . .

That thought got me going again. Harvey's house was pretty much out in the wilds up here on Martin Hill — but with the row we'd been making they'd probably heard us in St Kitts, never mind Luke's Village a mile or two away. I could expect the law to roll up at any moment.

Which made it time to leave — Mariano or no Mariano.

But first, there were things to be done. I took a last gulp of fresh air, then turned and walked unsteadily back into the house.

*   *   *

Coming in from the clean night, the smell of the bedroom hit me before I got to it — a foul, acrid stench of blood, gunfire, and faeces. I walked in through the main door from the anteroom — and then just stopped and stared, appalled.

In the dim light, the room looked like some primeval painting of hell. The atmosphere was heavy with hanging smoke and dust and the shocked, tingling silence of sudden death. The walls were pock-marked with bullet holes, mirrors and voodoo masks hung shattered and broken . . .

And there was blood everywhere.

It was splashed up the walls, spattered on the ceiling, and the corpses of Ruchter and his *leutnant* were covered in it. It glistened wetly, a vivid, stomach-churning scarlet. My stomach duly churned — and I shuddered from head to foot and shook my brain out and tried to remember what I'd come back in here for . . .

Ah yes — the Smith & Wesson. The one with my fingerprints on it. In Herr Leutnant's left trouser pocket.

I took a hesitant step forward — and my foot made a small wet *squidge*. I looked down and found I was standing in a widening, pink-tinged pool of water. For a moment I just stared uncomprehendingly — and then I realised it was coming from the water-bed, dripping with a rapid *plink-plink-plink* that seemed to echo in the stillness. Of course — Heurtaux's bullets had punctured the top of the water-bag, so . . .

Come ON, man! Bloody MOVE!

I shuddered again, and sploshed over to the dead man on the bed. He was lying more or less on his back, and he was practically under water, the sheets and the water-bag sagging under his weight. The body was a soggy mass of cloth and blood and red-coloured water. I leaned over him and fumbled for the revolver, trying to ignore the smell of gore and crap and the open, bulging eyes in the dead face.

I couldn't find it.

For seconds on end, I couldn't even find the pocket. His whole abdomen seemed to have been pulverised: the place where his hip-bone should have been was squashy under my fingers. I shivered in the heat while new sweat poured down my face and the sour taste of bile welled up in my throat. Maybe I was wasting my time: maybe the fingerprints wouldn't last after the body had sunk in the water anyway . . .

Then I had it.

I got a grip on it and pulled. It came out with a soggy *thrrrp*, bringing bits of cloth with it. And bits of something else, too. I wiped it roughly on the edge of the yellow coverlet, and pushed it into the under-belt holster.

Then someone moaned.

I did a panic-assisted take-off and ended up in a corner of the room waving the Luger around and listening to my heart trying to rev itself clean out of its moorings. For a frozen moment I stared wildly at the voodoo masks and heard my brain trying to tell me there *are* no such things as zombies and the un-dead . . .

Then it came again.

It was Heurtaux.

Somehow, the idea of him still being alive hadn't occurred to me. I prised myself off the wall, dragged a shaking left hand over my forehead, and advanced on him cautiously, with the Luger leading the way.

He was still where I'd left him. He'd slid down the wall more or less into a sitting position, with his legs straight out in front of him and the spreading pool of water soaking into his trousers. His hat was tilted to one side and pushed low over his eyes and his dark glasses were askew, sliding down his nose. He could have been a drunk passing into happy oblivion on a bar-room floor — until you saw the blood. His left shoulder and the right side of his stomach were soaked in it, shining blackly in the low red light from the nearest surviving voodoo mask. His left arm hung uselessly by his side, turned outwards at an unnatural angle, and his right hand was pawing weakly at the wound in his middle.

He seemed to hear me as I stepped up to him, my sandals making little squelching noises in the water. His head moved drunkenly as he looked for me, and his right hand fished under his shirt.

It came out holding a little automatic.

He giggled.

I shot him.

This time, with my ears more or less recovered, the Luger didn't go pop. It went off with a deep booming *crash*, as if I'd fired a field-gun in church. The muzzle-flash licked out at his chest, and through the instant haze of gunsmoke I saw him jerk like a man getting an electric shock. His hat rolled off, the dark glasses hung diagonally across his face — and his right hand, still holding the little pistol, flopped into his lap.

Slowly, his head bent forward, as if he was looking down at the new stain spreading across his shirt. There was a horrible gurgling rattle from his throat, loud enough to reach me through the post-Luger ringing in my ears.

Then his right hand moved again.

For a long second I could only stare at him sickly, the ghastly rattling noise filling my head and a voice in my brain saying 'he's *dead*. He *can't* still be moving . . .'

Then I stepped up, pressed the muzzle of the Luger into the woolly black hair on top of his skull, and squeezed the trigger again.

The sunglasses crunched soundlessly under my right foot as I turned away.

Heurtaux was the third man I'd killed in my life. I didn't regret it.

*　　*　　*

After that I seemed to move in idiot slow-motion. I knew what I had to do — but every tiny action was a slow, laborious process that went on and on for ever.

I squelched back to the bed, wiped the Luger all over with the sodden yellow cover, and carefully folded it into *Herr Leutnant's* limp right hand. The bed and body rippled sickeningly as I did it, and more pink water splashed on the floor. I didn't seriously expect the cops to believe that he and Herteaux had killed each other instantly and simultaneously — but I had to do *something* with the Luger, and as long as they didn't connect it with me I didn't give a damn what they believed. A few little touches like that might just complicate the issue so they'd never get it straightened out . . .

Then I went round the house from room to room wiping down door handles and anything else I could think of with the tail of my shirt, switching on lights with my elbow to do it and switching them off again afterwards. The last stop on the circular tour was the guest bedroom. I wiped the door from the anteroom, walked round the bed to the communicating door — and stubbed my toe on something that skittered away and fetched up with a clunk against the bedside table.

Another gun. A 9 mm Browning Hi-Power.

For a moment I just peered at it stupidly — and then I remembered. Someone — presumably Mariano — had fired the first shot of the battle from this room; the shot that had knocked over *Herr Leutnant*. Then Ruchter had started shooting back, and Mariano had run out of here and come into the main bedroom gun-less and dripping blood. So this had to be his gun: he must have dropped it when Ruchter clipped him. I glanced around. There were spots of red on the floor and the bed, and bullet holes in the far wall where the rest of Ruchter's slugs had gone.

I dithered for a moment, thinking about taking the Browning with me — and then finally left it where it was without touching it. If the cops could make anything of it, then good luck to them: at least it would give them a set of fingerprints to work on that weren't mine.

Then I left.

*   *   *

The night outside was hot, buzzing with insects — and bathed in pale silver moonlight. I whizzed out of the front door, darted into the deep black shadow beside the wall, and stood there panting and trying to tell myself that Mariano was winged, unarmed, and probably five miles away by now and still running. I didn't entirely convince myself — but after a minute or so I *did* realise that I was wasting time I might not have. Whether he was waiting for me or not I still had to move, still had to get the Moke out of here . . .

I took two or three deep breaths, and sprinted straight out into the moonlight.

Nothing happened.

I went across the lawn at about two knots under the speed of sound, dived straight into the driving seat of the Moke, and fumbled frantically for the keys underneath it. After an age or two I found them, got the right one singled out and into the ignition, and cranked up the engine. It fired on three, missed, picked up on four . . .

And then I was reversing round the red Maverick in a shower of dust and small stones, whanging the gearlever into first as I stamped on the brakes to slew the front end round — and finally walloping off down the track with the lights out and the suspension threatening to come up through the body as we bounced from rut to rut.

No-one shot at me. No police cars came the other way.

When I reached the narrow road at the end of the long drive I switched on the lights, turned south towards Sweets Village, and drove along sedately with my hands shaking violently on the wheel and my teeth chattering like a Wasp Junior's tappets. Banana trees and tropical scrub tumbled past in a blurry yellow-green tunnel, and the trilling of crickets and tree-frogs came in through the open sides of the warm wind.

I was still shaking when I reached the west coast twenty minutes later.

21

THE PLACE I'D got myself to was a deserted little by-road — or by-cart-track, to be strictly accurate — leading to Indian Town Point. There isn't a town there nowadays, but legend had it that the Arawak Indians used to have a settlement on it way back when. Personally, I very much doubt it: even the Arawaks couldn't have been daft enough to set up shop on a tiny peninsula of barren rock about two hundred yards across without a single blade of grass on it anywhere. But that's what the legend says — and the Antiguans certainly believe it. They think the place is haunted by ghosts or jumblies or whatever it is that ancient Arawaks use, and they won't come within a mile of it at night.

That was why I was there. I needed to be alone — and after a dose of René Heurtaux, I was willing to take my chances with the jumblies.

I pulled on to the little plateau, switched off lights and engine — and then just sat there slumped over the wheel, shivering with reaction in the hot night. The Atlantic wandered in and sploshed rhythmically against the rocks — but apart from that, the place was dead quiet and still. There wasn't even the sound of insects: maybe they were afraid of the jumblies, too.

After a long time I lifted my head up, got a Lucky Strike lit — and then remembered the part-worn bottle of Scotch in my flight bag. I hauled it out and took a couple of long, deep swigs. It went into my stomach with a bang, then flowed all over me with a warm, soothing fire.

I prescribed myself another dollop, and settled down to think.

The first item on the agenda was the cops. It looked as if I'd been wrong about them rushing up hot foot: if they'd really been in a hurry I'd probably have met them on the way out. So maybe no-one *had* heard the gunfire, after all. Now I come to think about it, it was possible: Luke's Village *was* over a mile away, and all the shooting had been inside the thick stone walls of the house. They'd get on to it eventually, of course — but with any luck it might not be for hours or even days.

So that brought the Brains Trust to item two — to wit, was there any reason for the cops to connect me with the carnage when they did find it? I thought long and hard about that, aided by the whisky bottle — and eventually came to the happy conclusion that there wasn't. Inspector de Lima might want a nibble at me on general principles — since by now he seemed to suspect me of everything up to and including swiping the trade winds — but all he'd have to go on was that the killings took place in Harvey's house and I'd been doing some work for Harvey. And he could hardly sling me in jug on the strength of *that*. In fact, it might even be a good thing: I could use it to explain any odd fingerprints I might have missed on the mopping-up operation. And then Harvey's disappearance would make *him* a natural suspect, too, of course . . .

I breathed out smoke and relief all over the windscreen, swallowed some more Scotch, and thought about Harvey for a while.

It wasn't a constructive exercise: he'd be in North America or Europe or some-bloody-where by now, tucked away behind a different name and set up for life on the proceeds of the first load of Krugerrands he'd swiped. That'd be — what? I looked out over the glittering moonlit water and calculated. If that first load into Caracas had been 4,500 coins — half of the 9,000 that Ruchter had said were missing — their market value would have been around $900,000 US. Harvey wouldn't have sold them for dollars, probably — you look a bit conspicuous carting a trunk-load of greenbacks round Caracas — and getting rid of them on the quiet, the chances were he wouldn't have got their full market value, either. But he *must* have got at least half a million, or it's equivalent . . .

Half a million dollars.

I tried to visualise that much money, but failed. It was too big for me. It was the price of blackmail, double-cross, and murder. The price of five deaths — and one shattered life.

After a while I lit another Lucky from the stub of the first, and turned my attention to worrying about Lashlee and Mariano.

There was plenty of scope for worry, there. Assuming Mariano hadn't been badly hit — and I didn't think he had, since it certainly hadn't impaired his running ability — then he'd currently be reporting back to Lashlee.

And once he'd done that, the pair of them would be coming to kill me.

From Lashlee's point of view, there couldn't be any other alternative. He'd wanted me badly enough before — and now, the stakes had been raised. Not knowing what had happened after Mariano had left, he'd have to work on the assumption that sooner or later I'd be arrested over the killings at Harvey's place — and he couldn't afford to have me babbling to the cops, because I knew too much about him. Left to his own devices he could probably talk his way out of his connection with Heurtaux — but if I went and Confessed All, he'd be sunk. His connection with the Krugerrands and Isla Bealta would come out, and the governments of about fifty-seven different countries would be looking for his head on a charger.

So — it would have to be Scott for the chop. After a quiet little talk about a few things such as where I'd delivered the Krugerrands to, of course . . .

I found I was feeling cold inside again. I had a short consultation with Johnnie Walker, then went back to thinking.

After a few minutes I'd come to the conclusion that short of me going after them first — which was a nice thought, but somewhat less than practical — the only thing I *could* do was take that sudden holiday I'd been thinking about yesterday . . .

Or maybe just clear out for good.

That thought brought me up with a jerk. I rubbed the back of my neck and pondered on it. At first glance it seemed preposterous: but the more I looked at it, the easier and more logical it got. I'd told myself yesterday that I needed time to sell up my business — but that had been yesterday. Today, with the Beech gone and my work permit going, I didn't *have* any business to sell: all I had was a scruffy Cherokee, a scruffier Moke, and a pile of debts like a film star's salary.

So I could leave the Moke to be sold by the bank, write to my beer magnate giving a month's notice on the house along with a month's rent, and island-hop the Cherokee up to Miami and sell it. The proceeds would have to come back to the Canadian

Imperial Bank of Commerce, of course — *and* they'd still be wanting the rest of their money after that — but all that was going to happen anyway, wherever I went and whatever I did. Just *when* I pulled out wouldn't make any difference one way or the other ...

So that was that.

I could leave in the morning.

* * *

Somehow, the realisation was infinitely depressing. It *was* the only sane thing to do — lose myself in the vastness of America and then move on and get another hack job somewhere else in the world — but it still opened up a pit of cold emptiness in my guts. It was the very easiness of it all that hit me more than anything: I'd been in Antigua nearly two years, flogged myself day and night to build a new business and a new life — and in the end, all it had come to was another time and place I could quit at a moment's notice. I had no ties, no pets, no friends to say goodbye to ...

Nothing.

I stared out into the wide, echoing night and tried to recall the hope I'd had when I first came to the island. The hope and the plans and the dreams and the schemes. But I couldn't: they'd gone, all of them, smashed and scattered beyond recall.

Like the dream of two red-and-white Chipmunks on an English airfield.

I looked up at the glittering tropical stars and felt small and cold and very, very lonely.

* * *

After a long time I stirred, climbed stiffly out of the Moke, and took the torch and a bar of El Convento soap down to the rough coral seashore to get rid of other people's blood on my hands. Then I came back to the Moke, had another go at the bottle, and stared out over the glinting moonlit ocean while I tried to work out a plan of campaign. First off, I ought to get myself home and packed up ...

Or did I?

I thought about it for a moment — and came to the conclusion that home was one place I *didn't* ought to go to. If Lashlee was on the warpath, staking out *Chez* Scott with a regiment or two would be the first thing he'd do ...

So home was out.

Well, it didn't matter too much. The only things I had there were clothes and a cheap record-player and a few other bits of junk: nothing worth getting myself shot over. My passport and all the other essential paperwork of life was in my flight bag, the aircraft documents were in the aircraft, and all the money I possessed was in my pockets right now.

The only thing I was going to miss was Jenny's picture, still on the dressing table.

After a little more thought I turned the ignition key, flicked on the lights, and drove away. The sound of the Moke's engine and the crunch of tyres on coral seemed small and insignificant in the vast cathedral of the night.

*   *   *

I woke up next morning in a peeling wooden bedroom with a beautiful brown girl lying beside me. For a moment I thought I'd died and come to heaven — and then sleep drained away and memory came back with a rush. I hadn't come to heaven: I'd come to Yolande's whorehouse, on the outskirts of St John's. I'd arrived late last night by taxi after eating in town and dumping the Moke in the bank's car park, and the services of the girl had cost me 130 Bee-wee dollars for the night.

Heaven comes expensive, these days.

I sat up, swung my legs cautiously over the side of the bed — and the Monday morning hangover hit me. The flaking walls of the bedroom blurred and rocked in front of my eyes and an artillery barrage started up in my head. The girl moved behind me, and when I twisted to look at her — slowly and carefully, in case my head fell off altogether — she was just stirring into consciousness. The big black eyes opened, gummy with sleep, and stared at me blankly and uncomprehendingly for a moment. Then she remembered where she was and what I was doing here, and the blankness washed out under a flush of professional sensuality.

"*Buenos dias, señor.*"

I found a sandpaper tongue in my mouth *buenos dias'd* back, which used up about thirty per cent of my Spanish in one go. I seemed to remember that we'd had a language difficulty the night before, since she was from Santo Domingo. Well — a *difference*, anyway: some things don't require any great grasp of linguistics.

The girl yawned, and then exercised what appeared to be her entire English vocabulary.

"Yo' wan' fucky-fucky now?"

I shook my head, then wished I hadn't. When the room stopped pitching and yawing I managed a sickly smile and said: "No thanks. But thanks anyway."

She shrugged indifferently. "*Como usted quiera.*" As you like. The eyes closed again.

I scooped up a towel and weaved my way to the shower.

*　　*　　*

Half an hour later I was out on the street. It was no thrill. It was only seven in the morning — but already the sun was hot enough to raise a sticky layer of sweat around my neck and bounce a blinding white glare off the dusty roadway and the peeling, heat-blasted Bee-wee shanties. To the south-west of St John's the peaks of Mt Thomas and Table Hill — known locally as The Sleeping Indian — stood out sharply against a sky of incredible burnished blue. There wasn't a scrap of cloud anywhere.

The trade winds hadn't returned. It was going to be another burning, breathless day.

I fished out my sunglasses, tried to ignore my throbbing morning head and the lead weight of nausea in my guts, and looked around for a taxi. There wasn't one, of course: not in the Villa area at seven in the morning. The people in the Villa area aren't in the taxi-riding class.

Somewhere in the shanties, the inevitable cock crowed in the sullen heat. I started walking, my flight bag bumping against my leg.

By the time I'd reached St John's proper, I was really sweating. My shirt clung damply to my back and armpits, my crutch was a blaze of soreness as the heat-rash chafed, and the gun under my belt was digging into my belly like a policeman's boot. I tried to look around and take an interest as I walked, telling myself it was the last time I was ever going to see the place, but I couldn't. I'd lived with it all for so long — the palm trees and dusty scrub, the goats and donkeys, the ragged children watching whitey go past with wide, distrustful eyes — that the last time held no impact. I was leaving, and that was that. *Finis.* No looking back.

I was good at leaving places.

At the corner of Athill Street and Dickinson Bay Street I

233

stopped, hauled out the bottle of Johnnie Walker, and took a long swig.

It helped — a bit, anyway. It was that sort of day.

I finally found an early taxi outside the Kensington Court Hotel in St Mary's Street. We drove into the airport just before eight a.m.

*   *   *

The first thing I did was lurk under a tamarind tree in the car park while I studied the activity on the terminal concourse. There were the usual clumps of rent-a-crowd people hanging around the airline desks, tripping over each other's baggage and complaining about mis-routed suitcases and all the other pleasures of modern air travel — but that was all. No sign of Lashlee, Mariano — or Inspector de Lima.

So far as I could see, anyway.

I gave it a couple of minutes for luck, then walked briskly across to the control tower to file my flight plan. The usual force-ten air-conditioning curdled the sweat on my back as I clumped up the steps into the control room.

One of the controllers on duty, a big black guy called Bert, swivelled round in his chair and gave me a big melon-slice grin.

"Ay Bill, *how a ya?* We hear yo' crash'n San Juan day befo' yes'day. Yo' okay nah?"

I reached for a pad of flight plan forms and said: "Yeah, sure. It was only a crash-landing. I walked away from it."

"Ay, yo' dam lucky den, man. We hear it go up in flames."

"Yeah, it did. But I was out of it by then."

He pursed his lips and said "Yo' lucky" again — and then thought of something. "Ay, me jus' remember. We gotta message fo' yo' here."

I ground to a halt in the middle of searching for a pen, and my stomach did a wheels-up landing in my sandals. If this was a message from Inspector de Lima grounding me pending police inquiries . . .

"What sort of message?" I croaked.

A LIAT Avro on the apron asked for start-up clearance. Bert turned back to his mike and gave it, then started searching casually through the mess of Notams and flight clearance forms on his table. "It 'ere somewhere . . ."

I managed not to scream.

Then he found it. "Oh yeh," he said. "It cum on de groun'-link from Le Raizet dis'mornin . . ."

I breathed out in a long, gusty sigh of relief. Le Raizet is the international airport of Guadeloupe: Inspector de Lima wouldn't be sending me *billets-doux* from there . . .

". . . It frum Missewer Jean-Claude Ca — ah — *Ca*rvell. De tower say Carvell bin tryin' to 'phone yo', but carn' get yo'. He wanna know if yo' can go to Dominica an' finish de crop-sprayin' job dat yo' know about. He say de 'plane bin fix but he got two pilot off sick wid 'flu and he carn' spare no-one. Dat make sense to yo'?"

I nodded. "Yeah, I know what that means."

It meant, in short, that Jean-Claude was up the creek without a paddle and wanted me to bail him out. The poor old sod wasn't having much joy with this particular Dominica contract: first I'd had that partial engine failure, and now this. It was the usual time for 'flu in the islands — the tourists bring it in from the colder countries and the residents don't have any resistance to it at the beginning of the season — but all the same, it was bad luck having two spray-jockeys go down at the same time. I'd've helped him out if I could, but as it was . . .

"Yo' gonna go, Bill? Me sen' a reply back t'rough de tower if yo'like."

I shook my head — to the last part, anyway. "No, I can't go. But I'd be obliged if you'd tell 'em that. Save me a phone call. Say I'm sorry, but I've got — er — other business."

"Hokay." He started jiggling buttons and bawling into the ground-link microphone. I went back to the flight plan form and started filling it in. Since I didn't want to land in Puerto Rico I was making my first re-fuelling stop in St Croix. So that was MKPA to MISX; time en route one hour fifty minutes; VFR flight level six-five . . .

". . . dey bin found, Bill?" I suddenly realised I was being spoken to, and looked up. It was the other controller, who'd just finished reading out the flight clearance to the LIAT Avro. He'd pushed his chair back, and was looking at me with raised eyebrows as if he'd just asked a question.

"Sorry, I didn't catch that."

He waved a languid hand. "I was jus' saying, had yo' heard dat dey found de wreckage o' 32 Romeo yes'day?"

*   *   *

235

After a long, quiet moment I found I was staring at him stupidly, with my jaw hanging open for the canned air to walk in and my right hand frozen in the act of signing the flight plan form. I jacked my teeth together, struggled to get a grip on the swaying universe, and finally said intelligently: "What . . . what was that?"

"T'ree-two Romeo. Yo' know — Missah McGrath's Twin Com, dat wen' down las' week. Yo' were on de search fo' it, weren't yo'?"

"Ah . . . er . . . yeah. You say it's been found, now?"

He nodded. "Dat's right. I t'ought yo'da heard. It foun' in de mountains in Dominica yes'day."

I swallowed hard and croaked: "No, I hadn't heard. Who — er — what happened, exactly?"

He waved his hand again. "It foun' by an Air Sport Cessna frum Guad'loupe. Dey say it 3,500 feet up de north-wes' face o' Morne Diablotins, deep in de trees. Somewhere near dat spray-trip yo' use, I think, on'y higher. I s'pose dat why it not seen befo': de mountain norm'lly hidden unner de cloud at dat height, but fo' de las' two days it bin clear 'cos o' de calm. De D'rector o' Civil Aviation talkin' 'bout organisin an expedition up dere some-time nex' wek, so p'raps we know what happen to de 'plane den."

I just said "Ah . . .", and waggled my head about. It had never occurred to me that 32 Romeo might have gone in on land some-where. You don't think of that in an area that's ninety per cent sea. My brain seemed to be wading through a thick, treacly swamp . . .

Then, very slowly, I tore the completed flight plan form off the top of the pad and scrumpled it up. Bert had finally got through to Guadeloupe on the ground-link and was yelling at them over the static that he'd got a message for Monsieur Carvell. No, not Caravelle — CARVELL, Charlie, Alpha, Romeo, Victor . . .

I tapped him on the shoulder.

"I've changed my mind," I said. "Ask them to tell Jean-Claude — M'sieur Carvell — that I'll do his spraying for him this evening if there isn't any turbulence, or tomorrow morning."

22

SEVENTY MINUTES LATER I eased the Cherokee's throttle back, pointed the nose downhill from flight level five-five, and watched the emerald-green spires of Dominica growing steadily larger in the windscreen. The island looked strangely small and unreal without its usual ramparts of cloud. The Dominica I knew was a land hidden and secret under thousands of feet of bellying, angry cumulus — nothing at all like this. This was just a green papier-mâché model, floating naked in a blue painted sea under a blue empty sky . . .

Still, I wasn't complaining: the stripping of the cloud cover was going to make me rich.

I hoped.

The air was crystal-clear — unusual for the third day of a calm — and I could make out the individual jungle-covered mountains twenty or thirty miles away. Morne Diablotins, Morne Concorde and Mang Peak in the north, Morne Couronne, Negres Marrons and Morne Trois Pitons farther south . . .

I bent the Cherokee's nose a touch to the right until it was pointing directly at Morne Diablotins.

Melville Hall control tower crackled through the speakers, asking for my estimate for the airport. I picked up the mike and told them I was going to do some flying round the north coast first, and I'd call them later when I was ready to come in. The controller said: "Okay, Eggo-Mike" in his thick Creole accent — and I slumped back in the sweaty heat of the cockpit and pondered idly on why the hell the island should be so French. Okay, the French *did* occupy it once — but they had it for just four years in the 1770s, and after that the British grabbed it and stuck to it for nigh on two centuries. You'd think we'd have made *some* sort of impression in two hundred years — but all the place names are French, the islanders still speak a French patois with English as a reluctant second language, and everybody drives French cars or rides on tatty old French lorries.

The northern coastline slid under the wings — and I jerked myself out of the cockpit-euphoria and back to the here and now. Levelled the Cherokee off at 3,500 feet, and kept her heading straight for Diablotins. The mountain grew larger until it filled the whole windscreen, and the distant green furriness materialised into the livid roof of the rain forest.

Then we were *there*. I stood the Cherokee on its right wing tip, rolled it out so we were flying parallel with the mountainside, and hung my chin on my left shoulder.

Close up, the forest was awe-inspiring.

I'd seen the trees of Dominica before, of course — spent many hours wandering around in them, in fact — but never up here, around the base of the normal cloud-line. *No-one* came up here: it was uninhabited and unexplored — unless you counted the monkeys and the parrots and the boa constrictors, that is.

Now, I could see why.

The mountainside sloped at forty or fifty degrees from the vertical — but in spite of that, you couldn't see the ground at all. All you could see was the roof of the jungle — a dense, impenetrable waterfall of brilliant green. The trees could be ten feet high or a hundred feet: there was just no way of telling. The forest soared up out of the green depths thousands of feet below and just kept right on going, up past my level and on into the burning blue dome of the sky.

I snatched my sunglasses off, wiped the sweat away from my eyes, and stared out over the bobbing left wing tip. The Cherokee bounced around in the turbulence — but apart from frequent glances at the altimeter to make sure I was holding 3,500, and ahead to make sure I wasn't about to try boring a hole through some mountain spur, I kept my eyes on the jungle. If I was going to spot the tiny splash of a wrecked aeroplane in this lot I was going to have to be hawk-eyed and then some . . .

The shape of the mountain was keeping me in a very gentle left turn. After five minutes I looked up and around — and found I'd flown almost round to the western face. I yawed the nose to the right and glanced down — and sure enough, there was Jean-Claude's little spray-strip just disappearing under the left wing root, about 1,500 feet below.

I peeled away from the mountainside and circled while I had a quick think. If the Twin Com was three-and-a-half thousand feet up the north-west face of Diablotins I ought to have flown right alongside the bloody thing — but I hadn't seen hide nor hair of it.

Well, maybe *alongside* was the trouble: maybe I ought to get *above* three-and-a-half so I could look *down* on the trees...

I poured on the power, climbed up to 4,000, and started another pass in a powered side-slip with my forehead jammed hard against the window, staring as near vertically downwards as I could.

I saw it two minutes later.

*   *   *

It was three or four hundred feet below me and deep in the trees — much too deep to see at first glance how much was left of it. All I could tell for sure was that it was *there* — or at least, some of it was. If I hadn't been almost directly overhead I'd never have it at all — and if the cloud cover hadn't gone on strike, *nobody* would have seen it for months or even years...

I slapped the throttle back, walloped the Cherokee into a steep descending spiral to the left — and instantly lost sight of the wreck as my angle of vision changed from vertically-above to oblique. Keeping my eyes on the spot, I kept the turn going until I was travelling in the same direction as before but three hundred feet lower. Then I rolled out and tucked in tight against the mountainside, slowed up and shoved two notches of flap down, and droned on towards where I thought it was.

A few seconds before I was ready for it, a Twin Commanche-sized clearing whizzed under the leading edge of the port wing. I slammed the Cherokee over to the left, the wreckage pivoted under the wing tip for a moment — and then it was out of sight behind the trees again.

I hauled her out of the turn and flew away into the open sky. I found I had a mind's-eye impression of a fuselage and a tail, a buckled up mass that might have been anything, and no signs of a fire.

Well, that was all I needed to know.

I flew around for another five minutes taking careful note of the position of the crash in relation to the spray-strip. The bad news was that it was three miles away or a bit more but the not-quite-so-bad news was that it was almost directly above the final end of the dirt road that led up to and past the strip itself.

Quite why the road bothered to go on beyond the strip at all, I couldn't imagine. There was nothing there but virgin jungle, and in the times I'd been flying the spray-kites I'd certainly never seen anyone using it. But then the West Indian islands are full of roads like that: either the people who build 'em can't read the map references on the plans, or the people who plan 'em intend to put things at the ends and never quite get round to it. I was bloody glad this one *was* there, though: not only would it save me hacking my way through the jungle all the way from the strip, but it would also give me some sort of chance of finding the wreck this side of next Christmas. Without a guiding land-mark you could wander around in that forest for weeks and find nothing but bugs and boa constrictors — but with the road to work from, all I had to do was get to the end, go about 150 yards farther on, and then head directly uphill until I was a thousand feet higher up the mountain. That way, I ought to walk straight into it. *Ought* to.

I took a last long look, then bent the Cherokee round to the west and headed for Melville Hall.

*   *   *

By midday I was back at the mountain — this time piloting Jean-Claude's old Chevvy truck, which I'd picked up at Melville Hall. My first plan had been to clear Customs and Immigration inbound at the airport and then fly the Cherokee up to the spray-strip — but then I'd remembered just in time that with the Chev at Melville Hall, where Jean-Claude's engineer had left it, flying up would mean being stuck at the strip without a car at all. And *that* would mean a six-mile hike from the strip to the end of the dirt-road and back, which on this hungover morning was some-thing I could very definitely do without. So I'd ended up leaving the Cherokee and driving all the way, churning my guts up on the Dominican roads and raising a new layer of perspiration in the Dominican heat.

I jounced to a stop at the very end of the dirt road to no-where, trod the parking brake on, and switched off the engine. The silence hummed in my ears.

For a long moment I just sat there in the high cab, feeling tired and wrung out and a million years old. Sweat rolled down my face in the still, sullen heat, and my hands were sticky on the wheel. I had a five-star headache, and my mouth tasted like a gorilla's armpit: I was in no condition to climb a flight of stairs, let alone a mountainside covered in dense tropical rain forest . . .

I shook myself, clambered down out of the cab, and tried to stretch the kinks out of my back. When that didn't work I walked away from the Chev for a long, slow look around. My sandals swished through grass and young ferns as I moved, and when I glanced down the track the wheel-marks of the Chev showed up clearly as twin furrows in a low tide of creeping vegetation. Mankind didn't seem to use this track very much — and as usual when mankind neglects something in the jungle, the jungle was taking it back. In six months it would be impassable, and in eighteen, gone for good.

Somewhere in the jungle a parrot squawked, getting over its suspicion of the rumbling Chevrolet. When it didn't get hit by a thunderbolt the rest of the forest took the cue and quit holding its breath as well. Monkeys chittered, birds cawed and whistled, and other things made low mysterious moving noises.

Scott, William, packed up philosophising and started looking at where he was supposed to be going. It was not an encouraging sight.

The dirt road had been hacked out of the jungle on a natural shoulder winding part-way round the mountain and rising to an altitude of about 2,800 feet — an extension of the same shoulder Jean-Claude had used for his airstrip, in fact. As I stood facing back down the track, the mountainside sloped steeply upwards on my left and rather more gently downwards on the right.

But it wasn't the slope I was worried about. It was the jungle itself.

The trees reared up fifty or sixty feet high on all sides. Not brand-leaders as Dominican rain forests go, but quite big enough to be going on with. The real problem was going to be the density of them, though: there were palms, bread-fruits, mahoganies, white cedars, calabashes, *gumjes*, mammee-apples, you name it — and they were all crushed together so closely that you couldn't see ten yards into the forest through the trunks. And where there *was* a foot or two of space it was invariably occupied by huge-leafed *frije* ferns and thick bell-ropes of liana vines.

I said "Bloody hell", aloud. My voice sounded very small and flat and was swallowed up instantly by the muttering forest.

I went back to the Chev and hauled out my flight bag and an oily old rucksack. Up-ending the rucksack produced a small cascade of tools: I selected a few, chucked the rest on the floor of the cab, then delved into the flight bag and came up with a bottle of water and the remains of the Scotch.

And the Smith & Wesson, in its little holster.

For a moment I weighed the gun in my hand — and then thought of the boa constrictors, took it out of the holster, and dropped it in the rucksack. So then I was ready to go.

I took a deep gulp of Scotch to wish myself luck, shrugged the sack on to my back, and pushed my way into the forest.

*　　*　　*

At first, the going was every bit as hard as I'd expected. In accordance with Plan A for getting myself directly down-slope of the wreck, I tried to cut along the contour of the mountainside from where the dirt road ended. It didn't work out too well: the jungle reached out and grabbed me at every step. If it wasn't ferns the size of Boeing mainwheels it was impenetrable clumps of tree trunks and vines that I had to squeeze round because I couldn't go through. Christ knows where all the trees found room for their roots — they must have had split-level accommodation down there. At the end of ten minutes I was sweating like an all-in-wrestler, panting as if I'd done ten rounds with Raquel Welch — and was all of twenty yards inside the forest.

I stopped for a breather, and thought about it. The jungle was full of unseen screeching and whistling, echoing through the cathedral of the trees. There was none of the dappled sunshine and shade you find in a temperate forest: the jungle roof, heavily intertwined foliage forty or fifty feet above my head, shut out the sun completely. Down here was a damp, stagnant world of permanent twilight and dark, sombre greens. It should have been cool to match the shade — but it wasn't: it was hot and steamy, and foetid with the bad-egg stench of rotting copra and plantains. I leaned against a jac-fruit tree and fanned my face with my right hand. It didn't do any good: after three days without the trade winds, the air under the trees was too exhausted to move.

Okay, mastermind — *now* what . . .?

Something screeched like a multiple car-crash above me, and I jerked my head up in time to see a green-and-yellow flash whipping through the trees and away towards the up-slope. Bloody parrot . . .

Although come to think of it, it might just be an *intelligent* bloody parrot, at that: maybe the undergrowth wasn't quite so thick up there on the hill . . .

It took me another ten minutes to reach the beginning of the rising ground — and then lo, it *had* been an intelligent parrot. The going didn't get easy, by any means — but at least it got possible, which was a start. The ferns thinned out a few per cent, the undergrowth shrank down to tread-on-able size in places, and some of the trees were that important few inches farther apart that left me room to squeeze in between them.

Against that, of course, there was the slope.

From the air it had just looked bloody steep — but down here, it was like trying to climb up the side of the Empire State Building. 'Steep' wasn't in it. There was no question of walking: the ground was tipped up fifty or sixty degrees from the horizontal, and the only way to move was by kneeling and lying on it — or, more accurately, *leaning* on it — and pulling yourself up by the trunks and roots and vines. It was like climbing a great big tree — except that this was a slimy, muddy tree with all sorts of knobs and obstacles and overhangs on the trunk which had to be negotiated, thick tangled patches of undergrowth which had to be skirted round, and ten thousand rotten branches which kept giving way under your hands and feet. About once a minute something on the oozing jungle floor would come away when I grabbed it: sometimes I was lucky and had a good purchase with a few other hands or feet when it happened — and other times I'd go slithering back downhill until I fetched up against something solid enough to stop me. It wasn't dangerous — there was no way I could have slid more than about ten feet without de-materialising myself in order to pass through a few tree trunks — but it was more than slightly abrasive on the temper. At the end of fifteen minutes, when I squatted on the slope with my feet against a sweetsop trunk for a rest, I was covered from head to foot in gooey filth and swearing under my breath in a steady, vicious monotone.

When I looked down I stopped swearing, though. I could see maybe a hundred feet through the trees in some places — and there was no sign of the Chev or the dirt road or any flat land at all. Maybe I was moving faster than I thought . . .

Or maybe you just can't see as far as you thought, Scott: quit straining your tiny brain and bloody get on with it . . .

I got on with it.

I got on with it for an hour and a half.

At the end of that time I was on the verge of exhaustion, sodden with jungle-slime from head to foot, and moving like one of the zombies which are supposed to inhabit the rain forests. I'd lost all sense of time and distance and orientation: the whole world had narrowed down to the next six feet of the interminable slope and then the next and the next after that. Every now and then I tried to remind myself of the crock of gold at the end of the climb — but here in the forest, $900,000 worth of yellow coins had no reality at all. There was nothing but the slime and the filth and the trees and the creepers and the grinding, killing, never-ending bloody slope . . .

I finally stopped, wedged myself against a tree trunk, and wriggled out of the rucksack. Then I fished around in it with shaking hands until I came up with the water bottle, uncapped it . . .

And stared disbelievingly as the water gurgled out *sideways*.

For a long moment my jaw sagged on my chest and the water dribbled over my soaking trousers — and then the penny dropped. I'd got the staggers — or 'spatial disorientation', as the flying manuals prefer to call it. I'd been staring at the steep slope and the crazily leaning trees for so long that the little balance tubes in my ears had gone on strike and quit telling my brain which way was up. It happens in instrument flying, too — and when it does, you have to ignore your senses and concentrate on the dials . . .

I stared hard at the bottle of water, and slowly righted it until the surface was level with the bottom. To me, bottle and water both seemed to be leaning 'way forward. I kept my eyes on it . . .

And after a few moments, the world moved back to its proper

place. The slope, which my mind had been trying to flatten out, looked like the side of a skyscraper again.

I shook my head, shivered in the heat, and drank most of my artificial horizon in three long gulps. Then I lay back against the rotting slime and listened to my breath coming and going in short, wheezing rasps. It wasn't achieving much: the air was hot and still suffocatingly humid, as if the jungle had wrung all the oxygen out of it and then just left it there, hanging limp and used up under the trees. My head was thumping with a dull, determined ache and I could feel the crawl of sweat all over my body, slippery and gritty as it mixed with the mud.

For five or ten minutes I just stayed flopped out, trembling with exhaustion. Then I sat up slowly, swallowed some more water, and took up thinking again. Or attempted to, anyway.

Without realising it, I'd climbed to a level where the trees were a little sparser — 'sparser' in this neck of the woods meaning sometimes as much as ten feet between the trunks — but the foliage overhead was still the same solid black-green mass. There were very few low branches — they saved their energy until they could shoulder their way into the jungle roof where the sunlight was, I suppose — so at my level the forest was a vista of bare trunks, vines, ferns and creepers. Some of the trees grew up vertically, others sprouted out at right angles to the slopes, and still others settled for a compromise. No wonder I'd got vertigo . . .

I squeezed my eyes shut for a moment to stop it happening again, and thought about how far I'd got. *That* was the real snag, not the staggers — because when it came down to it, I just didn't *know* how far I'd got. I could have covered five hundred feet or seven hundred or a thousand. There was simply no way of telling — and worse still, I wasn't even sure whether I'd come up the slope vertically.

An enormous lizard skittered out of the undergrowth ten feet down-slope, stopped to give me the fish eye for a moment, then zipped six feet up the nearest tree and hung there puffing out his throat.

I said "Bugger!" and the forest swallowed it up.

All right then — let's assume you're on track and you've climbed less than seven hundred feet: that means you've got to go along the slope 150 yards, and then carry on up. Right?

Right. Well . . . probably not right, actually, but it *was* the

245

only thing I could think of. I shouldered my way back into the rucksack, smeared the filth around my face in a useless attempt to wipe off some of the streaming sweat, and got under way again. It was two o'clock in the afternoon.

By twenty past, I reckoned I must have come sideways by the 150 yards I'd planned. I wasn't sure of it, of course — but it was easier moving across the slope than up it, and it *felt* like 150 yards. I swivelled my head round and peered up the slope. A hundred feet or so higher, barely visible through the trees, was a light-coloured out-crop of pumice or limestone or something. I'd make it that far, I decided, and then stop for another rest and a planning session. Providing I could think of something to plan by then, of course.

I was half way there before I realised that the white-ish patch wasn't a pile of rocks at all.

It was the tail of an aeroplane. I reached it ten minutes later.

23

SHE'D GONE IN almost vertically — and by the look of her, at something like terminal velocity going straight down. The trees had absorbed some of the impact — if they hadn't, she'd have been spread out over several acres — but in the process they'd become part of the wreck themselves. The clearing she'd made as she went in was a chaos of splintered trunks and crumpled aeroplane all mangled up together.

I stood on the perimeter, breathing like a racehorse, and tried to work out what had happened. Green and blue parrots flashed overhead constantly, their screeching and cawing echoing in the steamy heat of the jungle. The place had a rotting, putrifying smell about it.

The back end of the fuselage was sticking more or less straight up, the registration N2332R still readable on the rumpled white skin. It seemed to be resting against a couple of trees which had been broken off at their bases and were leaning over crazily, unable to fall down completely because the rest of the forest wouldn't let go of their tops. The tail unit was dented and battered but still there, with a couple of tangled vines hanging down from the port elevator. The left wing, complete with engine, had been torn almost off at the root in the crash and was buckled up crazily around a few more tree trunks.

The right wing was missing altogether.

I started to haul myself upwards, towards the underside of the fuselage. The crunching noises of my progress through the under-growth sounded like gunfire in a graveyard. I stopped again.

Come on, Scott: this is a graveyard you're going to rob, not just intrude on . . .

I pulled myself up a few paces nearer, and peered at the place where the starboard wing used to be.

The remains of the centre section were there — but the engine nacelle and the wing itself were just simply gone. The rear spar and the wing-skin near the trailing edge showed signs of stress-fractures and ripping — but farther forward, around the area of the mainspar, the inboard fuel tank had been blown open and the alloy structure was buckled and contorted and fused in a way that no impact or structural failure had ever produced. It looked as if some giant welding torch had been played over the remains . . .

I'd seen that sort of thing before. Two days before, in fact — when I'd looked at the remains of the Beech's engine nacelle where the bomb had gone off.

Now, I knew what had happened.

The bomb had been planted in the nacelle, as it had been in the Beech: up against the firewall behind the engine itself, or in the top of the wheel-well. Only it hadn't been an engine-stopping squib like I'd had — this had been the real McCoy, a slab of some really powerful explosive supplied courtesy of the Cuban government for the liberation of Antigua by the brethren of the Black Power. When that went off it probably blew the motor clean out of the airframe, and also disintegrated a foot or two of mainspar.

Goodbye starboard wing.

For a moment, I saw it. Cas McGrath and Larry Hawkins sitting side by side in the dim-lit cockpit. The engines snoring evenly as they droned through the smooth Caribbean night. Desultory cockpit-talk, or perhaps silence between them as each worried about the illicit cargo in his own way. Then the sudden shocking boom of detonation, maybe a quick metallic crunch as the wing came off — and after that, nothing but the maniac whirling of the spin and the howling of the airflow and McGrath fighting controls that weren't controlling anything any more . . .

And at the end, the final impact that neither of them could have felt. Then . . . nothing. Just the indignant screeching of the parrot colony round a new clearing in the rain forest.

I shuddered, feeling cold in the torpid heat of the afternoon. No wonder McGrath hadn't got a Mayday call out: even if he'd had time there'd have been no point . . .

After a while I found myself wondering vaguely why the wreck hadn't caught fire. I brought the thought into focus and looked at the remains in relation to it. It was fairly easy to work out: it wouldn't have gone up when the bomb went off because there hadn't been anything left on the starboard side to burn — and it hadn't gone up on impact because McGrath would have pulled the power off on the way down and the remaining engine would have had three or four thousand feet to get cool before the kite went in. You can never be sure with fire, of course — but the risk *is* statistically less if you haven't got an engine running at high power and heat at the moment of impact. That's why crashes on take-off tend to burn more often than any other kind of accident . . .

Come on, Scott — quit rolling your brain round your skull and get on with it. You're here to pick up 4,500 Krugerrands, not to do the Civil Aviation Authority's job for them . . .

I shook my head to clear it, ducked under a couple of slanting, fractured tree trunks, and emerged into a small patch of hot sunlight.

And came to the cockpit.

*   *   *

My first reaction was that I wanted to be sick — and not just from the stench, either.

The nose-section had telescoped completely — just sort of disappeared in a blurred mass of duralumin stamped flat on the mountainside. The cockpit itself was almost as bad: it was mashed to about a third of its normal length in a chaos of con-certina'd metal and shattered Perspex.

The bodies were still inside it.

I'd known they would be, of course — and I'd known they wouldn't be pretty. But *this* . . .

I'd come up on the right-hand side of the fuselage; the co-pilot or passenger side. In this case, Larry Hawkins' side.

He was literally smashed flat.

He'd gone into the instrument panel at two or three hundred knots. His head was sunk into the radios like a cannonball — except that it was incredibly spread out, and about two inches thick from front to back. There was a dark-ish brown stain all around it, lumpy and rusty, where blood and brains had exploded out in the impact and dried hard afterwards in the heat.

There was a lot of that rusty brown about. It was all over the roof and the shattered instruments and the mangled throttle pedestal.

Maybe it was something to do with McGrath having the control column through his chest.

If Larry Hawkins was a gruesome sight, then McGrath was horrific. The column, shedding the half-wheel yoke on the way, had gone clear through him until it stuck six inches out of his back in the mound of splintered bones and coagulated gore. His arms and shoulders were all mangled up with the flight panel in a dirty brown mass . . .

And that was the gentle part. The nasty part was his head.

His skull was jammed hard against the cockpit roof. An inch-diameter branch or a tree had come in like a spear and taken half his neck away during the final impact — but his head had stayed as it was, leering through the non-existent windscreen at the flattened earth six inches in front of his nose. The eyes were open and staring and glazed with a milky white opaqueness, and the mouth was gaping wide. Filthy, dried up tendrils hung from the lips like cobwebs.

The head was about one-and-half times its normal size, puffed-up like some dreadful balloon and ghastly with putrefaction.

The stench was indescribable.

The white ants didn't seem to mind it, though. The cockpit was a crawling, seething mass of them.

*   *   *

I don't have a weak stomach, and I'd seen dead men before — but *that* sight was enough to give anyone's guts the dry heaves. I stumbled a few feet down the slope so that the under-side of the aircraft was between me and the charnel-house of the cockpit, and sank down into a sitting position in the slime. I was shivering as if I had a fever, and cold clammy sweat rolled down my face in the heat. I fished out a crumpled pack of Luckies with trembling hands. It took me three matches to get one lit.

Down the slope, the foetid jungle suddenly seemed cool and clean and pure. I wanted to run and run and keep on running, slide down the mountainside between the trees and get back to the Chev and throw it down the track until I came to people who were alive and normal and everyday . . .

I stayed where I was. The parrots cawed over my head.

After a while I remembered the bottle of Scotch in the ruck-sack. I dug it out and prescribed myself a few medium-long medicinal gulps in between deep, jerky drags on the Lucky. Not a recommended beverage for mountain-climbing in the tropics, of course, but this was a special case . . .

It helped. A bit, anyway. Enough so I could get two or three brain cells together and start thinking again. I pushed the cigarette end into the mud and tried to recall what I knew about the spare spaces in Twin Commanches. It didn't amount to much: I'd never flown one, never even looked at a Flight Manual as far as I could remember. I had a hazy notion they had a luggage compartment aft and a lot of spare space in the nose, and that was about all.

Well, if the Krugerrands had been in the nose they could bloody well stay there. I wasn't going to start hauling those two bodies around for all the gold in Fort Knox . . .

I didn't really think they *had* been in the nose, though — or in the aft baggage compartment, either. McGrath's problems of weight and balance and security had been exactly the same as my own — and I was pretty sure he'd have solved them in the same way, by finding a space under the cabin floor in the vicinity of the mainspar housing. Hell — in that sort of kite, it was the only place he *could* have stashed them.

So all I had to do was get in there.

There was bound to be an inspection hatch in the cabin somewhere — but there was no way I was going looking for *that*, either. So that just left Plan B: hacking my way in through the bottom of the fuselage. It shouldn't be difficult: the outer skin of an aircraft is only light-gauge duralumin, and a good sharp chisel will go through it like a knife through butter. The chisel I'd brought from the Chev was neither good nor sharp — but with a five-pound hammer and the incentive of $900,000 behind it, I wasn't anticipating any real difficulty.

I dug hammer and chisel out of the rucksack, and pulled myself up to the belly of the aircraft.

The underside skin was rucked-up and ripped like a trodden-on cardboard box, and it took me a few moments of glancing sideways and comparing it with the wing stubs before I was sure where the mainspar housing was. When I'd got it sorted out I knelt down, lifted the chisel to the end of one of the rips . . .

And froze. Totally and utterly.

It wasn't a rip at all. It was a large L-shaped gash with the unmistakable crinkles of chisel-marks along the edges.

24

FOR WHAT SEEMED like a long time I just knelt there and stared, hammer and chisel poised and stomach draining away into my bowels. Then I dragged my eyes off the metal and looked slowly round the jungle. I don't know what I expected to see — zombies or jumblies or something, probably . . .

What I *did* see was a shadowy movement 'way back in the forest on my right.

I threw myself backwards just as something flicked like a camera-flash. The chisel whipped out of my hand with a tiny *spang* as I went — and then the gunshot was echoing round the forest like a slamming door, and I was tumbling and sliding down the slope. Confused impression of parrots exploding out of the trees . . . left hand numb and stinging . . . grabbing frantically for the Smith & Wesson as I skated past the rucksack on my stomach . . .

And then I was sprawled up against a tree with my heart trying to rev itself out of my chest and the gun muddy in my hand. I waved it uphill at the place where the shot had come from . . .

But there was nothing there. Only the creepers and the ferns and the dim cathedral-aisle of the trees. Parrots flashed across the clearing, screeching at the disturbance — but apart from them, everything was still.

Still as a graveyard.

My left hand was tingling-dead, as if it was frozen. It still seemed to be connected at the wrist, so I supposed it was impact-damage from when the bullet hit the chisel. I dragged it across my forehead to stop the sweat running into my eyes, and tried to think what to do next. Part of my brain howled *just take off downhill and get the hell OUT* — but that wasn't the answer. Not while I didn't know who they were, where they were, or how many there were: there could be a couple of battalions lurking behind the down-slope trees waiting for me to do just that. The same snag applied to moving in any other direction . . .

So that just left staying where I was.

The heat of the afternoon closed in around me like a damp suffocating blanket. I moved my head slowly from side to side, straining eyes and ears into the forest. The creepers and vines made a thousand shapes that could be a man, and the little rustling noises of the jungle floor were a million people with guns crawling towards me. I was being stalked by silent ghosts who moved invisibly through the trees and I was going to be dead before I'd even seen them . . .

Then something moved.

It was just a tiny flicker, on the other side of the clearing and about twenty yards from where the shot had come from. It could have been a fern stirring in the wind — except that there wasn't any wind. I cocked the revolver quietly with my thumb, gripped my right wrist with my left hand to steady it, and stared at the place over the short-coupled sights. Was I looking at a man's shoulder sticking out from behind that tree — or was it just part of the undergrowth? I squinted until my eyes watered . . .

And it moved again. Only a tiny jerk, as if the man had shifted his weight from one leg to the other — but it was enough. Now, I *knew*.

Now, *I* was the hunter.

The range was about thirty yards, uphill, and in bad light. I blinked several times to clear my vision, then took a deep breath and held it. The sights settled on the shoulder, wavered for a second, and steadied. As I took up the first trigger-pressure it suddenly occurred to me that I didn't know who I was shooting at — but after an instant's hesitation I decided I didn't bloody care, either: anyone who knew enough to hack into the underside of that Twin Com and then take potshots at me from the jungle was someone I wasn't waiting to be introduced to . . .

I squeezed the trigger.

And in the same split-second the shoulder disappeared as the man moved.

Bugger!

The crash of the shot walloped round the trees. The parrots

went up like multi-coloured shrapnel — but I wasn't sticking around to watch them. Having deafened myself and everybody else for a few seconds, I was only interested in changing position before the opposition got its head up and started filleting the place where the bang came from. I whipped off the ground like a Harrier in a hurry, catapulted five or six yards cross-wise along the slope, and splashed down in a dense carpet of ferns and ground orchids. I slid down-slope as I landed, got myself stopped and looking up again . . .

And the opposition had had the same idea. I was just in time to see Harvey's man Sherman darting across the clearing and going to ground behind the crumpled remains of the Twin Com's port wing.

His mistake.

I don't know why he went thataway: either he didn't realise I had something as powerful as a .38 Special — which was pretty unlikely in view of the racket I'd just made — or else he had a very optimistic idea of the stopping-power of aircraft wing-skin. I aimed between the rivet-lines on the rumpled section of wing that he'd disappeared behind, and fired twice. Two little black holes appeared where the bullets punched through, the wing *bonged* faintly in the echo of the shots . . .

And Sherman dived out into the open as if he'd been scalded. I shot him as he moved.

The bullet took him somewhere in the body. He spun round and crashed down, ending up half-sitting, half kneeling on the slope. There was blood on his filthy white shirt, his lips were drawn back in a snarl of agony — but he still had a big black automatic in his fist. He brought it up with the slow deliberation of a drunken man, holding it in both hands.

I took careful aim, and put my last round into the middle of his chest.

The gun jumped out of his grip as if he'd tossed it away. For a moment he looked mildly surprised about it — and then a red stain like spilt wine appeared suddenly on his shirt-front, and he pitched forward and dived into the undergrowth.

Then there was just the screeching of the parrots and the rustling of my shaking limbs.

After a long moment of breathing heavily, I started thinking again. Raised my head gingerly and stared all round, as far as I could without changing position or shaking the ferns too much.

Through the slowly drifting gunsmoke the forest *looked* empty enough — but I was bloody sure it wasn't. Sherman wouldn't have been up here all by himself . . .

And here was me with an empty gun. And no more ammunition nearer than my flight bag in the Chev.

Well, there's only one answer to that, Scott: nip up to the wreck and grab Sherman's gun from where the bastard dropped it . . .

Oh, yeah?

I thought about it, while the sweat rolled down my face and collected under my chin. The distance was only about twenty yards — but that twenty yards could take me the rest of my life. I was fairly well hidden where I was — well enough not to have had my head blown off yet, anyway — but as soon as I shifted I was going to be a big juicy slow-moving target.

Well, you're going to be that whichever way you go, chum. And at least they might not be expecting you to go uphill . . .

That was true. Maybe, anyway.

I took several deep breaths, a last, slow look round — and then came up out of the ferns in a rush. Scrambling furiously I got five feet up the slope, ten feet . . .

And then a voice behind me bawled: "Stay right where ya are Scotty!"

Harvey Bouvier, of course.

*   *   *

I froze, hanging on to a thick vine for support, and then turned slowly round. He was about ten yards down-slope from me, squatting behind a tree trunk. All I could see of him was his head and a fat hand holding a small pistol.

Cautious type.

"Hold ya hands out from ya body so I can see 'em."

I shifted my weight so I couldn't fall over, and did like the man said. Slowly and gently, so as not to give any wrong impressions. I could feel my clothes sticking to me all over with sweat and slime, and my heart was pounding wildly.

"Where's ya gun?"

I cleared my throat and said: "On the ground where I was lying. It's empty."

"Yeah?" He stood up and came out from behind the tree, keeping his eyes and the gun on me as he moved. He was wearing a long-sleeved shirt and long trousers — the first time I'd ever seen him in anything other than Bermuda shorts — and like me, he was covered from head to foot in the thick black slime of the forest floor. He didn't look happy about it.

"I'm comin' up ta ya. If ya move, I'm gonna let ya have it."

I nodded. I believed him. I was surprised he hadn't let me have it already

He pulled himself up three or four trees higher, then waded into the ferns where Scott's Last Stand had been. After kicking around for a few moments he stooped, groped, and came up with the Smith & Wesson. Still watching me, he pointed the gun into the air and pulled the trigger five times. All he got was five little clicks. He didn't seem to trust me — although why he thought I'd have left the damn thing there if there *had* been anything in it, I couldn't imagine.

Satisfied, he shoved the revolver into his pocket. Then he waved his own pistol and said: "Move up an' stand by the wing of the 'plane."

I moved. He followed a few yards behind me. When I got there, he said: "Siddown an' put ya hands on ya head."

I sat. Felt my hands trembling as they touched on top of my head.

Harvey backed across the slope to Sherman's body, keeping his gun pointed at me as he went. Now he was closer to me and out of the shade, I could see what it was: a little over-and-under Derringer-type-device. The sort of gun you sneer at if you don't know anything about it — but I *did* know something about it, and I wasn't sneering at all. It was the same shooter the local Mafia family in Antigua use, and I happened to know that it fired very soft .22 bullets out of enormous Magnum cartridges. It only carried two rounds and was about as accurate as a siege catapult — which may have been why Harvey hadn't chipped in on the gun-fight — but if you *did* hit somebody with it, they stayed hit: with the power of a .357 or more behind them, those little slugs went in like a pin-prick and came out like a hand-grenade.

I kept very still.

Harvey squatted beside the mortal remains and made a quick examination, glancing at me every few seconds to make sure I wasn't starting a civil uprising. After a minute or so he looked up and stayed looking up.

"He's dead." He sounded surprised about it. "Ya killed him."

I hadn't expected him *not* to be dead — not after stopping a .38 hollow-point square in the chest at twenty yards — and I didn't give a damn. Somewhere down the years I'd lost the capacity for worrying about how men like Sherman went out.

For a long moment, Harvey went on watching me. Him and the twin muzzles of the Derringer. Then he got his eyes down again, and started rooting around in the undergrowth. Searching for Sherman's gun. He scrabbled through the foliage with his left hand, and even rolled the body over to look underneath.

He couldn't find it.

After a couple of minutes, he gave up. Pulled himself upright and came towards me, staying a couple of yards down-slope.

"If ya go near Sherman I'll shoot ya," he said. "Unnerstand?"

I nodded.

"Right. Get yaself over ta that sweetsop tree past the end of the wing. I'll be right behind ya."

I got up and hauled myself along the side of the slope, taking care not to stumble. Harvey's heavy breathing followed a few feet behind me. We got to the tree without me getting shot, and when I turned round he gestured towards the up-slope side of the trunk with his gun. I looked for a moment without seeing anything in the undergrowth except undergrowth — and then I had it. An old metal ammunition box, brown-painted and scratched. A faded white stencil on the lid said *.303 Lee Enfield.*

"Bring it over ta the plane."

I bent down, grabbed the wire-loop handles at each end, and heaved. Nothing happened. I took a deep breath, tried again — and got exactly the same result. The damn thing felt as if it was bolted to the mountainside.

Harvey snapped impatiently: "C'mon, Scotty — get fuckin' movin'."

I glared round at him. "I can't lift it, you stupid sod. What the hell've you got in the bloody thi . . .?"

Silly question, of course. I realised it before I'd even finished speaking. I *knew* what he'd got in it . . .

$900,000 worth of Krugerrands.

And now I knew he hadn't shot me yet, too. With Sherman dead, he needed my help to get the 350 lb of dead weight down the mountainside. He was going to keep me alive until we reached the dirt road or the spray-strip or somewhere . . .

An then it would be goodbye Bill Scott. And there wasn't a damn thing I could do about it.

I straightened up. "Look," I said. "I just can't lift it, mate. Your man Sherman might've been able to, but *I* can't. If you want it moved, you'll have to help."

He didn't like it. His eyes went angry — and the little gun came up slowly at arm's length, until I was looking straight down the barrels. For a panicky moment I thought I was wrong, I'd overdone it: the forest was still and quiet, holding its breath, and I was going to die here in the damp heat under the tres . . .

Then he spoke. His voice seemed to come from a long way off, hoarse and infinitely menacing.

"Okay, Scotty," he said. "I'll help ya with it. But remember this, boy: one wrong move, just the tiniest thing, an' I'm gonna blow ya brains out first an' think about whether I was right after. Ya got that?"

I nodded. Slowly and carefully. The gun lowered, and the forest-sounds moved in again.

We picked up a handle each, and started moving across to the wreck.

*   *   *

Even with two of us, it wasn't easy. Straightforward carrying wasn't possible, not on that slope and through those trees. We ended up half-carrying, half-dragging the box, cursing when it caught on creepers and trunks, and constantly fighting its tendency to pull us downhill. Under the cover of tugging and hauling I studied the ground around Sherman's body as we struggled past it.

I couldn't see his bloody gun, either.

We got to the fuselage of the Twin Com eventually, and parked the box near the chiselled gash in the belly. The putrefying stench of the corpses made the ordinary rotting smell of the jungle seem clean and sweet. My stomach churned like a tired cement-mixer, and I backed away a few paces down the slope. Then I reached for my shirt pocket — and the little gun jerked threateningly.

I stopped reaching and said carefully: "The condemned man wants a smoke."

Harvey examined the idea for a moment, then grunted. I pulled out a very second-hand pack of Luckies, found one that wasn't broken in more than two places, and lit it. Then I looked up through the smoke, and found him watching me thoughtfully. Seeing me fishing in a pocket seemed to have reminded him of something . . .

"My money," he said abruptly. "What'dja do with my money, Scotty?"

It caught me off balance. With a fortune in gold at his feet, it hadn't occurred to me that he'd think about a couple of thousand in paper money. Silly of me, of course.

I said: "Ah . . . er . . . in the bank. I . . . er . . ."

The gun came up until I was looking down the barrels again. "Ya ain't had time ta put it in the bank. *Where is it?*"

Oh, what the hell — he was going to find it anyway after he'd shot me . . .

"In my pocket."

"Take it out and throw it to me."

I took it out and tossed it at his feet. Goodbye $2,400. I wouldn't be needing it where I was going anyway. Harvey stooped and picked it up without taking his eyes off me, then glanced down and riffled the notes with one thick finger.

"In the bank huh? Scotty, ya're a fuckin' liar." His heavy jowls shook as he chuckled about it. Big joke.

I just shrugged.

He went on gloating for a moment, then waved the gun at my stomach.

"Okay. Siddown an' put ya hands on ya head again."

I sat. Folded my hands on top of my head, breathed in smoke from the Lucky in my mouth, and tried to look like a man who wasn't watching for the smallest chance of making a break. The parrots squawked overhead and a column of white ants wound its way through the undergrowth a couple of feet away, trekking up-slope towards the stinking banquet in the Twin Com.

Harvey backed away cross-wise along the slope a few paces, then stopped to deal with the money. Keeping the gun pointed in my general direction he gripped the wodge of bills between his knees while he delved into his left trouser pocket and came up with a little draw-strung washleather bag. There was a lumpy bulge in the bottom as if the contents were small and solid. Spare rounds for the Derringer, probably. He opened it up, fumbled the dollars in on top of whatever-it-was, and re-tightened the string. I watched it vanish back into his pocket, making an expensive bump on his hip.

His eyes had never left me for more than two seconds at a time.

Having looked after the small change, he backed up the slope until he reached the belly of the Twin Com. He pushed open the lid of the ammunition box with his toe, then knelt down and yanked at the L-shaped rip in the aircraft underside. The thin alloy bent outwards without a sound. Still watching me, he transferred the gun to his left hand and started groping around inside the cavity with his right. From where I was, he looked like a Black Magic priest reaching into the corpse of some monstrous animal. From where *he* was it must have smelt about like that, too.

After a moment's fumbling, he pulled his arm out. He had two white-ish tubes in his hand, about three inches long. He glanced down at them, then looked back at me with a wolfish grin.

"Recognise 'em, Scotty?"

Tubes of Krugerrands. I nodded.

He tossed them carelessly into the ammunition box, then reached into the hole again and brought out more, two at a time. There seemed to be an endless stream of them: they must have heard me coming while they were in the early stages of unloading. I thought about the weight of the box a few minutes ago, and wondered how the hell we were going to get it down the mountain when it had the whole lot in it.

The point wasn't worrying Harvey, though. Right then, nothing was. Kneeling in the jungle slime scooping up gold in $10,000 handfuls seemed to be agreeing with him: he was almost laughing out loud. After about five minutes of it he stopped for a breather, wiping the dirt on his face into a new pattern as he tried to mop up the streaming sweat. I tensed every muscle in my body, ready to bolt — but there wasn't a chance. The little gun never stopped looking at me for a moment.

Then he said suddenly: "How'dja come ta be here, Scotty? I mean, how'dja know about this?"

I jerked out a mouthful of cigarette smoke, and shrugged. "I just guessed."

He frowned. "What'dja mean? How'dja guess?"

Here we went again. I said round the Lucky: "I knew you and Cas McGrath had been double-crossing Ruchter by selling some of his coins in Caracas, and I knew Cas was on his way to

Caracas with your guy Larry Hawkins when he went down. Even I could put that lot together: it *had* to mean there was a load of Krugerrands on board."

He said sharply: "How'dja find out I'd been shiftin' the stuff in Caracas?"

"That CIA man, Morgan. He picked me up in San Juan after your bloody bomb went off in my aeroplane, and one of the things he said was that they'd tracked down a load of coins in Caracas. After that, it was pretty obvious."

Harvey had gone very still at the mention of the CIA. "Does this guy Morgan know all this? About me?"

For a moment I nearly said yes, just to worry him — and then I realised I'd be signing my own death warrant. If Harvey thought the CIA were treading on his tail, he'd shoot me the way you'd wipe out a fingerprint. I didn't expect not to get shot — but there was no point in giving him a gold-plated motive that he didn't have already.

I shook my head. "No."

He went on frowning, and chewed at a fingernail to go with it. The gun sagged down a little, but not enough to make it worth trying anything. Keeping my hands on my head, I spat the remains of the Lucky on to the slope below my feet. The dog-end sizzled for a moment in the ooze, then went out. You didn't have to worry about starting fires in that forest: you could've dropped a stick of incendiaries and only got a slightly bigger fizz.

After a bit, Harvey said: "What about Ruchter? How much does he know?"

"Nothing. He's dead. Him and one of his men met up with two of Lashlee's crew yesterday evening. Ruchter and his mate and Lashlee's black gunman got killed." I didn't say where.

Harvey stared at me for a moment — and then threw back his head and laughed. A loud, triumphant Bronx cackle that echoed flatly in the still heat. A parrot screeched back at him — and I pulled my feet up under my thighs and bunched my muscles, trembling on the edge of launching myself down the slope...

"Don' do it, Scotty!"

I froze.

The laughter was gone, leaving just the indignant squawking from the tree. Harvey was tensed and still, the little gun raised and unwavering.

"Straighten ya legs out."

Breathing softly, I pushed my feet out until the backs of my legs squelched in the slime.

"Don' try that again, Scotty."

I shook my head.

Harvey relaxed a little, resting his gun-hand on the open lid of the box. Keeping his eyes on me, he reached out slowly with his right hand and fumbled in the belly of the Twin Com again. He brought out ten or twelve tubes, slower than before, then hitched a little nearer so he could reach farther in. The supply seemed to be drying up.

After a while, still going on with the job, he said abruptly: "What about Lashlee? Did he get hurt yesterday?"

"No. He wasn't there."

Harvey nodded, and went on fishing. Then: "Does *he* know anythin' about this load?"

I said: "No," again, quickly and definitely — since I didn't want him thinking he had *anyone* on his tail — then thought about it for myself. I was probably right, at that: Lashlee'd have no way of knowing about this unless Mariano had been listening in while I was talking to Ruchter — and Mariano hadn't seemed to be the listening-in type, to me.

Pity. I'd like to have thought of Lashlee catching up with Harvey sometime . . .

The unloading operation seemed to be coming to an end. Harvey was groping for longer, and coming up with single coins that must have burst out of their tubes.

To take my mind off the stench, I asked: "How did *you* get here?"

He hesitated for a moment — and then chuckled at me.

"Fuck, I was just lucky. I was waitin' f'ra plane at Coolidge when the news came in that this'd been found. One of the Immigration guys told me about it, 'cos he remembered Larry Hawkins'd been on it. So we got a plane to Guadeloupe instead, an' I went an' saw the pilot who'd found it an' got the position from him. Then we came on here this mornin' on the island-hopper."

I nodded. "I see. Just lucky."

He chuckled again.

After that there was silence, apart from the eerie cawing of the parrots and the clinking of the heavy coins. I stared down the slope through the trees, and thought about being dead. After the events of the last week it seemed stupid and futile that I was going to die *here*, in the stinking rain forest, at the hands of one man with a miserable two-shot .22 . . .

Then Harvey finished the unloading.

He pushed the flap of alloy fuselage-skin roughly back into place with his fist, then slammed down the lid of the ammunition box and produced a small padlock out of his pocket. When that was on he changed hands with the gun, grunted his way to his feet, and stood for a moment peering round. His eyes stopped on my rucksack.

"That yours, Scotty?"

I nodded.

"Okay. Go pick it up. We'll take it with us."

I pulled myself up and stumbled over to it on stiff legs, wondering *why* we were taking it. Then I realised: Harvey wanted to remove all traces of me so nobody'd start looking for my body round here when I turned up missing. I wasn't going to be a murder case at all: I was just going to quietly disappear somewhere in the vastness of the rain forest . . .

I shivered in the steaming heat.

The gun waved at me. "C'mon — move it."

I moved. Picked up the rucksack and the hammer that was lying near it, did up the buckles, and shrugged it on to my back.

"Okay. Now get up here an' take one end of the box."

I heaved myself up the slope to the wreckage, festering in its self-made patch of sunshine. The stench of putrefaction caught me in the throat as I got there. I coughed rackingly, leaving a buzzing in my ears when it stopped, then croaked: "Where're we taking it?"

"Down the fuckin' hill. Where d'ja think we're takin' it?"

"Yeah, but then what?"

He waved the gun impatiently. "Then we leave it by the track down there an' take a walk down ta that crop-dustin' strip of yours. I gotta hire-car there, an' we come back in that an' pick it up. See?"

Yeah, I saw.

And I also saw when I was going to die, too. My usefulness would be over when we reached the dirt road, and then Harvey would be picking a place and shoving the little Derringer up to my head and . . .

I coughed again, and the buzzing in my ears got louder. I

tried to push a bit of sweet reason into my voice and said: "Look, maybe we can do a deal about flying the stuff out of here..."

But Harvey wasn't listening. He wasn't even looking. He was staring up at the blue patch of sky over the clearing as if he'd just heard the Voice Of The Lord. The buzzing in my ears wound up...

And then it wasn't a buzzing any more. It was the approaching snarl of aero-engines.

For two or three seconds the noise swelled rapidly — and then a red-and-white Apache zapped low over the clearing in a blast of sound, cranking into a steep turn as it went and then curling away from the mountainside in a fading diminuendo.

I thought stupidly *Bloody Mariano* was *listening last night*...

Harvey jabbed the gun into my ribs and snarled: "Move!"

We moved. The parrots fluttered and screeched as we left.

*　　　*　　　*

At first, we tried carrying the box between us. That didn't work because the weight of it had one or other of us slipping over every few yards, and anyway the trees weren't far enough apart for us to go between them abreast. So then we did what we should have done in the first place — both got hold of one end of the thing and dragged it, half-stumbling down the slope on our feet and half-sliding on our backsides. That way, we moved surprisingly fast: the box tended to push us on rather than hold us back, and the only times we came to a full stop were when the front end got caught in creepers and roots and had to be lifted up.

After about five minutes, I glanced back up the slope. We seemed to have slithered down nigh on a hundred feet. The tail of the Twin Com was only just visible through the jungle of trees and vines, a little aluminium tombstone in the cluttered dimness of the forest. In a short time, even that would be gone: when the clouds came back with their warm constant moisture, the jungle would move in with its ferns and its moss and its all-pervading slime. In a year there wouldn't be a smashed-up aeroplane there at all: just an odd-shaped green hump on the mountainside and a thin place in the forest roof.

And the parrots, of course. They'd still be there.

I shuddered, and wondered what the Civil Aviation men from Trinidad would make of the bullet holes and the extra body.

We went on.

When we were about half way down — or at least, what *felt* like about half way down — Harvey called a short halt. We both sank down in the goo, wheezing like railway engines, with me watching him closely in case his attention wandered. It didn't, of course. He was plastered with black mud, streaked with blood from a score of cuts and grazes, glassy-eyed with exertion — but that bloody little Derringer still grew out of his right hand like a second thumb. He rested his forearm on his heavy stomach, and its vicious black over-and-under eyes bobbed up and down at my head.

After a bit, he said jerkily: "Would he'ya...seen us? Lashlee?"

I tried to cough up some moisture from my throat. My mouth felt like a bucket of sand. "Dunno. Shouldn't think so. He was going too fast."

There was a pause. Then Harvey said: "Where'll he land? At the crop-dustin' strip, or at the airport?"

"At the airport, if he's got any sense." I swallowed drily. "The spray-strip's a bit bloody short for an Apache. He'd get in all right, but he might not get out again."

Harvey nodded, then chewed his lip, thinking. I could see him working out the arithmetic. It would take Lashlee fifteen minutes to get to Melville Hall, clear inbound, and get himself a car or taxi: then, since there aren't any roads through the interior, he'd have to drive right round the north of the island, through Portsmouth, to get to Pointe Ronde and the start of the dirt road. Say an hour for that, or a bit more...

The time was now four twenty: just under half an hour since the Apache had appeared over the clearing.

Harvey hauled himself to his feet, grabbed the handle of the box again with his left hand, and waved the little gun in his right.

"Okay. Let's git."

We got.

Lashlee and Mariano caught us twenty minutes later, when we were slipping and sliding down the edge of a small gully with the dirt road in sight through the trees.

25

THE FIRST THING we knew about it was when they opened up with a machine gun.

The surprise was total and appalling. There was no challenge, no warning, no nothing. I never even *saw* them, never mind anything else. One second we were struggling downhill through the undergrowth — and the next, the whole world was full of the stammering blast of the gun. Chips of wood and greenery exploded all round us, the concussion-wave slammed in my ears . . .

And then I was down on the deck and trying to burrow into the mud, quivering with shock. For a moment the firing blared on over my head in short, vicious bursts — and then something plucked at the rucksack on my back, and something else *thunked* into the ammunition box a few inches in front of my nose. I twisted frantically and rolled right, tumbled over the edge of the gully, and spilled down into the bottom in a crackling of undergrowth. As I went, I caught a glimpse of Harvey. For a second he was standing on the edge of the gully waving the Derringer short-sightedly round the forest — and then the machine gun roared again, his legs whipped out from under him, and he came crashing down after me.

The firing stopped. Nothing but fading echoes and a huge hissing in my head.

After a moment I got my face up out of the slime. Harvey was three or four yards away, sprawled against the gnarled roots of a breadfruit tree in an awkward half-sitting, half-kneeling position.

And he was bleeding to death.

He'd stopped one in the inside of the right thigh, and his leg was laid open in a shattered red mass. The main femoral artery must have gone, because blood was pulsing out of the wound as if someone was turning a tap on and off. His trouser-leg was already soaked in it, glistening wetly as it mingled with the black jungle ooze that covered him. It started running off his turn-up in a thin steady trickle as I watched.

He hadn't even noticed it.

I'd heard of impact-shock numbing a serious wound, but never seen it before. Harvey looked at me blearily, like a man waking up with a bad hangover. After a few seconds he seemed to remember where he was and who I was — and then, incredibly, he brought up his bloody little gun. He waved it at me, and then towards the lip of the gully.

"Ge' . . . yore ass . . . up there," he mumbled.

I just stared at him. I could hear the trickling of his life running away in the silence.

"Hey, g'wan" — his lips worked for a moment while he panted heavily — "g'wan, geddup there. Wanna . . . wanna see where they are . . ."

I swallowed on a bone-dry throat and said hoarsely: "They've got a machine gun. They'll kill me." Something less than a bright observation, of course — but what *do* you say to a dying man who's trying to make you commit suicide?

Harvey actually grinned. A bit vacant, but definitely a grin.

"F'ya don' . . . don't, then *I'll* ki . . . kill ya." The grin faded, pushed out by a look of puzzlement as if he couldn't understand why it was difficult to speak.

I didn't move.

After a moment, he raised the Derringer and tried to sight it at my head. His gun-hand weaved around uncertainly for a few seconds — and then sagged tiredly into his lap. He blinked in surprise, looked down . . .

And saw his leg.

It took a while to sink in. When it had, his whole body seemed to slump. He spent several seconds staring at his own blood seeping away into the slime of the forest floor, then slowly pulled his head up and looked at me again. His face was deathly white under the mud.

"Shit, fuck," he said weakly. "I've . . . I'm gonna die. They killed me."

I thought of the bomb in the Beech and said: "Yeah. You're going to die."

"Fuck . . ." His head sagged back against the trunk of the tree, and his eyes closed. The squawking and rustling of the forest closed in. After a moment I found I was listening hard: there seemed to be more noise coming from up-slope than down.

Well, there would be, chum: that'll be Lashlee and Mariano working their way down to see if we need any first aid, like a bullet between the eyes . . .

I came back to life, took a couple of deep breaths — and launched myself at Harvey, scrabbling at the muddy slope with hands and feet and knees. I got a hand on the Derringer, wrenched . . .

And I had it. He didn't even try to resist.

For a moment I just knelt beside him, panting like a leaky bellows and trying to decide what the hell to do now. While I was thinking, I remembered something. I reached across his body, delved quickly into his pockets — and came up with the Smith & Wesson and the little washleather bag.

He must have felt them going. His head came down, and his eyes half-opened. His chest was rising and falling rapidly, the breath whistling in his throat. "Scotty?" His voice was thick and slow, between wheezes. "Tha' . . . you, Scotty?"

I nodded, then realised that he probably couldn't see by now. "Yeah, that's me."

The rustling-undergrowth sounds were coming closer. I stuffed the revolver and bag frantically into a pocket and picked up the Derringer again.

"Scotty, lis'n . . ." He made a feeble retching sound, and vomit dribbled out of the corner of his mouth. His head waved around as if he was looking for me in the dark.

"Fuck . . . ya c'n have . . . all that . . . f'ya get me outa . . ."

In the middle of it, he died

For a few seconds I just squatted there, looking at him. His last words had been typical of him: offering me my own money to draw back the curtain of death and get him away.

The rustling noises were very near, now.

I rose to a crouch, fired both barrels of the Derringer uphill to make them get their heads down, and then ran like hell.

* * *

I shouldn't have made it. I should have been mowed down as I came up out of the gully — but I got lucky. Either I happened to have a good selection of trees between them and me during the critical first few yards, or else I picked a moment when the one with the machine gun was re-loading or scratching his ear or something.

Whichever it was, I was thirty or forty feet down-slope and going like a train by the time anyone got round to shooting. Then the machine gun opened up in a series of short bursts, two or three shots each, as if the gunner wasn't seeing enough of me to draw a decent bead. The firing echoed round the forest like a thousand slamming doors — and I poured on the coal and went downhill at a speed I wouldn't have believed possible. I stumbled and slid, bounced off trees, smashed through ferns and undergrowth . . .

And suddenly, miraculously, I was bursting out on to the dirt road.

After the dim cavern of the forest, the sunlight was a blinding glare. For a moment I could only skid to a halt on all fours, blinking furiously and seeing nothing but misty red and whirling stars. Then vision came back — or enough to be going on with, anyway — and I was looking desperately up and down the track, expecting a new burst of gunfire out of the trees any moment.

Jean-Claude's Chev was about a hundred and fifty yards away to my right, with a blue Ford Falcon station wagon parked behind it.

I got up and sprinted towards them.

I don't know what the world record is for a hundred and fifty yards through low undergrowth in the tropical sun — but whatever it is, I hold it. By the time I reached the Chev my legs were turning to chewed string and my heart was pounding fit to squeeze itself out through my ears — but I hadn't been shot. I staggered the last few yards, dragging in air in great tearing gulps, snatched the driver's door open . . .

And the bastards had taken the ignition key.

I could get it going without it in time — or I could if they hadn't done anything else to it as well — but time was something I didn't have. Without stopping to think, I turned and stumbled back to the Falcon. Stupid, of course — since I could hardly expect them to have pinched my keys and left their own — but on the spur of the moment it was the first thing I thought of. I got there in a lurching run, and wrenched at the door. The first thing I saw was the empty ignition keyhole . . .

And the second thing was three roughly-bared wires dangling below the dashboard just underneath it.

For a few seconds I just stood there thinking idiotically *they must have stolen the bloody thing* — and then I was tearing the rucksack off my back, flinging it in ahead of me, and piling in behind the wheel with my mud-soaked shirt and trousers squelching on the hot plastic seat. I found I still had a handful of empty Derringer, stuffed it into my belt, and got to work on the wires with fingers that felt like bananas. The first two I flashed together churned the engine over on the starter without achieving anything, but the second two lit the ignition light. I twisted them up, touched the third one against the joint — and the engine ground over and came to life in a steady straight-six rumble.

Bingo. And now let's just get the hell OUT . . .

The Falcon was facing the wrong way — up the track towards the dead end. I yanked the park-brake release, stirred the column change into what felt like about the right place for reverse, and shot backwards on full left lock in a crunching welter of wheel-spin. Just before the back end punched a hole in the down-slope jungle I stamped on the brake, wound the wheel furiously, shoved the gears into first — and stalled the blasted engine. Fumbled with the wires, got it fired up again, and jerked forward until the bonnet crunched into the foliage on the up-slope side. Then back on left lock again — forward on right — back on left — the bloody thing about as handy as an aircraft carrier in the narrow track. Panic welled up in my throat because I was using up much too much time . . .

And then we were round. The left front wing smashing through branches and ferns on the up-slope — and then open track ahead. I gave it the gun in first, caught the slewing back end . . .

And I *had* used up too much time. Lashlee and Mariano popped out of the trees about a hundred yards ahead.

They were dragging the ammunition box, the same way Harvey and I had. They dashed straight out to the centre of the track and dropped it. Lashlee carried on to the down-slope side in two quick strides, reaching into his pocket as he went. Mariano stayed behind the box and brought up a sub-machine gun.

The track wasn't wide enough to go round him, so I did the

only other thing left: banged the gearlever into second, stamped the throttle on to the floor, and drove straight at him.

It was all over in seconds. The Falcon surged forward drunkenly over the ruts, rear wheels spinning and axle tramping wildly. Mariano loosed off a quick burst that seemed to be right at my face but hit the front somewhere with a single loud clang — and then we were *there*, doing forty or fifty, and he was diving sideways for his life. I got a flash-glimpse of the ammunition box disappearing dead-centre under the bonnet — there was a huge bone-jarring *crash* — a confused instant of the car trying to go into orbit and me trying to go through the roof — and then we were smashing down and ploughing on over it with a vast bonking and grating from the underside. The steering tried to rip out of my hands, the exhaust blared as the silencer got scraped off . . .

And suddenly we were clear and bellowing on down the track, bouncing and thumping with me playing Fangio on the wheel trying to stay out of the scenery. The speedo needle was waving past sixty — or something. The trees on each side were a rushing green tunnel, far too narrow for this great tank of a thing at this speed . . .

I whanged it into top and kept my foot down, dimly hearing the machine gun stuttering again behind me. The rear window blew out with a crack like a pistol-shot, three starred holes appeared in the windscreen — laminated and not toughened, thank Christ — and there was a noise like stones on a tin roof as more bullets hit the back somewhere.

Then the left rear tyre went, with a flat hollow *boom*.

I nearly lost it. The wheel thumped down, battered on the track — and the car weaved right and started to slide, lurching and bucking on the flat tyre. I lifted off for a moment and then put my foot down again, winding the big steering wheel frantically. The back end kept on coming round, smashed through undergrowth and low branches on the left — and then hit something solid with a resounding metallic crunch, and bounced back on to the track. I got the opposite lock unwound in a rush, caught the resulting tail-wag before it got properly started . . .

And then I had it, and we were slithering round a gentle left-hander which put a hundred yards of mountain between me and Mariano's gun.

Jesus . . .

I was shaking all over, guts churning with the hot sickness of terror — but I was still alive. Which was more than you could say for the car. I braked gently, sawing at the wheel as it snaked from side to side, until we were thumping along on square wheels at twenty with the engine making harsh open Pratt & Whitney noises. Even at that speed the steering kept trying to tie itself in knots — which it was entitled to do, since the blown tyre was probably shredding right off the rim by now — but I didn't dare slow down any more. Lashlee and Mariano would be pouring down the track behind me in the Chev at any moment . . .

Then I noticed the oil pressure light, glowing brightly red in the chrome-plated nest of the dashboard. It flickered off for a moment as we jounced over a couple of potholes, then came on again and stayed on.

Shit!

I could guess what had happened: I'd knocked a hole in the engine sump going over the ammunition box, and lost all the oil. As simple as that. So now it was only a matter of time before a piston or a bearing seized and poked a rod out through the side of the crankcase.

After which, of course, Scott would be back to walking.

I tried to think about it, while the Falcon banged and slammed over the ruts and did its best to shake my brain out of my head. I was quivering with mental and physical exhaustion, and there was a supercharged headache cranking itself up behind my eyes: I definitely wasn't in any condition to start hiking through the bloody rain forest again.

So go to the spray-strip and swop this car for the one Harvey left there. Right?

Right. Providing she holds together that far, of course . . .

The engine started to rattle as I leaned gently on the throttle and edged the speed up to twenty-five.

*   *   *

She made it. Just.

It was a hectic drive, what with the flat tyre and the engine sounding more and more like a concrete mixer with every yard — but she made it. Clanked on to the airstrip ten minutes later with the big ends hammering like a steel band, steam pouring out all round the bonnet — she must have taken a couple of bullets through the radiator, to add to her troubles — and me wondering why the hell Lashlee and Mariano hadn't caught me up already.

I jerked to a stop beside the hangar, yanked the ignition leads apart to stop the engine — and then just sat there for a moment, listening to the humming silence and peering round stupidly, looking for Harvey's car.

It wasn't there.

The only machines on the strip were the Falcon, expiring around my ears in a cloud of steam and a ticking of cooling metal . . .

And Lashlee's bloody Apache, poking its blunt snout out from the other side of the hangar.

For several seconds I just stared at it blankly. Then I found I had two thoughts running round my aching head. The first was that Lashlee was a bloody twit bringing an Apache into here — I hadn't been kidding when I'd told Harvey it might not get out again — and the second was that he must have pinched Harvey's car to get to the end of the dirt road.

Which meant, of course, that *this* was Harvey's car. The one I was sitting in.

The one that wasn't going to go another yard.

So okay — take the Apache. It ought to get off all right with one Scott-weight on board — and then you can leave it at Melville Hall with a few handfuls of sand in one of the engine sumps. That ought to put a bit of a crimp in Lashlee following you around . . .

I liked that idea, all right. I whanged the Falcon's door open, swung myself out, and reached in and grabbed the rucksack. Then I paused for a few seconds to wipe steering wheel, gearlever and door handles. Part of my brain screamed that I didn't have time for messing about like that — but after the last few days my instinct for destroying evidence went much too deep for me to leave fingerprints on a car full of bullet holes.

Then I sprinted towards the Apache.

As I passed the open front of the hangar I chucked the rucksack towards a pile of old bits and pieces in the far corner — and then skidded to a stop for a second and stared at the Pawnee. I'd forgotten about that. Maybe I ought to take it instead of the Apache: then Lashlee wouldn't be able to get me stopped by ringing up Melville Hall and screaming that I'd pinched his aeroplane . . .

Oh yeah, great idea: ruddy marvellous. Except that Lashlee's not about to start screaming anything anyway — not in his position — and if you leave him the Apache he'll be all set to follow you to the hot end of hell. Just quit spraining your brain and bloody move ...

I bloody moved. Reached the Apache, dashed round the tail, and grabbed at the handle of the single door.

The Goddamn thing was locked.

I leaned against the fuselage, sweat pouring down my face, and thought about breaking into it. It shouldn't be too difficult: the windows were only Perspex, and ...

The growl of a heavy car engine, not all that distant, floated across the clicking and rustling of the jungle and the squawking of the parrots.

Christ! Man! Get OUT ...

I sprinted back round the tail, shot into the hangar — and slipped on a pool of oil and went down like a ton of bricks. For a few seconds I just stayed where I ended up, unscrambling my eyeballs and wondering how many bones I'd broken — and then remembered that if I didn't get moving *now* it was going to be academic anyway. I scraped up the remains, limped painfully round to the Pawnee's starboard wing root, and hauled myself up into the high cockpit. You usually check an aeroplane over before flying it — especially after an engineer's been mauling it around — but there was no time for that now. There wasn't even time to strap myself in. I just plunked into the seat, stamped on the toe-brakes, turned fuel, master switch and mags on, reached for the primer and the starter button ...

And then stopped. The engine noise was very near now, changing pitch as if the vehicle was turning off the dirt road and pulling on to the strip itself. If I fired up the Lycoming now they couldn't help hearing it — and then all they'd have to do would be keep driving and park in front of the hangar, and I'd be bottled up here for the rest of my life. All two minutes of it. And even if I *did* get the Pawnee out of the hangar they'd only have to ram the tail or a wing tip or something while I was swinging into line with the runway ...

I stayed where I was, and sweated. Pulled up the starboard window-hatch and clipped it shut, then held the port one a few inches open so I could hear what was going on. Then just sat there and prayed that they wouldn't take it into their heads to park in front of the hangar anyway.

They didn't. The sound of the engine came near enough for me to recognise the distinctive clatter of the Chev — not that

I'd had any doubt about it anyway — and then tyres crunched on the gravel surface somewhere near the left wall of the hangar as the truck pulled up. They'd done the natural thing — stopped alongside the steaming remains of the Falcon. The engine died, I heard the *zzip* of the park-brake ratchet, and then the sounds of doors opening and footsteps crunching.

That was enough for me. I closed and clipped the window-hatch, gave the engine one stroke of primer — and then took a fast deep breath and pressed the starter button.

The propeller chunked over a couple of revs, the engine fired, missed, fired again — and then caught and ran, the deep snarling tickover sounding strangely hollow as it bounced back off the tin walls of the hangar. I released the brakes and shoved up the power . . .

And Lashlee and Mariano came charging across in front of me.

For a split-second I trod on both brakes out of sheer instinct — and then thought took over and I un-trod and whanged open the throttle. The engine noise blared round the hangar, the Pawnee jumped forward, and both of them tried to stop running. Lashlee made it — and Mariano didn't. He skidded, slipped, and the sub-machinegun flew out of his hand as he grabbed at the moving left wing to stop himself.

I stamped on the starboard brake, the Pawnee swivelled for a second — and the port leading edge hit him square in the face and he disappeared under the wing. As I tramped on the port brake to straighten up again I got a split-second glimpse of Lashlee, face contorted and heavy automatic spurting flame . . .

And then I was bursting out of the hangar and into the sun, the boom of the shot faint in my ears and the blare of the engine going suddenly flat as we ran into the open. I heaved frantically on right rudder and brake, the starboard wheel locked up in a crunching of gravel, and the long nose shuddered and swung quickly round the forest. I didn't have the full length of the runway from here — only about 1,800 feet — but it would have to do: I sure as hell wasn't starting any decorous taxiing exercises while Lashlee filleted me with the machinegun.

Before I was even lined up I had the throttle wide open and the stick forward to get the tail up. The Lycoming popped and banged and shook at the idea of full power from cold, my heart misfired with it — and then it chimed in on all six and we were off and running.

But not fast — not fast at all. An empty crop-sprayer ought to get off the mark like a Ferrari — but this one was behaving more like a tired Austin Seven. The tail came up slowly, and the airspeed crawled off the bottom of the dial. I snatched hands and eyes round the cockpit trying to find what was wrong — then suddenly realised that the bloody thing wasn't empty at all. The bloody engineer had filled up the bloody hopper — so I was carting along 900 lb of banana oil: the same weight as five-and-a-half people. I looked at the trees rushing at me, dropped my left hand on to the hopper-dump lever to jettison the load . . .

And then it wasn't necessary — I had the speed anyway. The controls were biting, responding, and the needle was flickering towards seventy. I eased back on the stick as we reached the shiny patch of oil I'd dumped on the runway a week ago — and the Pawnee snarled into the air, clearing the trees by forty or fifty feet. I sagged back limply in the seat as we ran up the burning sky. I was quivering from head to foot, and I wanted to be sick.

26

AFTER A PERIOD of time devoted solely to the shakes, I pulled myself together and started taking notice again. The Pawnee was still pounding away at full power, climbing heavily through 3,000 feet and pointing vaguely north-west towards the vast blue emptiness of the Caribbean Sea.

I pushed the nose down to the cruising position, eased the power back to 2,400 rpm, then went round the cockpit doing the chores normally done before take-off. Checked the gauges were all in the green, flicked the mags off and back on again one by one, gave the spray-pump brake a yank, and squinted at the fuel gauge, six feet away on top of the long cowling, to make sure I wasn't about to die of thirst. Then I bent my head down and peered under the instrument panel at the translucent glass-fibre wall of the hopper. It was muddy-black from top to bottom: filled to the brim with banana oil. For a moment I thought about dumping it there and then — since I'd go faster and farther without the excess weight — then decided to leave it until I was out over the sea.

After that I half-turned in the seat and scrabbled on the rear shelf until I came up with the shoulder straps and the crash-helmet, eyes-fronted again, fastened up the harness and clicked the inertia-reel toggle to Lock, then crammed the helmet on to shut out some of the racket of engine and slipstream.

Then I sat back and tried to decide what the hell to do.

It was quite a problem. The obvious Plan A was to lob into Melville Hall, pick up the Cherokee, and then get the hell out of the Caribbean as fast as the prop would turn — but as a strategy, it suffered from the equally obvious drawback that Lashlee would

277

be able to follow me in the Apache. If I was lucky and kept moving I might be able to stay out of his hands for a day or two — but since there were two of them and they had faster transport than me and I had to sleep sometime, there was no way I could avoid them catching up with me eventually.

And I knew what would happen when they did, too: I was the last living witness who could incriminate them, and I'd had ample evidence of how Lashlee felt about *that* . . .

I shuddered, rubbed a sweating hand over my face, and hoped fervently that they'd pile the Apache into the trees when they tried to get it out of the spray-strip. I was willing to bet they wouldn't, though: life isn't that fair. If they didn't have too much fuel on board, and if Lashlee was half-way clued-up on his short-take-off technique, they'd probably scrape out with a few feet to spare.

Unless, of course, I went and trod on them a bit . . .

The idea hit me like a slap in the face. I thought about it for maybe ten seconds — then hauled the Pawnee round in a crop-duster's wingover, pushed the power up to max continuous cruise, and headed back to the strip.

*　　*　　*

I got there three minutes later, and cranked into a steep turn 300 feet above the white slash of the runway.

They were still there.

They'd backed the Chev up close to the Apache, and two tiny human figures were moving slowly between the two. For a moment, I couldn't imagine what they were doing. I tightened the turn until my cheeks sagged and the stall-warning light flickered in front of me, and stared down over the revolving left wing tip. They seemed to be carrying something . . .

And then I got it: they were shifting the ammunition box full of Krugerrands. It was probably a bit frayed round the edges after I'd trampled over it with a ton-and-a-half of Ford Falcon — but it was still worth $900,000. Short runway or no short runway, Lashlee wasn't leaving *that* behind.

Well, it might kill him yet. Or help to, anyway.

The two figures stopped moving. I could see the blobs of their faces as they looked up, obviously wondering what the hell I was doing. Well, let them wonder: I was pretty sure they wouldn't guess. They'd probably think I was planning to land back there after they'd left — and unless Mariano had a Bofors in his back pocket there was nothing they could do about it anyway. I slackened off the turn before it pushed my spine up through my skull, and kept watching them while I tried to work out exactly what I *was* going to do. I needed to be downwind ready for a fast diving-turn when they lined up for their take-off roll . . .

After half a minute they seemed to decide that whatever I was up to it wasn't contagious, and got themselves back to the job in hand. The box disappeared into the Apache, and the two figures followed it. After a pause, the jungle behind the port engine started whipping around in a private wind. Then the same behind the starboard.

The shadows of the cockpit roll-cage dappled across my face as I kept turning and looking down. I wiped my sticky right hand on the side of the seat and took several slow, deep breaths. The Pawnee-smell of warm oil and simmering aluminium caught in my throat, making me swallow hard. I badly wanted a drink.

The Apache started to move.

It swung out from behind the hangar, back-tracked slowly to the very end of the strip, then pivoted round until it was facing the open runway.

I tightened my turn for a few seconds, hauling the long nose round the humpy green horizon of the hills, then slammed stick and rudder to the right and rolled out. The Pawnee snarled along parallel to the strip in the opposite direction to take-off, about three hundred yards out. I throttled back and pulled the nose up to reduce speed, and stared over the leading edge of the left wing at the Apache.

After a few seconds, the greenery behind the aircraft threshed in the slipstream as the engines wound up. Twin plumes of dust puffed back into the trees like blowing smoke. My nerves screamed *go* and my hands twitched on stick and throttle — but I didn't go. Lashlee'd just be running up the engines at this stage: I had to wait until he *moved*.

The airspeed slid back round the dial until the Pawnee was mushing along just above the stall, engine thrusting lazily and me correcting the heat-turbulence with big vicious jerks of the controls. The bitch might be viceless at low speed — but by Christ, she was heavy with it. Sweat poured down my face and ran into my eyes. I blinked it out.

The threshing and the dust-clouds died away.

Okay — he's finished his engine-run. Now he's doing his pre-take-off checks — so next time he opens up, he's going to mean it. Next time, you go . . .

The Pawnee's port wing tip reached the end of the runway. I dipped it so I could keep watching, then bent into a slow left turn, in towards the mountain, so as to stay the same distance away from the Apache. My hands were slippery with sweat, and I tried to will my legs into stopping their shuddering dance on the rudder pedals. But they weren't having any: I was wound up like a spring, quivering in the tension of waiting through the last few seconds when you know you're going to lash out, punch, kill.

I swallowed hard as the sour taste of bile humped up in my throat. Told myself I *was* going to kill; I was going to get this right . . .

I was curling round behind the Apache now, into its upwards and rearwards blind spot. Maybe they'd think I was going to land after they'd taken off. The Pawnee's matt-black cowling was tracking round the lush green slopes of Diablotins. In a minute, maybe less, I'd have to stand it on its ear and turn back the other way — and if Lashlee started his take-off roll then, I was probably going to miss him. I took another deep breath and went on staring down, trying to think myself into the other cockpit. Imagined the hands and eyes moving round the baking controls as they went through the checklist. *Trims — set for take-off; throttle nut — finger tight; mixture — full rich . . .*

The trees behind the Apache were blowing again. They whipped into a frenzy for five or ten seconds, and then the aircraft started to move.

*　　　*　　　*

I whanged on full throttle and slammed everything to the left. The Pawnee bellowed, rolled nearly through to the inverted — and then I was reefing her out in a power-dive, nose pointing downhill at the runway.

The airspeed wound up like a demented clock. The noise level wound with it, the blare of the engine merging into the rising thunder of airflow round struts and spray-booms. The controls were firm and responsive with speed now, all the mushiness gone. I wriggled the nose left then right with tiny movements of wrist and ankles, getting it exactly lined up with the target. The strip floated up towards me, expanding in the windscreen . . .

But the Apache didn't. It was off and running — and apparently pulling away.

It was an optical illusion, of course — probably something to do with the Pawnee's sloping nose and me going *down* as well as along. Passing 120 mph in a dive I was damn sure going to catch it eventually . . .

But eventually wasn't good enough. I had to be in the right place when it broke ground — not when it was trundling away a couple of hundred feet over the trees. I'd left it too late, got myself too far away: I was going to miss the bastard, and . . .

Then I was levelling out over the runway threshold at fifty feet — and suddenly, it wasn't pulling away any more. It was a third of the way down the strip and still gaining speed — but the illusion was gone: now I was catching it up hand over fist and I could see the gap closing. Four hundred yards. Three hundred . . .

And then I knew I was going to get it right. I was suddenly ice-cold in the hot cockpit, with everything moving like a slow-motion film. No nerves, no shakes — just the harness tight round my body and the controls an extension of my hands and feet. I wasn't a man in an aeroplane any more — I was the aeroplane. And now I was going to reach out and kill . . .

I was going too fast. The twin was a hundred yards ahead, and rushing back towards the Pawnee's down-sloping nose. I slapped the throttle shut and banged on right rudder and left stick. We staggered sideways for a moment with the characteristic shuddering of all Pawnees in side-slips — and then I was snapping her out of it and feeding the power back in. The speed was down to 100 or somewhere near — and now we were walking up on the Apache instead of running. It was moving like a silent film just ahead and below. I could see the rudder working and the elevators making jerky little attempts to get the nosewheel off before it was ready. It swayed and nodded over the bumps as it ran, getting light on its wheels, hopping . . .

Right — GO.

I poured on full power and pushed down to twenty feet. The trees closed in on each side, blurred green walls rushing past the wing tips. The Pawnee accelerated, bumping and shuddering as it hit the twin's wake-turbulence.

The Apache slid back under the nose.

The air smoothed out suddenly as we moved ahead of the

turbulence. I craned sideways against the straps, flying with tiny twitches of stick and rudder and flicking my eyes down behind the trailing edge of the right wing.

The Apache's tailplane appeared under the spray-boom and ran away backwards. Then the right wing, jolting, bumping . . .

NOW !

I grabbed the emergency hopper-dump lever and banged it all the way forwards.

* * *

There was a fast massive *gurgle* as eight hundredweight of banana oil poured out in two or three seconds. The Pawnee shied upwards — and I hauled back on the stick at the same time. We popped out from between the trees just before we'd have made another hole in my old friend the breadfruit at the end of the strip — and then I was whanging her into a steep left turn and trying to screw my head off my shoulders to see what was happening.

The Apache didn't make it.

I saw it a split-second before it hit. It was off the ground, clawing upwards — and then there was an explosion of greenery as it ploughed into the breadfruit. For a fraction of an instant it seemed to fly on through a barrage of debris — and then the starboard wing crumpled, it spun sideways, and the tail whipped up and over as it cartwheeled into the jungle. There was a fast impression of scything impact under a cloud of foliage . . . a glimpse of a buckled wing sticking out of the trees as the wreckage came to a stop . . .

And then it went up in a ball of fire. Ruptured tanks and hot engines, of course.

The suddenness of it was incredible. There was no warning flicker, nothing. One moment there was just the settling wreck — and the next, a huge silent explosion of yellow-orange flame boiling up out of the jungle. It twisted and swelled in seconds into a raging pillar of fire fifty feet high, belching out a vast red-hearted cloud of oily black smoke.

Goodbye Lashlee and Mariano.

And $900,000 worth of Krugerrands, of course.

I banked the Pawnee left and curled out from the Devil's Mountain towards the wide, clean sea.

It was over. All over.

* * *

It seemed to be a long time before my numbed brain got round to thinking again — and when it finally did, I started off by wasting several minutes wondering just what *had* killed Lashlee and Mariano. As far as I could tell, I'd dumped my load slap on top of the Apache's cockpit: I hadn't had the faintest idea what it would do — I'd just been pretty sure that 150 gallons of oil falling on an aircraft at the critical moment during a short take-off would have to do *something*. It might have swamped the windscreen and blinded him for a few seconds — or it might even have gone through it altogether, come to that. There *had* been 900 lb of it, and the windscreen *was* only made of Perspex. Or perhaps the shock of the Pawnee appearing over his head at the point of lift-off had been enough by itself. Or maybe they'd just never have made it out of that short strip anyway with the weight they had on board . . .

I shook my head angrily, and quit worrying about it. They'd tried to kill me and got killed themselves: when it came down to it, I didn't give a damn *how* it had happened. And I had much more important things to think about anyway — like, for example, what the hell I was going to tell the cops about two bodies in the forest, one car full of bullet holes on the airstrip, and one burnt-out aeroplane with 340 lb of melted-down gold dripping through its bones.

I turned the Pawnee back towards the interior, picking a course that would keep me away from the villages, and started thinking. The snarl of the engine echoed in my aching head like a tractor working in a deep, deep cave.

After a sweaty ten minutes, I'd come to the conclusion that I didn't have to tell anybody anything.

There'd been no witnesses to my oil-bombing pass over the Apache — or at least, none who were still alive — and I was damn sure nobody was going to learn anything by looking at the wreckage. Not after it'd finished burning up my oil and its own fuel *and* its aluminium skin along with everything else. There'd still be a splodge of oil on the runway, of course — but there'd been a splodge there anyway from where I'd dumped a week ago, so *that* wasn't going to prove anything.

So — if I landed back at the strip and re-filled the Pawnee's hopper, I could then go screaming to the cops with some horrific tale about how I'd come up to do some spray work in the calm of the evening and arrived just in time to see this mysterious

Apache attempting a take-off and hitting the trees. It would even explain the state I was in, covered in jungle slime: Valiant Rescue Attempt By Spray Pilot After Mystery Air Crash.

They might not altogether believe me — especially when they saw the Falcon and even more especially when the bodies of Harvey and Sherman got found in the forest — but providing I sorted out a few details such as Lashlee and Mariano's fingerprints on the Chev, they shouldn't actually be able to *prove* anything.

I could look after any distant witnesses who might have seen the Pawnee in the air by saying I'd taken it off the strip because I was frightened of the fire spreading to the hangar. That wouldn't explain how it came to be flying *before* the crash, of course — but I wasn't worried about it coming to that: the cops would be lucky to find a native Dominican who could tell a Pawnee from a Concorde anyway, never mind one who could give them reliable information about just *when* he saw it. And in any case they wouldn't be trying that hard: a crime like this with an all-foreign cast was well out of their league, and if they couldn't solve it immediately the best they'd be hoping for was that everyone would quietly forget about it and let them get back to the local stuff they *could* solve.

So — I ought to be in the clear.

Apart from having lost my business, work permit, home and livelihood, of course.

I sighed, dragged a trembling hand over my face, and bent the Pawnee round to the south, back towards Morne Diablotins. Stared at the bright green mountain crawling towards the nose, and wondered just what the hell I was going to do.

Back to running again, I supposed.

I felt very old and tired and lonely.

I coughed — something jabbed into my stomach. Harvey's little Derringer, tucked under my belt. I hauled it out, then tugged the Smith & Wesson out of my trouser pocket to go with it. For a moment I weighed them both in my left hand — and then opened one of the little storm-windows, made sure I was over virgin jungle, and dropped them out one after the other.

Goodbye incriminating evidence.

And *that* reminded me, too . . .

I fished into my right hip pocket, struggling and yanking and finally undoing the harness so I could get at it properly, and came up with Harvey's little washleather bag. Taking my feet off the rudder pedals and holding the stick between my knees I undid the draw-string, pulled out my roll of dollars, and stuffed it into a back pocket.

That left a small bundle of scrumpled-up tissue in the bottom of the bag, with several hard lumps in it about the size of pistol cartridges. I pulled the tissue out, opened it up to make sure it *was* cartridges before I heaved the lot out of the window . . .

And then just stopped and stared for a long, quiet moment. Or as quiet as you can get in a Pawnee in the air, anyway.

I should have thought of it, of course. In fact, I even had, after a fashion. If you were selling your first load of 4,500 stolen Krugerrands on the very-very quiet in Caracas, the last thing you'd want would be cash money. Nearly a million dollars in any paper currency is too easy to track down, too difficult to hide: you'd just be swapping one problem for another. So you'd be looking for something else — something small, virtually untraceable, and easy to sell anywhere in the world.

Something like a couple of dozen unmounted step-cut Columbian emeralds, for example. Each a deep flawless green, about half an inch long — and worth anything up to $30,000 a time, so I'd heard tell.

For a moment, I thought about two red-and-white Chipmunks on an English airfield. Then I banked the Pawnee slightly to the right, and growled on towards the north-west face of Diablotins.

Ahead, the fading column of smoke was a tall black stain against the bright blue and orange of sunset.

BRIAN LECOMBER

TURN KILLER

Ken Holland was a stunt flyer. Accidents and broken bones were all in a days work to him. But corpses were another matter. After his partner's plane crashed and killed him, and then his own Tiger Moth got engine failure while he was hanging below it on a rope ladder, Ken suddenly found that just then there were no such things as accidents — just murders, and some rare stamps, and a trail of terror that took him right through France to the steamy islands of the Caribbean.

'It isn't often that a new writer jumps right to the top of his class. But former air circus stunt man Brian Lecomber does just that with TURN KILLER.'

Sunday Mirror

CORONET BOOKS

IAN MACALISTER

THE VALLEY OF THE ASSASSINS

The map — doorway to one of the most evil mysteries of Islam's past.

Eric Larson was an adventurer. There were less polite names, of course, but Larson tried to stay on the right side of the law — when it was convenient.

He had a fine boat, a supply of good liquor, and an uncommitted future — until he picked up a shipwrecked stranger in the Persian Gulf. A stranger with a mysterious map.

The map was the key to the fabulous treasure of the ancient Assassins — a secret group of muderous fanatics long thought to be dead. But some were still alive — and waiting.

Waiting for someone like Larson to make a move toward the treasure . . .

CORONET BOOKS

ADVENTURE AND SUSPENSE
FROM CORONET BOOKS

BRIAN LECOMBER
- [ ] 20800 7   Turn Killer   80p

IAN MACALISTER
- [ ] 21004 4   The Valley Of The Assassins   60p

CHARLES MCCARRY
- [ ] 19942 3   The Miernik Dossier   60p
- [ ] 20452 4   The Tears Of Autumn   90p

DAVID LAVALLEE
- [ ] 17421 8   Event 1000   50p

OWEN SELA
- [ ] 19880 X   The Portuguese Fragment   50p
- [ ] 18289 X   The Bearer Plot   40p
- [ ] 20760 4   The Bengali Inheritance   70p
- [ ] 18774 3   The Kiriov Tapes   60p

ANNE ARMSTRONG THOMPSON
- [ ] 21825 8   Message From Absalom   80p

All these books are available at your local bookshop or newsagent, or can be ordered direct from the publisher. Just tick the titles you want and fill in the form below.

Prices and availability subject to change without notice.

-- -------------------------------- ....

CORONET BOOKS, P.O. Box 11, Falmouth, Cornwall.

Please send cheque or postal order, and allow the following for postage and packing:

U.K. — One book 22p plus 10p per copy for each additional book ordered, up to a maximum of 82p

B.F.P.O. and EIRE — 22p for the first book plus 10p per copy for the next 6 books, thereafter 4p per book.

OTHER OVERSEAS CUSTOMERS — 30p for the first book and 10p per copy for each additional book.

Name..

Address...

....